The Golden Cage

J D Oswald is the author of the epic fantasy series The Ballad of Sir Benfro. Currently, *Dreamwalker*, *The Rose Cord* and *The Golden Cage* are all available as Penguin ebooks. He is also the author of the Detective Inspector McLean series of crime novels under the name James Oswald.

In his spare time James runs a 350-acre livestock farm in north-east Fife, where he raises pedigree Highland cattle and New Zealand Romney sheep.

www.jamesoswald.co.uk
Twitter @SirBenfro

By the same author

The Ballad of Sir Benfro

Dreamwalker

The Rose Cord

The Golden Cage

The Inspector McLean Novels

Natural Causes

The Book of Souls

The Hangman's Song

Dead Men's Bones

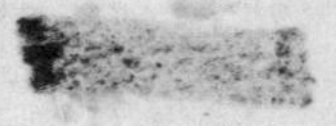

The Golden Cage

J D OSWALD

PENGUIN BOOKS

PENGUIN BOOKS

Published by the Penguin Group
Penguin Books Ltd, 80 Strand, London WC2R ORL, England
Penguin Group (USA) Inc., 375 Hudson Street, New York, New York 10014, USA
Penguin Group (Canada), 90 Eglinton Avenue East, Suite 700, Toronto, Ontario, Canada M4P 2Y3
(a division of Pearson Penguin Canada Inc.)
Penguin Ireland, 25 St Stephen's Green, Dublin 2, Ireland (a division of Penguin Books Ltd)
Penguin Group (Australia), 707 Collins Street, Melbourne, Victoria 3008, Australia
(a division of Pearson Australia Group Pty Ltd)
Penguin Books India Pvt Ltd, 11 Community Centre, Panchsheel Park, New Delhi – 110 017, India
Penguin Group (NZ), 67 Apollo Drive, Rosedale, Auckland 0632, New Zealand
(a division of Pearson New Zealand Ltd)
Penguin Books (South Africa) (Pty) Ltd, Block D, Rosebank Office Park,
181 Jan Smuts Avenue, Parktown North, Gauteng 2193, South Africa

Penguin Books Ltd, Registered Offices: 80 Strand, London WC2R ORL, England

www.penguin.com

First published by DevilDog Publishing 2012
Published in Penguin Books 2013
This edition published 2014
001

Set in 12.5/14.75 pt Garamond MT Std
Typeset by Jouve (UK), Milton Keynes
Printed in Great Britain by Clays Ltd, St Ives plc

ISBN: 978-1-405-91773-5

This one's for Juliet, who made it all happen.

I

Cuckoo-child in a nest of thieves
Bastard heir to mage's line
Stealer of souls, taker of lives
Harbinger of the death of worlds

The Prophecies of Mad Goronwy

Silence blanketed the world like an invisible fog. Even the trees gave off no sound, though they waved and flexed in the stiff breeze. Underfoot, the grass was wet with dew, but he could feel nothing of its texture on the soles of his bare feet. A shiver ran through him, but it wasn't the chill of the wind on his face, rather an aching leaching cold that he instinctively tried to get away from.

Not knowing how he had got there, Errol hunkered down between two large tree roots, pulling his cloak around himself and shivering. He was tired, but somehow sleep eluded him. Was he waiting for someone? He couldn't be sure, but he felt like he had been here before. His ankles ached at the thought of moving; he had no desire to stand up, no desire to do anything but huddle in his frozen hollow and try to sleep.

If only he could sleep.

She came to him as a scent. He could still hear nothing, not even the beating of his own heart, but the aroma plunged him back into happy memories of sun and warmth, holding hands, a lingering kiss. Everything was tinged with a deep comforting green, and for a moment he even forgot the cold and the pain.

From his dark hiding place Errol watched the path as it wound its way through the sparse ancient trees. He saw her first a good distance off, moving carefully, sticking to the shadows.

Closer now and he was sure. It was Martha as he had last seen her: serious eyes concentrating on the task ahead, dark shoulder-length hair pulled back and tied simply at her neck, still wearing her boot-length forest-green travelling cloak. She picked her way along the edge of the path, keeping as much as possible beneath the wind-swirled canopies of the great trees. Every so often she would look up at the sky, scanning the grey undersides of the clouds as if something terrible lurked there.

Errol tried to call out to her. Martha. But his voice was silent, echoing only in his head. Somehow he wasn't surprised. Neither did it alarm him that he couldn't move. He knew what was going to happen next.

For about two hundred paces she had to cross open ground, a natural clearing in the forest where a rocky outcrop rose out of the ground. She paused at the edge, glanced once more at the sky, then stepped boldly into the light. She didn't run; that might have drawn too much attention. Instead she seemed to draw in on herself until she almost disappeared. Almost, but not quite. Errol could still see her, shrinking as she moved steadily across the clearing. And others could see her too.

In the silence they were impossible creatures. They

appeared from nowhere, four great beasts with wings a dozen paces from shoulder to tip. Their landing should have shaken the earth, but they sank on to huge taloned feet without a tremor, surrounding her. Trapping her.

Errol could only watch, paralysed by something beyond fear. But Martha was not afraid. She stood among the dragons as if they were no more than placid cattle in a summer field. She looked at them each in turn, her mouth voicing words that had no sound. She held out her hand and a tiny sphere of light blazed forth, hovering above her palm. One of the dragons took an involuntary step back at this, slumping on to his tail as if in astonishment.

Martha must have taken this as permission to pass, for she boldly stepped out of their circle as if to continue to the other side of the clearing. Errol watched in astonishment and hope as she moved one step, two steps away while the four dragons merely looked at each other. Maybe this time she was going to make it.

This time?

Everything came crashing together. The dragon who had stepped back whipped around, grabbing Martha around her waist with one massive claw. Errol tried to wrench himself out of his hiding place even as he knew that there was nothing he could do. The dragons launched themselves into the air, the one carrying Martha clutched to his scaly breast struggling hard to clear the treetops. With a final wasted effort, Errol wrenched himself free, tripped over a root and plunged headlong.

He hit the ground much sooner than he expected, and with the impact, sound washed over him: the echo of running water over rocks, the chatter of early-morning birds.

His nose filled with a dusty spicy smell, making him sneeze then scramble to his feet. Pain shot through both ankles and he fell back on to the low bed of grass and heather that he had rolled out of in his sleep, his dream. Martha.

Errol rubbed the grit from his eyes and shivered at the cold. The ragged cloak that was all he had for a blanket lay twisted at the end of the bed, as if he had fought demons as he slept. Instinctively, he reached out for the lines, drawing enough warmth from them to push the chill from his bones. As they warmed his chest, he felt a moment's tightening at the scar where Beulah had stabbed him to the heart. Where Martha had healed him. Then he shifted his focus down to his ankles, trying to wash the pain out of them, wishing them to heal faster.

'They will get better. Give them time.' Errol didn't need to look up to know that the old dragon Corwen had joined him in the cave. Instead he leaned down and massaged first one ankle then the next, feeling the flow of the Grym through his fingertips. Finally, when he thought he might be able to cope with the pain, he slowly stood up, crossed to the fire and put some twigs on the ashen coals.

'You're up early, Errol. Bad dreams again?'

'Not dreams, just a single dream.' Errol shuffled towards the cave mouth and glanced out across the clearing. It was still, and the dawn light lit the scene only dimly. 'It's always the same.'

'Then it's likely she's trying to tell you something important.' Corwen was by his side, a presence, but also nothing at all. 'You must concentrate, try harder to communicate with her. Perhaps if you were to ask—'

'Benfro? He doesn't like me. Why should he? My kind

murdered his whole family.' Errol looked across the track to the small stone corral with its makeshift roof of branches, bracken and dried grass. It was so desolate he could almost taste the misery of the dragon who slept within.

'Besides, he's got trouble enough with his own dreams.'

'Your Majesty, you're not well. You should stay in bed.'

Queen Beulah looked up at her chambermaid with a mixture of contempt and weary resignation. Yet another sleepless night, and now she felt like her head was going to explode, shortly after her stomach had done so. At least this girl had some spine, unlike the other simpering maids, who stood in the doorway ready to flee from her wrath. Useless women, what did she need them for, anyway? She'd learned how to dress herself when she was two.

'I'm not my father. I won't rule the Twin Kingdoms from my bed.' Beulah hauled herself out of her pillows, wincing as the pain stabbed through her head right between the eyes.

'May I at least send for a physician?'

Beulah was surprised by the question; it was as if the woman was actually concerned.

'Very well,' she said, unsure what good it would do to be poked and prodded by the palace quacks. 'But find me a coenobite of the Ram. I don't want one of Padraig's useless bureaucrats treating me like a textbook.'

The chambermaid curtsied and left the room, taking the others with her. Beulah settled her head back into the pillows, wiping cold sweat from her forehead. It had been days now, maybe weeks, since this strange ailment had hit her. It came and went; sometimes she would be as fit as ever, the next day barely able to drag herself out of bed. It was difficult to keep food down, and what she did manage to eat left her feeling bloated. She would have suspected a poisoning attempt, but Clun, noble Clun, insisted on tasting all her food before she ate, and he was as fit as a fiddle.

Anger gave her a little strength, and Beulah used it to drag herself out of bed. She ached in her hips and back as she made her way to the bathroom. Warm scented steam swirled in the air, rising off the bath her chambermaids had already drawn. It was at once inviting and stomach-churning, and with a terrible sense of helplessness Beulah turned as fast as she could to the basin. She had not eaten much the evening before, but what was left of it came up in great heaves.

She leaned over the basin, catching her breath and fighting the waves of nausea that swept over her. How long had it really been like this? Had she felt this way before the debacle in the Neuadd when that strange young woman had run rings around a dozen highly trained warrior priests? When both she and the boy Errol had mysteriously disappeared in front of her eyes? It seemed to her that her symptoms had begun shortly after that. Perhaps she was suffering from some dark magical attack. And yet Beulah felt certain she would have known if that were the case. She was skilled in magic, after all. And she had the power of the Obsidian Throne to help her. Perhaps Melyn would have been able to divine what the problem was, but as ever when she needed him, he was elsewhere. She doubted she had the energy to try and contact him through the aethereal.

The raw burning pain in her throat seemed to counter her queasiness a little, and Beulah felt able to bathe. Warm water soothed her aches, and the perfumed soap washed away her night sweat, so that by the time she walked through into her dressing chamber, wrapped in a long white silk robe, she was beginning to feel almost human. In the mirror her face was gaunt, thin and drawn. Her freckles stood out like some disfiguring plague against skin as pale as a bloodless corpse. Her hair was straggly and matted, still damp from her bath, more scalp showing through than was healthy. She looked awful and was glad of the distraction when the reflected image of the chambermaid appeared behind her.

'I have summoned a physician, ma'am. A Ram, as requested. He awaits in your outer chamber.'

'Well, he's no use to me there, is he? Send him in.'

The chambermaid bobbed a curtsy and scurried out of the room. After a few moments there was a quiet knock at the door.

'Come,' Beulah said, not bothering to turn round. To her surprise, the figure who appeared in the doorway was not some road-weary travelling coenobite but Archimandrite Cassters himself. She remembered him as a chubby man, white-haired and slightly eccentric, but old age was catching up with him now.

'Your Majesty. I was told you weren't feeling well. Please, how may I help you?' The archimandrite made to bow, but Beulah stopped him. If he made it down on to one knee, he'd never get back up again.

'Come, Your Grace, sit. If I'd known the silly girl would fetch you I'd never have sent her. I only meant for her to find me a coenobite.' She steered the old man to one of the chairs arranged by the large window which overlooked an empty courtyard, settling herself down into the other.

'And why would you seek our help? Aren't Padraig's palace physicians to your liking?'

'They've used my blood to grow their leeches fat, and they've made my back sore with their cupping. I don't think they know the first thing about medicine.'

Cassters smiled, creases forming at the edges of his small clear eyes. 'So tell me, my queen. How long have you been suffering this malaise?'

'Perhaps three weeks now,' Beulah said. 'It comes and goes. Mornings are always worst. If I could just get a decent night's sleep. But I feel drained all the time.'

'If I may, ma'am?' Cassters reached out and took her wrist, feeling for a pulse. His touch was warm and dry against her skin as he felt her forehead and peered into her eyes. It seemed strange to be so close to someone, so intimate. Only Clun would dare to touch her face that way, and she had not had the strength to visit his chamber in weeks now. Dear Clun, so unlike his traitorous stepbrother Errol. But then Errol wasn't really Clun's stepbrother at all, was he?

'Did you know about Lleyn's child?' Beulah asked.

'Ma'am?'

'When she died, what was it, sixteen years ago now? She was with child. I assume you knew about that.'

Cassters looked her straight in the eyes. 'Only after she had died,' he said. 'Father Gideon was her physician. He told me afterwards what had happened. That Llanwennog prince, Balch, was the father, apparently.'

Beulah summoned up her strength. It was difficult with the headache pounding away between her temples and her stomach churning acid, but she could skim the edges of the archimandrite's thoughts and she saw no subterfuge in them.

'And the child died with its mother.'

'That's what I was told. It was a tragedy, but some might say a blessing too. A half-breed heir to the throne. There would have been civil war. Or worse.'

'So you believe the prophecies then.'

'What, Mad Goronwy? Not really, no. But for better or worse the people of the Twin Kingdoms wouldn't have taken kindly to a son of Ballah on the Obsidian Throne. Oh, there are some who would have welcomed it, true. Abervenn has always been close to the Llanwennogs. But others would have taken up arms against them: in Castell Glas and the west, not to mention Inquisitor Melyn and his warrior priests. No, it would have been a busy time for us Rams had that happened. Very complicated.'

Beulah felt the emotions skirting around the archimandrite's mind. He regretted that the two nations could not get along, but accepted it too. He had no part in the conspiracy, she decided.

'So what of me then? Have you any idea what's causing this infernal sickness and these grinding headaches?'

'That, my dear, is much less of a mystery.' Cassters patted her arm as the warm smile came back to his face. 'Really I'm surprised that Padraig's quacks couldn't see it for themselves, but then they would never think of such things, what with the vows they insist on taking. Your malady will cure itself in a while, but I can give you something to alleviate the symptoms straight away. I'll have an apothecary make it up, but given the circumstances I should probably administer it myself.'

'Why? What is it? What's wrong with me?' Beulah had noted the archimandrite's new informality and a sudden realization dawned on her which was both wonderful and terrifying.

'There's nothing wrong with you at all, my queen,' Casters said. 'You're simply suffering from a severe form of morning sickness. Your mother was just the same.'

'I'm with child?'

'Yes, Your Majesty. You are with child. May I be the first to offer you congratulations.'

The light was always different here, as if it were older, slower, thicker. It glowed with a golden sheen, dust motes hovering in the air like spiders on invisible threads. If he tried hard enough, he imagined he could make time stop, fix himself in one impossibly long moment. Stop doing the endless dreadful task his traitor hands persisted with.

But always he was helpless.

The pile of jewels was still large, but it was much smaller than it had been after he and Malkin had finished building it. Benfro picked his way through the jewels one by one, savouring briefly the flashing memories of those dragons who had lived so long before.

At first they had fought against him, ghostly forms swirling about his head, shouting at him to wake up. But Magog had done something to them so that all he could hear now was the soft chink of crystals rolling together and the silent screaming of tortured souls.

He was tired like he hadn't slept for a thousand nights. Weariness pulled at his arms, drooped his wings from his back, made every breath an effort, and yet he was powerless to do anything but sit in front of the pile, sorting jewels into smaller heaps. He always knew when the complete memories of a dragon were reunited. It was like the feeling of a voice abruptly cut off, a sobbing lament silenced by the slamming of a dungeon door. And when each small heap was ready, he would stand, scoop up the gleaming jewels in his shaky hands and carry them to the next stone alcove to imprison them in endless mad solitude.

Benfro knew that this was a dream. He knew that all the while he still slept in his draughty corral, shivering on his damp bed of twigs and grass. And yet he was here in Magog's repository, deep beneath the ruined castle of Cenobus, watched continuously by the brooding presence of the great mage himself. Corwen had tried to explain something to him of the art of dreamwalking, but Benfro was not all that receptive to the old dragon's teaching at the moment. Apart from his constant debilitating weariness, he couldn't forgive Corwen for bringing the young man, Errol, to the clearing he had begun to think of as home. Or was he just angry because Errol had saved his life? He didn't owe men anything but hate.

The jewels he had been carrying spilled out of his lifeless hands and into their alcove prison. Benfro imagined he could hear a howl of despair as the remains of some long-dead dragon succumbed to Magog's terrible working. Then with a start he realized that the noise came from his own mouth. He slumped forward, resting his head against the cold stone for a minute, sobbing with sheer frustration. He feared sleeping now, for every night brought the same journey to this terrible place; every night he was forced to do this horrific work, and every night he could feel Magog growing stronger. No wonder he spent his waking hours in a daze; there was no rest to be had from sleep. And nor could he easily escape from it.

Anger and frustration swept through him as he stood in the cold repository. Benfro hammered his hands against the rough stone, feeling the life surge back into him with the blows. Almost as quickly, the looming invisible presence of his tormentor coalesced into a solid form, the tendrils of control tightening in his mind.

'Come, young apprentice, your work is not yet finished.' Magog's voice was totally compelling, directing Benfro's muscles back towards the gleaming pile of stolen jewels. He fought against it with all his might, as he had done every night since escaping the mountaintop retreat, seeking out that weak spot in Magog's influence. He knew what he was looking for, the dull nagging ache between his shoulder blades, the root of his twisted wing.

'No more! Leave me alone!' Benfro twisted round as he shouted, feeling for the uneven branches he knew were underneath him, supporting his sleeping form hundreds of miles away. With a gasp he found them, found the spot of maximum tenderness, and drove himself backwards on to it. A searing pain ripped through his back as if some great wild beast had leaped upon him and was tearing the flesh from his bones with its teeth. The wind rushed out of him with a great screaming cry, his vision dimmed almost to black, and then he was back on his bed of dried grass and bracken, gasping for breath and juddering with shock.

The pale spring sun hung over the treetops on the eastern edge of the clearing as Benfro emerged wearily from the corral and trudged down to the river. The water was icy still, meltwater from the mountains to the north. He didn't care as he waded out towards the waterfall and plunged his muddled head into the flow. His wing ached like a sore tooth, something that had to be probed and prodded. It should have healed by now, but every night he wrenched it anew escaping from Magog's influence.

'He can help you, you know.'

Benfro looked around to see Corwen standing alongside him. The image of the old dragon was almost perfect, but the water didn't part around his legs and tail where they dipped into the river.

'How can he help? He can't even walk.'

'Errol's ankles are much improved, as it happens. He at least knows how to listen to those who offer help. Well, most of the time, anyway.'

'What can he possibly do for me?'

'He can watch over you while you sleep.'

Benfro snorted, water spraying from his nose. 'Why would he want to do that?'

'Because he can. Because he wants to help.'

'And why should I trust him, even if I did believe he could do anything for me?'

'Benfro, it's been three weeks now since you got back here. You've not slept properly in that entire time. Every night you're off to Magog's repository rebuilding his power, and every night you lose a little bit more of yourself to him. It's plain for anyone to see you're changing day by day. The kitling Morgwm raised would never have refused to help heal injuries, even if they were on a man, yet you left Errol to heal himself. That's the action of Magog, not Benfro.'

'I can defeat him. I will defeat him. And on my own.' Benfro trudged out of the river and shook himself dry. His wing root cracked painfully at the motion, but he ignored it, turning his attention instead to his aura and the insubstantial thin red cord that leached away from his forehead like some ghostly siphon. The knot he had tied around it had faded as he slept, and he spent weary minutes trying to fix it. Success brought a measure of relief from a pain he had not realized he had been feeling, like a heavy burden being lifted from his shoulders. He was surprised to find that he was seated on the riverbank; he didn't remember sitting down. Hunger rumbled in his stomach, but he ignored it for a moment, just relishing the feeling of the sun on his face. After a while Corwen came and sat beside him.

'I'm sorry,' Benfro said. 'It's hard to fight him sometimes.'

'I know. But you can do it. And you can win. But not alone, Benfro. If you don't take the help that's offered, and take it soon, there'll be nothing of you left to save.'

2

Although they have a reputation for terrorizing remote settlements and killing people for sport, there is no reliable documented evidence of dragons ever having caused anyone intentional harm. Mander Keece's fairy tales tell of ferocious battles fought between dragons and of unfortunate peasant farmers being caught up in the melee, but it is only in later, more derivative works of fiction that dragons actually go out of their way to do men ill.

This accords well with the nature of the beasts. Few and far between, they are peaceable, gentle creatures, only their savage appearance lending credence to the tales spun around them.

Father Charmoise, *Dragons' Tales*

'It's a miserable little place, really. You wonder why anyone would want to live here.'

Inquisitor Melyn looked across at Captain Osgal as they rode down towards the collection of rickety houses, noticing the sneer on the man's face. Melyn hadn't realized before quite how ramshackle and primitive the place was. The village hall had a sturdy simplicity about it, and the squat church was solidly functional, but the other buildings were little more than wattle and daub huts with reed-thatch roofs. Only two of the houses were more than a single storey high, presumably those of the village alderman and the merchant, Clun's father. The rest of them, clustered around the central green and along the line of the main route to Candlehall, were no more than ragged hovels. In the grey drizzling mist there was nobody to be seen as the small troop of warrior priests rode in.

'Don't you come from these parts, Osgal?'

The look of contempt deepened. 'And glad I was to leave. It's bastard hard farming here; you're off the main trading routes too. At least when the court was at Ystumtuen there was work to be had in the forests, but most of these people scratch and scrape just to keep alive.'

The troop rode on through the silent village until they arrived outside the alderman's house. One of the warrior priests dismounted and hammered on its stout oak door, the sound echoing across the damp green and fading into the mist. They waited for several minutes, and the inquisitor was about to order the door kicked down when finally the sound of a heavy bolt being drawn back rattled through the wood, followed by a tortured creaking as the door was opened a fraction.

'Alderman?' Melyn asked. The pale face peering out widened in surprise. Alderman Clusster pulled open the door and looked around nervously before stepping out of the house.

'Inquisitor, thank the Shepherd,' he said.

'What's the matter, man? Where is everyone?'

'Hiding, Your Grace. In fear of their lives.'

'What are you talking about?'

'Please, it's not safe out.' The alderman wrung his hands in agitation. 'Come inside.'

Melyn was going to protest, but there seemed little chance of getting the man to speak sense when he was so obviously terrified of the sky. Instead he turned to the captain.

'Wait here. I won't be long.' He dismounted, handing the reins over, then followed the nervous little man inside.

Once the door was closed and firmly bolted, Alderman Clusster seemed to regain some of his composure. He knelt, taking the inquisitor's hand and kissing it like a quaister.

'Please forgive my rudeness, Your Grace. But these past weeks have been hard for us all.'

'Hard? What are you talking about, man? What's been going on here?'

'Nobody has seen the creatures and lived to tell the tale. They come in the night mostly, but on days like today, when the mist flows out of the forest, you can hear them shuffling around the edge of the village.'

Melyn skimmed the edges of the alderman's thoughts, trying to make some sense of what he was being told, but all he could feel was the man's fear. It filled him completely, but it was irrational. There was nothing to be frightened of.

'Start at the beginning.' Melyn motioned for the alderman to stand. 'When did these . . . things first appear?'

'It's difficult to say, Your Grace. Livestock go missing all the time, but some of the more remote farmers started complaining quite a few weeks ago. Not just one or two beasts wandering off; they were losing whole flocks overnight. All the younger men left to join the army just as soon as the call went out for soldiers. Glad to go, they were. I'd have gone myself, but, well, I'm not as young as I was. And I have a responsibility to the village.'

'Quite so.' Melyn tried to calm the alderman's scurrying thoughts before he started babbling again. 'But what was it you thought was attacking you? What was taking your sheep?'

'Dragons, Inquisitor. It was dragons.'

'Dragons?' Melyn said. 'What makes you think that?'

'Tom Tydfil the smith swore he saw one up on the forest edge. A great beast of a thing, wings as wide as a barn, flying through the air as if it had every right.'

'Really?' Melyn had to admit he was intrigued by the story, though there could be no truth in it. The dragon hatchling Benfro was away up to the north and there couldn't be another creature like him. 'And where is Tom Tydfil now? I'd very much like to speak to him about this sighting. There's gold for information leading to the capture of dragons, you know.'

'He's dead, Your Grace. They killed him.'

'Killed him? How?'

'I don't know. We just found him out in one of the high fields, lying on his back, eyes wide open and stone cold. That's when most of the younger men left. I sent my daughter away too.'

'How many people are there left here?' Melyn surveyed the front hall of the alderman's house. It was cluttered and dusty.

'About twenty of us, all in.'

'The man who was getting married when last I was here, Godric Defaid. Is he still here?'

The alderman stiffened at the name as if he felt insulted to have it mentioned in his home.

'They say it was that witch he married that brought the beasts down on us. She put a glamour on him, that much is true. Why else would he give up his house here in the village and move up to that shack of hers in the woods? I've not seen either of them since the dragons turned up, but no doubt they're up there still, ordering them to destroy us all.'

Melyn looked long and hard at Alderman Clusster, and suddenly he understood. The man was quite mad. Something had tipped him over the edge, most probably watching the village he had once ruled as his own little kingdom slowly disintegrate as more and more people left. The raising of Queen Beulah's army would have sucked the life out of many villages like this one. There were no dragons raiding the livestock fields. Even if there were any of the beasts left in this corner of the Twin Kingdoms, it was very doubtful they would have dared to show themselves after what he had done to Morgwm and the sorry collection of beasts she had been hiding. If he remembered rightly, the smith had been a prodigious drinker, a great bear of a man. It was quite possible his heart had simply given out one night as he was walking home.

'Well, I wanted to speak with Goodman Defaid and his wife about their sons,' Melyn said. 'Now it seems there's another reason for my troop to seek out this cottage of theirs. I will of course be needing a guide.'

'A guide?' Melyn didn't need to read the alderman's thoughts to see the mad fear coursing through him. It was in his eyes.

'Don't worry, Alderman. I wouldn't expect you to do it yourself. You can send a boy. He'll be quite safe.'

'We . . . we sent all the children away. Father Kewick took them all to the seminary at Beteltown. There weren't many, and we thought it was for the best.'

'Very well.' Melyn felt a small surge of anger at the news, but he pushed it away. 'I've no doubt we can find this place ourselves. In the meantime I want you to gather all the remaining villagers together in the hall. I've some important news for you all.'

The alderman's eyes were nearly popping at the thought of having to leave his house, but Melyn grabbed him by his shirt front and pulled him outside. Captain Osgal still sat on his horse, holding the inquisitor's and waiting patiently. Behind him the troop had not moved a muscle.

'Change of plan, Captain,' Melyn said. 'We're taking a ride out into the woods. Seems there's been a bit of dragon trouble here lately. I want you to help Alderman Clusster here round up the rest of the villagers. Take half of the troop and make sure they're all waiting for me in the village hall when I get back.'

Osgal nodded his assent as Melyn climbed back on to his horse. Without being told, half of the warrior priests fell in behind him. They rode out of the village on the track indicated by the alderman that led uphill towards the forest edge.

It took less time to reach the cottage than he had expected. The path was well worn, testimony to Hennas's skill as a healer, no doubt. Melyn signalled for his warrior priests to fan out, surrounding the building, before he approached it. He needn't have bothered; the place was empty and looked like it had been for several days. Inside were signs of a rushed departure: clothes strewn over the floor, a food store hurriedly ransacked for provisions, the fireplace filled with charred wood, cold and damp. He pushed his way through the chaos into the back of the house, finding a slightly tidier state of affairs. One room, obviously the master bedroom, was dominated by an unmade bed and a huge oak wardrobe, its doors hanging slightly open to reveal assorted clothes within. The room smelled damp, like it hadn't been used for a while, and the same was true of the smaller bedroom, though this was tidy. Errol's room, Melyn thought as his eyes fell on the narrow cot-like bed, the neat desk arranged under the window and the heavy wooden chest that no doubt held the boy's clothes. He hadn't come here, that much was certain.

'Inquisitor, I think you should see this.'

Melyn turned to the warrior priest who had interrupted him. The young man had a name, he was sure, but for the moment he couldn't think what it was. Cursing his forgetfulness, he followed him out of the house and across the small clearing to the trees.

'It's through here.' The warrior priest pushed aside some bushes, making a narrow path for Melyn to scramble through before leading him into the thickening trees, then, finally, out into another clearing.

It was littered with trees smashed and splintered as if by some giant. The ground was churned, pools of oily

water collecting in the holes where roots had been ripped from the earth. Something had beaten a path fully thirty paces wide leading away from the cottage and up the hill towards the deeper forest.

'What in the name of the Shepherd could have done this?' Melyn asked, though he had a horrible feeling he knew already.

'It gets worse, sir. Over here.' The warrior priest picked his way through the carnage to the far side of the clearing. Melyn followed, slowly taking everything in. Overhead the sun was beginning to burn through the mist, painting the scene with a surreal golden glow, and something glinted in the mud at his feet. He bent to pick it up, but before he could examine what it was, his eyes fell on the sight he had been brought here to see.

In the crater left by the roots of a particularly large oak tree someone had piled the bones of what must have been several dozen animals. They had been stripped of meat until they gleamed white, scraps of wool and hide still clinging in odd places. Flies buzzed around the charnel pit with frenzied motion, stirring up a stench that reminded Melyn of the battlefield. Rotting meat, blood and ichor, the smell of guts violently spilled. These creatures had not died easily.

They were mostly sheep, a few cattle and perhaps a couple of horses, judging by the shape of the skulls that hadn't been cracked open. But two sets of bones to one side dragged Melyn's attention away from the animal remains. They lay together like grossly entwined lovers, one somewhat larger than the other, both reduced to torn

shreds of flesh and gristle, their limbs ripped from sockets, skulls trailing vertebrae.

Human skulls.

'Maybe Godric and Hennas didn't escape after all. A pity. I had planned on killing them myself.' Melyn wiped his face with the back of his hand. He remembered the shiny object he had picked up, and held it up to the light to get a better view. It was about the size of his palm, triangular in shape and thicker along one edge than the other two. It curved slightly to the thin point and had ridges along its flat side that reminded him curiously of a fingernail.

'What is it, sir?' Melyn looked up at the warrior priest. His name was Tegwin, he remembered now.

'It would seem that Alderman Clusster's not as mad as I had thought,' he said. 'This is a dragon's scale. Perhaps the largest I've ever seen.'

Benfro whittled away at the log with one extended talon, covering his feet in pale yellow shavings. He wasn't carving anything in particular, nor did he need to light a fire. It was simply a distraction, something to keep him from drifting off to sleep and Magog's unwelcome embrace. Leaning against the rough stone wall of his corral, he had taken the weight off his damaged wing root, but he knew that it would wake him if he began to nod off.

Movement at the cave mouth caught his attention. The young man, Errol, stepped out into the light, wincing slightly with each footfall, even though he supported his weight on a crude pair of crutches fashioned from some of the longer pieces of firewood. Benfro watched him, saying nothing, as he hobbled painfully to the river and knelt for a drink, then inched slowly across the ford to the far side. Without looking back, Errol shuffled slowly off into the forest.

'He really shouldn't be walking that far. Not yet.' Benfro looked round to see Corwen sitting down beside him. The old dragon's sudden appearances no longer startled him.

'Where's he going?'

'A bit deeper into the woods, to set a few snares. I think he's getting tired of the roots and herbs he's been eating.'

'Can't he just get stuff? You know . . .'

'Like Ynys Môn used to? Sir Frynwy and the others? That's a skill it takes years to master, as I think you probably know. What was it you managed – a melon and a turnip? And that was with the greatest mage that ever lived directing you.'

'Magog wasn't there. I did it on my own.'

'Magog is always there, Benfro. You won't be free of him until you find a way to reckon that jewel.'

'Then I might as well give up now. Let him take me over completely. There're no dragons left with that kind of skill.'

'Perhaps not in this land, no. Maybe you need to look further afield.'

The piece of wood snapped in his hands. Benfro looked down, startled to see that he had stripped it to almost nothing. Thin shavings covered his feet and sprayed out on to the path, as if he had been caught in a woodchip snowstorm. He stood up, dusted himself off, suddenly bored.

'Where are you going?' Corwen asked as Benfro made his way towards the ford.

'To check on those snares. I doubt very much that boy has a clue what he's doing.'

The forest was cool and still. Benfro walked silently through dappled light, tasting the air and straining with his ears for the telltale signs of Errol's trail. It wasn't hard to follow. He found the first snare in minutes. It was a makeshift thing, made from long threads that must have been teased out of the boy's cloak and plaited together for strength. It was placed too high, but at least it was on a regularly used animal trail. He picked it up and moved it to a position that would be more likely to guarantee a catch, then moved on to look for the next one.

There were ten in all, each platted from the same material. It wasn't ideal for making snares – Benfro had better ones in the bottom of his leather bag – but the work showed remarkable ingenuity. Errol had nothing else to work with, he realized – less even than Benfro himself. Just the clothes he stood in. And yet he was making the most of his situation. It was a pity that the boy had no real skill as a hunter. He would have to learn, or he would surely starve out here in the forest.

Errol limped from the trees, leaning on his crutches as he struggled across the shallow ford. The afternoon sun was warm on his back, but it was a small pleasure compared to the pain in his ankles. That he could walk at all was miracle enough, he reminded himself.

There was no sign of Benfro apart from the mess of wood shavings where he had been splintering logs all day.

Errol bent down, picked up a handful and took it into the cave. The dry wood caught easily on the last few embers of the fire, and he soon had a reasonable blaze going again. It was just a pity he had nothing to cook on it but tough roots and the few woodland salad leaves that had started to shoot now that the winter's cold was turning to spring. He only hoped that his snares would be strong enough to hold whatever they caught. If they caught anything at all.

'You won't starve, Errol. Don't worry about that.'

He looked up to see Corwen's vast bulk seated on the other side of the fire. The image of Corwen, he reminded himself. Corwen was long dead, but somewhere nearby his jewels lay at a nexus of the Grym, just like Sir Radnor's. Only where Sir Radnor had appeared as a magnificent beast with wings greater even than Benfro's, Corwen chose to appear as a doddery old creature, bent with age, his scales chipped and broken.

'Why do you look like that?' Errol asked.

'This is how I appeared when I died. It would be vain to present myself otherwise.'

'But you must have been younger once, stronger.' Errol struggled to say what he was thinking without sounding rude. 'Does it not hurt to be old like that?'

'I'm dead, Errol. I feel nothing in my bones; they were burned away in the Fflam Gwir hundreds of years ago. This image you see is just how I had come to regard myself.'

Errol massaged his ankles as he sat on the low bed. Walking had pained him more than he liked to admit. He shifted his focus on to the Grym, meaning to pull some of its warmth and healing into him, to disperse some of the discomfort, but as he watched the lines shimmer into view, so he noticed something about the image of the old dragon.

Corwen glowed with a pale translucence. He was suffused with it, as if formed from the Grym itself. He sat on a point where two thick strands intersected, and it seemed that power flowed through them and into him. But whereas the Grym surrounding him was golden like spring sunlight, the lines immediately beneath him were tinged with pink.

'You see it, don't you?' Corwen said. 'The canker that he spreads through the land. This is only a fraction of what Benfro feels.'

'I don't understand. Who are you talking about?'

Instead of answering, Corwen stood up and turned to face the cave wall. 'Follow me,' he said, then vanished.

Errol stared at the spot where the old dragon had been. The pink was gone, but one line glowed brighter than the others, spearing away through the rock. For a moment he was confused. He couldn't possibly see through solid stone, and yet he could sense the line reaching out to a destination. He could almost see another cave, circular, dark, with a small raised plinth in the middle of it. The more he stared, the clearer it became, so that the wall of rock between him and the strange scene faded to air, and then nothing. He could see the plinth clearly now, and on its top, at the centre, sat a pile of clear white jewels. Towards the edge sat a single red gem. Without thinking what he was doing, Errol reached out for it.

'I shouldn't do that if I were you.'

He stopped in mid-reach and realized with a start that he was standing up. He didn't remember leaving his bed, but the air felt different, cooler. The smell of woodsmoke was gone and it was darker than it should have been. Looking around for an exit, Errol saw smooth rock forming an almost perfect circle a few dozen paces across. Only a dark opening broke the shape, bringing the distant sound of running water along it.

Corwen shimmered into existence, his form covering the plinth but not obscuring it.

'Two hundred years have passed since Benfro's mother performed the ceremony of reckoning and set my jewels in here. No dragon has entered this cavern since then. No man has ever entered it. You should consider yourself quite privileged, Errol Ramsbottom.'

Errol shuddered, both at the chill and the realization of what he had just done.

'Why . . . ? What . . . ?'

'These –' Corwen indicated the pile at the centre of the plinth '– are my jewels. This –' he lifted a single pale jewel that had been obscured behind the pile '– is all that Benfro has of his mother, Morgwm the Green. Your friend Inquisitor Melyn has the rest. And this –' he indicated the small irregular nugget of crimson crystal '– is an unreckoned jewel from the great Magog, Son of the Summer Moon.'

'But I thought Magog was just a myth. The way Sir Radnor told it, the story was a lesson, a warning about being too arrogant and proud.'

'And so it is. But that doesn't mean it's not true. Magog lived thousands of years ago. His exploits were never exaggerated, nor his cruelty. But what none of us ever realized was the extent of his madness. He used the darkest perversion of the subtle arts to remove some of his own jewels while he still lived. Through these he has maintained an influence over men and dragons for thousands of years.'

'And that's one of them?' Errol pointed at the ugly red gem.

'No. That's the last of his true jewels. Benfro found it. Or more correctly, he was drawn to it. What Magog never anticipated was that Benfro would rescue the jewel and carry it with him. He was supposed to leave it behind. That way he would never have noticed the link that had been forged between the two of them. At least not until it was too late.'

'What link? Too late for what?' Errol felt like he was back in the classroom at Emmass Fawr, only this time he hadn't a clue what the lesson was about.

'Through this jewel, Magog is slowly taking over Benfro. His mind, his body. He gave him his wings. That's powerful magic even for a living dragon. And that gift formed an almost unbreakable bond between the two of them. I've done what I can to help; before, Benfro only had to move a few paces away from the jewel and he was totally incapacitated. But I've only lengthened the time it takes Magog to succeed, not foiled him completely.'

'And it's destroying you too, isn't it?'

'An unreckoned jewel is a very dangerous thing, Errol. This one immeasurably more so.'

'But it can be stopped. You said the bond was *almost* unbreakable. Not unbreakable.'

'The jewel must be reckoned. And for that it must be burned along with the body that contained it. You need only burn one jewel and all the others will turn white, even if they are on the other side of Gwlad. But one jewel must be burned.'

'But surely Magog's body must be long rotted away. If the legends are true, he was slain by King Diseverin over two thousand years ago.'

'If Benfro's story is correct, and I've no reason to disbelieve him, then some of Magog's bones remain. But they're hidden by an ancient and powerful spell at the place where both brothers were hatched. The only way you can find it is to be invited there by either Magog or his brother Gog.'

Errol couldn't be sure, but it seemed as though the red jewel pulsed with an angry fire at the mention of the name. And Corwen's image seemed to fade slightly, as if the dragon had been hit by some powerful force.

'But if they're both dead . . .'

'If both brothers were dead, then the magic that hid their hatchplace would slowly begin to dissolve. Any who had been there would be able to find their way back. Benfro has no clue as to where the place is, so it is still protected. Wherever he is, Gog must be very much still alive.'

Again at the name that flash of angry power seemed to sap Corwen's vitality.

'But why are you telling me this? You want me to find Gog? I wouldn't know where to start.'

'You know more than you realize, young Errol. And you've far more skill at the subtle arts than any man. And yes, I would like you to find him. Or to help Benfro find him. But there's another reason why I wanted to show you this; to explain it all as best I understand it myself. Magog must not be allowed to rise again. I've no love of your kind, but if Magog succeeds in taking over Benfro, then he will rip the whole of Gwlad apart looking for his brother. And when he finds him they will fight. If anything is left when they've finished, it won't be worth living in, for man or dragon.

'So yes, I want you to help Benfro free himself of this curse, and me too, for that matter. But if you fail there's something else you must do. You'll know when there's nothing left of Benfro and Magog has taken his place. If that moment comes, you must kill him.'

Errol looked up at the old dragon in surprise.

'Surely there must be –'

'I won't make you promise, Errol. You don't owe either of us anything. But I hope you can understand. Magog must not be allowed to live again. Now come. Follow me back to your cave. Or go on your own, if you feel you can.'

Errol knew he was being dismissed, and even though Corwen's words made his thoughts a turmoil, still he felt he should try and walk the lines back to where he had started. He focused on the Grym, searching for the way he had come, but it was too confusing. The lines went everywhere, each one a tantalizing glimpse of something different, somewhere else. Briefly he glimpsed the cave, or something that looked a lot like it, but it was overlaid with an image of a stone-walled room dominated by an enormous fireplace and a huge reading desk. Another, more shadowy place of pillars and low ceilings hovered in the background of his mind like a mist. Frustrated, he gave up.

'It's no use. I can't concentrate.'

'Perhaps understandable, given the circumstances.' Corwen shuffled forward and past Errol to the dark opening in the far wall of the cave. 'Follow me then, but I'm afraid you're going to get wet.'

It was slow painful going without his crutches for support. Errol leaned against the walls as best he could to minimize his weight as he inched along a wide tunnel that wound in a spiral pattern, climbing up until it opened into a much larger cavern. Light spilled in through a curtain of water cascading down directly opposite, and yet the air was dry, as was the furniture that filled what had once been someone's home. Corwen's home, Errol realized, as the old dragon continued to walk, straight through the wall of water, which showed no sign of his passing. Errol hobbled up to the edge, paused, then stepped through.

He dropped about three feet into the roiling water at the base of the waterfall. The bubble-filled water couldn't support his weight and he sank to the bottom like a stone. Cold drove the air out of his lungs, and for a moment he was back at Jagged Leap, struggling to save himself. Then the current swept him swiftly away, towards the ford, and he was soon able to pull himself out and on to dry land. Gasping and shivering, he limped slowly back to the cave mouth, where Corwen stood, a wicked grin on his face. Benfro was nowhere to be seen, though the pile of shavings where he had been whittling earlier was even bigger than before. Errol assumed he was inside the corral, sleeping or perhaps just moping. He wondered if he would ever be able to help the young dragon. Or kill him.

Inside, the fire was warm, filling the cave with welcome

heat. Errol stripped off his soaking clothes, hanging them as best he could to dry before wrapping himself in his cloak. Only then did he notice what looked like a pile of blackened leaves on the edge of the hearth. Intrigued, he dragged it towards him with a stick, and a heavenly aroma of cooked meat burst forth. He pulled the leaves apart to find a large rabbit, gutted and skinned and cooked to perfection. Its empty stomach cavity had even been stuffed with a few choice herbs to add flavour, but Errol didn't care. He would have eaten it raw.

He only remembered his manners when the last bone was licked clean. Wrapping his cloak around him, he limped out of the cave into the evening dark. Across the track there was no sign of Benfro, who had presumably taken himself off to bed.

'Thank you,' Errol said anyway, if only to the night.

3

Dragons are naturally magical creatures; any trained mage will tell you of the aura of power they exude. The jewels that grow within their brains are prized above gold for their ability to focus the Grym. They are not, however, intelligent practitioners of magic, any more than they are masterful intellects in any other way. More, dragons are like precocious children who sometimes amaze their parents with acts of seeming great skill, yet nevertheless stumble upon those acts by chance.

There are some who say that dragons indeed have magical lore, and that it is written down in great and powerful books. Anyone who has read the simple runic scratchings that pass for dragon writing will see this for the fanciful nonsense it is.

Father Charmoise, *Dragons' Tales*

'My lady, are you sure you should be out of bed? The palace physicians said you should get as much rest as possible.'

'The palace physicians couldn't heal a cut finger. I've a mind to have them flogged for what they did to me. Useless quacks.' Beulah wished she had thought of it earlier, but the sheer joy of being rid of her tiredness and nausea had driven everything else from her mind. Even her condition didn't concern her. If anything, the knowledge that she was pregnant had displaced the fear and revulsion of having to produce an heir with a kind of giddy excitement she hadn't experienced in years. But there were serious matters that had to be considered: her heir had to be legitimate.

'Where are you taking me, my lady?' Clun followed her like a loyal hound; Beulah was certain that he would follow her into the lair of the Running Wolf if she asked him. But as they descended deeper into the old parts of the citadel, the basements and tunnels cut into the rock of the Hill of Kings, so he had fallen a little behind her, as if uncertain he should be seeing the things he was being shown.

'It's a surprise, my love.' Beulah waited for him to catch up, took him by the hand and led him to the next door, its heavy panel of oak blackened with age and studded with great iron nails. Two locks yielded to the huge keys she had brought with her, and with a great deal of theatrical creaking the door swung open. Beyond, a narrow staircase hewn out of the rock climbed down in a spiral. Darkness seemed to ooze out of the doorway, bringing with it a strange chill and the near-silent whispering of countless voices.

'Should I bring a torch?'

Beulah smiled. She could hear the fear in his voice, though Clun hid it well.

'There's no need.' She held out her hand and a ball of pure white light appeared, hovering just over her palm. Holding it ahead of her, she stepped on to the stairs.

'What I'm about to show you is a secret few have ever seen. Down here are the collected treasures of over two thousand years of the House of Balwen. Only the royal family and the heads of the three religious orders are allowed to see them.'

'My lady, I shouldn't . . .' Beulah reached for Clun with her free hand and pulled him towards her, planting a kiss firmly on his lips.

'I order it,' she said, handing him the keys. 'Now follow. And lock the door behind you.'

He said nothing but did as he was told. Beulah could sense his trepidation, but she could also feel his wonder and excitement at this new adventure. It was a mix as potent as any of her father's sweet Fo Afron wines, and she savoured it as they stepped carefully down the narrow winding staircase.

Towards the bottom, light began to seep up from below, dull red but more than enough to see by. Beulah let her conjured light extinguish, absorbing the power of it into herself with a little surge of warmth that spread across her whole skin and made her tingle. Instead of the sensation slowly ebbing away, as it would normally, it grew with each step further down.

'My lady, I feel . . .'

'Powerful? Intoxicated? Aroused? Don't worry, my love. You will come to no harm in this place.' She reached out for his hand again, and as their fingers brushed together sparks flew between them. All of a sudden Beulah could see his thoughts as clearly as if they were her own. He was scared, but also awed and a little confused. He had been told about this place, she realized, but only as the sort of barrack-room rumour all novitiates might hear. He had no real idea what it truly was, only that the punishment for entering it was an unpleasant and messy death.

With a practised thought Beulah wiped away Clun's fears, assuring him that he had every right to be here. Then, because she couldn't help herself, she went deeper into his mind.

He loved her with an unquestioning, unconditional devotion, she realized. With a start, she discovered that he had loved her since first he had seen her, at his father's wedding. He had never harboured any hope that she would even notice him, but he had dedicated himself to her service. Silently, personally, but with a good deal more conviction than his stepbrother Errol's drunken proclamation.

The image of Errol flickered through Clun's mind, and with it there was a deep sorrow. He believed that the boy had turned traitor, perhaps had always been a traitor, and yet his betrayal didn't square with the Errol he had grown up with. The weedy little book-obsessed outsider had turned out to be far more of a friend than any of the other boys in the village. Clun desperately wanted Errol to have been under some kind of mind control, to have been turned by King Ballah. Beulah left him that small comfort and quietly withdrew from his thoughts. Grasping his hand more firmly, she led him around the last corner.

It was a vast underground store. Squat pillars marched off in all directions, holding up a ceiling that was higher than it felt. Into each pillar had been carved hundreds of small niches, and in each niche sat a collection of red jewels, glowing dully in the darkness.

'King Balwen's treasure. The jewels of more than ten thousand dragons.' Beulah watched Clun's open-mouthed expression, his eyes growing wider and wider as he took in each new sight. She walked slowly along the main aisle and he followed her as if hypnotized. His reaction delighted her. She well remembered the first time Melyn had shown her this place, the secret behind the power of the royal house. Then she had been too awestruck to speak, astonished by the endless whispering voices that spoke the thoughts and feelings of her people to her. Later she had learned how to distinguish those voices, how to focus on groups or even individuals. Even the strongest of minds could not long hide its thoughts from this place. The royal house had used that to its advantage down the centuries; no man could keep secrets from the ruler who sat on the Obsidian Throne.

'It's best you don't touch them, my love. They are powerful things, but they are dangerous too. It takes decades of discipline and study to be able to handle a dragon's jewels without losing yourself in them.'

Clun had been reaching towards a niche, but he snapped back his hand as if the alcove had contained a venomous snake.

'Why are these ones white when all the others are red?'

Beulah walked over to where he stood at the end of the long aisle. The niches in the pillar before him were only half filled. Most of the jewels were blood-red, small and irregular in shape, but the ones Clun had pointed out were the size of hens' eggs, brilliantly faceted as if they had been cut by a master jeweller and as white as a bridal gown.

'These are the jewels Melyn brought back from his last hunt. Sometimes they turn white like that, but it's very rare.'

'They sing such a sad song, so lonely and incomplete.'

Beulah stared at the young man who had suddenly come to mean so much to her. She could hear the whispering of the jewels all around her, telling their endless tales of petty lives, the little triumphs and disasters that made up each day for her subjects. With an effort of will she could focus her attention on a single niche, find her way into the mind of a single person, but from the white jewels she heard only silence.

'The white jewels are of little use here. I don't know why Melyn bothers collecting them at all. But come, my love; there's one more thing you must see.'

Clun seemed almost reluctant to leave the pillar and its curious white stones, but he dragged himself away and followed Beulah as she strode along the aisles towards the centre of the vast room. The central pillar was ten times as thick as the rest and made from stone that was pitch black. It had been polished to a mirror-smooth finish, reflecting the glow of the thousands of jewels surrounding it, and underneath the shiny surface strange markings scrolled like an ancient language.

'We are directly underneath the Obsidian Throne,' Beulah said, once more taking Clun's hand. He looked nervously up as if expecting the massive structure to come crashing down through the ceiling at any moment. She reached up to his face and pulled his gaze back down to her. 'It's stood there for more than two thousand years, my love. It's not going to fall down today.'

'Why are you showing me this?' Clun asked.

'Because you need to know. The father of my child must share the responsibility of raising the heir to the throne.'

He was in the forest again. Errol stood on legs blissfully free of pain and looked out over a familiar landscape of ancient trees. Close by, shaded by great cooling canopies of pale green leaves, the path meandered its way past their massive trunks. High overhead, the sky was duck-egg blue and dotted with the whirling forms of distant birds at play. The air smelled sweet and fresh, overlaid with the subtlest fragrance of spice. He was happy just to stand and breathe, free from pain, free from worry.

And then he caught it, a lingering odour on the slightest of breezes. Complex and beautiful, it was spring flowers and autumn leaves, sun-baked rocks and cold water, the smell of soft soap and clean hair. He knew at once who was coming, and his heart soared at the thought of seeing her again.

She came along the path, keeping to the leafy shade. Every so often she would look up at the gyring birds so high above. Then she would bustle across to the next tree, not running but moving with deceptive speed nonetheless. Errol was content to wait for her; he knew that she would reach him soon. Then they could be together. But when she reached where he stood, she didn't turn to greet him. Instead she hurried on towards the next clearing.

He tried to call out to her, but there was something wrong with his voice. He could hear her name as he spoke it deep in his head. But his ears heard nothing, only the constant hiss of the breeze in the leaves. He wanted to run after her, but his legs seemed fixed to the ground. And now she had reached the edge of the tree, pausing briefly before stepping out into the clearing.

He knew what was going to happen next. He had seen it dozens of times already. Every night since he had arrived at Corwen's cave. He was dreaming the scene. Martha was going to be captured by dragons and there was nothing he could do about it.

He watched helplessly as first she confronted the dragons, seemed almost to convince them to leave her alone, then finally allowed herself to be carried off. Any minute now I'll wake up, Errol thought as he realized that Martha hadn't put up a struggle, had almost gone willingly with her captors. But instead of waking, he found himself out in the clearing. The ground was scuffed and marked where the dragons had landed; otherwise there was nothing remarkable about the scene. Looking up, Errol could see birds wheeling and turning in the sunlit sky. They seemed so free, so joyful as they played. Then he realized they weren't birds. They were dragons, dozens of them, chasing each other back and forth, clashing together in mid-air, tumbling down, over and over, before breaking apart at the last possible moment and climbing back into the sky on huge wings.

Then they seemed to notice him. As one, the whole group turned and dived. Errol tried to run, but once more he was fixed in place. He tried to scream, but his voice would not come out. The great beasts grew bigger and bigger as they closed the gap with impossible speed, and he could see the bloody wounds of their play, the scars and missing scales of earlier battles. The dragons were filled with bloodlust, their eyes devoid of any intelligent spark. These were not magnificent creatures of magic and learning. These were feral monsters, wild as the birds of prey for which he had mistaken them.

Errol shut his eyes against the rushing mass. He could hear their screeching and the dreadful sound of their leathery wings beating the air into submission. Louder and louder, they narrowed the gap, and he instinctively turned away at the moment of impact.

It never came.

Instead there was a roar of frustration, a great billowing wind that threatened to topple him over, then silence.

At first he didn't dare open his eyes, but Errol could tell that he was no longer in the forest clearing. There was a different quality to the air, a stillness that spoke of being indoors. Then through the silence he began to hear sounds: the soft clinking of stone upon stone, the near-silent creak of someone moving and a low miserable sobbing. Unsure whether he was awake or still slept, Errol opened his eyes.

He was in a vast chamber carved from the rock. Pillars held up the ceiling, marching off into darkness in all directions. Only the area immediately in front of him was lit, and that by an enormous pile of jewels, luminous and white. The noise seemed to be coming from the other side of the pile, and Errol took a tentative step, unsure whether he would be able to move or not. His view shifted, though it didn't feel like he had moved at all, and now he could see.

Benfro sat on the floor in front of the mountain of jewels, his tail tucked around him like a patient dog waiting to be fed. Behind him a huge old writing desk looked like it had been pushed to one side, long-extinguished candles little more than globs of shiny wax in their sconces. At his feet were three small piles of the white crystals, and he was pulling more from the vast heap, weighing them in his palm one by one, before either adding it to one of the piles or returning it to the heap. Errol had not met many dragons, and wasn't an expert on their expressions, but even he could see the terrible pain that this task seemed to be causing Benfro. His arms moved with a reluctant rigidity, as if he were fighting his own actions with all his strength. He held himself awkwardly, back pressed against the writing desk, pushing it hard with the base of his wing.

And then Benfro stopped his sorting. Oblivious to Errol's presence, he scooped up all the jewels from one small pile, hauled himself to his feet and set off with them into the darkness. Errol followed him bodilessly, devoid of any sensation of movement except his changing viewpoint. They passed down a long aisle between two rows of columns, coming finally to a wall carved with little holes. Some of these, Errol saw, were filled with the pale white jewels – less luminous here, almost dead. Benfro slowly poured the jewels he was carrying into an empty hole, leaning forward and resting his head against the cold stone as he did so, his whole body racked with sobs. All the while he seemed to be fighting, twisting around as if he wanted to smash his back against the wall and demolish it, tumble the jewels all back together. And yet he was powerless to do anything but head back to the large pile at the centre of the room.

Too late Errol realized he was standing in the way. Benfro would have to trample him to get past. But the dragon simply walked straight through him. And at that moment of contact Errol felt a terrible presence all around him, a malignant evil that grew into a form visible in the darkness of the vaulted ceiling. It was a dragon's head larger than any he had ever seen, and it stared into him, through him, with eyes as red as burning coals. It reached out for him with massive hands, fingers tipped with razor-sharp talons. Instinctively Errol took a step backwards, tripped over something and overbalanced. As he fell, he thought he heard an enraged scream, those crushing hands grasping the air where his head had just been. Then, with a great jerk of motion that nearly threw him out of his bed, he woke up.

Melyn brushed a low-hanging branch aside, causing a cascade of rainwater to pour over his cloak, saddle and horse. The track through the trees was a lot more overgrown than he remembered, though scarcely a year had passed since last he had come this way.

'Is there no end to this forest?' He ducked under yet another branch, precipitating another deluge of water down the back of his neck. The icy cold against his skin brought his anger to the surface, and with a quick flick of the wrist he conjured up a blade of light, using it to hack away the branches ahead of him. When he saw that this was merely dislodging more water, he stopped, but not before his horse was soaked to the skin, his cloak a sopping rag pulling heavily at his shoulders.

'Your Grace, I think we're here.' Captain Osgal wheeled his own horse to face the inquisitor. Melyn was pleased to see that the captain was just as wet as him, the rest of the troop possibly wetter. He spurred his horse forward under one more overhanging branch and out into the clearing.

At first he wasn't entirely sure it was the same place. The track that ran through the village to the green and the great hall was completely overrun with moss, grass and weeds; the burned-out shells of the houses had crumbled almost to nothing, made barely recognizable by encroaching vegetation. They rode through the jungle in silence. Of the troop only he and Osgal had been present during the previous visit, but everyone knew they were looking at the sort of growth that should have taken a decade, not a year.

The green in front of the great hall was a sea of grass that tickled the bellies of the horses as they rode through it. The hall itself still stood, in frame at least. Its roof had collapsed, the plaster infill between the oak beams turned brittle and crumbly. Leaded glass windows sagged in their frames, loosed panes lying broken on the ground.

Melyn dismounted, handing his reins to a warrior priest before pushing his way through the long grass to the heavy doors, still standing in their twisted, blackened frames. They sagged half open, and as he pushed on the weathered oak they swung inwards with a smooth action quite at odds with everything else in the ruined village.

Inside, daylight flooded through the ruined roof to reveal a heap of burned and charred timbers, heavy stone slates and half-collapsed walls. In the middle of the room a huge table lay smashed in half. Benches along either side had been broken into so much firewood by the collapsing roof. Only the large carved wooden chair at the head of the table was unscathed, miraculously missed by falling masonry. Rain-streaked and weathered, it was otherwise almost perfect.

Except for the sapling growing from the wood of its seat, reaching for the open ceiling and already twice as tall as a man.

Melyn trod carefully over the debris, testing beams and huge stone slabs for stability before trusting his weight to them. He scrabbled over to the great table, even though he knew there was no point. There should have been the charred skeletons of thirty dragons in here, their skulls weakened by exposure and ready for splitting, their jewels waiting to be scooped from within. Instead there were more saplings, each one where a dragon might have been expected to sit.

'Where did they go?' Captain Osgal bent forward and pulled one of the saplings towards him, then cursed, let it go and put his hand to his mouth.

'Bastard thing's got thorns.' Osgal held out his finger and Melyn could see a long ragged-edged tear in the skin. Blood welled out of the new cut, splashing to the floor to mix with the damp dust and ash.

'Let's get out of here.' Melyn retraced his steps to the door, Osgal following and grumbling all the while.

As he climbed back on to his horse, Melyn felt a shudder run through him, as if someone were watching him in the aethereal. Slipping into the trance state with practised ease, he looked around the clearing for Queen Beulah's form; he doubted anyone else could master the skill well enough to find him here and was surprised that even she had managed.

She was nowhere to be seen, but the clearing looked completely different from his new perspective. For a start it was whole, undamaged and unclaimed by the surrounding forest. The hall was better than it had been when he had set it aflame, crisp and new like the day it was completed. The green below his horse's feet was smooth and flat, the grass neatly trimmed. Over the arrow-straight and smooth-cobbled track, the houses stood solid and welcoming, the nearest and largest seeming to glow as if someone lived within.

'Inquisitor?' Melyn dropped out of his trance, turning to face the captain, who had wrapped his hand in a white cloth that even now was turning red with his blood.

'What is it, Captain?'

'Should we search the area? Try to find who took the jewels?'

Melyn felt a surge of irritation at the man. He was a skilled warrior, if rather brutal in his manipulation of the Grym, but he was singularly lacking in imagination.

'No, Captain,' he said. 'That would be a waste of time. The jewels are gone. Leave it at that. I should have sent a party to collect them earlier, but I had other things on my mind. I let myself get distracted. I shan't make that mistake again.'

He turned away from the captain and looked back in the direction of the glowing house that he had seen in his trance state. It stood taller than those around it, some of its shape still visible under the heavy blanket of brambles, bushes and ivy. Spurring his horse forward, he crossed the fast-disappearing track, using the animal's bulk to force his way as close to the front door as possible. When he could go no further without risking injury, he conjured a blade of light and hacked at the vegetation. Silently, without being commanded, the warrior priests appeared at his side and began to help.

It took a good half-hour to clear a path wide enough. The building had burned, but the fire had only consumed the top storey, leaving the ground floor largely intact. Melyn forced the door open to reveal a weed-choked hall with two further doors leading off. A scorched staircase climbed to the clouds.

The first door opened on to a mass of leaves where a thick bush had grown to fill the available space. Beyond the staircase the fire had eaten away most of the back of the building, but the other door still stood firm. He tried to open it, but it was locked. His blade of fire should have made short work of the wood, but as he brought it to bear, it fizzled out and died. Astonished, Melyn looked more closely. The frame was dark and ornately carved with strange stick-like sigils – Draigiaith. As written by the dragons themselves, it was a poor alphabet and difficult to decipher, so many words being depicted by the same symbol. He really needed Andro to read it, or at least give him some idea of what he was dealing with.

Slipping once more into his trance, Melyn studied the doorway as he would study the Grym, and sure enough he could make out protections weaved over the room beyond. They would have been all but impossible to break had the creature that had woven them been still alive, but any spell began to unravel and lose its potency once its creator died; all he needed to find was the right point to start.

It was slow work, but rewarding. The skill with which the protections had been wrought was breathtaking, certainly far more sophisticated than anything he had seen in many years. Still, he knew he could beat them, and eventually he did. With a quiet sigh of satisfaction he slid back from the aethereal and into his body, pushing forward on the door as he felt its solid form against his outstretched hand. It gave, creaking slightly as it opened on to a dark room, musty and dry smelling despite the damp and vegetation all around it.

Conjuring a light, Melyn stepped into what was quite obviously a library. Heavy leather-bound books lined the walls, and were piled on and around a wide reading desk. Two chairs, shaped for dragons to sit in, sat one each side of a large fireplace, the ashen shapes of logs still sitting on the hearth. With the door opened, a breeze kicked up the ash, crumbling it away to dust that floated up the chimney.

Melyn looked slowly around the room, wondering how it had been missed when the troop had searched the village. But then half of them had been novitiates; they would never have even seen the door, let alone been able to get past the wards that protected it. While the dragons had still lived, perhaps even he might have overlooked it.

He reached out and took a book from the pile on top of the reading desk. It was a thick volume, bound in dark leather and bearing more of those impenetrable runes inscribed in gold on its cover. It felt too heavy in his hands, and the tips of his fingers tingled where they touched it. Voices whispered seductively in his ears as he made to open the cover and look inside.

'Inquisitor?' Captain Osgal stood in the doorway, not daring to come in. For once Melyn forgave him the interruption. He pushed back the urge to open the book, shuddering slightly at how quickly it had gone to work on him. Pulling off his travelling cloak, he wrapped the book in it, feeling its lure diminish as physical contact was broken.

'Gather the troop together, Captain,' he said. 'I want all these books transported to Emmass Fawr immediately.' Andro would know what he was dealing with. He would decipher the runes, and then Melyn would understand the secrets that lay within.

4

> The history of Abervenn is one of constant change. What might have grown to be a powerful dukedom, perhaps a rival even to Candlehall, has been kept in check down the centuries by the clever patronage of the House of Balwen. The gift of a grateful monarch, Abervenn has equally often lost its duke to a capricious king. Divitie III most notably appointed four and executed three dukes of Abervenn during his tumultuous reign.
>
> Barrod Sheepshead, *A History of the House of Balwen*

Benfro wandered aimlessly through the forest. He had intended hunting, but there seemed to be little prey out in the twilight gloom. Or maybe it was just that he couldn't be bothered with stealth and silence, instead tramping through the undergrowth with all the subtlety of a herd of cattle. He was tired, bone weary in a way that made it difficult to think straight, almost impossible to maintain his control over his aura. His damaged wing was a constant niggling pain that he dared not deal with; he needed it to help him stay awake and to wake him when he did finally succumb to sleep.

He dreaded the end of each day. In the light he could

find things to do, useless tasks that took his mind off the gnawing lethargy that constantly pulled at him. But at the end of the day there was nothing, no distraction but to sit in his rude little corral, shivering with the cold. He never lit a fire; the warmth would have had him sound asleep in seconds. He would battle against the waves of tiredness that dragged him down, and sometime in the night he would lose. Magog would break through the last loose knot of his resolve and come crashing in. Sleep had once been a time of wonder for Benfro, a place of magic dreams and adventure, a safe haven from the trials of growing up. Now it was the enemy, his own private torment.

With a wail, he found himself back in Magog's repository. His first reaction was anger. How could he have fallen asleep so easily, out in the forest, walking? But soon weary resignation took over. His thoughts might be free to wander, to rail against the unfairness of it all, but he was a slave to the master of this place. It mattered nothing to Magog that Benfro's mind was addled by lack of sleep, his body weak with too little food. Perhaps the mad old mage even intended him to be that way. If Magog could control his sleep this easily, soon he might take over his waking hours too.

Wearily Benfro began his struggle against the force that made him sort the jewels. It was so difficult to concentrate; he just wanted to close his eyes and fade into oblivion. But Magog would not allow it, and the central of the three small heaps in front of him demanded he fight.

It had been building slowly over three nights, as if the

jewels he sought had burrowed their way into the pile, spreading out through the other memories rather than staying where they had been. Almost as if they had known what was coming and sought to make it as difficult for him as possible. Benfro knew that sooner or later he would start to find old friends with his traitorous hands, and now in front of him, almost complete, lay the sparkling white reckoned jewels of Sir Frynwy. He had no desire to find the final jewel, but he knew with a terrible certainty that tonight he was going to consign his old friend to a terrible lonely fate.

Benfro struggled with all his might, trying to keep his hands from the large pile of jewels. In the back of his head he could hear Magog laughing. Or was it just that he felt the old mage's glee more strongly with each passing hour? Either way, he was powerless to do anything but watch as he reached for the first jewel, picking it out with rock-steady fingers and hefting it in his palm.

It wasn't Sir Frynwy.

It wasn't either of the other dragons whose smaller piles lay in front of him, but a fourth memory, as yet unchosen, still free to commune with the other souls that Magog had trapped so many thousands of years before. Benfro placed the jewel back on the heap, slightly off to one side, then reached for another.

The progress was painfully slow. He didn't know how many nights he had come back to the repository and sorted jewels. It would have been madness to count. He could see that the great pile had diminished, but it wasn't yet half the size it had been when he and Malkin had first created it. There were some nights, joyous nights, when he found no complete sets of jewels before he managed to shake off Magog's influence and wake himself. But even as he fought against it, a part of his mind couldn't help thinking that there must be a more efficient means of sorting. Then again, if Magog wanted him ground down by a slow process of crushing tedium and demoralization, this was probably the best way to do it.

His fingers brushed another jewel, shaking Benfro out of his musings. He cursed himself for being sidetracked from fighting at the same time as his hearts sank in defeat. There was no mistaking the dragon whose memories he held; he shared many of them himself. Slowly, shaking as he tried to stop himself, Benfro lowered Sir Frynwy's last jewel down to the pile in front of him, forcing out a whisper through reluctant lips as he did so.

'I'm sorry.'

His body no more than a puppet, Benfro got to his feet, bending to scoop up the completed collection. This was the worst bit, when the dragon whose memories he held would speak to him, chide him, plead with him to stop what he was doing.

'You need to fight him, Benfro.' Sir Frynwy's voice was in his head, as clear as if he stood beside him.

'You don't know what it's like.' Benfro replied only in his mind, his lips locked shut in a grimace. 'He's so powerful.'

'I know, but you're powerful too. You fought him off before, and you can do it again.'

'But I'm so tired. I can't think straight half the time. It's like fighting your own shadow.'

'Listen, Benfro. Remember how Frecknock put that

glamour on you, to stop you from telling anyone what she was doing.'

Benfro felt a momentary surge of anger at the mention of Frecknock's name. It was her fault that the villagers were all dead, that his mother had been slaughtered in front of his own eyes, that he was in the mess he was now in.

'Yes, she has a lot to answer for.' Sir Frynwy's voice seemed unreasonably forgiving. 'But think about how you dealt with that. You fought it as hard as you could; you tried every trick you could think of to get round the spell. I remember thinking you'd gone quite mad, the way you kept coming up to me and asking odd questions. Of course, once I knew what had happened to you, they all made sense.'

'But it's hopeless.' Benfro wailed the words in his head. He could see the stone wall with its collection of alcoves all too close now as he walked with stiff legs towards it. 'I couldn't break her spell. It took months for any of you to see what was wrong. And by then it was too late.'

'Benfro, it was too late before you were hatched, long before Frecknock even came to our village. Don't be so quick to condemn her. Us old dragons had chosen to live together; she was forced. Some day you'll understand what that means. But that's not the point. The point is, you had a problem you couldn't solve on your own, so you brought it to us. You brought it to your friends.'

Benfro was at the wall now, leaning towards the nearest empty alcove. Tears welled up in his eyes as he reached out with his cupped hands to drop the jewels in.

'I'm sorry, Sir Frynwy. I don't want to do this, but I can't stop.'

'I know you can't, Benfro. Not on your own. Don't worry about me. I'll be fine in here on my own for a while, and I know you'll win. You'll defeat Magog and come back here to free us all again. But remember what I said. You don't have to fight him alone. You have friends out there who can help you. If you'll just ask.'

'What friends? Who are you talking about?' Benfro screamed out the questions in his head, but the last jewel had tumbled from his hands into the alcove, and the voice of Sir Frynwy fell silent.

The Neuadd was considerably less than half full. Admittedly it was almost impossible to fill it entirely, so vast was the area it covered, but nevertheless Beulah felt it would have lent more gravitas to the occasion had her people shown a bit more enthusiasm. Perhaps she should have insisted that the city merchants pay their respects in person.

Representatives of all the noble houses were there, of course. The court hangers-on were jockeying for position, still playing the game as if her father were alive. She watched them from her vantage point on the Obsidian Throne, trying to work out who was sleeping with whom, trying to remember some of their names.

Seneschal Padraig sat on a simple wooden chair to one side of the throne, Archimandrite Cassters alongside him. Beulah wished that Melyn was here too. Not that she needed his support or even his approval, but he was her power base. Without him she felt the responsibility of state rested on her shoulders alone. She had tried to contact him, but the one thing Cassters' potions had not been able to cure was her frustrating inability to achieve the trance state necessary to reach the aethereal. And she had no idea where the inquisitor might be right now.

A few latecomers darted through the doors at the far end of the hall, no doubt hoping their tardiness went unnoticed. Beulah knew that Padraig had scribes posted throughout the citadel; she would be presented with a list of all those who had attended and all those who had not, along with their excuses or lack thereof some time in the next week. With the raising of an army throughout the Twin Kingdoms, plenty of the heads of the noble houses had a reasonable excuse for their absence – at least this time. Still disappointed at the attendance, she decided it was time and nodded at the seneschal to get the proceedings under way.

Padraig shuffled to his feet, a sheaf of papers in his hand as if he needed reminding of what he was going to say.

'My lords, ladies and gentlemen. You have been called here for an important royal proclamation.' He tried to project his voice across the hall, Beulah noticed, but he didn't have the skill, nor the power of the Obsidian Throne behind him. It was likely that most of the gathered audience couldn't hear a word he was saying.

'As you all well know, the ducal House of Abervenn was recently implicated in a plot to overthrow our beloved Queen Beulah, a plot backed and financed by the godless Llanwennogs.' Looking down at his sheaf of papers, Padraig's voice faltered slightly at these words. He glanced briefly over at her and Beulah scowled at him. Clearing his throat quietly, he continued.

'This unprovoked attack is an act of war on the Twin Kingdoms, and it will not go unanswered. Even now armies are being recruited and trained. We will bring the queen's enlightened rule to the lands of the north.'

A muted ruffle of sound fluttered around the great hall, losing itself in its own echoes as the seneschal's words were relayed from person to person. It wasn't news to anyone: the draft had been pulling able-bodied men from villages and towns across the land for weeks now.

'By his treason Duke Angor has forfeited all the lands and titles of Abervenn. His co-conspirators have been rounded up and executed, his wife and daughter stripped of their titles and privileges. This is the punishment any can expect who plot with our enemies.'

Beulah cast her mind out over the crowd, judging the mood as Padraig droned on. She had read his speech earlier, added to it herself the passages he seemed to have most difficulty with. Now she wished he would just hurry up and get to the point.

'It is the right of the queen to bestow lands and titles as she sees fit, and it is for this reason that she has brought you all here today. Come forward, Clun Defaid.'

He had been standing in the front row, his nervousness at complete odds with the studied nonchalance and self-confidence of the nobles surrounding him. At his name Clun stiffened as if someone had poked him with a sharp stick. Beulah could feel his unease beginning to turn to fear, and she sent calming thoughts towards him. He still looked like a rabbit hearing the shriek of the raptor, but he seemed to pull himself together enough to take first one step, then another, and another, each one easier than the last until he reached the podium. A low bench had been placed in front of the throne, and he knelt upon it on both knees, bowing his head.

Beulah stood and the whole hall rose with her. She looked over Clun's prostrate figure and fixed her audience with her gaze. She paused just long enough to make people feel uncomfortable, the silence hanging heavy in the vast space of the Neuadd, then with a single thought conjured up a thin blade of light.

A palpable gasp ran through the crowd. All eyes were on her – she could feel their full attention as she reached out with the power of the throne, projecting her words so that everyone would hear as if she stood alongside them.

'Clun Defaid. You have proven yourself selfless in service to the House of Balwen. As a warrior priest of the Order of the High Ffrydd, I would expect no less.' Beulah noted Clun's involuntary flinch at the inappropriate rank. She couldn't very well introduce him to the other noble houses as a mere novitiate. Melyn might not like it, but Clun would be his equal soon, so the inquisitor would just have to promote him to a full warrior priest, and the traditions of the order be damned.

'Your actions succeeded in foiling an attempt on my life. You took a poisoned quarrel meant for me, and now I offer you this in reward. Do you swear, in front of the assembled noble houses of the Twin Kingdoms, to serve the House of Balwen and to pledge the service of your issue from this time henceforth?'

Clun's voice was thin, scared. It barely travelled beyond his lips. Beulah took the thought behind it and pushed it out to the audience as loud as her own words.

'I do so swear.'

'And do you swear to uphold the laws of our nation, to act as arbiter in matters of justice?'

'I do so swear.'

'Do you swear to maintain an army of able-bodied men, equipped and trained in such numbers as are commensurate with the lands and titles I choose to bestow upon you?'

'I do so swear.'

'And do you swear to honour me in whatever task I set before you?'

'Unless death prevents me, I do so swear.'

Beulah was almost taken aback by the deviation from the set protocol, but delighted at Clun's new-found confidence. She could tell by the murmuring of the collected witnesses that they approved. Good. It would make her next proclamation easier for them to accept.

Bending forward to the still-kneeling Clun, she touched the shimmering blade of light to his left shoulder, then his right, smelling the slightest odour of singeing cloth and leaving two almost imperceptible dark lines on the simple shirt that he wore.

'Then rise, Clun Defaid, Duke of Abervenn.'

Clun stood slowly as the murmurs fluttered back and forth through the hall. There were some among the crowd who thought him perhaps too young to take on the responsibilities of a whole province, others who saw in his elevation a fairy story turned real.

'Now take my blade, my love.' Beulah whispered the words just for Clun as she held out her hand, offering him the blade of light. His eyes widened in surprise. This had not been a part of the ceremony he had rehearsed with Padraig the night before. She smiled at him, then released her control, directing the flow of the Grym towards him. An unskilled peasant would likely have been burned alive from the inside, but he caught it naturally, as if he had been practising all his life. Beulah could see the near panic in his face as he realized what he was holding. She didn't need to skim the edge of his thoughts. But she took his free hand, turned him to face the crowd, which stood silent, enthralled.

'Duke Clun has proven himself worthy as my protector.' She pitched her voice to thunder through the hall, drawing power from the throne even though she wasn't sitting in it. The moment was perfect. She felt like she could have taken on the whole of Llanwennog single-handed.

'Now hear me, all of you, when I make this proclamation. Today will be a day of celebration for the new Duke of Abervenn. Tomorrow will begin two weeks of festivities, at the end of which I will take this man as my consort.'

Errol slipped into the ice-cold water, shuddering as it rose to his waist, his chest and finally his neck. Downstream of the ford it deepened rapidly, the flow slowing into a long pool. Taking the weight off his ankles was bliss, but the main reason for this morning dip was hygiene. He swam to the opposite side and ripped off some of the soft grass that overhung the bank, tearing it in his hands and pulping it as best he could to form a basic soap. Kneeling in the shallows, he scrubbed at his skin until he began to feel clean, trying to remember the last time he had bathed properly.

The sun had broken over the treetops and was shining down on the flat rocks closer to the ford and the waterfall. Errol let it dry him, the light breeze causing involuntary shivers to run across his bare skin even though he drew warmth from the Grym. Then he turned his attention to his clothes.

His shirt was frayed and thin, crusted with ingrained dirt and blood; a ragged tear ripped the fabric where Beulah had stabbed him. He plunged it into the cold water then laid it flat on the rock, using a smooth stone to try and work out the worst of the stains. He was pummelling away at the blood on his breeches when Corwen appeared.

'Is it worth all the effort?' the old dragon asked.

'I've nothing else to wear.' Errol thought of his novitiate's robes hanging in their locker in the monastery at Emmass Fawr; the selection of unfashionable but well made and hard-wearing clothes in the chest in the back room in his mother's cottage. 'And I can't wander around naked.'

'Dragons do.'

Errol laughed. 'Yes, I suppose they do. But I'm not a dragon. I don't have thick scales to protect me.' He picked up his shirt, which had almost dried in the sun. It crackled stiffly in his hands as he inspected it. 'I wish I had a mending kit.'

'Why not just get a new shirt?'

'Where from? There's no shirt maker for hundreds of miles, and I haven't any coin to pay him with even if there was.'

'But there are shirt makers in Gwlad, and tailors,

cobblers – craftsmen whose purpose in life is to fashion clothes and boots for others. I remember a man in Talard-deg who used to make funny little hats with tassels on the top.'

'But they're not here, are they.' Errol hauled his breeches from the water and squeezed them out a last time. Some bloodstains would never shift, he realized, and pretty soon the knees would be gone.

'Neither were you, four weeks ago, and yet here you are now. Did you walk here, Errol?'

Errol could remember very little of his arrival apart from the pain. He had walked the lines, that much he knew. But he had intended to go home to Pwllpeiran, where his mother could heal him. Instead he had heard Sir Radnor's voice, felt a gentle but firm force push him elsewhere, and then he had woken up in the cave with Corwen staring down at him.

'So I could go back,' he said. 'I could go home and pick up some clothes. Check on my mother. Let her know I'm all right.'

'That would be one way. Inadvisable but possible.'

'Except I've never managed to do it on purpose. I've always had help. Or it's been a matter of life and death, and I don't want to end up in Ruthin's Grove again. Or Melyn's chapel.' Errol shuddered at the thought of being back in that cold miserable place.

'You don't have to go anywhere at all, Errol.' The old dragon sat himself down on the rock, resting his feet in the water, where they made no impression whatsoever. 'You can reach out to a place and bring what's there to you. It's one of the first of the subtle arts a dragon learns.'

'I'm not a dragon.'

'So you keep saying. And as long as that's how you think of yourself, you never will be. But humour me. Since Benfro has gone off on one of his sulks in the woods, I've no one to teach right now. Perhaps you'd like to learn something new.'

'Of course,' Errol said. 'Always.'

'Well then, try this for me. Close your eyes and imagine your mother's house. Imagine the room where you used to sleep and the chest where all your clothes are stored.'

Errol tried to build the picture in his mind, finding it remarkably hard. He knew the house so well that he couldn't remember ever having studied it in any great detail. Nor did it help that his memories of home had been comprehensively rewritten by Inquisitor Melyn. Errol thought he had sorted out the truth from the jumble of incongruous images, but there was always that doubt at the back of his mind.

'Concentrate, Errol. Describe the chest. See it.' Corwen's voice was inside him, all around him, and in that instant Errol felt himself slip from his physical body. His eyes were still closed, but suddenly he could see everything around him – the clearing, the trees, the river cascading over the falls past the rock on which he sat and on towards the forest. And he could see the lines linking everything, painting the form of Gwlad, each point linked to every other.

He looked south, in the approximate direction of his mother's house so many hundreds of miles away. It was daft to think that he could see it, but suddenly he was there, standing outside the front door. It looked dilapidated, lifeless. He supposed that made sense; his mother would have moved into Godric's house in the village. He wondered if she would have taken his things with her, and with that thought he was standing in his bedroom.

It was dark and dusty, even to his strange new sight, but everything seemed to be pretty much where he had left it. His small collection of books sat on the shelf above his narrow bed, and there, under the draughty window that looked out on to the woods, was his clothes chest. He remembered it perfectly.

'Come back to me now, Errol.' Corwen's voice sounded impossibly distant, and yet at the same time right there with him. Errol realized he could hear the rush of the waterfall and the splashing of the river over the ford. The image of his room was fading, but he could still see the chest and, linking it to where he sat, the endless impossibly complicated web of the Grym. He felt the rock under his backside and feet, anchoring him to the clearing, and yet his clothes chest was only a hand's reach away. He just had to –

A great splash whipped Errol's eyes open. He was suddenly, painfully, fully back in himself, his heart pounding as if he had just run up six flights of stairs. He looked around, first at Corwen, who was still sitting on the next rock along, then at the river, where something had upset the flow just in front of him. Something large and square and wooden.

'How . . . ? Did I . . . ?' He dropped down into the shallow water, dragging the heavy chest out on to the bank before it was completely ruined. His fingers touched its surface, and he noted the long tracks of dust they left behind. How long had the house been abandoned? Why had his mother left his things behind?

'I had thought you might just fetch a shirt perhaps, or maybe a pair of breeks. This, this is splendid.'

Errol barely heard Corwen's words. The sudden magical appearance of the clothes chest was a wondrous thing he couldn't comprehend, let alone acknowledge that it had been his own doing. But seeing his old home, his old life abandoned and left to ruin, he was overcome with a loneliness so bleak, so total that it choked his throat and brought tears to his eyes.

'Your Majesty, I see you've created a new Duke of Abervenn. My congratulations to the Lord Lyon on his subtle work with the new coat of arms.'

Melyn climbed the dais and knelt briefly before the Obsidian Throne before standing again. He had noticed the new pennant fluttering in the breeze and flying from almost every second flagpole in the citadel. 'So tell me, who presented themselves as such an obvious choice you did not feel the need to consult your old mentor?'

'Do I detect a note of jealousy, Melyn?' Beulah smiled at him from the throne and he couldn't help notice a change in her. She seemed somehow softer, more feminine.

'My queen is of course free to take counsel wherever she chooses,' he said.

'Don't be so po-faced, Melyn. You weren't here, and circumstances forced my hand. I don't think you'll disapprove of my choice. You sent him to me, after all.'

'Clun! You made a novitiate duke of the most important region of the Twin Kingdoms?'

'That's only the half of it, Inquisitor.' Melyn turned to see Seneschal Padraig emerging from a side room. 'She intends to marry him.'

Melyn looked back at the queen, seeing again that difference in her. He knew she had something of an infatuation with the boy, but he hadn't realized things might go so far. Still, given the choice, he'd take Clun as prince consort over any of the vacuous sons of the noble houses.

'Padraig disapproves,' Beulah said, an unusual amount of tolerance in her voice. 'Both about Abervenn and my marriage choice. He thinks I should have forged greater ties with Tochers or Castell Glas.'

'It's true that a union with either of those houses would have strengthened your position, Your Majesty,' Padraig said. 'And marrying a commoner is a snub to your courtiers.'

'Whoever I'd chosen, even if it had been one of those pathetic little lordlings, it would have been seen as a snub to the rest of them. Elevating a common man, then taking him as my consort, makes me popular with the people. It's a fairy tale come true.'

'Of course, Your Majesty. And that's what my predicants are telling everyone as they spread the news throughout the Twin Kingdoms. Although I would have preferred a little more time to make all the necessary preparations.'

'More time?' Melyn asked. 'How soon are you planning on having the ceremony.'

'Next Saddith, by the Shepherd!' Padraig settled himself down at a small desk placed close to the throne and shuffled through a pile of scrolls. Melyn looked back at the queen, trying to work out what it was that was different about her. She was wearing a long dress of gold silk rather than her usual boyish suede trousers, for one thing. Was her hair a little longer than he remembered? It was difficult to tell. Her face looked thinner, as if she'd not been eating properly, but she looked healthy, almost glowing with the power of the throne. Then the penny dropped.

'Your Majesty, would you like to take a walk around the courtyard? It's a beautiful morning.'

'Why, yes, Inquisitor. I think I should.' Beulah held out her hand and Melyn took it, helping her down from the throne. Beside them Padraig scowled but continued with his paperwork.

At the great oak doors to the Neuadd two guards tried to follow as Melyn escorted the queen outside. She dismissed them with a casual wave.

'Do you think any harm can come to me when the Inquisitor of the Order of the High Ffrydd is my personal escort?'

They walked across the grass, keeping away from the cloister that surrounded the great hall. Only when Melyn was sure they were beyond eavesdropping range did he speak.

'How long have you known?'

'Known what?' Beulah feigned innocence, but he had known her too long for that to work.

'That you were carrying Clun's child.'

'Cassters came up with the diagnosis. I'd been sick as a dog for a fortnight before that.'

'You had the archimandrite examine you himself?'

'It wasn't my idea, actually, I just wanted a Ram rather than one of those useless Candle physicians Padraig's filled the palace with. They tried to treat me with leeches.'

'So Padraig doesn't know.'

'No one knows but Cassters, Clun and myself. And you, I suppose. Cassters has even found a pregnant maid-servant in the castle to treat for morning sickness. Some of her medication comes my way.'

'And you think no one will suspect there's a reason behind your sudden rush to get married?'

'There are ways of lengthening my term, by a few weeks if necessary. My child will be conceived on my wedding night. It won't be delivered until nine months have passed. No one will be able to cast doubts on the legitimacy of my heir.'

'That's dangerous magic, Beulah.' Melyn dropped all pretence of royal protocol. 'You could damage the child, or yourself for that matter.'

'It's necessary. You know how little the noble houses respect me. I need them for their armies and their taxes, and they know it. Angor wasn't the only one with sympathies towards the Llanwennogs; there are others with no stomach for war. I don't want to give them any reason to think my dear sister Iolwen might have a greater claim on the throne than my heir.'

'Have you any news from Tynhelyg?'

'She and Dafydd were married months ago. They went east towards Fo Afron for their honeymoon and nobody's seen them since. Our spies are concentrating more on tracking Ballah's army; they're not too concerned with his grandson.'

Melyn was about to ask about the plans for the wedding, but they were interrupted by a guard running across the grass. He stopped several paces away as the inquisitor and queen both produced blades of light. Dropping to one knee, he bowed his head low.

'Please forgive this intrusion, Your Majesty. But there's been an attack. In the citadel. An assassin.'

'Who?' Melyn asked as Beulah mouthed the same words. 'Who's been attacked?'

'Your Majesty, it's the Duke of Abervenn.'

5

There is nothing so good as time when it comes to the healing of bones. Yet time alone cannot force a fracture back to its proper shape. A limb can be splinted with wood and cloth to hold it in position while it heals, but where many small bones are broken, or where immobilization might lead to seizing of a joint, then the subtle arts may be used to speed the healing process.

Care should ever be your watchword when tapping the Llinellau, but even more so when using the power of the Grym to heal. Be sure when you work not to draw strength from your patient, nor yourself. That way lies exhaustion, illness and death.

Morgwm the Green,
The Herbwoman's Guide to Healing

'Your Majesty, please, get behind me. Stay with the guards.' Melyn cursed his age as he tried to keep up with Beulah. She ran with most unregal haste, despite her dress, sending servants and minor nobles alike flying as she sped down the corridor. The sensible ones stayed on the floor or ducked into alcoves and doorways to avoid the party heading for the royal chambers.

He managed to catch up with her as she stopped to

wrench open an ornately decorated pair of double doors. Melyn grasped her arm and held her back.

'Remember what I taught you, Beulah. Don't go rushing in unprepared.'

He already had his blade of light at the ready, its steady fire a reassuring pressure in his mind. When he was sure that the queen was not going to go running off again, he released her arm and opened the door himself. A grisly scene awaited him on the other side.

It was a reception chamber in one of the guest suites, well appointed for the most noble of visiting dignitaries. Tall windows hung with elegant curtains looked out on to a lawned courtyard. Sumptuous armchairs were arranged around an open fireplace, currently unlit. Two ornate desks sat at the far end of the room, one split in two as if by some crazed axe-wielding giant. Chairs lay on their backs, and two very dead bodies sprawled on the floor.

It looked like something had ripped them apart. Their blood splattered the walls, innards oozing out into the richly patterned rug. A heavy stench of burned iron and shit hung in the air.

'By the Shepherd! Clun!' Melyn was astonished to hear the wail in Beulah's voice.

'My . . . my lady.' Movement behind the desk dragged Melyn's gaze away from the eviscerated corpses on the floor. He looked up and saw a man-shaped blood spatter shift, a clear shadow appearing on the wall as Clun stepped forward. He was covered from head to toe in gore, his ducal robes ruined.

'By the Shepherd, boy, what happened here?' Melyn heard Beulah's sudden intake of breath at his words and remembered that he was no longer addressing a novitiate but the Duke of Abervenn. 'Your Grace,' he corrected himself. 'Are you all right?'

'I think so . . . sir.' Clun seemed to be unsure of the correct way to address him. Given what he must have been through, Melyn was prepared to forgive him, just this once.

'What happened?'

'I . . . They were here to see me about trade agreements.' Clun motioned with his hand towards the broken desk. Papers lay all around it, some stuck to the green leather top with blood. 'Then one of them said something about Abervenn never again being a plaything of the House of Balwen. He conjured a blade of light, used it on the desk. He was trying to get at me.'

Beulah ran across the room, ruining her dress in the process, and began wiping blood from Clun's face with a white handkerchief. Melyn was so astonished by the sight that it took him a few moments to gather his thoughts. What had happened to the ruthless queen he had left behind?

Two sets of double doors led from the reception room; one stood open. Silently Melyn crossed over to the doors, approaching so that he could see what lay beyond. It was a large bedchamber dominated by a huge four-poster. For a moment Melyn thought that was all there was in the room, but something pulled at his attention, a feeling of incongruity. He stared hard, trying to work out what it was, and then he saw her, at the foot of the bed, cowering, her head covered by her flimsy wings. Quite how he could have missed her bulk he didn't know, but the question was lost in his contempt and hatred for her kind.

Melyn crossed the room in swift strides, lowering the point of his blade until it sizzled just a hair's breadth from the dragon's face.

'Well, if it isn't sweet Frecknock. I'd been meaning to have a word with you. Get up!' He spat out the words, a cold fury sweeping over him as he remembered the death and destruction caused by the dragon in the woods near Pwllpeiran. A dragon she had failed to tell him about. 'What are you doing in the duke's bedchamber?'

'Your Grace, Master Def— the duke asked me to attend him.'

'Nonsense. What would the likes of him want with the likes of you?'

'He said that he wanted to learn more about the Grym. What little I know, I was happy to share.'

Melyn came close to lopping off her head there and then, but he remembered the other reason he had kept Frecknock alive: her knowledge of the passes through the Rim mountains to northern Llanwennog. He stayed his hand, let his blade evaporate into nothing. The pent-up force of the Grym took some of his anger with it as it went.

'What happened out there?' He pointed towards the reception chamber.

'Some men came. They said they wanted to talk about trade agreements. His Grace the duke invited them in, started talking to them about commerce. He knows a great deal about it; I think his visitors were surprised.'

'And where were you while this was happening?'

'I was sitting under the window by the door over there.' Frecknock pointed back out to the main chamber. I suspect the duke likes to have me around when he conducts his negotiations; my appearance is . . . unsettling to some men.'

Melyn hastily revised his opinion of Clun. His knowledge of trade was understandable, given that his father had been a moderately successful merchant, but using a dragon to put his competitors on edge during negotiations? That showed a subtlety of touch beyond his years.

'So. You were lying there taking up space, and what? You just let these men attack the duke? You ran in here to hide? You didn't think to help?'

'No, Your Grace. It happened so fast I barely had time to react. I would have done anything to help Master Defaid. He's always been kind to me, ever since the attack on the queen. I didn't run from his attackers.'

'But you were hiding in here.'

'I didn't run from his attackers,' Frecknock repeated. 'I ran from him.'

'What are you talking about?'

'The first man leaped up, shouted something and then slashed at the desk with a great fiery blade, much like yours. His Grace took a step back and then . . .' She paused, her expression changing from deferential and scared to one of total puzzlement.

'Then what, dragon?'

'I . . . I don't know. I think His Grace reached out for the blade. Then there was this screaming sound, and both of his attackers sort of . . . exploded. No, that's not the right expression. It was more like something tore them apart. But I couldn't see what. And then His Grace was standing there alone, with the blade in his hand. And he looked at me with such a light in his eyes. I thought he was going to kill me. I . . . I fled.'

Benfro sat under the trees at the edge of the clearing and watched as the boy dragged a heavy wooden chest from the riverbank back towards the cave. He managed a couple of paces, then slipped and fell, staying down for a long time. Then he sat up, rubbing at his ankles as if they were sore, climbed wearily to his feet and started again. Two more paces and he fell once more. At this rate it was going to take him all day to get the chest to the cave.

Leaning back against the rough bark of an old oak tree, Benfro felt the reassuring ache in his wing root. It was his anchor, the only thing that he could rely on to help him escape from Magog. But slowly, inevitably, the damage was healing. Despite the endless nights of twisting and turning, digging his back into roots and branches, bashing it against rocks or just lying on it badly, it was getting increasingly difficult to raise the necessary pain out of his injury. Soon he would be as good as he had been before his fall, and then there would be nothing to stop Magog from possessing him throughout the night. He would sort jewels until he was so exhausted he fell into a stupor, and as soon as he was rested, he would be back in the repository. Even now he could feel the weariness pulling him down, as if he weighed three times as much as he should, as if the earth were a warm welcoming bed just waiting for him to sink into its comforting embrace.

Benfro jerked his head back, smacking it against the tree and blurring his vision for a moment. He had been so close. He could see the outline of the ancient writing desk fading away from his sight as he snapped back into himself, and deep in his mind he heard the insane laughter of his tormentor, echoing away to nothing.

He tried to focus on his aura, to tighten his grip on the rose cord that linked him with Magog's jewel, but to see it properly he needed to relax, and to relax was to succumb to sleep. To sleep was to condemn more of his dead friends to an eternity of terrifying solitude. Like he had condemned Sir Frynwy.

The old dragon's spirit had told him to look to his friends for help, but Benfro couldn't think of anyone he could consider a friend. His mother was dead, most of her jewels stolen by Inquisitor Melyn; the villagers were dead and at the mercy of Magog; he supposed Frecknock was still alive, but she would never be friend. And besides she was responsible for the whole mess he was in. Perhaps he could consider Corwen a friend, but the dragon mage was only a projection of his memories. If he'd been able to help Benfro fight Magog, then he would surely have done so already. So who had Sir Frynwy meant? Malkin? The mother tree? Benfro was sure they would help him if they could, but how could he find them? He didn't know where to begin looking. It was all helpless. He was alone.

Glumly he watched as once more the boy hauled

himself to his feet, his pain obvious even this far away, and tried to move the heavy chest. He was persistent, Benfro had to admit, but couldn't he see that the task was beyond him?

More for the want of something to do than anything else, he levered himself to his feet and headed down into the clearing. The boy didn't hear his approach; he was too intent on straining at the chest. As Benfro neared, he let out a short gasp of pain and crumpled to the ground again, clutching at his ankles and grimacing.

'Where do you want it?' Benfro picked up the chest as if it weighed no more than air.

'I . . . In the cave, please. If it is fit.' The boy spoke halting Draigiaith with a strange accent that reminded Benfro of Gideon. He remembered his first meeting with the man, and how his mother had said that of all their kind he was perhaps the only one she would have trusted.

'Who taught you our language?'

'I learn what I can from to read scrolls.' The boy was very pale, now that Benfro looked at him. He didn't know much about men, but he was sure their ankles weren't meant to look like that either. Not twisted at such an odd angle to the leg, and not swollen, bruised. He shifted his perception a little, trying to see the boy's aura. It was a pale thing, as if he was hanging on to life by the thinnest of threads. But around his ankles and feet it swelled out, pulsing and livid with purples and reds. Benfro remembered his own aura when he had damaged his wing root and knew that these injuries were much worse. How had the boy managed to walk at all?

'Wait there,' he said as if it were necessary. He carried the chest into the cave, setting it down close to the bed. Then he went back out to where the boy was still lying, reached down and scooped him up. He weighed even less than the chest.

'What am you do?'

'Your ankles are broken.' Benfro spoke Saesneg, even though he hadn't used the language since his mother had taught him. He carried the boy to the cave and set him down on the bed, then turned his attention to the fire. The coals were almost burned out; it would take too long to stoke them up to a decent flame. Instead, he piled thick logs on top of the ash, then breathed out a steady flame. The wood caught, blazing a welcome warmth. On the bed the boy shivered, moving towards the heat.

Benfro went to the chest, opened it and peered inside. There were assorted clothes, piled on the top, some damp from the river, but at the bottom he found a couple of dry wool blankets which he handed over.

'Rest,' he said, then left the cave before the boy could say anything more. Outside the sky had darkened with clouds, threatening rain. The tops of the trees whipped back and forth in the strengthening wind, suggesting a storm might be coming. Benfro looked over at the makeshift roof on his corral, wondering whether it would withstand a good blow. He didn't really fancy finding out.

'He can help you. If you let him.' Corwen appeared beside Benfro as if he'd been there all the time.

'How? The boy can't even walk.'

'His name's Errol, Benfro. As you well know. Don't you think it's a bit kitlingish, ignoring him the whole time?'

'I just helped him.'

'For only the second time in a month. He saved your life.'

'How? You've said that before, but just how exactly did someone I've never met before save my life?'

'You have met before, Benfro. You and Errol are far closer than you can imagine. And who do you think it was told you to jump when you were surrounded by warrior priests at Emmass Fawr?'

Benfro remembered the voice in his head telling him to jump. 'That was him?'

'That was him. He was kidnapped, brainwashed by Inquisitor Melyn. He was taken to their monastery and trained to be their spy. But he still managed to break free. Help him, Benfro, and he'll help you fight Magog.'

Benfro doubted very much there was anything the boy could do for him, but the simple act of helping with the chest had made him feel better. It had been something to do rather than sitting around trying not to fall asleep. He needed activity, things to occupy his body as much as his mind. And Errol was in need of medical help. Even if he was a man. His mother had never refused help to anyone. It would shame her if he left the boy untended.

'I need to gather some herbs.' Benfro stepped into the woods, dark with the coming storm. Corwen said nothing, but Benfro was sure the old dragon smiled as he faded from sight.

*

'Your Majesty, this is too soon. Half of the provinces don't even know of your betrothal yet. How can they be expected to send tribute?'

Beulah looked up at her seneschal sitting beside the Obsidian Throne, his little desk once more strewn with scrolls as he delivered his daily report on the state of the Twin Kingdoms. Every day since her announcement he had used the briefing to moan about her upcoming wedding.

'I neither expect their tribute nor their presence, Padraig. I fully intend travelling the whole country myself, just as soon as Clun and I are wed.'

'A royal tour? But no ruler has done that since –'

'My great-grandfather. I know. And even he missed out most of it. I saw more of my kingdom travelling with Melyn for the choosing than my father saw in all of his reign. It's no wonder the people aren't happy with my call to arms. They don't know who I am. I shall show them and recruit them to my army.'

'Your Majesty, is it wise to pursue this war? No one has ever succeeded in breaking through the passes before.'

Beulah let the seneschal make his case, unsure quite why she was so tolerant of him. Perhaps it was because he ran the palace and citadel so effectively. Beyond Candlehall the entire machinery of state was kept running by predicants of the Order of the Candle. Avoiding the upheaval his replacement would cause was well worth the hassle of his arguments for peace. And Beulah knew that Padraig's loyalty to the throne was unquestionable. He would never ally himself with the factions that plotted against her; he just didn't want a messy war mucking up his accounts.

'King Ballah has made three attempts on my life since I came to power, Padraig. We know he has plans to put his grandson and my traitorous sister on this throne. I'll not sit back and let him do that.'

'You know I will always serve you, my queen, but I must advise caution. Ballah provokes you with these attacks. He wants a war. What better way to thwart him than to refuse?'

'No, Padraig. I understand your reluctance, and I value your counsel, but I cannot tolerate a belligerent nation to the north. Ballah will have his war, but he won't like the outcome. I don't intend fighting it by his rules.'

'Very well, Your Majesty.' Padraig went back to his scrolls, but Beulah knew that she would have the same argument, couched in different terms, the next day.

Errol didn't need to look at his ankles to know that he had undone weeks of healing. The pain was constant even when he kept as still as possible. Movement sent waves of agony rushing up his legs so intense he felt he might vomit. He lay back on his bed of grass and tried not to twitch.

It had been monumentally stupid, he realized, to try and move the entire chest at once. Far easier to have taken all the clothes out, piece by piece if necessary, and carried them to the cave. Then he might have been able to shift the empty chest without doing himself harm. But at the time he had been so amazed to see it, so determined to get it out of the water and into the cave, he hadn't thought of the consequences of putting so much strain on his partially healed bones. Now there was little else he could think about.

He tried to sit up, the better to examine the damage, but the pain dimmed his vision and forced an involuntary gasp past his lips. It seemed worse now than in the dungeons below King Ballah's castle, when the hammer had first fallen. Back then he had been able to tune out of the pain somehow, to move out of his body and observe it from a distance. It was the same when he had recalled his bedroom and the chest: it hadn't been memory but a part of him actually there.

Errol searched for that feeling, a strange mixture of anticipation and indifference which had come over him as he had followed Corwen's instructions. The throbbing in his ankles made it impossible to concentrate. Giving up, he listened instead to the noise of the wind outside. It was strengthening with the promise of a fearsome storm, and he was glad of his shelter, the warmth of the fire. He wondered what had caused Benfro to help. He wondered too where the dragon had gone.

Almost as if it were waiting for him to stop trying, the strange feeling of otherness slid over him. The pain of his ankles didn't so much diminish as become something that was happening a very long way away, to someone else. He felt light, as if his already skinny body had turned to air, and all around him the lines of the Grym shimmered into view, adding their own form to the shape of the cave.

Errol sat up and experienced the disorienting feeling of watching his body stay where it was. He lifted his hands to inspect them, and saw an image of muted flickering colours, pale as he flexed his fingers. Looking down at his legs, he could see the same swirl of pastel shades, closely hugging his real shape like a second skin. And then, surrounding his shattered ankles, a livid pulsing mass of purple and red.

'There are very few of your kind who can master this skill.' Corwen sat on the far side of the fire. But it was a different-looking Corwen to the one he was used to seeing. This dragon was old, yes, and he bore the same scars as Corwen, but he was fully twice his size, with huge wings folded neatly at his back. He glowed with a rainbow of colours that shifted and flowed over his form in a mesmerizing pattern that shouted vitality. All except for one arm, his left. It was small, like the arm Errol was used to seeing, only now it seemed shrivelled and useless. It hung limply at the dragon's side, the hand twisted into a crude fist, talons digging into the palm. And it glowed with a malignant red shimmer that hugged the leathery skin like sweat.

'It is a manifestation of the Grym,' Corwen continued. 'Those who can see it call it the aethereal in your language. We have another name for it, an mhorfa, but it doesn't translate well from the Draigiaith.'

'I . . . What am I seeing?'

'You're seeing the Grym with your mind's eye. Freed from the physicality of your body. This is an intermediate step between the magic of men and what we call the subtle arts.'

'And these colours, my ankles?'

'Your aura, Errol. The power of the Grym that flows

from you, that defines you. Your ankles are badly damaged, and your aura reflects that.'

'So what's wrong with your arm?'

'I think you already know that.'

'Magog.'

'His influence is insidious. His power infects the very Grym itself, turning it into something I've never encountered before. I am holding him back as best I can, but in time he will prevail. I don't want to think what I will become when that happens.'

'We'll find a way to stop him,' Errol said, feeling the pull of his body dragging him back to a world of pain. 'There has to be a way.'

'Your concern is admirable, Errol. But you've got to heal yourself first. And you need to help Benfro. Then you can worry about me.'

Errol wanted to ask more. There was so much he didn't understand, so many things he needed to know, but his leg twitched and a wave of pain sparked through him so intense it leached all the colour out of his new vision. He was back in his body with a terrible snap that had him sitting bolt upright. For a moment he could see nothing at all but sparks of red light flickering in front of his eyes. Wave after wave of nausea washed over him. His mouth ran wet with the promise of throwing up.

And then there was a hand on his forehead. In his confusion Errol thought it must be his mother, come to soothe his fever away. But the hand was too big, its texture rough on his skin. Another hand pressed something into his palm and he heard a voice say, 'Chew this. It will take away the pain for a while.' Without thinking, Errol put what felt like a rolled-up leaf into his mouth and bit down on it. A bitter taste filled his mouth briefly, then turned sweet, making his mouth water more. He chewed reflexively, feeling the agony recede almost immediately. With the relief came a crushing weariness that pulled him downwards, back on to the soft bed of dry grass and into a deep warm sleep.

Benfro looked down at the sleeping boy, glad that he had found the sedda leaves on his forest search. Too many and they would knock out even a fully grown dragon, but one, chewed for a few minutes, would make what he had to do next at least painless if hardly pleasant.

He set about arranging the ingredients for the potion around the edge of the hearth, then realized he had no pot in which to mix them. On the ledge above the bed his battered old leather bag still sat with its contents of purloined gold from Magog's repository. He opened it, sure that he had taken a wide goblet along with the other treasures. Sure enough he found it, wedged in the bottom of the bag, but it was too small. He had seen a cauldron somewhere, he was sure, but had it been in Magog's retreat on Mount Arnahi?

Benfro's eyes lost their focus as he tried to remember, and unbidden the Llinellau Grym swam into view. They patterned the walls and the floor, thick lines intersecting under the hearth. He could almost hear them calling to him, inviting him to investigate their endless paths, but he knew better than to give in to that temptation. He was too weary to concentrate, and he knew that Magog would whisk him away somewhere if he tried to walk the lines, like he had done the last time, diverting his attention away from Corwen's cave and across the miles to his mountain-top retreat.

Corwen's cave. Benfro remembered now where he had seen a cauldron. And many other things he might find useful. They were just a few dozen paces away, through a wall of solid rock. He could see the way there. It was as simple as stepping over a fallen branch in the forest. All he needed to do was take that first step. In an instant he would be there, with the familiar old furniture, the writing table with its unfinished manuscript laid out waiting, the bookcase with its store of ancient knowledge, the fire and comfortable bed alongside.

Benfro shook his head, driving away the stupor that had crept up over him. He had seen the room at the top of Mount Arnahi, Magog's retreat. Even with his jewels dislodged from their pillar-top resting place, the ancient dead dragon mage was trying to drag him back to that inhospitable place.

Benfro turned away from the cave wall and headed out into the clearing. The storm had darkened the sky almost to black, though nightfall was hours away. The trees writhed around in a frenzy, their fresh new leaves ripping in the wind. As he watched, a squall of rain lashed across the track, kicking up the dust and turning it to mud. He hunched his shoulders against the wet and made his way to the ford, turning upstream into the deeper water and wading to the waterfall, pushing through into the cold dark cavern beyond.

With almost no light filtering in from outside, Benfro

had to wait long moments for his eyes to adjust enough to see what he was doing. He thought of conjuring a flame – there was fire just the other side of the cave wall – but he was terrified of manipulating the Grym. Magog lay in wait for him that way. So instead he hauled himself out of the icy water and stood shivering until the gloom resolved itself into familiar shapes.

It took a while to find the cauldron, and by feel a set of long iron spoons. All the while he wondered why Corwen didn't appear to him, but the old dragon's movements were a mystery. Sometimes he was absent for days, other times he was always around, watching, making occasionally helpful comments. Benfro was about to head back to the water's edge when he realized what else had been bothering him the whole time he had searched the cave. There was an unusual odour, as if someone had visited the place recently, certainly in the last week. He tried to pin down the scent, but it was very faint and the ground underfoot had that faint spicy smell that covered everything else. Then, finally, he realized what it was. The boy had been in here.

He wasn't sure whether he was more angry or surprised at this. It seemed somehow wrong that Errol should have been in here, but there was no way he could have found it without Corwen's help. Confused, Benfro pushed through the curtain of water, pausing to rinse the cauldron thoroughly in the strong current. When he was halfway across the clearing, a squall peeled the makeshift roof off the corral with a great crashing noise, branches splintering and careening off into the darkness. He stood staring at his sleeping place as the rain rattled off the inside of the walls, no doubt soaking the once-dry grass that was his bedding. Shrugging in defeat, Benfro turned away and entered the cave.

The warmth was welcoming after the chill of the storm. He put some more dry logs on the fire and placed the cauldron on top of them, then checked on Errol. The boy was still asleep and probably would be for hours yet, which was just as well. Benfro recalled the times before when he had prepared this medication, back at home with his mother watching over him to make sure he made no mistakes. Would she be proud of him now? Would she praise him for what he was doing? He hoped so.

The preparation took almost half an hour, during which time Benfro examined the damage done to Errol's ankles. He had never studied the anatomy of men, but it was fairly easy to see that the damage had been healing badly. Not set properly, the bones would likely have fused into one unyielding mass, making walking extremely difficult and painful. In some ways the boy had done himself a favour by breaking them again.

It wasn't going to be easy to set them right though; he might not even be able to do it at all. Errol's ankles were much smaller and more complicated than Ynys Môn's shoulder, and he had only watched his mother heal that. But it was a task that would require his full attention, that would take his mind off sleep and the endless weariness that pulled at him.

Steeling himself to the task, Benfro let his perceptions

shift until he could see Errol's aura, stretched thin over him like a second skin. Only those ruined ankles glowed with any colour, and that was a livid shifting mass of purples and reds. Settling down in the best position he could manage for both comfort and light from the fire, he extended one talon and set to work.

6

And the Shepherd called forth his followers, bidding them come to him at his most marvellous palace. They gathered together, Grendor and Malco, Wise Earith and Balwen the Brave. Though they had travelled to the far corners of Gwlad, spreading his good words, still they heeded his call and returned.

Each one in turn attended him, curious as to why he had summoned them. But none was so bold as to question him. And to each one he gave a gift of power, of understanding and wisdom. Grendor received the knowledge of all the languages of men, Malco the strength of the mountain bears he so resembled. To Earith the Shepherd gave the power of healing, so that any she touched would be cured of all illness.

Then came Balwen, last into the hall. And when he knelt before his master, the Shepherd rose from his throne and went down to meet him.

'A great war is coming,' the Shepherd said, 'and I must leave Gwlad to fight the Wolf in his lair. But do not despair, my loyal servants, for I shall return. Until then I have touched you each with some measure of my power. Use it wisely, for only thus can you guard my throne.'

And he laid his hand on Balwen's head. And with that touch, Balwen the Brave was filled with the power of Gwlad such as no man had ever known.

The Book of the Shepherd

Melyn pushed through the doors into the royal chambers, ignoring the startled looks of the ladies-in-waiting who hovered around the queen like so many flies around a corpse.

'Your Majesty, once again you look ridiculous. Must you insist on wearing these outrageous costumes?'

Beulah laughed without any mirth. 'You know as well as I do that I hate this pomp and show, Melyn. I hate it as much as you do. But it's what the people expect.'

'True,' Melyn conceded. 'Padraig may be an insufferable bore, but he knows how to manipulate public feeling. The whole city celebrates today.'

'That's because they don't have to go to work.'

'Well, that could have something to do with it, I suppose. But they're feeling well disposed towards the royal house too. The people seem to approve of Clun.'

'I didn't choose him for his public appeal, Melyn. He has other qualities.'

'I'm sure he does, but now is perhaps not the time to discuss them. You're due to be married in about twenty minutes.'

'Is it that late already?' Beulah looked over at the window as if trying to gauge the time by the light filtering in. The sky was overcast, a grey pallor marring an otherwise fine warm spring day. It had rained earlier, washing down the yellow sandstone walls of the citadel and making everything smell fresh. All they needed was a little sunshine and it would be perfect.

'His Grace the Duke of Abervenn left for the chapel about ten minutes ago,' Melyn said. 'I don't think I've ever seen a boy look more nervous.'

'Boy, Melyn? He's a grown man.' Beulah shooed away the ladies-in-waiting. 'Go now. I will speak with the inquisitor alone. You may wait for me downstairs.'

The ladies left the room, fussing that the queen was not yet ready, though Melyn could see nothing wrong with how she looked beyond the sheer ridiculousness of her costume itself. White and large was the best way he could describe it, with all manner of extraneous bits trailing off here and there. He understood the need for the symbolism, but he couldn't help disliking the extravagance of a dress costing so much gold which would be worn just once, for less than half a day.

'Has he asked about his father?' Beulah took up the brush one of her ladies had placed carefully on the dressing table, and began pulling it through her hair. Melyn realized he was staring and looked away. He didn't think he'd ever seen Beulah brush her hair before. It had always been too short to worry about, but now it was down to her shoulders

'His father?'

'Clun. Has he asked about his father? I assume you took care of that little problem.'

'Clun hasn't asked about his father, no,' Melyn said.

'Not that I've had that much time to talk to him. Or you for that matter. I should have delivered my report to you as soon as I arrived.'

'As I recall, you were doing that when we were interrupted. Never mind, Melyn. Tell me now.'

'But your wedding?'

'Can wait a few minutes more. It never hurts to keep a man waiting. A lady, on the other hand . . .'

Melyn told her what they had found at Pwllpeiran and how they had tracked signs of a dragon travelling north into the great forest of the Ffrydd. 'I don't think it was the kitling, Benfro. I think this is another beast entirely, something completely wild. I've never heard of their kind eating people before. Killing us, yes, but not eating us.'

'What about the boy Errol? Was there any sign of him?'

'No,' Melyn said. 'I don't even think he'd gone back to his home. We found only signs of the two adults living there, and their bones.'

'And you're sure it was them?'

'As sure as I could be. They were picked clean, but it was definitely a man and a woman. You could say the beast did us a favour, but I'll still track it down and kill it. I'll break the bad news to Clun tomorrow. Let him enjoy his wedding day.'

'No, I'll tell him,' Beulah said, standing and gathering her voluminous dress around her, taking Melyn's proffered arm. 'He's going to be my husband, after all.'

Errol sat on a cliff, looking out over hauntingly familiar mountains. He hugged his knees to his chest, shivered at the cold and stared at the impossibly large building across the narrow steep-sided ravine. He had seen Emmass Fawr, walked its endless corridors from the highest tower to the deepest dungeon. The castle he saw now made the monastery of the Order of the High Ffrydd look like a doll's house.

It spread around the whole of a single mountain peak, encircling it with concentric rings of battlement-topped stone walls. Windows glinted in the sun like the myriad facets of some vast spider's eye, and thin towers reached skyward from every corner. In the middle, atop the highest peak, a single fat circular tower rose five or six storeys higher still, capped with a conical roof of dark slate.

As he watched the huge castle, looking for signs of life and wondering how he had come to be in this place, Errol heard a screeching noise behind him at once alien and terribly familiar. He turned to see four great beasts beating their way through the sky. One, weighed down with something, flew lower than the others, and as they approached one of its companions dipped down in a complex spiralling motion, dropping even lower still and catching the burden as it was released. Errol's heart lurched as he realized what that burden was.

Martha.

She was being passed from dragon to dragon in mid-air, hundreds of feet above the ragged mountains, tumbling from one set of talons to another like a child's discarded doll, and all the while the dragons were screeching at each other in what sounded like hideous laughter. Before he could do anything, before he could even register that he must be dreaming, they had passed overhead, ignoring him completely, and were making the short trip across the ravine to the massive castle. In only a dozen beats of their wings, they were there, passing over one of the high walls and disappearing from sight.

And then Errol was sitting on the castle wall, looking down over a wide courtyard laid with flagstones and neatly mown grass. The four dragons had landed, their captive now lying on the ground motionless. They bickered among themselves like crows dancing around a dead animal, so absorbed in their dispute that they completely failed to notice a fifth dragon approach on foot from a huge arched doorway that led into the building. It had to be a male dragon; Errol had never seen a creature so big and magnificent. He towered over the other four, making them seem like children, and he clipped them around the heads until they stopped their arguments and formed a sulky line.

It was so like old Father Drebble knocking a bit of discipline into his more unruly pupils that Errol almost laughed, but his voice choked off before he made a sound. The large dragon leaned down to inspect the still bundle on the ground, stooping further to pick it up and inspect it more closely. He turned away from the four youngsters, walked a few paces back towards the door, then turned and shouted something at them. As one, they leaped back, crashing into each other in their haste to get airborne. Errol ignored them, straining to see the older dragon and the too-still form of Martha as he carried her away towards the building. Was it his imagination? Was it just the rolling, bumping motion of the dragon's gait, or did she move her arm to her head, like someone waking from unconsciousness? He prayed she was unharmed even as he knew she was in serious trouble.

He wanted to rush after her, follow as stealthily as he

could, find wherever it was the dragon was taking her and free her. They could escape together, if he could just get down to the courtyard. But it was a forty-foot drop on to hard flagstones. Behind, he knew without looking, it was ten times that on to near-vertical scree-covered slopes. To either side the wall snaked away, impossibly narrow, hitting him with sudden heart-stopping vertigo.

And then he was enveloped in noise, a terrible screeching as the first of the four young dragons dived at him, claws reaching for his head, talons outstretched. Instinctively Errol ducked and felt himself tipping over the wall backwards. Into nothing.

'It is written that in the earliest days, when he still walked among his chosen, the Shepherd directed King Balwen towards fair Myfanwy and filled his heart with love for her as he filled hers with devotion to him. His blessing upon that union was the foundation of our people, the beginning of the Twin Kingdoms.'

Beulah tuned out the words, barely hearing Archimandrite Cassters' droning voice as he worked his way through the marriage ceremony. She knelt on a hard cushion in front of the altar in Brynceri's chapel, staring through her veil at the ornate carvings on the wall behind, at the archimandrite's heavy silk robes, at her hands. Darting a quick glance sideways at Clun.

'Our lord no longer walks among his flock, but he watches over us at all times. From our first breath he is there, even until we depart this life and make that final journey to the safe pastures. He is our guide through life, our protector from the Running Wolf.'

She had not expected to be so nervous. It was such a cliché; only empty-headed young maidens panicked on their wedding day. And yet here she was, fidgeting and quite unable to concentrate.

'His compassion knows no bounds, his wisdom is infinite, and nowhere is his generosity more amply demonstrated than in his blessing of the union of man and woman. For if we search our hearts, we can see that he has brought together Clun Godric Defaid, Duke of Abervenn, and Her Majesty Queen Beulah of the Speckled Face, just as he has brought together every man and woman since the beginning of time.'

Beulah winced at her full title, hating her father for his cruelty in naming her so. She would have dearly liked to change it, but her people were a superstitious lot, and nothing would alarm them more than abandoning the name bestowed upon her. The history of the House of Balwen was littered with sorry tales of those who had tempted fate that way.

'We gather here, in the shelter of this chapel, built by King Brynceri himself on the spot where the Shepherd instructed him to unite the whole of Gwlad in his love, to act as witnesses to this union.'

There was a power to this place, Beulah had to admit. She was not one for spending hours in religious contemplation, preferring to serve her god in her actions, but Brynceri's chapel glowed with an energy like the Obsidian Throne, though perhaps not as potent. She tried to relax, letting herself slip into the aethereal. Once more it seemed she was unable to reach that state that had been second nature. She suspected it was something to do with her pregnancy, but it was frustrating nonetheless. She didn't like the feeling of helplessness, and she longed to teach Clun the art. His aethereal image was so strong, he would surely master it as swiftly as had she under Melyn's tutelage. There were few enough adepts as it was and she would need them all for the coming war.

'Your Majesty, would you please stand now.' The archimandrite's words were a whisper, meant only for her. Beulah realized she had tuned him out completely, not hearing the ceremony at all. Behind her the chapel was an echo of silent anticipation, as if everyone assembled simultaneously held their breath. Then she felt a hand touch her arm lightly and looked round to where Clun hovered in an almost squatting position, offering to help her up. She took his arm and they rose together.

'To be joined in the eyes of the Shepherd is no trifling thing. Do you, Clun Godric Defaid, take this woman to be your wife? Do you swear to protect her, to honour her for all of your days?'

Clun's nervous 'I do so swear' was the greatest gift he could have given her. Beulah could see in his thoughts that he was in awe of her. There was no artifice in him: he didn't see her as a source of power or wealth or influence, only as the woman he wanted to be with for the rest of his life, to serve with unquestioning loyalty, faith and love. It was almost humbling, but also unsettling to be faced with such devotion.

'And do you, Queen Beulah of the Speckled Face, First of the House of Balwen, Ruler of the Twin Kingdoms and Defender of the Faith, take this man to be your husband and consort? Do you swear to protect him, to honour him for all of your days?'

'I do so swear.' Beulah heard the words, recognized them as her own, but she had no memory of saying them. For an instant she was in the aethereal, looking at the two figures standing in front of the altar, faced by the indistinct shape of the archimandrite. Clun was a shining form of gold, handsome and self-assured, and tinged with that soft roseate glow that had suffused him the night he had come to her possessed by the spirit of the Shepherd. Beside him she looked small and slightly pale, all the energy and colour swirling around her belly, as if her unborn child were leaching the life out of her.

And then with a nauseating swirl she was back in her own body, staggering slightly as if she had been hit. Clun held her firm, lending her strength as she knew he always would. Behind her, she sensed the approach of Inquisitor Melyn.

'Hold steady now, Beulah. It's nearly done,' he murmured as he handed two rings to the archimandrite. Cassters took a sharp breath as he saw them. One was a plain gold band inscribed with intricate sigils. The other, larger than its companion, was white silver, ancient in design, and held a single small ruby surrounded by tiny diamonds. As he held them up for the congregation to witness, a ripple of astonished whispering flickered through the chapel

'Your Majesty, this is King Balwen's ring.' The archimandrite spoke quietly, a look of horror on his face.

'One of them, yes,' Beulah said, and added nothing else but a smile. As if aware that he had interrupted his own service, the archimandrite shuddered slightly, then collected himself. He blessed the gold ring first, handing it to Clun. Then he blessed the silver ring, taking far longer over it than was necessary before passing it to the queen.

'These . . . rings.' The archimandrite hesitated, struggling to regain his composure. 'These rings are a token of your troth, a reminder of the promises you have made to each other today, in the presence of the Shepherd and of these witnesses. By taking them, by wearing them, what was two is become one.'

As he spoke the words, Beulah felt Clun take her hand and gently push the golden band on to her finger. He looked at her through her veil, waiting patiently, but didn't reach out for the ring she held. It was hers to give, he was saying. He would not take it from her. Or had he picked up on the archimandrite's hesitation? Did he realize that there was something yet more in the exchange of this particular ring?

Beulah found she no longer cared. She had made this decision weeks ago. She took Clun's hand in hers, feeling its warmth and strength. Turning slightly, so that everyone in the chapel could see, she pushed the ring on to his finger.

'It is done. What the Shepherd has joined, only he can ever part.' Archimandrite Cassters' voice faltered slightly as he made the benediction, sounding higher than its normal deep baritone. 'You may kiss the bride.'

Clun lifted Beulah's veil and bent to kiss her. There, in front of witnesses, she felt a sudden sense of embarrassment, as if this union were a private matter and not something for all to see. It was a fleeting moment, however, and she reached up and took his head in her hands, pulling him into a fierce embrace that lasted a good few seconds.

As she reluctantly pulled away, taking Clun's hand in her own, he leaned towards her and whispered, 'My lady. The ring. What does it mean?'

'It is King Balwen's ring,' she said as they stepped slowly down the aisle. 'Legend says that it was made for him by the Shepherd himself. It has been worn by every king of the House of Balwen for the last two thousand years.'

'But I'm not a king.'

'No, my love. You're not a king. But you are my consort and you will rule the Twin Kingdoms by my side.'

The pile had grown depressingly small now. Benfro didn't know how long he had been sorting through it, but the screams of protest that echoed through his head as he sifted jewel after jewel were much quieter than when he had started. He had found two more of the villagers. Both had been calm, telling him much the same as Sir Frynwy had done, forgiving him for his actions, trying to reassure him that he would win his fight, return and free them all once more. Now parts of Ynys Môn sat in front of him, incomplete but close to the point where he too would be consigned to a solitary hell. The old dragon was quiet, choosing only to send images of the hunts they had shared and the small triumphs Benfro had achieved as he learned the skills of forest craft. The aim was obvious and laudable, to show him that he could succeed. But Benfro felt only sadness in the memories.

He was going to lose. Soon the whole pile would be

sorted, each dragon's memories trapped once more for Magog to tap for whatever strange power they held. Then he would be overcome. He wondered if he would drift away to nothing, or if he would just be pushed to the back, left a spectator as the greatest mage ever to master the skies of Gwlad rose again and took his revenge on the creatures that had killed him. It was becoming increasingly difficult to care.

Jewel after jewel after jewel, he lifted them, weighed them in his palm, felt the flavour of the thoughts they contained and compared them with the small piles he had already sorted but were still incomplete. Sometimes he had to lift a jewel from these piles and weigh it in his other palm, holding both as if he were some kind of strange balance, measuring their similarity. There were memories subtly different yet so intertwined they could only belong to dragons who had shared a lifetime together. To part them was to live through his mother's death over and over again, and yet he was powerless to stop. Even the pain in his wing root was little more than a minor irritation now, and nothing he could use to break out of the endless loop of his nightmare.

A shudder ran through him as Benfro's fingers found the next jewel. There was no mistaking it, no denying it was the last piece of Ynys Môn.

'Do not despair, Benfro. This is a torment for us, I won't pretend otherwise. But we're safe here. And I know you'll defeat him.'

Benfro wanted to scream. As his traitorous hands cupped the pile of shining white jewels, he strained every sinew of his mind to throw them back on to the pile. Bad enough that Meirionnydd, Sir Frynwy and half the other villagers had already been consigned to the alcoves, but not this. Not Ynys Môn. There had to be a way to stop it from happening. But as if his effort were nothing, he scrambled to his feet, heading off into the darkness in search of the correct alcove.

Something blocked his way.

Something long and low, like a rolled-up rug or an animal sprawled on the floor. Something, in fact, remarkably like a young man, hardly more than a boy.

In his puppet-like state, he walked straight into the shape, rolling it over as he lost his balance and tipped forward. Benfro had just enough time to make out Errol's startled face before he was plunging down, tumbling head over heels as cracked and eroded cliffs rushed past him in the opposite direction. Astonished, he almost dropped the precious jewels still cupped in his outstretched hands, and as he clutched them, he realized he had control over his body. He snapped open his wings. For a few moments he continued plummeting towards the bottom of what looked like a deep ravine, but then he felt them catch the wind and slow his fall, and then with a single great sweep he halted his descent and swooped up.

As he climbed, Benfro could see that he was surrounded by mountains, though he didn't recognize any of them. Neither had he ever before seen the enormous castle that squatted on top of the nearest, surrounding its peak with concentric rings of high walls, rising to a single thick tower on the top.

Curious, he wheeled about, climbing higher until he could get a better look. The scale was almost impossible to comprehend; nothing could be that big, surely. He needed to get closer or to see something recognizable within one of the open spaces surrounded by those tall thin walls. But for the moment Benfro was content just to whirl in the air currents, feel the wind in his ears.

Some indefinable seventh sense kicked in at the last possible moment. It was almost as if a voice in the back of his head had shouted, 'Duck!' Not knowing why he did it, Benfro folded his wings in with a snap, clasped his hands to his chest and hunched his head. He dropped like a stone just as something vast swooped through the place in the air where he had been. It screeched like an enraged buzzard, and now Benfro could see it was a dragon, clawing at the air in an undignified attempt at a fast turn.

That sense tickled him again, and Benfro swept his wings wide, slowing to a halt and pirouetting as a second dragon speared through the point where he would have been had he continued falling. There was a great clattering of wings and two other dragons tumbled past him, looking as if they had just collided in mid-air. The first dragon had recovered from its dive and was heading straight towards him, screeching, talons drawn for blood. Beneath him the other three had sorted themselves out and were climbing back up through the air.

Benfro folded his wings and dived again, still clasping the jewels to his chest. His move took his attackers by surprise. They must have thought he would try to turn and flee; instead he plummeted between the three, heading for the castle, looking for shelter before they could regroup and attack again. They tumbled out of his way, bashing into each other and lashing out like bickering kitlings. He sped himself onward with huge sweeps of his wings, surprised to find that he felt no pain at all in his wing root.

Too late he remembered the first dragon.

Wiser than his three companions, he must have wheeled round, watching the fight and flight, taking his time to see what was going on. This time his dive connected, and Benfro felt the wind knocked out of him. Sharp pain lanced across his shoulders as talons sank into his flesh. He twisted in the air, trying to shake his attacker loose, but without success. And all the while he was falling towards the huge castle.

They were over the wall now, tumbling towards an area of grass criss-crossed by wide flagstone paths. Benfro twisted again, trying to wrench the talons from his back, but they stayed firm, the pain lancing through him anew. His hands flew open reflexively, spilling their precious collection of memories to the air. Ynys Môn's jewels tumbled towards the grass, Benfro watching them with a mixture of horror and relief. Wherever it was he had brought them, they weren't going to be trapped in Magog's repository.

His hands free now, Benfro was able to reach up to grip his attacker's talons, all the while fighting with his wings to keep aloft. He felt scale and leathery skin taut over trembling muscle. Extending one talon, he ripped at the other dragon's feet and ankles. With a screech, his attacker let go, and Benfro once more snapped his wings shut, diving away for a moment before whirling round to face his vicious enemy.

Or at least that was what he meant to do. But he was suddenly too close to the ground and travelling too quickly to stop before he hit. In the instant before impact he heard the dragon shriek in maniacal triumph.

'Your Highness, is there anything else I can get you this evening?'

Prince Dafydd looked up at his manservant, hovering by the door. No doubt the man was on a promise. One of the kitchen girls most likely. Sometimes he wondered that the palace staff managed to perform their duties at all, the amount of time they seemed to spend jumping into bed with one another.

'No,' he said, grateful that he would be left alone now. 'That will be all. Goodnight, Jevans.'

The servant bowed and retreated from the room, pulling the doors closed behind him. Dafydd settled back into his armchair and studied the patterns of flame in the fireplace. Through the doorway in the bedchamber Iolwen was sleeping. She did a lot of that these days. And eating. The slim lonely girl he knew and loved was filling out as her condition began to show, but there was more to her brooding than pregnancy. Ever since she had met the boy Errol she had been different, almost homesick for the country that had abandoned her so many years ago. She took far more interest in the news from the Twin Kingdoms than ever she had before, and she spent long hours up in the tower where he had been imprisoned, reading the words he had written as if there were something profound in them, rather than a rather naive attempt at a Llanwennog grammar.

What had it been about that boy? King Ballah had been fascinated by him too, had let him get far closer than was wise. Was it yet one more sign of the old man finally losing his mind, that he could be so easily swayed by a likeness to his dead youngest and favourite son, Balch? Or was there something else about the young spy that Dafydd hadn't noticed? He didn't think he'd ever met someone so naturally powerful in magic, and yet so unskilled, so unwise in its application. And then there was the nature of his disappearance. His escape from the executioner's block still defied any explanation. It was a worry too. If Melyn had uncovered some new conjuring that could make his spies invisible, whisk them away from danger even when their ankles were smashed beyond walking, then Llanwennog was in far greater danger from the Twin Kingdoms than the war council realized.

Dafydd despaired at the council. Tordu was so wrapped up in his spite, hating everything and everyone, and he was as stubborn as a pack mule. Dondal was a coward, terrified of Ballah but always looking to play both sides. He would agree with anyone, as long as it meant he could keep his head on his shoulders. And Geraint, dear old dad. Dafydd supposed he should have more respect for his father, but the man was a foot soldier to the core, lacking any imagination.

Which left the king. Ballah was still a force to be reckoned with, still the sharpest mind of the lot. And his experience counted for a great deal. But lately he seemed less the all-powerful ruler, more the grandfather in a dynasty grown fat and complacent. Perhaps familiarity bred contempt; certainly he'd seen more of the king these past few months than in the rest of his life. Since his wedding. Since he had been invited to join the council.

The knock at the door was so quiet Dafydd couldn't be sure it hadn't been going on for minutes. It dragged his attention back to the room, the hypnotic swirls of the flames becoming just fire flickering as it consumed the logs. He focused his mind and reached out to the figure who stood without, trying to work out who it was from the colour of their thoughts.

There was nobody there.

Another knock, slightly louder this time, came from the door.

'Who's there?' Dafydd brought forth his puissant sword, feeling the power of it surge through him. He crossed to the door in a half-dozen paces. Still he could sense no one standing on the other side. Or was there something? He reached out with his mind again, visualising the corridor outside. He knew it well enough, but now there was something different. A shadow in the darkness, perhaps. Or a hole the shape and size of a man.

Dafydd whipped the door open, blade forward. For an instant he saw nothing but the corridor, he was certain. And then there was a hooded figure in front of him, motionless, waiting.

'Who are you?' Dafydd raised his blade to the man's throat. Unperturbed, the stranger held up his hands, palms outward in a gesture of peace, then slowly reached up to his hood, pulling it back to reveal his features.

'My name is Usel, Your Highness. I mean you no harm. Quite the opposite in fact.'

Dafydd almost dropped his blade in surprise. The man who stood before him was quite plainly a southerner, from the Twin Kingdoms. He wore the simple robes of one of their travelling monks, a healer coenobite of the Order of the Ram. His face was pale, as if he didn't often see the sun; his skin smooth save for a light fuzz of stubble, his dark hair streaked with white; but it was his eyes that held Dafydd's gaze. They were palest grey, bright with intelligence. As he looked at the man, those eyes shifted focus to behind him and creased at the edges with a warm smile.

'I heard voices . . . Oh.' Dafydd looked around to see Iolwen, wrapped in silk bedclothes and a heavy shawl, standing in the middle of the room, staring.

'Princess Iolwen. It's good to see you again. I hope you're well.' The stranger spoke softly, but his voice carried. Dafydd cursed himself for being distracted like a novice. He whipped his head back round, tensed for an attack, but there was no need. Their unannounced visitor had not moved.

'Usel, what in the Shepherd's name are you doing here?' Iolwen said.

'You know this man?' Dafydd asked.

'Of course, love. So do you. He's Usel. He was with the party that brought me here. He stayed almost a year while I settled in. I cried for a week when he was called away, when it was just me and my ladies-in-waiting.'

'Your Highness, might I ask you lower your blade? And might I come in? I don't want to be seen by the guards if at all possible.'

Dafydd didn't know whether to be offended by the request or amused. He remembered little of the arrival of Iolwen at Tynhelyg; he had been only eight, far more interested in games of war. Perhaps there had been a foreign adult who had stayed longer than the rest; he supposed that it could have been this man. Whoever he was, Usel certainly had courage. To come back now and appear like this.

'I couldn't sense you,' he said. 'How did you do that?'

'A trick I learned from someone in Eirawen. I'll teach you if you're willing to learn. And if you wish to sense my intentions, my mind is unguarded now.'

Dafydd concentrated, trying not to be distracted by those piercing eyes, that disarming smile. He skimmed the surface of Usel's thoughts, seeing glimpses of the man's journey through the mountains, his slow progress across a country grown hostile to people who looked like they came from the south, the shadowy and ill-defined route across the city and into the palace past guards who were supposed to protect the king and his family. And there were other images too: a hasty escape from an enormous stone building, endless damp and twisting tunnels lit only by a smoky flame from a guttering torch, a pale-faced young boy lying on a bed unconscious, his legs wrapped in white bandages turned crimson at the feet.

'You saw the spy? Errol?' In his astonishment Dafydd let his blade extinguish itself, his hand falling to his side. 'Where?'

'Errol was never a spy.' Usel stepped into the room and closed the door behind him. 'He appeared quite unexpectedly in Ruthin's Grove, just beneath the monastery at Emmass Fawr some months ago. I was trying to treat his injuries, but he kept on disappearing, ending up in the most unlikely places. He has a rather unique talent, that boy. Something I don't really understand.'

'Is he all right?' Iolwen settled herself into a chair by the fire.

'The last I heard, he was being taken to Candlehall to be questioned by Queen Beulah. I'm sorry to say I failed him. I was forced to flee before I could help him escape. Melyn uncovered his secret, you see. Something I'd tried to cover up.'

'His secret? What secret?' Dafydd heard the concern in Iolwen's voice and felt a moment's irrational jealousy.

'He's Lleyn's child. And Balch's too, Prince Dafydd. Your cousin, both of you.'

7

Strategically located at the mouth of the rivers Abheinn and Gwy, and with the sheltered Bay of Kerdigen giving access to the southern sea, Abervenn has long been a centre of trade. With the dukedom a plaything of the king at Candlehall, true power in Abervenn has most often resided with the merchants who base their operations in the city. Quite happy to trade with Llanwennog and Fo Afron to the north, as well as distant Eirawen to the south, the loyalty of the merchants of Abervenn has most often been to their money, rather than the crown.

Abervenn, *A History of Trade*

Dafydd strode down the narrow streets of Tynhelyg, marvelling at how well the foreigner, Usel, seemed to know his way around. He was taking a circuitous route, avoiding areas where there might be more than a few people, keeping to the narrow streets overhung with tall buildings, their upper storeys canted out until they almost touched in the middle. The shadows seemed to swallow him, so that Dafydd had to strain every sense to keep track of him. He recalled the way the man had hidden before, how he had managed to sneak into the royal palace and evade guards who were meant to be skilled in throwing off magical glamours. Usel had said he would teach Dafydd the trick, and he was very keen to learn.

They were heading for the merchant quarter, passing elegant houses that appeared lifeless, their lower windows shuttered tight, iron bolts barring entry. These were the houses of Twin Kingdoms traders, empty now save for a few servants. Few men from the south dared show their faces in public these days.

'Your Highness, may I beg a favour of you?'

Dafydd stopped short, nearly bumping into Usel, who loomed out of the darkness in a completely different place to where he had thought him to be.

'I came alone because Iolwen said you could be trusted. Is that not favour enough?'

'You're right, of course. Perhaps favour is the wrong word. Perhaps I should just say that the people you're going to meet have put their lives on the line for you. If they're found here, they'll be executed. If their actions are uncovered at home, their families will be executed.'

'I'll hear what they have to say. As long as they do nothing to antagonize me, I'll say nothing about their presence here. You can all go home and no one need be the wiser.'

'Thank you, sir. I could ask for no more.' Usel disappeared once more into the gloom, and a door opened, spilling muted light into the alleyway. Dafydd followed the healer into a low-ceilinged rear entrance hall of the sort more often frequented by tradesmen and servants. He was led through an empty kitchen, along a corridor with a creaking wooden floor covered in a threadbare rug, and out into the more formal area of the house. Usel opened a door leading into a small but richly appointed reception room. Dafydd stepped through to see a small group: four men he did not recognize, and one young woman he did.

'Lady Anwyn, I was distraught at the news of your father and brother. Please accept my heartfelt condolences.' Dafydd bowed. Behind him Usel closed the door and turned the key in the lock.

'Your Highness.' Anwyn curtsied, flustered. 'I had hoped you would come, but I never dared believe . . . I'm sorry, please let me introduce Lord Ansey, Lord Meygrim and Count Vespil. And this is Master Holgrum.'

'The spice merchant,' Dafydd said, as he nodded in turn to each of the men.

'You know of me, Your Highness?' Holgrum asked, his piggy face flushed, though whether this was from alarm or the man's natural complexion, Dafydd couldn't be sure.

'I know of your business. It's said that you're richer than King Ballah himself.'

'Would that it were so, sir. Would that it were so. But please, have a seat. Can I get you come wine?' The merchant bustled over to a side table and poured rich dark liquid into fine crystal glasses without waiting for an answer.

'Healer Usel tells me you have a proposition to make.' Dafydd accepted the offered wine but didn't drink. 'It must be something important for you all to have risked coming here to make it in person.'

'Indeed it is,' Anwyn said, settling herself down in a chair by the fire. 'I come to offer you Abervenn.'

'As I understood it, Queen Beulah took back those lands and titles when she declared your family traitors.'

'The people of Abervenn were loyal first to my father. They loved him, and they loved Merrl too. They've no loyalty to Beulah. Ansey, Meygrim and Vespil control all the towns in the province; I command the city itself. We can bring together a sizeable army, well equipped and far better trained than the rabble being pressed to serve in the queen's name.'

'And why would they fight their own? Why would they help the likes of me?'

'Because you are Iolwen's husband.'

Dafydd took a chair beside the fire opposite Anwyn. She was far younger than he had thought, still in her teens, but her face was hard, her eyes wary. He skimmed her thoughts, trying to sense her sincerity, but he was overwhelmed by her desperate hope and behind that an obsessive hatred for the woman who had destroyed her family.

'My father always believed Beulah's claim to the Obsidian Throne was false,' she said.

'Why would he believe that? Surely Beulah's the oldest.'

'You've never met her, have you?' It was Lord Ansey who spoke. 'Of Diseverin's three daughters, Lleyn and Iolwen were like twins, only born years apart. Beulah was different in so many ways, not least her complexion. I remember well the intrigue in court leading up to her birth and after she was born. More than one whisper said that Queen Ellyn had cuckolded her husband.'

'Really?' Dafydd was intrigued. 'With whom?'

'Inquisitor Melyn spent a lot of time at Candlehall in those days. And he gained great influence in court too.'

'I knew nothing of this,' Dafydd said.

'The rumour died as quick as it began,' Lord Ansey said. 'People accepted Beulah as princess because the alternative was unthinkable. But Duke Angor thought otherwise, and he was close to Ellyn. The only person who knows the truth is Melyn, and I doubt he'd tell.'

Dafydd looked from the three noblemen to Lady Anwyn and back, absentmindedly taking a sip of his wine – an excellent vintage, he noted. It stood to reason that these noblemen would dislike Queen Beulah, but their willingness to commit treason, to sell out their own country to the enemy, seemed too much. It almost offended him that they had no loyalty, no sense of honour. Skulking about with plots and intrigue was not the way of a soldier. But then soldiers died on the battlefield, with their guts spilled out on the ground and ravens pecking out their eyeballs. Wars were won by strategists, by people prepared to compromise their morals.

'So you say you can give me Abervenn,' he said. 'What you really mean is you can give Iolwen Abervenn, but I'll accept that. The question is, what do you want me to do with it?'

'Queen Beulah is scouring the whole of the Twin Kingdoms for men to fight in her armies,' Lord Ansey said. 'She intends to force her way through the passes by sheer weight of numbers. You can ask Master Holgrum here how the taxes have grown since she took the throne. There's only so long she can continue like that before there's open revolt through all the provinces. But if her plan succeeds, if she makes it to Tynewydd or Wrthol, then her people will love her.'

'She'll never make it through the passes,' Dafydd said. 'No one ever has.'

'Don't underestimate her, sir. And don't forget Melyn. His warrior priests are a force to be reckoned with. But if her invasion can be delayed to next winter, then her army will disintegrate. She'll have a hard time holding the Twin Kingdoms together when that happens.'

'So you want me to delay her by attacking from the rear.'

'Exactly.'

'It won't work. At least not the way you think.'

'Why not?' Anwyn asked.

'You say you can give me Abervenn, but I don't think you can. Even if your captains tell the people to follow me, they won't be happy about it. And a reluctant army's less use than no army at all. No, they need Iolwen to return. To stand at my side. They need to see that I command them in her name.'

'Your Highness, may I make a suggestion?' Dafydd turned to where Usel still stood at the door, as if on guard. He remembered the sound of the key turning in the lock and wondered if it were to keep others out, or him in.

'Go ahead,' he said.

'Despite his age, King Ballah shows every sign of living for many a year yet. Prince Geraint is, if anything, healthier still. Provided he doesn't get himself killed in some battle, he'll likely rule just as long as his father. You'll be an old man before your turn comes along. But you could rule the Twin Kingdoms at Iolwen's side. And your child would be rightful heir to both thrones.'

It was a tempting thought. Dafydd well knew that he would have to wait many years to be king in Tynhelyg. The thought of ruling alongside Iolwen in Candlehall was beguiling. He could bring an end to the petty bickering between the two countries that so often spilled over into needless bloody war. But it would be no easy thing overcoming centuries of hostility, the almost inbred antipathy of men from the north to their paler cousins in the south, and the other way around. Some might see his marriage to the princess as evidence the two peoples could live in harmony. Others would see it as something entirely different, a corruption of the Twin Kingdoms' most pure and innocent soul, their young princess, by the evil heathen northerners. That would be the battle: to show that his wife was not under some demon spell.

'You seem very certain that the people of Abervenn would follow Iolwen.' Dafydd chose his words carefully. 'But she's been among my kind for more than fourteen years now. And our child will have my looks, you can be sure of that. Would the Twin Kingdoms be ready to accept such a one as their ruler?'

Usel bowed slightly, and Dafydd got the distinct impression this was the point the healer had been trying to get across all along.

'Yes. I believe they would. If the child were born in Abervenn.'

Benfro didn't know where he was, but neither did he care. He was warm, comfortable. The ache at the root of his wing had gone, and he lay curled up on the edge of dreamless sleep.

A tiny niggle of unease spoiled his perfect rest. Sleep was bad. Sleep was when Magog came to him, forced him to be his slave. But Benfro could sense nothing of the long-dead dragon mage. Maybe he wasn't asleep then. But if that were the case, where was he? He felt more rested, more relaxed than he could remember.

Sounds seeped back to him: the rush of water over stone, wind in trees still putting out their first spring leaves, the crackle of flames. He could smell acrid smoke and a rich spicy aroma that was instantly recognizable. He knew where he was, and with that realization came the memories of his strange dream. His flight, his fight and the headlong plummet towards the ground.

Snapping his eyes open, Benfro sat up in a rush, as if doing so would stop him crashing into the flagstones. But he had never reached that ground; that impact had never come. He had gone . . . somewhere. He didn't know where. Nor did he know how long he had been there; only that it had been time enough to rest.

'You have wakened. That is good.' Benfro looked round to see Errol sitting against the rock wall of the cave. His voice sounded strange as he tried to speak Draigiaith, and it occurred to Benfro that men's mouths were not well shaped for the task.

Shaking the last of the sleep from his face, Benfro looked around the cave. He was sitting between the fire and the makeshift mattress of dried grass, exactly where he had settled himself down to attend to Errol's broken ankles. As he thought of them, Benfro looked at the boy's legs, then at the fire. The cauldron sat a little away from the flames, the last of the poultice he had mixed turned dry and flaky inside it.

'I must thank you,' Errol said, 'for what you did to my ankles. The pain is gone now.'

'It was nothing. You'll need to keep the weight off them for a while though. No more trying to drag heavy wooden chests across the clearing.' Benfro looked out of the cave entrance to a sunlit day well progressed. The storm had blown through, and bright sunlight painted shadows on grass strewn with branches torn from the surrounding trees. 'How long was I asleep?'

'I am not know . . . I don't know.' Errol corrected his mistake and Benfro realized quite how much effort the boy was putting into Draigiaith. 'I woke at dawn. You have been sleeping for some hours since then. I tried to keep the bad dragon away from you. Did it work?'

'I . . .' Benfro thought back to his strange dream, and then before that when he had been in Magog's repository. 'I . . . Yes. I saw you. And then I was somewhere else. How did you do that?'

'I'm not sure.' Errol slipped back into the language of men. 'I tried to close off the link he has with you, like I've seen you do sometimes, with your aura. I didn't know if I'd be able to do it.'

'Well, you did, and I'm grateful. You've no idea how much.'

'Then can I stop now?'

Benfro looked back at Errol, noticing for the first time the uncomfortable way the boy sat, wedged up against the rock. He was pale, and a thin sheen of sweat shined his forehead and cheeks, as if he were recovering from a fever. Benfro lifted his hands and let his vision relax until he could see Errol's aura. It looked healthier than he had seen it for a long time. Errol's form glowed with a thin veil of white, almost the colour of the Grym itself. Benfro noticed that the breaks in his ankles were healing well, no longer angry red welts of fire. But what most amazed him was the thinnest strand, little more than a horse's tail, that floated from the boy's right hand, stretching out to the thin red cord that still looped away from his forehead, disappearing into the Llinellau nearby.

As he watched, the gossamer thread dissolved into nothing, and the red malevolence pulsed back up the cord like an angry snake. Instantly Benfro felt the dread presence of Magog battering against him, trying to take him over. But it was a weaker attack. Or if not weaker, Benfro felt stronger, more hopeful than he had in the months since he had first encountered the spirit of the dead mage. He reached out with his own aura, knotting it tight around the cord in an almost reflex action.

'You should sleep now,' he said, seeing the boy slump down on to the grass. 'You need rest for your ankles to heal properly.'

'Corwen said we could help each other,' Errol said. 'I think that's why he brought me here. Or maybe why Sir Radnor sent me here.'

'Brought you here? Sir Radnor?' Benfro suppressed the questions bubbling up in his mind, which was clear for the first time in weeks. The boy was on the verge of collapse. 'You can tell me later. Sleep now. I'll make up a fresh poultice for your ankles. And then I'll see about getting us something to eat.'

'I didn't think I'd be seeing this place again any time soon. And certainly not like this.'

Beulah looked over at Clun sitting tall on his horse as they passed through the gates of Beteltown. They rode at the head of what looked like a small army, accompanied by Inquisitor Melyn and several hundred warrior priests as well as the wagons that inevitably slowed down any royal procession. She had put off most of the nobles who had suggested they accompany her by insisting all would ride on their horses rather than in carriages. Those that had still been keen to come were the men she felt she could trust.

'I didn't know you'd been to Beteltown,' she said. 'I thought you lived further north.'

'Pwllpeiran's only a day's ride by wagon train. My father did most of his trading here.' Clun's face darkened, and Beulah remembered the moment she had told him of Godric's death. He had not wept, though his eyes had shone with tears as he repeated the oath of allegiance to the Order of the High Ffrydd. It was all the mother and father he would ever need. She had seen something of the man he was growing to be then, and he had made love to her with a fierce passion that night, clinging hard to her as he fell into a disturbed sleep. Since then he hadn't said a word about his family. Until now.

'Perhaps we should go there. Melyn buried their remains, but you should see for yourself what happened.'

'I'd like that.' Clun's words were quiet but hard. 'I'd like to know how they died, know something about the creature that killed them. Then I intend to track it down and kill it.'

Beulah said nothing, but she smiled as they rode through the streets towards the castle that dominated the town from a spur of rock high above the river. The crowd was perhaps smaller than she had been expecting but made up for it with genuine enthusiasm. Some of her people loved her, it seemed.

Duke Moorit of Beteltown was an elderly man, forgetful of where he was at any given moment, but like many old men he seemed to have near-total recall of events that had happened much earlier in his life. Beulah endured many hours of stories about her grandfather and the week-long hunting parties he used to arrange. She suffered it all with greater grace and patience than she knew she possessed while a string of minor nobles came from the outlying settlements to pay their respects. The recruiters had already been through most of this region, so there were few new conscripts to be had for the army. Meanwhile, Melyn was busy carrying out his own investigations into dragon sightings in the area. Finally, when she could stand the gloomy halls and corridors of Castle Betel no longer, she assembled a small troop of warrior priests, Clun at their head, and rode out heading for Pwllpeiran.

The road was easy going, though empty of people. Close to Beteltown there was evidence of agriculture, fields showing the first breard of crops fuzzing the dark earth with green. But as they climbed the series of hills towards the forest edge so the crops gave way to grass grown matted and thick with lack of grazing. There were no sheep to be seen, no cattle. Even the birds seemed subdued. Then, as they breasted the last rise towards the village, they saw a bank of cloud hanging over the land like a curse. What little conversation there had been among the troop dried up completely. This was no natural weather; more as if the trees of the forest had exhaled a toxic fog over the whole valley where the village of Pwll-peiran once had stood.

They rode on in silence past the low walls that marked the field boundaries, and then to the first building.

'By the Shepherd, what happened here?' Clun slid off his horse, dropping the reins as he walked to the ruined empty house. Beulah watched him peer through the broken door into the wreckage beyond, knowing full well he would find nothing there. The roof was gone and one wall had collapsed. It looked for all the world like a tree had fallen on it, yet there were no trees around.

The next house was the same, and the next. They made slow progress into the village, seeing only destruction. There were no people here any more, just broken things and the dull misty cloud. Still, Clun insisted on checking each ruined home. Beulah watched him go from door to door, his footsteps light and familiar across the ground where he had been born, his shoulders dropping lower and lower with each new piece of destruction uncovered. It looked like a tornado had ripped through the village.

And then they reached the village hall.

At first glance it looked more or less intact, the roof still in place and the shutters closed to protect the windows. But the large double doors at the front of the building had been pushed inwards with enough force to buckle their frame. And then whatever had gone in had ripped its way back out, leaving splintered wood spread across the track and the village green.

Beulah cast her mind out across the hall, feeling for the telltale patterns of thoughts, but there was nothing. Further out, into the rest of the village, the surrounding fields, nothing. Out to the edge of the woods, their ancient ranks a different feeling in her thoughts. Nothing. Apart from herself, Clun and the small troop of warrior priests, there was nothing alive that could frame a conscious thought.

Still concentrating on the emptiness, Beulah dismounted and followed Clun up the creaking wooden steps to the hall where she had first met him, where he had made his silent declaration of allegiance to her. She was about to enter through the broken doors when he stopped, held her back. Startled, she almost lashed out at him, but then the stench hit her and she knew what he was doing.

'My lady, I don't think you should go in there.' Clun's voice was dead, flat, as if he too knew what was inside.

'I don't need to be protected from this. These were my people. I have to see what happened to them.' She pushed past him and stepped into the hall.

It was barely recognizable from the place where Godric and Hennas had been married. All the furniture was smashed, the wooden floor gouged as if someone had set about it with a pick. The shuttered windows kept most of the pale daylight out, but they let in enough to illuminate the source of the stench. Over in the far corner, where the dais and the bridal throne that she had usurped had been, Beulah could see what looked like a pile of discarded clothing, ripped and matted. She walked carefully across the creaking splintered floorboards, and as she came closer to the pile, held up her arm with a conjured ball of flame for illumination. What the harsh light revealed made her retch.

They were clothes, but they hadn't been discarded. They had been ripped from the bodies they had covered, limbs still in coat arms and trouser legs. And then those bodies had been eaten. The flesh had been stripped from bones, leaving scraps of skin, tendons, rotting red meat.

Beulah felt a presence beside her and looked round to see Clun staring white-faced at the mess.

'They didn't stand a chance.' He hunkered down close to the pile, his own light shining brightly over the carnage. 'It ripped them apart like . . . I don't know. Why did they stay here? Why not go with the others to Beteltown?'

'Melyn told them to stay,' Beulah said. 'He posted two warrior priests here to wait for the creature and slay it if it returned.' She looked once more over the pile of rent clothing, searching for the drab robes of the Order of the High Ffrydd. Looking up at the windows, she could see that they had been bolted, as well as shuttered from the outside. 'It came back all right. And it was more than a match for them. By the look of things they tried to barricade themselves in here.'

'It didn't do them much good.' Clun leaned forward,

took a handful of material and pulled it towards him. Beulah watched in fascinated horror as a pile of wet bones rolled forward with the cloak. The severed head of a warrior priest tumbled from the pile, rolling to a halt at her feet, staring up at her with accusing eyes.

Suddenly Clun had her by the arm, was pulling her away from the pile and back towards the door.

'It's coming back,' he said. 'We have to go.'

Beulah looked at him in surprise, and then she too felt the disturbance. It wasn't like a person's thoughts, the spark of a mind that she could sense over great distances. It was alien, almost impossible to grasp. It was confused and angry and hungry. Oh so hungry.

'Why are we running? I thought you wanted to kill it.'

'I do, my lady.' Clun hurried her over to her horse, helped her up into the saddle and hauled himself into his own. 'But it's more powerful than I imagined. It's killed two experienced warrior priests. I can't risk any harm coming to you while we fight it. We have to get you to safety.'

The warrior priests formed a circle around Beulah as they rode out of the village at a canter, all eyes alert. She could feel the terrible thoughts of the creature, clouding her mind with an intoxicating fear. For a moment it almost overwhelmed her, and then she remembered Melyn's lessons. Fear was an easy emotion to project, a good way to paralyse your enemy, to stop him thinking straight, force him into making stupid decisions. Shaking her head as if the feeling were just water in her ears, Beulah pushed the fear aside. She tried to get a fix on where those terrible thoughts were coming from, but her horse was responding to the fear now, its ears flat, nostrils wide, and she needed all her strength just to hold it back.

A terrible scream behind her was cut short by a horrible ripping noise. And then a great wind buffeted the whole troop, unseating several riders. A vast dark shadow flashed overhead and something wet splattered on to Beulah's face and hands. She looked down expecting rain, but saw red. Blood.

'Regroup! Protect the queen!' She heard Clun's voice and realized her horse had carried on while the others had stopped. It was heading down the path back towards Beteltown, its canter rapidly turning into a gallop. She pulled hard on the reins, feet pushing forward in her stirrups as she tried to halt the terrified beast. Then something roared out of the mist, dark and improbably large. Her horse reared and she slipped from the saddle, falling to the ground with a crash that drove the wind out of her. Before she could gather her wits, a head as large as a man loomed over her, huge fanged jaws clamping down on the struggling body of her horse. A snap, and the poor creature was bitten clean in two, pieces falling to the ground with a sound like wet laundry being bashed against a rock. The ground shook as the shadowy form of a dragon far larger than any she had ever seen stepped forward, slavering, blood-smeared hands the size of cartwheels reaching out for her with talons extended. It screeched in what could have been pain, could have been rage, could have been words. Whatever it was, the sound cut through Beulah's last reserves of self-control, flooding her with a fear she'd not known since the day of her mother's burial, the day she'd been sent off to Emmass Fawr.

And then there was a light at her side, flashing away like a piece of the sun. Clun stood between her and the dragon, his blade held high. The dragon seemed momentarily taken aback, rearing away. But it was just a feint. It lunged at him with its fearsome claws and he had to dive to the ground to avoid being decapitated. He rolled with the agility of a trained warrior, swung his blade and caught the dragon's outstretched arm. The blade passed through scale, leathery skin, muscle and bone with a fierce charring. Howling, the creature leaped back as its severed forearm fell to the ground.

The rest of the troop had regrouped now. Beulah watched as they spread out, meaning to encircle the beast. Each held aloft a blade of light, though some seemed less certain of themselves than she had ever seen. It was a long time since any warrior priest had battled a dragon of this size and ferocity.

For its part, the dragon held its bleeding stump almost in a daze. Then it looked directly at Clun, who was pacing carefully, keeping himself just out of reach. With a roar, it lunged, the stench of its breath reaching even Beulah as she lay on the ground. Clun retreated a step, which was all the dragon needed. It turned with remarkable swiftness for its size, lashing out with its tail and knocking two warrior priests to the ground. Then it leaped into the air. Huge wings beat at the ground and in seconds it had disappeared into the mist.

8

Nothing is more important to a kitling than the galwr, or naming ceremony. It is the first great celebration of any young dragon's life, and is usually accompanied by much feasting and merriment. But there is more to the galwr than a simple giving of a name. It is a recognition, in front of gathered witnesses, of lineage, status and birthright. To be named is to be accepted into the tribe. To go anghalwyr, or without name, is the worst of all possible punishments.

Maddau the Wise, *An Etiquette*

'Your Majesty, Queen Beulah has married a commoner, a novitiate of the Order of the High Ffrydd. Rumour at Candlehall is she already carries his child. She has made him Duke of Abervenn.'

'That won't be popular with the people, I'm sure. What of her army?'

Prince Dafydd sat quietly to the side of his grandfather's throne, watching as the odious Duke Dondal delivered his latest report from the border. Tordu stood nearby, his sour face describing eloquently his utter disdain for the duke. Dafydd's father, Prince Geraint, slouched in a chair behind a table topped with charts and papers, eyes closed, apparently asleep though Dafydd knew better.

'Peasant forces are mustering at Dina and Tochers, sire,' Dondal replied. 'Not many at the moment, but they're being trained by the accursed warrior priests. And a call has gone out to all the provinces. She's building a considerable force.'

'Which will need to be fed, equipped, clothed. She can't hold an army of any size together for more than a year. Beulah's young, impulsive and foolish. Let her throw her peasant army at the passes. No one has ever succeeded in breaking through before.' Tordu's words were clipped, impatient. Much like the man himself. 'We have nothing to fear from her, and she has everything to fear from her own people. The way she treats them, there'll be an uprising within months.'

'You're forgetting that she's an adept at magic fully the equal of Inquisitor Melyn himself, uncle.' Geraint opened his eyes and stared at the palace major domo. 'And she's just as skilled at manipulation. Take this boy she's married, for instance. Yes, he's a commoner, but that works in her favour. She knows she needs an heir as soon as possible, what with young Dafydd here knocking up her little sister. If she takes a commoner, the people love her for coming down to them, and the nobles grumble but see no favouritism. They'll stay on her side for now. Especially after what she did to Angor.'

'And her army?' The king leaned forward, his attention fixed on his son. From his seat Dafydd could see how the movement pained the old man. His joints were swollen and stiff, the fingers on his hands twisted and claw-like.

Ballah had been unwell for a long time, but lately his infirmity had begun to show more obviously. For now his reputation and sheer presence were enough to keep people in line, but how long would it be before the jackals began to gather around the throne?

'Melyn will assemble enough men to attack through either of the passes, or perhaps both at once,' Geraint said. 'If he can train them sufficiently well before the autumn, then we can expect him to move several weeks before the first snows. He won't want to retreat in the depths of winter or risk having his supply trail cut.'

'Why doesn't he train them over the winter and launch his attack next spring?' Dafydd asked.

It was Tordu who answered. 'An army that size eats like a glutton and drains gold from the treasury faster than the most profligate of kings. Beulah will have to tax her merchants to the point where they feel they're working for nothing. She'll have to pull almost every able-bodied man from the provinces to fight for her, leaving the old and the very young to tend the animals and bring in the harvest. If she has two big camps, then it won't be long before her soldiers start dying of disease. It's one thing to die fighting for your queen, quite another to drown in your own phlegm on some litter in a hospital tent. No, if she tries to keep her forces together over next winter, they'll rebel against her. She has to mount her attack this autumn. And like her predecessors before her, she will fail.'

'So we just sit here and do nothing?' Dafydd asked. 'Is that not a cowardly thing to do? Shouldn't we be taking this fight to them?'

'The passes are no easier to get through from this side, Dafydd.' Geraint leaned forward, rolling out a large parchment map of the Gwahanfa ranges and the country to either side of the mountains. He stabbed it with a blunt finger. 'A large force, an invasion force, would get bottled up here. You wouldn't need a very big army to stop us dead, and the sort of numbers Beulah's gathering would wipe us out.'

'But what if there wasn't a large force waiting for you? What if they'd been drawn away?'

'Beulah's scouts will know if we make a feint to one pass, to draw the bulk of her army from the other,' Geraint said. 'And anyway she could easily defend each pass with half of her forces. A diversion won't work.'

'I agree,' Dafydd replied. 'The two passes are too easily watched. But there are other ways to create a diversion. An army of skilled mages could break through from Tynewydd and take Tochers. I've seen the lie of the land around there; if you control the city, you control the pass. An invading army could march through unchallenged. In less than six weeks we could be at Candlehall.'

'You have an idea for this diversion, don't you?' King Ballah shifted in his throne to look Dafydd in the eye. The old man might be frail, but he still radiated power. Dafydd felt the brush of that terrible mind against his thoughts.

'Yes, Your Majesty, I do.'

'In all my years I've never heard of such a thing. Not even in our histories. For a dragon to eat another sentient creature. It would be like cannibalism. No, worse than that. It would be feral.'

The lower levels of Castle Betel were gloomy and

damp, lit only by yellow flames from widely spaced torches. Melyn stood in a storeroom that had been turned into a makeshift cell; all the others had doorways too narrow for Frecknock to pass through. She had been brought in under cover of darkness, following the queen's train in a wagon. He had wanted her presence kept secret to avoid disturbing the people. Given the rumours circulating and the general state of unease in the province, it had turned out to be a wise precaution.

'Something killed five of my warrior priests and ate two of them along with at least twenty other people they were meant to be protecting. Are you trying to tell me the creature that did this wasn't a dragon?'

'I don't know, Your Grace. I didn't see it. I just know it's not the kind of behaviour I'd expect of our kind.'

Melyn seethed, as he always did in her presence. His every instinct urged him to kill her, to cut off her head like he had that of Morgwm the Green. But one small part of him held back. She knew so much, had so much innate skill, and she was so afraid, so attached to her life she would do almost anything to avoid death. Unlike most of her kind she was relatively young and inexperienced. He would break her spirit, if she even had one, and force her to divulge the secrets of her skill.

'Tell me about your kind.' Melyn settled himself on to a squat barrel still sitting in the storeroom several feet away from where Frecknock sat in that oddly dog-like manner dragons had, her tail curled around her heavy feet. That was what made her look so docile, he supposed. It didn't fool him; he knew she would dissemble as much as she could get away with.

‘What do you want to know?’

‘How many of you are there out there in the forest?’

‘I have no idea. None, I suppose. You killed us all.’ Frecknock’s voice was not accusing, not sorrowful either. It was just matter of fact, as if she were discussing one of Seneschal Padraig’s drier treatises on logistics. It put Melyn on edge.

‘And what about the rest of Gwlad? Where might this creature have come from? What brought it here, of all places?’

‘Again, Your Grace, I don’t know. Before you came, before you . . . Well, back then I thought our village the only dragons left in the whole of the Twin Kingdoms. I’d heard of a few living down in Eirawen, and it’s said that in Llanwennog they parade us like circus animals, but those of our kind who chose the long road are surely all dead now. I called and called for someone to come, but all I got was you – a man. Your warrior priests have hunted us so long. Never would I believe one of us capable of what you describe. It can’t be a dragon you’re talking about. It’s just so wrong.’

‘Do you think your queen a liar?’

‘Of course not.’ Frecknock seemed to shrink in on herself.

‘Then what would you say this was?’ Melyn nodded to one of the silent warrior priests who had accompanied him to the storeroom. The man stepped forward, carrying a wrapped bundle, which he laid on the ground in front of the dragon. ‘Open it up. Tell me what you see.’

Frecknock stooped, seeming almost to sniff the package before gently picking it up. She unwrapped the cloth with slow, methodical movements. Melyn studied her face, looking for any telltale signs on those alien features. Dragons were difficult to read, but not impossible, and he had spent a lifetime studying them.

'By the moon!' Frecknock shrieked, letting the bundle fall to the floor with a dull slap. The severed hand and forearm of the beast that had attacked the queen rolled over, claws clenched into a fist as if it were trying to pull down the ceiling.

'This . . . this came from the creature?' She gestured towards the limb but seemed disinclined to touch it. 'How did you . . . ?'

'His Grace the Duke of Abervenn cut it off. I think he might even have killed the beast had it not turned tail and fled.'

Frecknock looked again at the grisly remnant, only this time she leaned forward, peering closely.

'Could I possibly have a little more light?' she asked.

'I know full well your capabilities. Make your own.'

'Thank you, Your Grace.' Frecknock lifted her hand and a sphere of white flame appeared in her palm. She held it over the forelimb, pinched between finger and thumb, then released it to hover exactly where she had placed it, casting a harsh light over her task.

Bending down further, she took up the arm in both her hands, lifting it to her nose and sniffing it deeply from one end to the other.

'It is definitely a dragon,' she said. 'I'm sorry for ever doubting your word, Your Grace. But I still don't understand how such a creature came to be in the woods here. Nor have I ever encountered a dragon so large. Look.' She held the forelimb alongside her own extended arm and even Melyn had to admit she had a point. The talons alone were as long as her entire hand outstretched; the muscle where the limb had been severed was almost as thick as her thigh. She put it back down on the cloth and re-wrapped it, then reached up and extinguished her light as if it were no more than a candle. For an instant, as his eyes adjusted to the gloom, Melyn thought he saw her bathed in a thin skein of light, as if he had seen her form in the aethereal, but this disappeared as quickly as it had come.

'So where did it come from? Where might it have gone?'

'I really don't know, Your Grace. This is far beyond anything I've ever encountered before. A creature this size is something from legend, but the dragons of our tales never ate people. We never ate people. I can only assume this is something wild, a distant ancestor somehow brought here. A dragon in form, but mindless, soulless, a true beast.'

'Then perhaps you can explain this.' Melyn reached into his pocket and pulled out a heavy silver band, its circumference large enough to fit over his hand. He threw it at Frecknock, who caught it easily, even in the poor light. 'We found it on the creature's middle finger. Looks to me like a signet ring.'

Frecknock turned the band over in her hand, feeling the figures let into its surface.

'Your Grace, may I try something?'

'What did you have in mind?'

'A simple conjuring. There may be a message within this ring for those who know how to read it.'

Melyn stared at the dragon, trying to decide whether she was up to some trickery. As always, her mind was almost impossible for him to fathom, though he could sense something of her thoughts. She looked on the world in so different a way, he found himself not knowing where to begin. And yet there was an underlying curiosity in her that reminded him of nothing so much as a classroom full of eager young novitiates. She truly had no idea where this other dragon had come from, and its behaviour appalled her in a profound way, but she was determined to solve the mystery.

'Very well,' he said finally. 'But don't do anything to upset your guards.' He nodded to the two warrior priests, who responded by conjuring their blades of light and moving closer. Frecknock nodded her understanding, then bent to the ring, holding it in one palm, sweeping the other a few inches over it and muttering in Draigiaith under her breath. Melyn felt the hairs on the back of his neck rise at the sound. It seemed to be right inside him. And then he could hear other voices speaking in the language of the dragons.

It was a strange sensation. He was sitting on the barrel in a storeroom beneath Castle Betel, but he was also in a clearing in the middle of a forest somewhere. Snow-capped mountains ringed the view, distant and glowing against a sky of deepest cloudless blue. And right in front of him a party of twenty or more dragons seemed to be engaged in some ceremony.

A youngster, little more than a hatchling, knelt in front of a rude altar crafted from a fallen rock. Behind the altar several larger dragons stood tall and still, their heads bowed as if in prayer. In front of it a dragon so old and withered it seemed almost a dried husk mouthed the words he could hear, which overlaid Frecknock's mutterings. Melyn knew Draigiaith, but this dialect was so thick, the words so ancient-sounding, he could only understand the barest minimum. It seemed to be a naming ceremony, the hatchling being welcomed into some kind of extended family. He heard a name, Caradoc, and then a list of what may well have been ancestors' names. But as these continued they seemed to fade away, along with the scene itself, until he was once more in the storeroom staring at Frecknock. Her muttering had dwindled to almost nothing, and as he watched she fell silent and slumped forward as if exhausted. After a few moments of silence, she pulled herself together, straightened up, then rose on unsteady feet.

The two warrior priests stepped forward to bar her way, but Melyn stopped them with a shake of his head.

She walked up to him, holding out the ring. He took it from her, feeling a tingle of power in it not unlike the thrill he felt when he conjured his blade, or when he was in the presence of the Shepherd.

'It's a naming ring,' Frecknock said, her voice trembling as if her resolve had finally left her, as if what she had seen was more terrible even than the slaughter of her extended family, her capture and enslavement. 'The dragon you seek is called Caradoc, son of Edryd. He has a long and illustrious family history, according to the ring, but I don't recognize any of it. I've no idea who he is or where he came from. But I can help you find him. At least, I can try.'

'And why would you do that, sweet Frecknock? Are you still looking for a mate?'

Frecknock physically recoiled at his words, her face a picture of horror.

'No, Your Grace. No! He is an abomination. By Rasalene and Arhelion, the moon and the sun, he cannot be allowed to walk Gwlad. He must be found. He must be stopped. He must be killed.'

Benfro stood on the edge of the cliff, gazing down over the waterfall, the river and the clearing beyond. Low spring sunlight picked out the hollows and rock-strewn areas he would have to avoid, and was it his imagination, or were the trees taller than they had been the previous autumn? The spiky conifers were in flower, fluffy pale green tassels hanging from the ends of their branches. It made them look slightly softer, but he knew that a collision with any of them would be at least painful.

'Are you sure you're ready to do this?' Benfro looked to one side, seeing the image of Corwen hovering in the air. The old dragon seemed somehow less solid than he remembered, which was strange given that he was no more than an apparition anyway. His appearances had become less and less frequent too.

'I have to try,' Benfro said. 'I'm going mad stuck here all the time with nothing to do but scavenge in the forest for food.'

'And treat Errol's ankles.'

'He's doing that himself now. I just had to reset the bones so they knit properly, didn't fuse together in one great big lump.'

'What changed your mind, Benfro? Why did you decide to help him?'

'I remembered when I was about seven. Ynys Môn broke his arm quite badly. My mother taught me about bones and how to heal them. She showed me how to mix up the right poultices, how to apply them and when to remove them. She was a good healer, but she didn't just heal dragons. She would use her skill to help anyone who needed it. She wouldn't have sulked around while Errol was in pain; she'd have taken on the job regardless of what she thought of him and his kind.'

'Your mother could have been a great mage, if she'd wanted to. But she chose to be a healer instead. And a teacher, it would appear.'

Benfro shrugged, feeling the breeze on his face and chest. 'She tried to teach me to listen to what people were saying, but she failed there. You told me to ask Errol for help and I ignored you. If I'd done as you said, I could have saved hundreds of those dragons.'

'Don't punish yourself, Benfro. Your reaction was perfectly understandable, especially given your circumstances. How long had you been without proper sleep? How long has Magog been working away at you, building up your hate and shrinking your compassion? His influence is insidious. Trust me; I know.'

Benfro looked more closely at the old dragon. The image was definitely less substantial, and as he let the lines ease into his vision, he could see a halo of sickly red surrounding Corwen's head and shoulders. It shocked him to see how far Magog had spread his foul control. He reached out to touch his tutor, but Corwen drifted back from him like a ghost.

'He's destroying you.' Benfro felt a stab of guilt as he realized that this was his fault. He had taken Magog's jewel from the bottom of the pool. He had carried it halfway across the land to Corwen's clearing. The old dragon would be fine if it hadn't been for him.

'I'm not finished yet,' Corwen said. 'Don't worry about me, Benfro. I can look after myself. And I can keep Magog from giving you his full attention.'

'But you can't easily maintain your illusion any more, can you? You can't appear to me at will. When you do, you risk losing a little bit more of yourself.'

'It's not quite that bad. Not yet, at least. I'll be around for a good while yet. You just won't be seeing so much of me.'

'There must be something we can do. Some way to break the link.'

'There are many things that you can do, Benfro. And the first of them is to learn to use those wings Magog gave you. I seem to remember that's what you were working on before he whisked you off to Mount Arnahi. So if your back is really healed, you must get back to your practising.'

Benfro felt the soft rebuke in Corwen's words and realized how foolish he had been. The old dragon had lived thousands of years, forgotten more than he would ever know, understood the subtle arts in all their mystery. Who was he, Benfro, to worry about the likes of Corwen? The mage would not have willingly put himself into deadly peril, and even if he had, there was nothing that Benfro could do about it. He had to trust that Corwen knew what he was doing and accept what teachings the old dragon was prepared to pass on to him.

Standing on the cliff edge, he unfurled his wings, let the sun warm them. The muscles in his back stretched and took their new load. The knot of pain that had been his constant companion these past months was no more than an area of stiffness, a slight limit to his mobility that felt good to be stretched. Bending his knees slightly, Benfro allowed his body to tip forward and launched himself into the air.

His first thought was panic. He fell far faster than he remembered, the ground hurtling towards him like a falling tree. For far too long he was paralysed, unsure what he was supposed to be doing. In his dreams it had always come naturally, and when he had launched himself from this cliff before, he had managed to swoop majestically down before climbing effortlessly up again. But now he was as helpless as a hatchling.

At the last possible moment instinct kicked in. He swept his outstretched wings forward in a desperate lunge and felt his fall slow, his motion turn from the vertical to the horizontal. Whipping them back, he repeated the action and felt his wing tips brush the grass. It tickled his belly scales and tugged at his tail until with a couple more wing beats he finally began to climb. Only then did he remember the trees.

Looking ahead, Benfro could tell that they were too high for him to clear. He would have to bank and turn, head back the other way and try to leave the clearing on the other side. But he had never before turned so sharply, so close to the ground. He wasn't particularly scared of heights, but his momentum was such that he knew hitting anything, even with the tip of a wing, would hurt and probably do serious damage.

In the end there wasn't much time for thought. The approaching trees focused his mind quite enough. He banked hard, felt the temperature drop as he flew into shadow, then warm again as he levelled out and sped towards the centre of the clearing. He was low, almost too close to the ground. Wings working as hard as he could remember ever having worked, he fought his way up into the sky. And then with a few great sweeps of his wings Benfro was above the clearing. He scanned the canopy, marking the shapes of nearby hills and holding them in his mind. He didn't want to lose himself, nor stray too far from home. The last thing he needed was to run out of strength and end up crashing into the trees.

A screech overhead diverted his attention. He looked up to see two buzzards wheeling in the warming air. Not sure whether he was still tapping into another dragon's experiences or simply doing something innate, he climbed towards the birds, who eyed him with suspicion, and spread his wings wide. He felt the warmth of the updraught on the undersides of his wings almost as a pleasure. Like having his brow stroked by his mother, or tucking into a feast in the great hall with Ynys Môn sitting on one side of him, Meirionnydd on the other. What would all three of them have made of him now, circling in the rising air, testing the edges of the invisible column with wing tips far more sensitive than he had realized.

By the time the thermal had grown too weak to lift him further, he was high above the forest. He could glide for a hundred miles in any direction, lock his wings open and just go. East, the sun cast shadows on the cliff-like wall of the Rim mountains, far closer than he had thought them. West, the forest rolled on into hazy distance. To the north Mount Arnahi was a siren call, even blanketed in cloud. South, and he fancied he could make out the stone mount of Cenobus climbing out of the endless undulating green.

Benfro was struck with the idea of flying there now. He could force his way into the repository and undo the work of his dream self. Pull all the jewels from their alcoves and return them to the pile. Before he had even begun to dismiss the thought as foolish, his wings were turning him that way, angling into the long slow glide that covered the ground with such deceptive speed.

'No!' He had to shout the word to make himself obey. He didn't have the strength to make it that far, even if he could find other thermals on the way to help him along. With an effort of will, he banked and turned again, heading back for the clearing. It wasn't far, still safe and familiar just a few wing beats away. He circled, losing height as he sized up the ground, looking for the best place to land.

Something made him look up, back to the south and invisible Cenobus, too far for even his sharp vision. And yet in that moment he saw it as clearly as if it were just a few hundred paces away. It was unchanged from the time he had left, the ruined buildings poking from the top of the mount like the rotted stumps of teeth on the jaw of some gargantuan beast. Only there was something moving around the ruined tower, circling it like a moth around a candle.

It was another dragon. And it was flying. It appeared to be looking for a place to land, hugging one hand to its chest as if it were injured. It looked strong, bold, and Benfro was reminded of the dragons who had attacked him in his strange dream. This wasn't one of them, but he radiated the same aura of difference, the same casual mastery of the air, the same impression of violent rage.

It was as he was wondering how he could see this beast from so far away, how he could know so much about it, that Benfro realized he had stopped beating his own wings. Too late, he looked down to see the ground rushing towards him. He thrashed and twisted at the air in a desperate attempt to slow himself, to position himself over the river.

He succeeded in one of those aims.

Errol sat outside the cave entrance, his back to the warm rock, feeling the sun on his face for the first time in too long. He watched as Benfro leaped from the cliff top above, wincing and ducking instinctively as the dragon almost crashed into the ground, then the trees, before clawing his way up into the air. Still, it was a magnificent sight to see him fly, wings fully outstretched, wheeling slowly up like some incredible eagle.

'He needs to practise his take-off and landing a bit more.' Errol didn't need to look round to know that the old dragon Corwen had joined him. 'How are your ankles?'

Errol looked down at his legs, pulling up the loose

material of his breeks to show the scarred flesh, still slightly swollen but no longer livid red. They were stiff, and he had no doubt they would never be quite as good as they had been before King Ballah's torturer had set about him with a hammer, but they were remarkably free of pain.

'Much better, thank you,' he said. 'I don't know what Benfro did to them, but it was miraculous. I doubt any of Melyn's surgeons could have done as well. Not even Usel.'

'If it had been Benfro's mother, you'd never know they'd been broken in the first place. Morgwm could heal almost anything. You're lucky she taught her son so much in the few years they had together.'

'I never realized she was a dragon,' Errol said, hearing the name and remembering it from years earlier.

'What?'

'Morgwm. My mother used to speak of her. She said that Morgwm had taught her most of the herb lore and healing she knew. I always assumed she was some wise woman.'

'She was wise,' Corwen said, 'but also quite the most stubborn dragon I ever met. She studied with me for over a century before deciding to be a healer rather than a mage. I still don't know what it was changed her mind. She could have been great, far more skilled than me.'

Errol thought of Sir Radnor and the form he had taken when first he had shown himself. That was how a great dragon mage looked, but most of the dragons he had seen had been shrunken downtrodden creatures. Even Benfro, with his huge wings, was still small in comparison. And the image of Corwen was not much bigger.

'What happened to you all? Why did you shrink?'

'Shrink? What do you mean?'

'Sir Radnor was huge. In your legends dragons stood as tall as trees. We know now that they weren't legends, so even if the stories are exaggerated, that doesn't explain why you're all so small.'

'All of us?'

Errol was about to continue, but suddenly the image of Corwen towered over him. No longer old and decrepit, he was strong and fit, his face scar-less, his scales shining in myriad colours. Even his folded wings were magnificent, their joints rising to points level with his head, though not as large as Benfro's. If Sir Radnor had been magnificent, then Corwen was majestic. He looked down his long nose with an imperious stare, thin wisps of smoke coming from his flared nostrils, and Errol understood what a rabbit must feel like in that tiny instant of lucidity before the hawk strikes.

And then he was his normal self again, short, stooped, wrinkled and scarred.

'That was how I looked when I was a hundred and fifty years old. This is how I looked the day I died. You're right, Errol: we've shrunk in on ourselves. We were faced with a choice when your kind started to kill us: either fight back and die glorious but futile deaths, or slink off and hide. Most of us took to the deep forests, but some of us chose the former path. We call it the long road, and the last dragon I know who travelled it was Benfro's father. No one's seen or heard from him since before Benfro was hatched, so I must assume he fell to men somewhere out in the wider world. Morgwm certainly thought so; that's why she gave Benfro the title "sir". She accepted him as the male head of her family.'

'I didn't – What's that?' Errol had seen something in the corner of his eye that dragged his attention away from Corwen and towards the river. A brief flash of movement as if something large had tumbled from the sky. And then with an noise like a thunderclap the surface of the water exploded upwards and outwards, sending the birds screeching from the treetops.

9

All novitiates know of the Grym, and all warrior priests of the High Ffrydd are highly trained in its manipulation. Less well understood by all but the most adept is the aethereal. This is linked to the Grym – some say it is but a higher manifestation of the life force that links us all – but it is also separate. To reach it requires both years of diligent practice and an uncanny mental self-discipline.

Many a skilled warrior priest has tried and failed to achieve the necessary state of trance, but once achieved, the aethereal is a place of immense power. With but the slightest thought a practitioner may transport his mind halfway across Gwlad, may influence the unwary and, most of all, may communicate with those few blessed others who possess the skill.

Not that communication using the aethereal is easy; far from it. Even those who reach the higher plane may still be unable to recognize fellow travellers. Most easily seen are those closely related, and the innate skill runs deep in some families.

Inquisitor Melyn,
A Short Treatise on the Aethereal

Errol scrambled over to the riverbank as fast as he could manage. He had fashioned a pair of crutches out of branches, but he still needed to put some weight on his ankles. Not wanting to think about the damage he might be doing or what Benfro would say if he had to mend them all over again, he pressed on regardless. The pain hit him soon enough, but it was a dull ache rather than the stabbing, burning sensation from when he had tried to move his clothes chest.

The bank was soaked, slippery grass flattened and slick, making the going even more perilous. Then as Errol reached the edge, he saw the thing he most feared: Benfro lay face down in the sluggish water, unmoving.

Without a second thought he dropped his crutches and slid himself into the water. It was cold after the morning sun, but it took the weight off his legs. Reminded of the old dragon and their unfinished conversation, Errol looked around to see if he had followed, but he was nowhere to be seen. One more puzzle to worry about.

The water was deep downstream of the ford, and it moved slowly. Errol swam across to the unconscious dragon and only then stopped to consider what he could do to help. He tried grabbing Benfro's hand and levering him over on to his back, but the dragon was too large and the water too deep. Benfro's outstretched wings were like great sheets on the water, stopping him from sinking but also preventing him from being rolled over.

Errol reached out for one wing, trying to push it closed. Remarkably, this seemed to work. At his touch the huge limb flinched. He touched it again, more firmly, and it folded away. Swimming awkwardly around, he did the same with Benfro's other wing. Then he tried once more to push the dragon over on to his back.

Still no success. It was almost as if Benfro wanted to drown.

'Come on, you great beast,' Errol shouted. 'Give me some help here.' But Benfro remained stubbornly unconscious. He wondered how long a dragon could survive without breathing, then it struck him that Benfro might already be dead. He must have fallen from a great height to have hit the water hard enough to knock himself senseless.

'Think, Errol,' he said to himself. He ducked under the water, draping Benfro's arm over his shoulder and then kicking up with his feet as hard as he could. The dragon rolled a little but not far enough. His bulk was just too much. Spluttering, Errol bobbed up again, taking in a deep breath and coughing out a mouthful of river.

They were drifting slowly downstream towards the rocks. Once they got there, Errol knew it would be all over. He might be able to reach the river bed then, but there was no way he could turn over the dragon if he was wedged tight against boulders. Even if his ankles hadn't been weakened, Errol didn't have the strength. He needed leverage.

And then it hit him. He kicked out hard with his legs, lunged out of the water and clambered unsteadily on to Benfro's back, heedless of any thoughts of indignity. Kneeling in the small of his back, where those massive wings rooted, Errol leaned over and grasped one floating arm, pulling it out of the water. Benfro's body started to roll, and Errol leaned back as far as he could, trying to keep the momentum going.

It was slow. He thought it wasn't going to work, but gradually, as if he were pulling a foot from deep sticky mud, the dragon rolled over. At the point of no return Errol collapsed backwards into the water, his feet finding the bottom just in time for him to brace Benfro's flailing arm and stop the roll going all the way round. And then they hit the rocks.

Errol swam around to Benfro's head, which lolled sideways in the water. He felt his feet sink into mud and was thankful for the small support it gave his ankles as he tried to lift the dragon's mouth and nostrils out of the river. He had never been so close to a dragon before, never really noticed the way their mouths were formed, the way their fangs poked out from thick leathery lips. There was, he realized, no way he was going to be able to resuscitate Benfro like he had Martha.

'Come on, Benfro. Breathe.' He slapped painfully at his scaly neck and chest, but the dragon remained coldly still. Errol stared at his bulk, wondering what to do, wondering again whether he was already dead. But his wings had responded to Errol's touch, so Benfro had to be alive, somewhere deep down.

The river cold began to chill him, and he shivered as he struggled to hold Benfro's head out of the water. There was only so long he could last before his strength gave out, but he couldn't give up. There must be something he could do to make the dragon breathe.

And then he noticed the pale colour clinging to

Benfro's body, a tight second skin. His aura was very weak, but it was there, even that malign rose thread that connected him to Magog in a manner Errol couldn't begin to understand. But it meant that the dragon was alive.

Errol looked at his own hands, seeing the pale colours surrounding them, weak but certainly more vital than Benfro's. For over a week now he had been practising the art of stretching his aura, using it to hold back Magog while Benfro slept. That was a hard thing to do, but what he planned now was even more so. Still he had to try.

Ignoring the cold, Errol concentrated only on his aura, imagined it swelling out from his hand, flowing over Benfro's face. He tried to shape it into a mask, tried to see it covering Benfro's mouth and nostrils, turning hard, sealing them tight. Then he extruded a long cylinder from them, narrowing it until it reached his own mouth. Taking a deep breath, he let the thin-stretched film of colours touch his lips, felt it like the lightest of threads blown on the wind. Then he exhaled with all the force he could muster.

Whether it was the effort of concentration, the cold, or the effect of breathing out hard, Errol's vision dimmed, lights sparking in the air in front of him. He dropped Benfro's head back into the water as his knees began to buckle under him, too weak to do any more.

And then with a great roaring splutter, the dragon convulsed, spewing out a wave of water. Freed of the weight, Errol found just enough strength to swim for the bank. He hauled himself out of the water, shivering and soaked as Benfro continued to retch and cough.

It took a few minutes for the dragon to come

completely to his senses. Meanwhile Errol hugged his arms close to his chest, shivering while the sun and wind dried his exposed skin and hair, too tired even to draw warmth from the lines. His clothes would need to be wrung out and hung by the fire, but that was several hundred paces away, the other side of the river. Looking over to the far bank, he could see just how far they had drifted downstream while he had struggled to turn Benfro over. His makeshift crutches were a long way off.

Eventually, Benfro's coughing and retching turned to regular, rasping breaths. He had hauled himself over on to his side, almost kneeling in the water, and now he pulled himself to unsteady feet, looking around at his surroundings, up at the pale blue sky and then back down to the water as if only just realizing where he was. Errol sat silently until those bewildered eyes finally came to rest on him.

'Are you all right?' It seemed like a particularly stupid question, but he couldn't think of anything else to say. Benfro looked at him as if trying to remember what words were, then waded slowly through the water and clambered out on to the bank, setting himself down with a heavy thump before belching loudly and coughing up another great spume of river water.

'What happened?' His voice was raw with coughing, the Draigiaith thick and difficult to understand.

'You fell out of the sky,' Errol said. 'You were face down in the water. I didn't know how long you could survive like that.'

'You saved me?' Benfro's tone was one of surprise.

'I could hardly let you drown.' Errol shivered, noticing that Benfro too was suffering from the cold. Or more likely delayed shock. 'We should get back to the cave. Warm up a bit.'

Benfro looked at him, taking time for his words to sink in. Finally he nodded slightly and rose to his feet; he was about to set off on his own when something occurred to him.

'Your ankles?'

'They're fine, a bit sore,' Errol said. 'I was in the water most of the time. I didn't put any weight on them.'

'But you can't walk back to the cave.' And before Errol could reply, Benfro had stooped, picked him up and slung him over his shoulder like a large sack of grain.

The trip was uncomfortable but uneventful. Errol was treated to a close view of Benfro's wings, and he marvelled at the intricate patterns of tiny scales that covered them. They shimmered in the sunlight and seemed to move as if alive with images of tiny dragons wheeling and turning in the air. Then the shadow of the cave entrance froze them all back into random flecks of silver and black and gold. Errol winced slightly as Benfro squeezed him, lifting him bodily and placing him down on the bed of dried grass. The dragon was immensely strong.

Benfro selected several heavy logs from the pile and dumped them awkwardly on the banked-up coals from the previous day's fire. Sparks flew in all directions, and Errol had to brush several away from his mattress. Without the rough woollen blanket from the chest covering it, his bed would have gone up in flames.

'Whoops, sorry.' Benfro almost giggled, if a dragon could giggle. 'It looks like I've put it out.' He bent down close to the hearth, peering at the dully glowing coals. He took in a deep breath, and Errol thought he was going to blow on the embers to get the logs to catch. But instead of breath, a gout of pure flame burst from the dragon's mouth, engulfing the wood and setting it instantly ablaze. Then, with an awkward bump, Benfro fell backwards on to his tail and sat silently, his hands held out to soak up the heat.

Errol was so amazed at the sight that he didn't notice the smell of burning until it was too late. The smoke was not the sharp acrid tang of charring wood, but the thicker, more cloying smell of hair. And underlying it a sweeter odour. Looking down, he saw the edge of his blanket burning away merrily, the bed beneath it catching alight.

He leaped up, pulling the blanket over itself and smothering the flames eating the wool, but they had too great a hold on the dried grass. All he could do was step back and let it go, glad that his clothes chest was on the other side of the cave. For his part, Benfro stayed motionless and silent, staring at the burning grass with an unfocused glaze over his eyes. Errol was surprised it had taken this long for the shock to hit him fully.

Hobbling slightly, he moved around to the other side of the fire to wait for the grass to burn itself out. Once it was reduced to ash, he would sweep it out of the cave and then make up a new bed with blankets and old clothes from the chest. It would probably be more comfortable, Errol thought.

Then he saw the bag.

How he had missed something so large before, he couldn't have said. It was at the end of the bed where he had laid his feet, and must have been covered by the dried grass, but even so he should have seen it. The brief fire hadn't been enough to char the leather, but he hobbled back around the fire to retrieve the bag anyway.

It was too heavy for him to lift. Perhaps had his ankles not been so weak and stiff, he would have managed to drag it, but he remembered the pain when he had tried to move his chest and let its thick strap fall to the ground.

'I can't move it,' Errol said to Benfro, who was still staring at nothing. At his words, the dragon seemed to regain a little of his composure, looking through the crackling flames.

'What happened to the bed?' he asked.

'It caught fire.'

'Oh.'

'I tried to pull your bag away from the flames, but it's too heavy. What's in it?'

'See for yourself,' Benfro said, obviously still not fully recovered from his fall. Errol slumped down on the cave floor next to the bag. The black ash from the burned grass smeared his breeks and shirt, still damp from his earlier swim. They would be a nightmare to get clean, but he didn't have the energy to do anything about that now. Instead, he reached over and unclipped the buckles that held the bag closed to let the front flap drop.

It was full of gold. No wonder it had been so heavy. There were mounds of coins, a couple of goblets, some elegantly worked cutlery with fine carved ivory handles and a small selection of rings and brooches. But perhaps the finest piece in the bag was a torc, made from several strands of gold wire wound around each other in an intricate series of loops and coils. The two end caps were wrought to look like dragon's heads, the detail exquisite, and encircling it was a smooth round shank of gold bearing a worn coat of arms, polished almost to nothing by centuries of warriors' braids.

'Where did you get this?' Errol asked, feeling the age of the piece. Holding it in his hand, it was as if he could see the long line of previous wearers stretching back into the mists of time.

'I found it around the neck of a human skeleton just outside Magog's repository. Back at Cenobus. Why, what is it?'

Errol ran his fingers over the smooth insignia, bending towards the fire to get a better look. He breathed on it, misting the shiny gold surface, but it was difficult to be sure.

'I think it might be King Balwen's golden torc.'

It was hard to explain away the mass of warrior priests as an honour guard any more. Even with the news of the queen's recent brush with a dragon and the Duke of Abervenn's brave fight to save her, Melyn worried that the sheer numbers would draw the wrong sort of attention. He was certain that King Ballah had spies in all the towns and cities on the queen's grand tour, and all would report back to Tynhelyg the most seemingly inconsequential details, but he was fairly certain there were no Llanwennog sympathisers in the party that travelled with the queen.

It had always been his plan to disguise the gathering of his small army. Individual troops were under orders to meet him at certain points along the route from Beteltown to Castell Glas, where the main road skirted the edge of the great forest of the Ffrydd and the western Rim mountains tumbled down into the plains of the Hafod. But some of his captains had heard stories of the dragon attacks and taken it upon themselves to join the main party earlier. As it was, the stretch of country they were riding through now was sparsely populated, the chances of the large column of men being noticed by a spy minimal. Still, Melyn was nervous. His whole plan could fall apart at this point. Before it had even begun.

A lone man on horseback appeared at the crest of the next rise in the road. He stopped and stared for a moment, then spurred his horse down towards them. Riding beside Melyn, Beulah tensed even though she was in the heart of her own kingdom. She had been on edge ever since riding back from Pwllpeiran on a dead warrior priest's mount, but she need not have worried. Melyn had known who it was from the moment he appeared, recognized the horse long before he could make out the unsmiling features of his senior captain

'Your Majesty, I'm glad to see you've arrived safely.' Osgal turned his horse to match the slow pace of the moving column, bowing in the saddle and clasping his clenched fist to his chest by way of salute. 'I heard a wild dragon had attacked you. Is it true that young Master Clun drove off the beast on his own?'

'The Duke of Abervenn cut off the animal's arm.' Melyn emphasized the boy's new title, aware how touchy the queen was on the subject of Clun's status. The last thing he wanted was to have Osgal flogged for insulting a member of the royal family. 'He would probably have killed the beast if it hadn't fled.'

'He was the best of his year's choosing,' Osgal said, which Melyn had to concede was high praise indeed from the captain. 'It was a shame to lose him.'

'Captain, do you have something to report, or have you just come here to insult my husband?' Beulah's tone was cold, her face icier still as she stared at Osgal. Melyn could understand the man's familiarity; the captain had known the queen since she had first arrived at Emmass Fawr as an eight-year-old girl. In many ways he had raised her. It surprised him that Osgal didn't have the sense to defer to her now that she had such power over him, but then he had never been the most imaginative of men, just strong and dogged. Something in the queen's words must have filtered through though. He bowed to her again and once more thumped his chest in salute.

'Your Majesty, I meant no disrespect. Clu— His Grace the Duke of Abervenn is a skilled and courageous warrior. It's selfish of me to want him for the order when his place should be at your side. I was riding the perimeter of our camp and saw the column. I came down to bid you welcome.'

They rode over the crest of the hill and looked down into a wide valley. Ancient trees grew in small clumps, surrounded by fields of lush green grass on which a few sheep munched thoughtfully. A small river lined on each bank with willows and hawthorn meandered through the middle of the valley. A cluster of derelict houses stood where the road forded the water, their roofs long gone. Arranged around them in neat circles, a series of tents fanned out into the grassland. Beyond them, horses grazed loose, trusted not to stray far from the camp.

'This place, is it secure?' Melyn asked as they rode towards the circles of tents.

'I've patrols sweeping the area for miles in all directions, Your Grace,' Osgal said. 'And I know this country well. No one lives nearby. We'll not be detected as long as we don't stay here for more than a couple of days.'

'Days? I hope to be gone tomorrow at first light,' Melyn said. 'As long as our wild dragon doesn't turn up and spoil the party.'

'You think that likely?' Beulah asked.

'No, I don't. Clun gave it something to think about. If it doesn't bleed to death from its wound, it's going to take weeks to recover, if not months. And it won't be so keen to attack us now it knows we can fight back.' Melyn looked over his shoulder, back towards the ranks of mounted warrior priests and the slow wagon train trailing behind. 'Where is His Grace anyway?'

'He went to speak with Frecknock,' Beulah said. 'Something about wanting to know more about its kind. I think he's grown a bit too fond of it, Melyn. Perhaps it would be best if it doesn't come back from your expedition. Use it to find this pass through to Llanwennog, then dispose of it.'

'Of course,' Melyn said, quietly pleased to see some of the queen's old ruthless streak resurfacing. He had no intention of letting Frecknock live one minute longer than she was of use to him.

The warrior priests were quick and efficient, well used to pitching camp at a moment's notice and in the worst of conditions. Their tents were up and their horses grazing with the others in short order, but the queen's camp took longer to prepare. The last of the wagons, in which Frecknock rode, arrived fully two hours after Beulah had first dismounted and gone to review her troops. By the time her marquee had been erected and the last of the entourage found a place to sleep, the evening sky was turning black.

The derelict farmhouse was no use for a camp, but Melyn had ordered the main room cleared so he could have some privacy. It wasn't as good as a chapel, but it would do. In its time the house had been a substantial building, more a manor than the home of some humble farmer. As he stood in the centre of the empty room, stars visible through a jagged hole in the ceiling, he wondered what had happened to the family that had lived here. Presumably at some point in the past this had been a busy little place, supplying wool and meat to the lowlands. Now it was deserted, and the buildings had begun their slow return to the earth. Where once there had been an organized pattern of enclosures, the forest was slowly reclaiming the land as the trees oozed out of the rift of the Graith Fawr like honey from a broken pot. It was all decay, the sweat and toil of men come to nothing, order unravelling into chaos.

This was what he was fighting against, the inquisitor thought. This was what he had struggled for all his life. The Llanwennogs, with their casual godlessness and degenerate mores were one symptom of it. Dragons like the upstart Benfro and now this other beast, Caradoc, were another. They were creatures of the Wolf, bent only on destruction. It was his sworn duty to push back the darkness, to bring the Shepherd's wisdom to those who would embrace it and to destroy those who wouldn't.

Alone in the empty room, Melyn reached into the pocket of his cloak and drew out the slim wooden box he carried close to him at all times. He fumbled with the stiff metal clasp that held it closed, his fingers no longer as dextrous as once they had been. Inside, Brynceri's ring looked almost lost in the velvet lining, the desiccated remains of his finger little more than a dusty stick.

Melyn placed the open box on the floor in front of him. The single rough jewel was black under the starlight, but it radiated power, the touch of his god. He knelt on the dusty flagstones and bent his head in prayer. He was barely into the second cycle of the litany when he felt the presence of the Shepherd, that blessed feeling of being young and all-powerful, the banishing of all self-doubt.

'You are troubled, my servant. You think your plan might fail.'

'My lord, please forgive my weakness. There is so much at stake, and I fear the queen will not regain her skill in the aethereal before her child is born. So much hinges on my ability to communicate with her.'

'There are others who possess the skill. But you do not

trust them with such momentous news. That is wise, my servant, but you do not need to look so far from the queen to find your answer. She has chosen her man well.'

'Clun? But he's only a novitiate, my lord. He knows nothing of this skill.'

'I have gifted him with the sight. He will hear you when you call him.' Melyn felt the displeasure of the Shepherd, a rebuke for his lack of faith. It shot through his joints with a flash of unbelievable pain that made him gasp out loud.

'Forgive me, my lord. I do not mean to question, I only seek to know how best to serve.'

'Of course you do, Melyn. You have always been my most faithful servant. But there are others who work to spread my word. You do not need to do it all yourself.'

The pain began to ease, his penitence accepted. Melyn relaxed a little, realizing how tense he had become. A trickle of sweat ran down his spine, and his brow felt damp.

'You worry about your motives for this mission.' The Shepherd's voice was all around him, inside him. Like nothing else in the whole of Gwlad could, it made him feel small and vulnerable. Quite unbidden, an image flickered through his mind of a huge bear of a man towering over him, red with rage and drink, blood-streaked fist raised ready to bring down another blow. A memory of his earliest childhood, before the Shepherd had found him and set him on this lifelong quest.

'The hatchling has escaped me twice now, lord. As long as he lives, my authority – your authority – is questioned.

I want nothing more than to track him down and finish what I started with his mother. But the chance to take your message to the godless Llanwennogs is more important still. I fear that I will be tempted to pursue this Benfro and my mind diverted from the true task. And then there is this other creature, Caradoc, son of Edryd . . .'

The ring burned like a red-hot coal. He felt the heat blister his skin. The rage of the Shepherd was a terrible thing, ripping through him like he was nothing. In his mind Melyn saw a tumble of images: the abandoned cottage and behind it the discarded skeletons stripped of all flesh, Frecknock in the cellar at Castle Betel holding the severed arm, the naming ring, the strange ceremony. With each new image the ring blazed hotter still.

'My lord,' he whispered. It was not his place to question, and he pushed the thought from his mind. At the same time the burning stopped and a soothing calm swept over him, instantly blotting out the pain.

'You should have prayed to me for guidance as soon as you encountered this creature.' The rage evaporated as quickly as it had appeared. The voice of the Shepherd soothed him, but it was tinged with a sense of irritation that filled him with dread. 'This is no ordinary dragon, Melyn. I think even you know that. This is one of the beasts of old, the creatures the Order of the High Ffrydd was charged with destroying. The dragons you've hunted all your life can be tolerated as long as they hold to my laws, but this . . . this creature has given itself to the Wolf. It must be hunted down and destroyed before it can turn more to its evil.'

'I will not rest until I have its head,' Melyn said, recalling his conversation with Frecknock. She too had been shocked by the rogue dragon.

'You plan to use your captive dragon as bait. That is a wise plan. A beast of the Wolf will come quickly to such a call. It is driven by base lusts and nothing else. But you must be careful, my servant. Bind Frecknock to you with the ring, make her swear a blood oath upon it, or she may be swayed by the servant of the Wolf and turn on you.'

'I have a thousand warrior priests with me, lord,' Melyn said. 'The beast will die before it can utter a single word.'

'Do not underestimate this foe, Melyn. The likes of Caradoc have not been seen in this land for millennia. It is cunning and ruthless, a creature of pure evil and great power.'

The words echoed in the inquisitor's head as the spirit of the Shepherd departed from him. His lord was the creator of all things, the master of Gwlad, and yet Melyn couldn't help a tiny, rebellious, blasphemous part of his mind thinking that the Shepherd had been surprised to learn of this new dragon. His initial reaction had been one of frustration and rage, as if a foe long vanquished had suddenly risen again strong and fresh to renew the fight. And if that were the case, if the Wolf was once more walking the land of the living, then surely the Shepherd would come down among his faithful soon and give them the tools to fight for the side of light and good.

Melyn didn't know how long he knelt in prayer in the derelict house, giving thanks that it would be during his lifetime that his god chose to walk among the people again. It was obvious now that he thought about it. The war against Llanwennog was just the start. This was the end time, when the Shepherd and the Wolf would fight the final battle. The scriptures had always spoken of it, and now it was coming true.

10

A few brave souls eke out a living on the fringes of the forest of the Ffrydd, but none would be so foolhardy as to try to live within its bounds. Strange magics fill the place, confusing even the most skilled hunter into turning back on himself. Stories abound of travellers lost within its endless miles, returning years later to civilization yet not aged a day. Or worse, gone from their loved ones no more than a few hours, yet returned old and bent before their time, telling tales of a lifetime spent wandering amidst the trees.

Treat it with respect, and the forest will merely send you on your way. Force yourself against it and it will destroy you utterly.

Father Keoldale, *The Forest of the Ffrydd*

The palace was always quiet at this early hour. A few bleary-eyed servants stumbled about their morning duties, and sleepy guards wilted at their posts, waiting for their relief to arrive, but mostly the long corridors and echoing halls were empty. Prince Dafydd liked this time of day. He could go about his business unchallenged, and without the constant worry that he might bump into either King Ballah or, worse, Tordu, the palace major domo.

That his great-uncle disliked both him and Prince Geraint was no great secret; Tordu had never forgiven Ballah's eldest for allowing Balch to be sent to the Twin Kingdoms. He viewed Dafydd's marriage to Iolwen as a betrayal, their unborn child as an ill-fated omen heralding the destruction of the royal house. Lately Tordu had been seeing omens in everything, from the patterns of migrating birds to the strange disappearance of the spy Errol. Dafydd wondered whether the major domo knew that the boy had turned up back at Emmass Fawr. Almost certainly he did; he seemed to have his own spies everywhere. It would no doubt feed his paranoia even more.

The stables were quiet as Dafydd entered the courtyard, though light spilled from the open door of the tack room. The sky was just beginning to show the first sign of dawn, the tinge of pink on the undersides of the clouds that heralded unsettled weather. He cursed under his breath. Spring had been fine so far, if cold. He hated travelling in the wet. Well, it couldn't be helped now. His mind was made up, and the messages had been sent. There could be no turning back.

A lone dog raised its head and stared at him as he pushed the door wider, feeling the warmth of the stove on his face. Recognizing him as a friend, it thumped its tail twice on the floor then went back to snoozing. Dafydd slipped silently through the rows of immaculately clean harness, the leather shiny and supple, the bits and buckles gleaming. He breathed in the heady aroma of saddle soap and liniment, the smell of horses. As a child this had been one of his favourite places, a retreat from the endless bustle and protocol of the palace proper. Here he had played games with the stable boys, heedless of rank or deference. Prince Geraint had been happy for him to mix with the rougher lads, keen for him to learn real horsemanship; it was one of the few things Dafydd had done that had pleased his father.

'Your Highness, you should have sent word. I'd have had your horse ready.'

Dafydd turned to see the ruddy-faced figure of Teryll, the senior stable hand. Teryll and he were of an age, had grown up together. If a prince of the royal house of Ballah could have a friend among the common people, then Teryll was just that. Dafydd knew he could count on his loyalty and above all his discretion.

'I can saddle a horse as well as any man, Teryll.' He slapped the man hard on the shoulder. 'And you know it.'

'Ah, but if you tend to your own beasts, then where'll a useless layabout like me find work, eh? What were you after, sir, taking one of the fillies out for a dawn canter?'

'No Teryll, not today.' Dafydd looked nervously around the tack room, trying to see if any of the other stable hands were about. It seemed empty, but he knew they would all be starting to wake. Their dormitory was directly overhead, stretching the upper length of the long building that formed one side of the courtyard. Not wishing to be overheard by any other early risers, he lowered his voice, bending close to Teryll. 'I need two horses made ready for a long journey. One for Princess Iolwen, so I'll need a side saddle.'

'I'll get Keffl and Melly ready straight away, sir.' Teryll made to turn, but Dafydd stopped him.

'No, Teryll. Not those two. I don't want . . . people

thinking we've gone far. This is a secret mission so nobody must know. And we'll need another two horses to carry provisions and luggage.'

Teryll nodded, his eyes showing a gleam of excitement that reminded Dafydd of some of the more daring escapades they had undertaken in their childhood. 'I'll have them ready in twenty minutes, sir.'

'Thank you, Teryll. I knew I could count on you. But we can't come for them here. Take them to the corner of Philum Street, at the back of the merchants' quarter. We'll meet you there in one hour.'

Teryll nodded his understanding, reaching up to select bridles from the rack. Dafydd saw that they were from the common stock, not the elegant and expensive harness reserved for royalty. He smiled once more at his old friend, turned and hurried away, hoping that Iolwen would be ready by the time he returned to their chambers.

Benfro's head pounded as if he had been drinking wine by the flagon the night before. It was worse even than the time he had first eaten at Magog's table, in the retreat at the top of Mount Arnahi. Back then his whole body hadn't ached like he had fallen down a mountainside, and his throat hadn't been raw as if he had shouted at the top of his lungs for an hour. Now he could scarcely move without a thousand different parts of his body screaming at him to stop.

Opening one eye slowly so as to avoid any more pain than was necessary, he tried to work out where he was. It was difficult to remember anything except talking to Corwen, then almost crashing when he had tried to fly. But that felt like it had been a lifetime ago. There were disjointed, jumbled images of things that had happened since, but he could put them in no logical order. Carrying Errol back to the cave, both of them soaking wet; flying with buzzards, reading the air currents to gain maximum height with minimum effort; seeing the whole of Gwlad spread out beneath him, a world to conquer; watching a winged dragon wheel around the broken towers of Cenobus.

Benfro blinked both eyes open, sitting up too fast as all the memories tumbled into place. No wonder he felt like a tree had fallen on him. Of all the feelings that could have swept over him, it was embarrassment that heated his face. He had allowed himself to become so distracted, he had forgotten to fly. He was lucky to be alive.

'You're awake. Good. How do you feel?'

Benfro looked over to the alcove where the grass bed had been. Only now there was just an empty space, the floor a mix of dark earth and black ash. The cave walls were black too, and he dimly remembered breathing fire. Too much fire. His leather bag leaned against the wall, its flap open, revealing the glint of gold within, and the last few bits of missing memory dropped into place

'Dreadful.' He looked down at the floor where he had lain, brushed soft red earth from his arms and breathed in that alluring spice smell. It was overlaid with something even better, a meaty soup aroma, and he finally looked round to where Errol was sitting between the fire and the back wall of the cave. He had propped the small cauldron against the banked-up fire and was stirring something within. Benfro rubbed at his face with his palms, easing away his headache, then shuffled closer to the flames. Every muscle in his body creaked and complained.

'You fall from the sky.' Errol's command of Draigiaith was much better than Benfro's ability to speak the language of men, but it was still far from perfect. At least they could communicate. He was grateful for that.

'I was distracted. I saw . . .' Benfro wondered how he could explain what it was he had seen. It made no sense to him as a memory. He was hundreds of miles from Cenobus, and yet he had seen the place as if he were just a few wing beats away. And he had seen the dragon's features as if he were flying alongside him. 'I saw another dragon, flying. But I don't know how that can be.'

'Are there no other dragons that can fly?'

'I don't know. I wish . . .'

'No dragon has flown in this sphere for many hundreds of years.' Benfro looked around to see Corwen sitting in the same spot where he had first appeared all those months ago. 'Our legends tell of a time when we were lords of the air, and you know now that our legends have more truth in them than we thought. I grew up with wings far larger than those that burned with me when I died. But I never flew. We had made our choice long before my hatching.'

'You said that before,' Errol said. 'About making a choice. What did you mean? Did you choose to become smaller?'

'In a manner of speaking, I suppose we did. We chose to become less noticeable, and so we shrank physically, though our minds stayed sharp. Over time the difference became more and more ingrained. Frecknock is fully grown, but she would have been mistaken for a hatchling of one or two summers by my parents.'

Benfro scowled at the mention of Frecknock's name. He didn't care if she shrank away to nothing, if Queen Beulah sliced her head off with a blade of light.

'What of the dragons who took . . . What did you call it? The long road?' Errol spoke in his own language and it took a moment for Benfro to grasp the meaning of his final words. He had heard something similar before but couldn't place it.

'Fewer and fewer of us made that choice, though it has always been open to us.' Corwen switched to Draigiaith and turned to Benfro. 'Your father was the last dragon I knew to make it, though I suppose you have too, in a way.'

'My father?' Benfro forgot his headache, his aches and pains, even the gurgling in his stomach that Errol's cauldron of broth had provoked. 'What do you know of him?'

'A great deal, Benfro,' Corwen said. 'Sir Trefaldwyn was once a pupil of mine, like your mother. He was quite her opposite though. Impetuous and headstrong, impatient too, now I come to think of it. And his head was always full of the most wild nonsense. I guess he passed a lot of that on to you.'

'What nonsense?' Benfro felt a flash of anger that the old dragon could be so rude about his father, then wondered why he should feel that way. He'd never met Sir Trefaldwyn after all.

'Well the last time I saw him he was full of some story he'd heard from a dragon who lived down in the Hendry boglands, far to the south of here. He said he was searching for the portal to another world, identical to this one, but where dragons ruled the air and men knew nothing of the subtle arts. It was a fool's quest, and I told him so at the time. But he insisted on . . . Oh.'

'What?' To Benfro's horror, Corwen had faded almost to nothing, his face contorting in apparent pain. Benfro hauled himself to his feet, heading across the cave to try and help his master, but the old dragon waved him away. He seemed to be struggling with something and Benfro had a suspicion he knew just what it was. He concentrated for a moment, shifting his view until he could see the Llinellau and his own aura, the long pale rose cord looping away from him to fuse with the nearest of the lines. It was unprotected, and instinctively he knotted his aura around it, cutting off Magog's malign influence even though for once he had felt nothing of the dead mage's presence. Looking into the corner of the cave, where the shrunken ghostly image of Corwen struggled against an unseen foe, Benfro realized why.

Magog wasn't attacking him; he was concentrating all his efforts on Corwen.

Without a thought for his own safety, Benfro leaped forward. He didn't know what he was going to do, but he wasn't going to let the one friend he had left in the world be destroyed. He tried to see where Magog was mounting his attack from; there had to be a point, a connection like the one that tied him so tightly. But Corwen was not alive. He was a projection of memories, and as he struggled and faded, Benfro could see only a dull blood-red glow seeping over him, washing him away.

'Find . . . Sir Trefaldwyn . . .' Corwen's voice was a distant echo in the back of Benfro's mind. 'Find . . . Gog.' At the name Benfro felt a surge of anger, a hatred so visceral it almost knocked him out, even though his best defences were up.

'I have to help you first.' He moved closer to the almost invisible image. Part of it repelled him, as if the old dragon was pushing him away, but part of it drew him in. He could see beyond the fading figure into a dark cavern where a pile of jewels sat on a raised stone dais. They were white, but a miasma of red filled the whole cave, pulsing out from a familiar lone jewel placed on the edge of the dais. One small stone should not have been able to overcome so many, and yet it radiated an evil power that was like a wall of heat.

'You . . . must . . . not . . .' Corwen's voice was forced, but it had about it something of that power that had once immobilized him completely. Benfro felt himself receding from the cave even as he understood that he had been travelling the Llinellau towards it. Then at the last moment he noticed one other jewel, pale and white, shielded from Magog by the bulk of Corwen's memories. He knew without a doubt whose it was; knew also that he could not leave it. Reaching out as he had done when bringing himself food, he tried to summon his mother's last remaining jewel to himself.

'No, Benfro. You must leave that here. It will only be a burden to you.' Corwen's voice was gone completely, his thoughts barely brushing the turmoil in Benfro's mind. 'We will endure, but I won't be able to appear to you any more. I realize now what I should have seen years ago. Your father's quest – he was looking for another world. I thought it a stupid fantasy, but it makes perfect sense. If everything else said about Magog is true, then why not this? His brother made a world apart, and he still lives there. Your father believed there was a way to get to it. He went north, to Llanwennog. You must find him. Find a way back to Magog's bones.'

'But how can I find him? I don't know where to begin. I don't even know what he looks like.' Benfro spoke out loud, and the sound of his own voice seemed to pull him back into himself. He was standing in the corner of the cave where Corwen had first appeared, staring at the rock wall, his hand reaching out for something that wasn't there.

Melyn had never much liked the great forest of the Ffrydd, not since the first time he had entered its uncharted depths as a novitiate too many years ago now to even try to remember. There was something oppressive about the endless ranks of trees blocking off a decent view of the sky. He preferred to be above the world, looking down, not skulking around in the undergrowth like some rodent.

There were tracks through the forest. At the southern edge these snaked into the trees for miles and some of them were reasonably well mapped. Mostly they were used by hunters and trappers, though a few hardy woodsmen lived among the trees far from civilization. And dragons had taken to the woods of course, seeking their protection centuries ago. Few lived there now, only two that he knew of, and neither of them would survive this foray if he had anything to do with it.

From his earlier expedition, and others like it that the warrior priests occasionally mounted, Melyn knew that the forest was not entirely close-grown trees. There were clearings all over the place, some as large as the agricultural estates of minor nobles, others no bigger than the rude garden that Morgwm the Green had tended. In places the wood was thick, the undergrowth all but impassable; then it might open up into good hunting country, huge ancient broadleaves each surrounded by hundreds of paces of clear grass, saplings kept down by vast herds of deer.

The paths that wound their way uphill towards the interior of the forest were in the main narrow, although wide enough for a cart to make good progress. Three or four men could ride abreast along the clearest of them, narrowing to maybe only two at the worst. Still Melyn forced his small army on at a relentless pace, setting destinations from his memory and using teams of warrior priests to hack the path wider where necessary. From the air, he had no doubt, the mark of their passage would be a wide scar of destruction, spearing towards the heart of the forest. For some reason that image made him happy.

They were a week into their long march before the tracks began to betray them. Melyn detected the subtlest play of ancient magics, tricking compasses, fooling even the most competent of navigators. Parties sent forward to scout out likely watering holes and good grazing would appear hours later, galloping from the rear of the column in confusion, certain they should be miles ahead. Still he pushed on, measuring the army's progress by the position of the stars at night.

This was the confused time. He had read enough of Father Keoldale's account of Prince Lonk's failed expedition to know what to expect. He even remembered it from his own journey all those years ago. Father Helnas, leading the troop of novitiates on what was meant to have been a month-long dragon hunt, had almost lost his mind as they looped back on themselves, headed east and ended up west, climbed hills only to find themselves looking down on the evidence of their earlier passage ahead of them. Melyn had learned more from the healer on the trip, Father Colter. He had known how to read the stars, and he was the one who had led them out of the forest, on to the calling road some three months after they had left.

During the day, as the column made its slow progress, Melyn would slip into the aethereal and scout ahead. Freed from the constraints of his body, he could soar above the highest trees and look down on the mass of ill-formed self-images riding their solid-bodied horses through the woodland. He could see far enough ahead to plot out their course and pass adjustments on to Osgal, but it was exhausting work.

The army started with first light and pushed on well into the gloaming of each day, and it was all Melyn could manage to sit up long enough to eat the rations prepared for him before he crawled into his bedroll and slept. Never before had he felt his age so much. He began to worry that he had made a rash decision. So many before him had tried to tame the forest, and all had failed. But he was different. He didn't want to search out treasures or cut down the trees for cultivation; he wanted to pass right through and out the other side. As quickly as possible. If the rumours were true and the Ffrydd really did have a rudimentary mind of its own, then he hoped that it would realize its best course of action was to let him through. He had no intention of ever coming back.

They were making camp in a vast clearing, the horses enjoying a rich feed of spring grass and plentiful water from a wide river, when Osgal came to Melyn in the deepening gloom one night. If he had to make a guess, Melyn would have said they'd been in the saddle for almost three weeks. They should have been roughly halfway across, but he was too tired from a day battling against waves of disorienting colours that flowed across the aethereal like some improbable camouflage. Little things like where they were and how long they had taken to get there were not nearly as important as sleep to him right now. The sight of the captain approaching with what was probably bad news put him in an instant ill humour.

'What is it, Osgal?' Melyn's voice was too tired even to show the anger and irritation he felt.

'Your Grace, the dragon Frecknock has asked if it might speak with you.' Osgal's dislike of their captive was unwavering, a constant rock in a sea of change. Melyn found himself oddly grateful for that small certainty, even if he had no intention of ever voicing his gratitude. Still, mention of the dragon bothered him. He had meant to speak to her weeks earlier, to force her to swear an oath to serve him just as the Shepherd had commanded, but he disliked her presence and hated even more the thought of letting her touch Brynceri's ring. If there were any other way to bind her to his will . . .

'What does she want?'

'It says it has information regarding the feral dragon that attacked the queen, sir.'

Melyn took a swig of water from his bottle, wishing it were wine. He could do with something to lift the cloud of weariness from his mind. He needed his wits about him.

'Bring her to me,' he said, then slumped against the trunk of the large oak tree under which he had unrolled his bedding. The evening was warm, the sky part obscured by high cloud that promised a mild night, so he had not bothered with his tent. Noises from the growing camp spoiled what otherwise might have been an idyllic spot.

'Your Grace?' Melyn looked up to see the dragon standing beside his fire. Weeks on the road had slimmed her down, turned some of her flab to muscle, but she was filthy with dust and the very sight of her disgusted him.

'You have information for me?'

'Indeed yes, Your Grace. I have been around this clearing and I believe the feral beast, Caradoc, was here not more than two days ago.'

'What makes you think that?' Melyn wanted to ask by whose authority she had been wandering around the camp, but that was a question for someone else. A punishment for someone else.

'Over where the track fords the river there is a hearth. There are freshly blackened logs on it. The fire was left to go out by itself, not banked up. And it only burned out recently.'

'So there have been woodsmen here. This is a good place for a camp. There's water and fish from the river, plenty of dry wood under these old trees, grazing for horses.'

'This hearth is about the size of one of your arm spans, sir. I don't think a trapper would build something so large. Nor would he easily have lifted the logs that have been burned.'

Melyn looked at the dragon, his hatred of her kind mixing with irritation and, oddly, gratitude. He would have to see this hearth for himself. His bedroll would stay cold for an hour or more still. But this was something that none of his highly trained warrior priests had noticed. Or more likely had been too tired, too preoccupied with finding forage for their horses, a meal for themselves and somewhere to lay their heads to notice.

'Show me.' He hauled himself to his feet. For her part, Frecknock seemed light-footed, full of energy as she walked back through the camp towards the river. The warrior priests ignored her as if their sacred oath to King Brynceri's charter and the teachings of the Shepherd meant nothing. Most of them, Melyn realized, had stopped thinking of her as a dragon. Forced to march at the rear of the column, with the packhorses, she had become part of the army. It was dangerous thinking, he knew, but also seductively appealing. An army that marched with a tame dragon in its midst was surely invincible. But was she tame?

'See, here.' Frecknock stopped in the shade of a tree whose canopy reached out over the flowing river. The hearth was much as she had described it, perhaps even larger. One vast stone had been dragged out of the river and dug into a hole in the ground. Smaller but still substantial boulders were arranged around it in a circle to form a fire pit, now choked with black ash and chunks of dried logs twice the width of a man's thigh and at least ten paces long. This was no trapper's campsite fire.

'So what does this tell me?' Melyn asked. 'Other than that this beast was here and that it had a good meal of fish from the river.' He nodded towards a pile of fish bones in the grass beside the fire pit.

'He was here quite recently, or crows would have taken those bones. He stayed here for several days judging by the ash in the fire. And he was trying to get his hand to regrow.'

'Regrow? Is that possible?'

'Morgwm could have done it.' Melyn heard the rebuke in Frecknock's tone but chose to ignore it. This was fascinating information, worth far more than his anger.

'It's not an easy healing,' Frecknock continued. 'And it's not quick either. Even properly done it might take six months for something the size of the arm and hand you showed me to grow back completely.'

'And how do you know that's what he was doing?' Melyn stepped closer to the fire pit, wishing he had brought a torch with him. He was weary and the thought of conjuring a flame filled him with foreboding. Magic was always best performed with a clear head, especially where fire was involved.

'Here, and here.' Frecknock pointed at the darkening grass around the base of the tree trunk. The day's light had all gone now, and only the faint glow from the stars and a sliver of pale moon lit the scene. Melyn felt he might as well have been in the fifth portal of the library back at Emmass Fawr for all he could see.

'What am I looking at?'

Frecknock whispered something under her breath that made his skin crawl, and bright light appeared in her outstretched hand. Beneath it Melyn could see a number of flat-sided stones laid in a circle on the grass about ten paces across. Perhaps just big enough for a very large dragon to sit within. Some of the stones were discoloured in odd patches.

'He's set out the ingredients for the potion in the correct order. And here there's some left over.' Frecknock moved towards the tree, reached into the hollow between two massive roots and pulled out a handful of something that looked like mud and straw but smelled of brimstone. She dropped it back into the hollow with a wet slapping sound, then pulled something dry and powdery out of another. 'He must have searched all over the forest for these herbs and minerals. The . . . magic part of it is best done on a new moon. That was three nights ago, was it not?'

'How would a beast that eats people know about this healing? That's not the action of a wild creature.'

'I don't know, sir. It's almost like the field surgery your men perform. I think Caradoc has done this kind of thing before, but I don't know of anywhere a dragon might learn these skills.' Frecknock had almost glowed as she showed Melyn the evidence, proud that she had discovered something of use to him, almost like a shy pupil seeking praise from her teacher. But now she pulled in on herself again as if expecting to be punished. He truly didn't understand her. She should have been surly and uncooperative, or passively accepting of her death like the others in her village, and yet she seemed genuinely to want to help him.

'Well then, keep looking.' He wanted to be angry with her but found he couldn't. There were warrior priests who would feel his wrath this night, but he would use the dragon far more for scouting from now on.

The horses awaited them in the dark alleyway Usel had taken him down just days earlier. Dafydd led Iolwen through the shadows though she was quite capable of looking after herself. Her child showed as the tiniest of bumps; an uncharitable soul might have said she was putting on a bit of weight from too many dinner parties.

The horses that Teryll had chosen were solid beasts, well capable of long distances and reasonable speed. They were harnessed for comfort rather than fashion, and the luggage beasts bore capacious leather saddlebags that would doubtless hold a fortnight's travel provisions and camp gear. Besides them, their own meagre travelling bags seemed paltry as Dafydd roped them in place.

Looking around to see if he was being watched, he helped Iolwen up into her side saddle, then made to climb on to his own horse. Only then did he notice that there were six beasts, not the four he had asked for.

'Well, you didn't think I was going to let you go riding off on your own, did you? Not with six of my best horses.' Teryll stepped from the dark doorway of a nearby house and Dafydd cursed himself, both for not noticing the two extra mounts, or realizing the horses were unnaturally calm. Had they been left alone, as he had requested, they would have been more skittish and nervous at his approach.

'I don't suppose there's any point in my arguing, is there?'

'No, sir. Morning, Your Highness.' Teryll nodded a bow to Iolwen, then swung himself up on to the third saddled horse, taking the lead ropes of the other three. 'Now, my lord. Where are we going?'

'East, through Palmer's Gate.' Dafydd sighed. He had really wanted to do this alone, but he could have thought of worse company than Teryll.

They made quick progress through the empty streets, arriving at the gate before the first morning bell. Two sleepy guards stumbled to attention as they approached, stepping forward to block their path.

'No one passes until sunrise,' one of the guards said.

'Unless he bears the king's seal.' Dafydd tossed a roll of parchment at the man who had spoken. He dropped his halberd and scrabbled for the scroll before dropping that too. He went down on his hands and knees to retrieve both, then fumbled with them as he tried to unroll the one and balance the other in the crook of his elbow. Finally he succeeded in breaking the seal on the roll and opened it up. The look on his face as he deciphered the inscription written inside was one of supreme astonishment.

'Beggin' pardon, sir. I wasn't told –'

'You've no need to apologize for doing your job,' Dafydd said. 'Just open the gate and let us through.'

'Of course, sir. Of course.' In his hurry to obey, the guard dropped both halberd and scroll again. He looked down at them lying in the dry dirt of the track that passed through this minor gate, then decided they were less important than an order backed up by the king's warrant. He turned for the gate and heaved at the massive beam that locked the two iron-studded oak doors closed.

As soon as the gap was wide enough for a horse, Dafydd kicked forward, leading his small party out of Tynhelyg and into the dark plain beyond. Five miles to the forest edge, three weeks to the Sea of Tegid, if the weather held. He felt a surge of excitement at the beginning of this most glorious of adventures.

'Your Highness.'

Looking around, Dafydd let out a silent curse at his luck. At the head of a group of twenty-five mounted cavalry, Captain Pelod of the Royal Guard sat on his charger.

'His Majesty the king thought you might choose this gate to make your exit.'

11

Beware the blood oath for it is a two-edged sword. Bind a person to you by their sworn word, and be sure that you too are bound to them.

Maddau the Wise, *An Etiquette*

'You're very quiet, my love. Is there something on your mind?' Beulah sat down beside Clun, who was staring from a castle window out over the rain-swept town below. The building material of choice was dirty-grey granite, with slate roofs lending everything an air of gloom under the lowering clouds. Three days of confinement in Castle Derrin and the royal party was beginning to fray at the edges.

'I'm sorry, my lady. I was trying to see into the aethereal, like Inquisitor Melyn asked. I find it hard to focus when there are distractions.'

'It's remarkable you can do it at all. Few have the skill. There are perhaps only three people in the whole of the Twin Kingdoms who can use it reliably to communicate.'

'Three?'

'Melyn, myself and Master Librarian Andro at Emmass Fawr.'

'And no one else can see this . . .' Clun swept his hand

around the room, staring at things Beulah herself was denied. ' Ah, it's gone.'

She felt a moment's twinge of envy that her gift had left her, then thanked the Shepherd that he had seen fit to give her a substitute. Without any direct way of contacting Melyn, his whole plan would have to rely on message birds or even his leaky network of spies across Llanwennog. Delays would ruin any chance of surprise, and without that taking the passes without horrendous losses would be all but impossible. Clun had to be encouraged to hone his talent, but not being able to join him in the aethereal Beulah was at a loss as to how she could help.

'My lady, can you not see this place at all?' Clun's question was well meant, but it irritated her nonetheless. Even though she knew it was hopeless, Beulah slipped into the familiar trance state she had practised many thousands of times before. Ever since Melyn had introduced her to the wonders of the aethereal as a girl of ten, she had thought of it as her personal kingdom. Lleyn had never known its splendour, and for all she knew, Iolwen was not aware of it either. Her father had shown little interest in anything other than his base senses, choosing to drown out the more subtle forces of Gwlad with endless wine. Only she had the skill, but now it failed her. The life growing in her womb tipped the balance of her mind and closed that door almost completely. Almost, but not quite. Tantalizingly, she could see flickers of the vibrant life that pulsed around everything. Clun himself was aglow, as if the sun that couldn't fight its way through Derrin's clouds instead focused entirely on him, outlining his form in fiery gold.

‘I can see some.’ Beulah let go of her trance, realizing as she did that the effort had made her tense. She breathed out deeply, stroking her belly through the heavy silk of her gown. It was still flat, no sign yet of the force that leached her skill from her. ‘But it never lasts long. I see only glimpses, like hallucinations. Who would have thought something so small could make such a difference.’

‘He’s growing strong, our child. Do you feel him yet?’ Clun reached over and pressed his own hand over Beulah’s. It was warm, his touch sending tiny sparks through her bare skin as he radiated the power of the aethereal.

‘Not yet, but it’s early still. I don’t show at all.’

‘You do to me. I can see our child in your eyes, in the way you carry yourself. And when I see you the way Inquisitor Melyn taught me, it’s as if there are two of you, shadowing each other. And there, in your belly, is a fire of brilliant white.’

Beulah wanted to be cheered by these words, but in truth they pained her. She had seven months or more of this weakness still to endure, and she knew that it would get worse as her pregnancy progressed. Already she woke at odd times in the night longing for foods she had always hated, or so heated with passion she had to wake Clun from his sleep and demand satisfaction. The sickness that had plagued her mornings still claimed her occasionally, although Archimandrite Cassters’ medication helped with that. But more than anything she felt restless, nervous and fidgety. It was hard for her to concentrate even on the lines, and conjuring a blade of light scared her. A hideous and painful death awaited should she not be able to maintain her self-discipline. For the first time in many years she had taken to carrying a short steel sword with her, hidden in her sleeve.

'I think we should leave this place tomorrow. Whether the rain has stopped or not.' Beulah tried to snap her wandering mind back to the here and now. 'It should weed out the less hardy of our followers. And I really can't stand another day cooped up like this. I was always meant to be out on the road.'

'I agree, my lady. We should move on soon. It's a long way to Castell Glas, further still to Abervenn. If the inquisitor holds to his plan, we need to be ready to play our part.'

'Has he contacted you?' Beulah felt an unexpected surge of hope that there might be news from Melyn. She had not realized how much she missed him, how much she had grown to rely on his counsel.

'No, not yet. I practise as he instructed, try to hold myself in the aethereal at the appointed hour each day. But as yet he has not come to me, and I dare not move far from myself, lest I not be able to find the way back.'

Beulah shuddered, remembering the almshouses outside Emmass Fawr where the casualties of magical training were kept. The mindless. Melyn had shown them to her when she began her training. Most of them had been like the idiots that graced every village from Candlehall to Dina, drooling, moronic but capable of eating, sleeping and maintaining some control over their bodily functions. One man had been different. Young, and with the air of nobility about him, he had sat motionless, unaware of anything around him. The duty quaisters fed him, cleaned him, walked him, but everything had to be done for him. Lift his arm and it would stay where it was put, turn his head to one side and his blank stare would gaze in that direction until someone moved his head back again. Novitiates would sometimes pose him in undignified positions, stick his hands down his loose trousers as if he were playing with himself, but he didn't care. He wasn't there any more. He had learned to see the aethereal, but before he had mastered the basic skills had chosen to explore beyond his own body. Where his mind had gone, no one could tell, but it had never come back.

'No, my love. You must not risk that. Not without someone to watch over you while you try. When our child is born, when my skill returns, as it surely must, then I will take this training on myself. Then we will walk the aethereal together.'

Melyn squatted in the undergrowth watching the small clearing as the light fell. At the edge of the trees, hidden from view, two dozen warrior priests knelt motionless, waiting, all eyes focused on the figure huddled at the centre of their wide circle.

They were a day's ride from the main camp, where Melyn had ordered the bulk of the army to rest their horses, hunt for supplies and prepare for another long march. He had brought this elite band with him for one purpose: to kill the feral dragon. In the centre of the clearing, sitting cross-legged astride a point where two bright glowing lines of power intersected, Frecknock bowed her head in a risible parody of prayer, making her calling as she had done those many months before.

'Hear me, dragons of the Ffrydd, of Gwlad. It is I, Frecknock the Fair, daughter of Sir Teifi teul Albarn and Morwenna the Wise. I am alone now, seeking out the companionship of my kind.'

Melyn tuned out the pleading Draigiaith and fixed his eye instead on the darkening skies, searching for any sign of movement larger than a woodpigeon. Four hours now they had been at this task, and still nothing had happened. Soon it would be too dark to safely continue with their planned attack. Any other dragon he would have thought nothing of tackling alone, in the middle of the night, but he had seen what this one was capable of and was no longer willing to take chances.

'Hear me, lonely souls on the long road. I would gladly join you, be your companion in your search. Answer my call and I will hasten to your side.'

Frecknock had assured him that Caradoc would be nearby. He would have found himself a place where he would be comfortable for months. Not a simple camp, but perhaps a cave or a bower formed by a fallen tree that he could take shelter in when it rained. Food was plentiful in the forest, and the only other thing he needed to heal was rest. As night fell Melyn wondered if the beast hadn't drifted off into a sleep so deep he couldn't hear Frecknock's ceaseless whining.

'Enough. Stop now. We'll try again at first light.' He tapped into the dragon's calling and sent his own words back at her, unsure quite how it was he did it. It was not unlike the way he communicated with the Shepherd, though his presence was nothing like that of the pathetic creature who sat up stiffly at the centre of the clearing.

Motioning to the other warrior priests nearby to follow him, Melyn levered himself to his feet, joints creaking in protest at being made to move after so long motionless.

'Well. Where was he?'

'Your Grace, I tried my best.' Frecknock had shrunken in on herself again, Melyn noticed. It was a defence mechanism, he supposed, remembering the time back at Candlehall when assassins had attacked Clun. Then she had almost disappeared. Another secret he intended to extract from her.

'But your best wasn't good enough. When you called before, it was like a lasso around a steer, tugging any who heard towards you. I remember it well. Even I wanted to rush to your side. Yet today all I heard was words. Where was the passion?'

'Sir, I had . . . help then.' Melyn noticed the hesitation. So the dragon was holding something back.

'Don't play games with me, Frecknock. I don't need you to show me the way through the mountains. I can find that myself. It's enough to know the pass exists. I won't hesitate to leave your body here in this clearing if you don't give me your complete cooperation.' Melyn conjured a blade of light, letting it sizzle in the night air, pointed at the ground. Reflected in its light, Frecknock's face was a gaunt picture of fear.

'Please, Your Grace, I don't mean to trick you. I had a . . . a magic book when I made my calling before. It acts as a focus for the spell. It increases my allure. I'm trying my hardest. Please trust me when I say no one wants this feral monster killed more than I do. But without the book . . . I'm not a skilled mage.'

'Osgal, fetch the horses.' Melyn ignored Frecknock's whining protestations, keeping his blade low, letting it sputter like a blacksmith's forge. The other warrior priests followed their captain back towards the trees, one by one disappearing from view. Melyn waited a moment, unsure why he wanted to be alone with the beast, save that he could enjoy the power he had over her. Finally the silence began to unnerve him. 'Come. Let's get out of here. I don't want to make camp near our trap.'

He led the dragon back across the clearing to the trees, her obvious obedience going some way to lessen his anger at the wasted evening. As they pushed through the undergrowth towards the nearby path, Melyn turned back to Frecknock.

'How long had you been calling before you found me?'

'Years without the book,' Frecknock said. 'As soon as I learned the spell I tried it out.'

'Why? Why risk your family in that way?'

'They weren't my family. You killed my family. They were just the first dragons I stumbled across after a year of wandering this cursed forest on my own. I had hoped they might take me away from it, but no. They were set in their ways, slowly fading away into senility. Even Morgwm. She was younger than most of them – she could have been anything – but she chose to settle, to serve. She healed the old ones, and she healed men who came to her as well. I couldn't stand that, seeing her help the people who had wiped out our race.'

'And yet you help me now.' For a moment Melyn had seen a spark in Frecknock's eyes, an anger that almost matched his own. It was a fleeting thing, but it cheered him to know she had some life in her. There was no challenge in breaking a creature that had no spirit.

'I have no choice, do I?' The dragon wilted in front of his eyes, her wings drooping by her sides like dead leaves on an autumn tree. 'There is no one out there to come to my rescue. My only potential saviour is a monster from my worst nightmares, a feral beast. If I help you I stay alive. If I don't I die. I'd rather live in fear or in the service of my enemy. I'm not like the old dragons you killed in the village. They had made their choice. They had settled. If you hadn't found them they would have faded away to nothing in time.'

They broke through the undergrowth on to the path to find Captain Osgal waiting with the horses. Frecknock fell silent in the company of the other warrior priests, and Melyn wondered if she hadn't decided to adopt him as her companion anyway. In an odd manner it seemed appropriate. He had answered her call, after all. He had come, as she had requested, and taken her from her life of drudgery, as he had promised. It was almost laughable had there not been that knowledge, right in the forefront of his mind, that there was far more to the dragon than he could see.

'Follow me.' He swung up on to his horse. Frecknock fell in behind him, keeping up with his swift trot with her own strange rolling gait. For all the world an obedient hound following her master on the hunt.

Their campsite was an hour's ride from the clearing where Frecknock had attempted her calling. Night was fully upon them by the time the fires were lit and the evening meal prepared. Melyn sat apart from the men, the dragon curled up by his side as he chewed on charred venison and drank from his water skin. She had not eaten all day, he was fairly certain, and had walked without complaint where they had ridden.

'Are you hungry?' He took the haunch that still hung on a spit over the glowing coals and tossed it over to her.

'Thank you, Your Grace.' Melyn returned to his own meal, trying not to listen to the noises of chewing and swallowing behind him, wondering why he had even thought to offer her food.

'This magic book that made all the difference to your spell. It wasn't yours, was it.'

'No, Your Grace.' The sound of ripping meat ceased. 'It belonged to the village elder. Sir Frynwy.'

'He'd be the one whose house was closest to the big hall? Two storeys high?'

'Yes.' Frecknock's voice was uncertain as if she were considering her answer carefully. Good, Melyn thought. Far better to know that she values her knowledge. Tricking it out of her will be so much more enjoyable.

'And when you used it, you did so without his knowledge, didn't you? You knew they'd never let you make such a powerful calling. Not to the whole of Gwlad like you did. That would put them in too much danger, wouldn't it?'

Melyn looked over his shoulder, seeing the dark eyes of the dragon staring up at him from her supper. By the look of the haunch, she had been ravenous, but she had not complained. Now she seemed to be struggling with her conscience, as if to answer was to damn herself, to admit that she had been responsible for the deaths of her fellow dragons. Finally, she seemed to come to some resolution.

'Yes, I took it. I needed it. I asked Sir Frynwy time and time again. But he wouldn't hear of it. He was so old he couldn't begin to understand my need.'

'Or maybe he was wise. It's of no importance now. He's dead, as are all the others. The forest has reclaimed them. But you still live, Frecknock. And as long as you are of use to me, I might just let you stay that way. So tell me. To trap this creature Caradoc, you really need to perform the same spell of calling that you used when you found me?'

'Yes. I might get lucky and contact him with the spell I used today. He's close by, I can feel it. But to make it so he can't resist, so he has to come to me straight away, to do that I need the book. I will keep trying, Your Grace. But it will take time.'

Melyn hauled himself to his feet, crossed to where his saddlebags were propped up against a small tree and reaching inside for the package he had been carrying for months now. It was much heavier than a book its size should be. He carried it back to where Frecknock was now sitting up, her eyes wide, her meal forgotten.

'Would this be your magic book?' He didn't need to ask. Her face was answer enough. She hungered for it like an addict for the burning weed. 'Then swear to me on it. A blood oath binding you to my will. Then I will let you use it, and together we will track down and slay this monster that pretends to be a dragon.'

Errol sat on the pallet of branches and dried grass he had constructed for himself across the cave from the alcove. After the fire he had insisted that Benfro have his old sleeping area back, and had even helped to gather grass and moss for new bedding. It was a better arrangement. The cave seemed small when the dragon curled himself up on the floor to sleep; at least with Benfro confined to the alcove Errol didn't feel like the walls were squeezing in on him.

The days since Corwen's last appearance had slowly formed into a kind of routine. Benfro would practise flying in the mornings while Errol slept. In the afternoons the dragon would head off into the forest in search of food, usually returning before sundown with some dead beast which he would prepare and cook. Errol spent the hours of solitude either sleeping or studying the lines, trying to tap their power to speed his recovery. He exercised a little, often walking down to the river and swimming in the icy water, flexing his ankles to improve their mobility.

Come evening, they would eat, perhaps talk a while, and then Benfro would settle himself down to sleep. He never asked for any help, but Errol could see the dragon's aura relaxing as he drifted off, the knot around that terrible red line untying itself and leaving him open to attack. And so he would sit up through the night, his own aura keeping Magog's influence at bay.

It would be dawn soon, Errol realized. He could tell both by the change in the texture of the blackness he could see through the cave entrance and by the change in the colours of Benfro's aura. As the dragon rose from deep sleep into dreams, so he seemed to change and grow. Sometimes he would turn in his sleep, twitch like a dog or mutter strange words under his breath. Errol was learning Draigiaith fast, but he still didn't understand its more subtle nuances and understood little of what it was Benfro said as he dreamed, but he could tell that the dragon was experiencing something painful, something he didn't want to go through.

Errol leaned his head against the rock, feeling its coolness against his cheek as he stifled a yawn. It was hard to sit up all night, even if he had slept through the day. He had always risen with the sun, even before Melyn had taken him to Emmass Fawr. If anything, his months in the library archives before his birthday had lessened his need for sleep, so that when the time had come for him to take on the mantle of novitiate, it had been no trouble keeping his candle long. He wondered idly whether his small flame still burned in the novitiates' chapel. Had he extinguished it before leaving with Captain Osgal for Tynewydd? So much had happened since that fateful day he couldn't remember, but he hoped that it had burned down to nothing, then extinguished itself. He would dearly love to be candled out of the order. Even if he had already been cast into the Faaeren Chasm.

Benfro rolled over, mumbling in his sleep. He would wake soon, Errol knew. Then he could settle himself back on his comfortable pallet, pull his battered old cloak around him for a blanket and doze off to sleep himself. He wondered whether he would dream of Martha and the group of dragons carrying her off to the vast castle. Every night he drifted off hoping to see her, but mostly his nights were filled with darkness, pain and memories of King Ballah's dungeons. He could see the rough stone walls, vaulted arches reaching high overhead, echoing his footsteps as he walked down a seemingly endless corridor.

Torches hung in sconces at regular intervals, stretching off into the distance, pulling him onward.

Confused, Errol tried to look round for the guards who were supposed to escort him to the torture chamber. But he couldn't move his head. Nor could he control his feet, and as he realized this, so he understood that he was dreaming. And he wasn't in Ballah's dungeons, nor in the depths of Emmass Fawr, though the place bore some striking similarities to the monastery.

Trapped in someone else's body, Errol watched the corridor slowly roll past him until, finally, he arrived at a set of stairs winding up in a wide spiral. He paused a while here, as if steeling himself for a long climb, then set off. It seemed both to take for ever and no time at all. Errol experienced the frustration and tiredness of a long and arduous climb, but he was also aware, somehow, that no time had actually passed from the moment he had put a foot on to the first step to the point where he stopped. He could see that he was at the top of a high tower, but frustratingly he could only see a narrow part of the room he guessed must fill the space.

It was vast, that much he could tell. And it was filled with bizarre pieces of machinery, long wooden benches with their tops higher than his head, piles of books strewn over the floor. He wanted to explore this strange place, but instead he found himself turning, walking to the high arched opening that flooded light into the room. It was filled with vast panes of glass, thick as his hand and yet clear as the finest crystal. They were set into heavy iron-framed doors which reached down to the floor and opened out on to a wide balcony. Errol found himself stepping out, felt the wind tug at his face and clothes as he looked this way and that as if expecting to see someone. But there was no one there. Then he walked to the edge and looked down. His gut twisted in fear at the impossible drop to the base of the castle, and then further into the depths of a chasm. There was no balustrade around the balcony, nothing to stop him plummeting to a horrible death. He looked up again, across to the other side of the chasm. There was something terribly familiar about the rock formations and the shape of the mountains beyond, but he couldn't work out what it was.

A noise behind him caught his attention and he turned, walking carefully away from the edge and back inside. He still had no control over his movements: it was as if he was riding someone else's senses, seeing only what they chose to look at, going only where they chose to go.

Back in the tower room, he looked left and right, trying to pinpoint the source of the noise he had heard. There was so much clutter in the vast space it was difficult to see over to the other side, but something was moving rhythmically, scraping and squeaking like a mouse in a wheel. Movement flickered in the corner of his eye, and he looked up into the conical jigsaw of rafters and beams that formed the ceiling. More strange intricately wrought devices hung in the gloom, some twisting gently in the breeze from the open window, others glittering and shiny in the sunlight that streamed through the glass. And in the middle, rocking gently in time to the squeaking noise, a cage had been winched towards the apex.

It was big enough for a large man to stand up in, perhaps

twelve paces across and circular in plan. The floor of the cage was stuffed with dried reeds, their ends poking out of the bars like a badly made scarecrow. But what was most striking about the cage was the material of its making. As a novitiate, it had been one of Errol's tasks to clean the candlesticks and other decorative metalwork in the quaisters' chapel at Emmass Fawr. More recently he had held King Balwen's torc in his hands and felt its solid weight. He knew the difference between gold and highly polished bronze. This cage was not made from bronze, and if the thickness of the chain holding it up was a reliable indicator, the bars, each as thick as his wrist, were solid. He couldn't begin to conceive of the value of such a thing, or why anyone would want to construct a cage so large from such a precious and rare metal. But whatever the reason, it was plain that the cage was occupied. Something was inside it and trying hard to get out.

Errol thought to get closer, to climb on to something and peer inside, but the eyes through which he saw darted away as he heard another sound behind him. He turned and saw a dark shadow pass the window. A sudden sharp wind buffeted the open doors and, with a lurch that made him dizzy, he was running for the staircase.

He made it just in time, or so it seemed. He stopped in the relative safety of the stairwell and looked back into the room. There was a noise like the shaking of a heavy tarpaulin, then the oldest dragon Errol had ever seen stepped through the window and into the room, folding his wings behind him as he did so.

Corwen was ancient, Errol knew. The dead mage had lived for over a thousand years and kept his decrepit form in death. Although less battle-scarred, and presumably still alive, this dragon had to be ten times Corwen's age. His scales were worn and chipped; around his shoulders and neck they were missing entirely, just wrinkled, leathery skin hanging off his frame in folds. His skeletal head poked forward from his body as if all the fat and muscle had wasted away, leaving just skin pulled tight over bone. As he walked, his skull rocked back and forth like a cockerel strutting in a farmyard. The tufts of hair sprouting from the tips of his ears were white, his fangs blunt and yellow. He carried himself like an old man, stooping, moving slowly on arthritic legs. And yet his wings must have worked well, for he had flown to the room.

Errol watched as the beast moved through the piles of accumulated junk towards the far side of the room. Old and shrivelled he might be, but he was still huge. Far bigger than Benfro, bigger even than the image Corwen had worn as the memory of his one-hundred-and-fifty-year-old self. How magnificent, how enormous this dragon must have been in his prime.

He had reached the middle of the room, which was much smaller-looking now that its occupant had returned. The tables and chairs, books and other odd apparatus were perfectly in proportion to the dragon as he reached up and pulled the cage down, tilting it so that he could peer in. From Errol's position he could still only see the base with its mat of reeds, but whatever was inside the cage shrieked.

Then a hand, a human hand, pushed through the bars, the arm stretching far enough forward for Errol to see. It was difficult to tell from a distance and against the vastness of the dragon's own hand, but it seemed to him whoever was in the cage was small, not fully adult, and female.

To his surprise Errol then heard himself speak in a voice quite unlike his own. It was a quiet exclamation of surprise, spoken under his breath, less than a whisper, but the dragon's head instantly whipped around, eyes piercing the gloom and staring straight at him.

'A spy?' he said, and Errol felt even more helpless than before. Fear pinned him to the spot. Pinned whoever it was whose senses he rode. 'Come, Xando. Oh yes, I know it's you. No one else would dare venture up here.'

Errol felt himself backing away into the shadows, ready to turn and run headlong down the stairs to the cellars so far below. But the dragon merely smiled, muttered something under his breath and reached out towards him. A tug with one long taloned finger and he was walking out into the light, powerless to do anything else.

'Curiosity isn't a sin, boy.' The dragon's voice was unusual, at once high-pitched and yet more guttural than Benfro's or Corwen's. It reminded Errol of Sir Radnor more than anyone.

'What brings you up to my eyrie anyway? Is it my new pet? Did you want to see her for yourself?' Errol found himself stepping further into the room, drawn helplessly by the power of that voice. The dragon turned away for a moment, muttering something else under his breath but still tilting the cage, which descended further. As Errol reached the end of one of the huge benches, he saw that the centre of the room was clear. Beyond it logs burned in a huge open fireplace, alongside which had been arranged a reading desk and a pair of vast chairs, clearly designed for dragons to use. The walls were lined with shelves untidily stacked with rolls of parchment, more books and yet more bits and pieces of machinery. He took it all in with a quick glance, his eyes never straying far from the descending cage. The chain clanked over noisy pulleys high up in the darkness overhead, jerking and snapping so that the cage came down in a series of bumps.

Closer and he could see that more reeds had been woven around the bars, as if a nesting bird was inside and not a person at all. For an instant Errol wondered if the dragon had been feeding people to whatever creature he had trapped within. Had the hand merely been the remains of its supper? Then, just as it thudded on to the floor, the dragon righted the cage with his hand as if the weight of it were nothing to him, so that now Errol could see what was inside.

'There you are, young lad. And since you've shown yourself spirited enough to serve me, you can start by attending to the needs of my pet. If you can understand the gibberish she spouts.'

She was half lying, half sitting, shoved up against the bars. Her hair was tangled and awry, fallen across her face, her clothes dirty and torn. But Errol didn't need to see any more to know who it was, nor to feel her keening sense of despair and hopelessness. She reached out her hand, grubby and bruised, and Errol willed himself to take it. But the boy whose thoughts he rode stayed motionless, petrified, aghast. He could feel himself slipping away, the sounds leaching from the scene as if someone slowly closed a door on the world, the light fading away from the edges inwards.

Martha reached out to him with pleading in her eyes, and her mouth formed words of desperation. But he could hear nothing, and slowly, agonizingly, she faded away to black.

12

In Llanwennog it is called a puissant sword, in the Twin Kingdoms a blade of light or sometimes blade of fire. In Eirawen men called it marwyr or deathbringer. But whatever its name, it is the most terrible manifestation of man's brutality. The Grym connects all living things; in a very real sense it is all living things. To take from it for such destructive ends is a travesty, an affront to Gwlad, who gives life to us all.

Corwen teul Maddau,
On the Application of the Subtle Arts

'You didn't honestly think you could slip out of the city unnoticed did you, Dafydd?'

Captain Jarius Pelod of the King's Guard wore the kind of smile that Dafydd would happily have run through with his sword, if he hadn't been both a lifelong friend and backed up by twenty-five heavily armed guardsmen. Still, it was humbling to be caught out so soon.

The war council had been adamant. There was absolutely no way that the second in line to the throne was going to be allowed to go anywhere near the Twin Kingdoms, even if his intelligence – that Abervenn would rise to fight for him and King Ballah against its own queen – was gold standard. The idea of taking the pregnant princess with him, and on a dangerous sea journey at that, only showed that he had no idea of the bigger picture, perhaps wasn't even fit to be a full member of the council. Dafydd remembered all too well the arguments that had rattled back and forth. The king had kept silent, watching from his throne with that indulgent expression of his as Tordu and Geraint were for once united in their disapproval of his mad scheme. In the end he had conceded that it was likely to end only in his delivering himself to Beulah as a valuable hostage, or worse yet losing both his head and that of his wife. He had accepted their ruling that he should stay in Tynhelyg and oversee the city guard while the bulk of the army was split between Tynewydd and Wrthol.

It was only when Tordu had announced that he would be supervising the army at Tynewydd himself, and that Duke Dondal would be sent to tour the northern regions to drum up more fighting men, that Dafydd had decided to ignore the council anyway. There was nothing he could do in the capital and it was an insult to keep him so far away from the action. That same night he had contacted Usel and outlined his mad plan, persuaded Iolwen of it too, though she had needed little convincing. He had thought himself so careful, so well organized, and yet the council had known all along what he was doing. He knew Tordu's spies were good, but he thought he had identified all of them. Now he wasn't so sure.

'So, Jarius. They sent you because they knew you wouldn't hesitate to use force against me, and I'd be unlikely to hurt my old sparring partner.' Dafydd edged his horse closer to the line of guardsmen, trying to recall their names. They were some of the best soldiers in the king's own troop and perhaps too many to bring in one wayward prince and his pregnant wife.

'King Ballah said something along those lines,' Pelod said. 'He also said I should see that you didn't get yourself into any difficulty, and that if you were in danger I was to protect you with my life. But that if it came to a choice between you and your unborn son, I should err in favour of youth.'

'He would say something like that. So tell me, Jar. Am I to be taken to the West Tower like my grandfather's previous guest? I can't promise to escape the executioner's blade in quite such a spectacular fashion.' Dafydd joked, but he knew he was in deep trouble. King Ballah had executed family before when they showed overt signs of coveting the throne. He only hoped he could find a way to exonerate Teryll. The stable hand deserved reward for his loyalty, not punishment.

'His Majesty said nothing about taking you anywhere. Merely that I should follow you and see you kept out of trouble.' Jarius' smile was wider than ever.

'He did what?' It took a moment for Dafydd to catch up with the words.

'No prince of Tynhelyg should sit behind stone walls when the enemy masses at the borders. And besides, you have two brothers to take your place if you fall. I think those were the king's actual words. He sent me and my men to escort you on this mad quest of yours, Dafydd. We are at your command.' Jarius bowed in his saddle

'What does the major domo think of this?' Dafydd asked. 'What does my father think?'

'As I understand it, they will think you're sleeping late. They most likely won't miss you until the next meeting of the war council, which the king sees fit to call in two days' time. By then we should be well on our way to Talarddeg. If you're ready for a hard ride.'

Dafydd turned back to where Iolwen and Teryll waited with the packhorses. Where moments earlier he had felt despair, now he felt a reckless abandon. Not only was his plan still achievable, now he had the tacit backing of the king and a troop of the finest warriors in the land to help him. What could possibly go wrong?

'What say you, my princess? Do you fancy a morning gallop?'

Cold rain fell in sheets from lead-grey clouds driven by the ceaseless wind. The train of riders and wagons moved slowly across the open plain, huddled against the weather. At the head of the column Beulah wrapped herself tight in her heavy woollen travelling cloak and muttered curses. Two weeks out of Beteltown and the weather had dogged them the whole time. The past three nights of wet camps had been the worst, their only fires those lit by the cook to prepare their evening and morning meals. Beulah's canvas tent was soaked through, put away each new day still wet. It dripped constantly through the night, keeping her awake more effectively than if she had slept wrapped only in a coarse blanket. She was an adept and knew how to draw warmth from the lines, but with each new hour of unremitting grey, her mood blackened further, her enthusiasm for the whole tour the only thing evaporating.

'By the Shepherd, will this rain never end?' Beulah nudged her horse close to Clun, who rode at her side. The beast baulked at her direction and she cursed the dragon that had killed her favourite mount. Melyn had given her Pahthia for her sixteenth birthday. A flighty young filly for a flighty young filly, he had said, but over the years they had grown accustomed to each other. She missed her horse more than she cared to admit, as much, perhaps, as she missed the man who had gifted her. Another sign of reliance on others, Beulah noted, only adding to her anger.

'They say it can rain for forty days without let up here, my lady. I know my father used to complain that the wagons always took longer to cover this ground than anywhere else on the route from Castell Glas.' Clun's face darkened, his brow furrowing at the thought of his father. He didn't complain, Beulah noted. Clun never complained. But he felt the loss perhaps even more keenly than she missed her horse, and every time something reminded him of his past the blackness fell over him. She hated to see him so sullen.

'Melyn will have tracked down the dragon and killed it by now, my love,' she said. 'He'll bring you its jewels and you can add them to the collection at Candlehall.'

'We'll see.' He fell silent, drawing his cloak around him, though he hadn't pulled the hood over his head. The rain plastered his fair hair to his scalp, ran down his face in rivulets and dripped from the end of his nose and chin, but he didn't shiver, barely moved a muscle except for the rhythmic sway that kept him in balance with his horse's steady walk.

The road took them over bleak, empty moorland, visibility never more than a few dozen paces, the occasional fords swollen and wild. The sun moved through the sky somewhere overhead, but the clouds hid its position so effectively they moved in permanent twilight, heedless of the passage of time. It might have taken them a few hours, or a few days, but eventually the road crested a final hill and began its slow descent towards the River Hafren.

After a while they saw trees looming out of the mist, ranks of moss-decked spruce and pine flanking the road like silent sentinels. Then the rain eased, first to a steady drizzle, then to a hanging cloud of moisture in the air, and finally it petered out altogether. Beulah sighed with relief, digging deep into the lines, pulling the power of the Grym into her so that she might dry herself out. It was hard work, no longer the instinct she had known all her life. The child growing within her made even the most simple of magics an effort. But slowly the warmth suffused her skin and she basked in it as she might enjoy a long soak in her deep bath back home at Candlehall.

So wrapped up in the sensation was she that Beulah didn't notice the first cry of alarm. Ahead of her, the point guard stiffened on his horse, then toppled sideways, falling to the ground with a wet slap. Before she could react, dozens of armed men swarmed out of the trees, screaming like demons and running straight at the column.

'To the queen!' Clun shouted beside her, his blade of

light flaring into existence with a smell of burned air. In no time at all Beulah was surrounded by guards on horseback, obscuring her view of the attackers.

'Out of my way, you fools!' she shouted, drawing her thin steel sword and wishing for her own blade of light as she kicked her horse on. The enemy had avoided the riders and were heading for the few wagons. Beulah didn't wait for anyone to follow her, spurring on alone towards the running men. The first two went down before they knew what had hit them, heads neatly severed by her blade. The third dodged, wheeled round and flailed at her horse's legs with an evil-looking curved blade. Steel sliced through muscle and bit into bone as her horse squealed. It reared up, kicking out at the man, who expertly dodged the hooves and brought his blade round in an arc that half sliced through the creature's neck.

Beulah leaped from her saddle as the horse went down, blood spraying over the road. The blade she carried with her was completely inadequate, but such was her rage, she had no difficulty focusing the Grym along its length. Not as good as a pure blade of light, but more than enough for her needs. The man who had killed her horse turned on her, a strange smile on his face. His eyes were bright black buttons in a face swollen and red. Whatever he had taken before the attack, it had relieved him of any sense of self-preservation, any inkling of fear, but had left his skills intact. He moved lightly on his feet, swinging his sword through a short arc, back and forth, as if searching for the right place to strike. And all the while he giggled like an insane girl.

'Who are you people?' Beulah shouted, though she

knew there was no chance of getting an answer from the man. She doubted he knew what his own name was right now. At the sound of her voice, he lunged with his blade. She parried it, then stepped aside as his momentum took him past her. A flick of the wrist and his head parted from his shoulders, his body crumpling to the ground with a noise like a dropped coal sack.

There wasn't time to stop and consider his worthless life. All around her the battle raged as the warrior priests struggled to regroup after the initial surprise. There were crossbowmen in the trees, judging by the whizzing of quarrels. Standing still was not a good idea, so she rushed towards the wagons and the band of attackers hacking wildly at the horses and terrified passengers. Beulah launched herself at them, spearing and slashing, heedless of the screams of agony, the stench of spilled guts and the blood that drenched her front, splashed her face and hands. She wasn't scared; there was no time for fear. In its place a cold fury directed her arm and primed her senses. How dare these people attack a peaceful convoy in her country?

'My lady, are you hurt?' Beulah paused a moment, hearing Clun's voice behind her. At the same time another blade of light flashed past her head, removing the arm of one attacker. Eyes mad, her attacker simply reached down and picked up his sword with the other hand. As he stood back up again, Clun removed his head, and his body crumpled to the ground.

'What manner of men are these?' he asked. 'I've never seen bandits fight so hard.'

'They're drugged with something,' Beulah said, then let

out a shriek as something slammed into her arm, spinning her round.

Her knees were suddenly weak and her legs buckled under her as Clun screamed, 'Beulah!' She tried to look up at him, to see his face, but her head was unresponsive, her stare fixed on her bloodstained arm and the sword clutched in her hand. White heat burned through its leather handle and into her hand as the Grym sought a way back to the land. Reluctant fingers dropped the melting steel, and she was grateful that it had taken the force of the blow, rather than herself. For a moment that was all she could think of, and then her focus shifted. A crossbow bolt had buried itself in her upper arm, the wicked barbed point poking right through. Dark red blood oozed down her arm to merge with the slick that already covered her. Royalty mixing with common thieves.

Without a word the remaining bandits around the wagons broke off their individual fights as if they were puppets controlled by some invisible hand. All eyes turned to her; Beulah thought there were at least twenty men. How many had there been in the original raiding party? There were dozens lying dead on the ground.

She tried to stand, but her legs wouldn't cooperate, and her head was fuzzy with pain and shock.

'Stay down, my lady.' Beulah looked up at Clun's determined face. His travelling cloak was stained dark with blood, his face splattered with gore, his hair tinged pink at the ends. He watched the approaching brigands calmly, as if this were just a training exercise.

He held a blade of light in each hand.

Beulah blinked. She had to be hallucinating. No one

could conjure two blades. Not even Melyn. But as she knelt on the wet road, he wheeled, slicing one attacker clean in two, following up with the second blade through the next. Further away, mounted warrior priests hacked at the backs of the bandits as they piled in on her, eyes more feral even than the dragon that had attacked her out of the mist.

Time seemed to slow down. The attackers came at her as if they cared nothing for their own lives. Every time one launched himself forward, Clun was there, his blades whirling like lightning. But as soon as he moved one way, they surged in from the other side and he had to swing round to counter their onslaught. Beulah was surrounded by a wall of insane contorted faces, throwing themselves on Clun's blades, hoping to overwhelm him by sheer numbers, something driving them that was more terrifying even than painful death.

And then with a shriek it was over. Warrior priests cut down the remaining attackers from behind, chopping them like so much autumn wheat. Clun finished off the last one with a swift backhand cut that sliced the top off the man's head. His eyes shot up as if looking for the missing section of his skull, then he slumped to his knees, wavered a moment and toppled forward. Beulah stared at the grey bloody mess that oozed out on to the ground and noticed the silence that descended on the scene. She felt a momentary rush in the Grym as Clun extinguished his blades, and then he was kneeling beside her, taking her arm in gentle hands and inspecting her wound.

'I'm sorry, my lady. I wasn't fast enough to stop this one for you.' Clun's voice trembled slightly. Beulah looked up at his face, felt his all-enveloping embrace and knew that she would always be safe with him to guard her. She allowed him to pick her up. As he carried her to the nearest wagon, she saw the carnage of their small battlefield, the dismembered bodies of dozens of brigands. Most of them were piled around the area where she had fought and fallen. The warrior priests were walking among the rest, making sure no one was still alive.

'I've never heard of bandits operating in such large groups before,' Clun said.

'These weren't bandits, my love. These were mercenaries. Someone paid for them to be here. Paid them to kill me.'

'Merciful Arhelion, hear my prayer. Show me the ways and the paths to the world.'

Melyn stood motionless in a thick-leaved bush, watching the still form of Frecknock as she began her calling.

'Great Rasalene, hear my supplication. Lend power to my voice that I may be heard throughout Gwlad.'

She had the book in front of her, along with a small metal cauldron in which she had mixed some herbs. Smoke wafted in the air and Melyn could smell a faint aroma, an indefinable scent that would turn any head.

'Hear my voice, all who walk the long road. I am Frecknock and I would call you to me.'

Her voice was inside Melyn's head, louder than he had ever imagined anything could be and yet not painful. Behind it there was a pull so strong his muscles tensed, ready to step forward. At the last moment he managed to stop, realizing what he was doing. All around the clearing a sudden rustling of the bushes showed how powerful Frecknock's calling now was, how all-pervasive.

'Come to me, dragons of Gwlad. As Angharad called Palisander, so I, Frecknock, daughter of Sir Teifi teul Albarn, call to you.'

Frecknock fell silent, but the potent force that demanded he respond still tugged at Melyn as if he were a fish caught on a hook. He had known the dragon book was valuable and powerful; it had been hidden with great skill and even he could sense the weight of knowledge locked within its pages. Perhaps that was why he had kept it with him when all the others had been sent off to Emmass Fawr for Andro to catalogue and translate. Seeing for himself the difference in Frecknock's ability with and without it confirmed its importance, but it also concerned him. The dragon had sworn a binding oath, and all he had read, all he knew about their kind, told him that the creatures would rather die than break such a thing. But he worried still she might turn on him, use the book to make her escape. He couldn't bring himself to kill her. Not yet, not while she was of use. But he determined to watch her closely and keep her away from the book as much as possible.

'What manner of mage art thou, to so proudly summon all to your side?'

The voice broke into Melyn's head with a roar like thunder in the mountains. Unmistakably male, it was at once profoundly alien. He recognized the Draigiaith, but the dialect was thick, inflections in all the wrong places.

'I am Frecknock.' Across the clearing the female dragon tensed, raising her head as if scanning the sky, though her eyes were still tightly shut. 'I have walked these paths alone for too many years. I would have some company.'

'And where exactly are these paths? Just where in Gwlad is this cursed place?'

'Can you not see me? Do you not know where I am?'

'By the moon, kitling, I see well enough where you are. What I don't know is where that place is. What do you call this cursed country?'

'I am no kitling.' Frecknock's reaction to the perceived insult made her seem very much like a child, Melyn thought. Her voice was petulant, and for a moment he thought she might ruin everything by sulking. Instead she drew herself up to her full height and spread her wings to the sky. It was a bit like watching a chicken trying to take off, and Melyn had to stifle a laugh.

'You are but a dozen winters old, kitling. Skilled in the subtle arts for one of your age, I will give you that. But you should live a century or two before tying yourself to a mate. Now tell me, Frecknock, daughter of Sir Teifi. What is this place, this accursed forest of shadows? What is it called?'

'You do not know? But this is the great forest of the Ffrydd. How can you not know that?'

'The Ffrydd? You speak madness, kitling. The Ffrydd is a place of rocks and sand, a barren wilderness, and has been ever since Gog slew his brother Magog there millennia ago.'

'I am no kitling. I have watched two hundred summers pass. And this is the Ffrydd as I have known it all my life.

Gog and Magog are creatures of myth. What is your name, good dragon, who are so confused?'

Frecknock's irritation had weakened her spell; Melyn no longer had to fight off the urge to run to her side and could instead concentrate on the words echoing in his head. It was a strange sensation to eavesdrop on dragons; few of them had been foolish enough or desperate enough to make a calling in his lifetime. Frecknock's earlier contact had been the first time he had heard the strange language flowing through the aethereal in decades. But if the call was intended for any to hear, then presumably any reply was too. What other dragons might be listening in? He doubted there were many left alive, aside from Benfro. What would he make of Frecknock's calling? Would he flee from his forest retreat or come rushing to her aid?

'If you are truly two centuries old, then why are you so small? I've seen twelve-month hatchlings your size. Larger.' The dragon's voice was a loud rumble that made thought difficult. It pervaded every corner of Melyn's mind, and he had to fight to keep control of himself. There was something about the language that spoke of an indulgent adult patronizing a small child, spoke of looking down on something scarcely worthy of attention.

Looking down.

Melyn cursed himself silently, raising his head to scan the skies. How could this dragon know Frecknock was small? He had to be close by, watching her. But had he flown here, or had he walked? Melyn had banked on the creature flying in, landing in the clearing and being distracted by Frecknock long enough for his warrior priests to get close. Once they had it surrounded, it would just be a matter of swift dispatch with a dozen blades of light. The beast would be slain, and they could get on with their journey. But if it walked in, pushing through the trees and bushes, then it would almost certainly discover the trap before it could be sprung.

'Come to me, stranger. You will find me full of surprises and wonders. I have travelled all of Gwlad, studied the subtle arts at the feet of great mages. I am entrusted with many secrets I would gladly share, would you just tell me your name.' Frecknock resumed her spell of allure, though it was not as potent as before. No doubt her confidence had been shaken by the unusual turn her magic had taken. Melyn cared little for her discomfort; he only needed her to bring the creature to him.

'I am Caradoc, son of Edryd, son of Tallyn, son of Mortimer, son of Gog.' Something dark shot overhead, blanking out the sun for an instant. Melyn ducked instinctively. A great wind buffeted the trees, pushed the leaves of the bush into his face, temporarily blinding him, and he felt something massive hit the ground with a thud that reverberated around the clearing. The wind died as quickly as it had come. Silence settled so heavily, he thought for a moment that something had deafened him. And then he realized he was no longer listening to Frecknock's words in his head. The pull of her spell had evaporated completely, leaving only a faint disgust that he had shared that connection with her.

Shaking his head as if to get water out of his ears, Melyn peered out through the leaves and almost gasped. Only a lifetime of discipline stopped him from letting out an audible shriek. If this was the creature that Clun had faced down, almost defeated, then the newly elevated Duke of Abervenn deserved his rapid promotion to the status of warrior priest far more than Melyn had realized.

The dragon had landed in the middle of the clearing right alongside Frecknock, and was now looking down on her with a curious expression on his massive face. Side by side the differences in them were so striking that they might have been mistaken for different species altogether. The top of Frecknock's head scarcely came up to Caradoc's chest, even though the beast stooped. His tail was as long as her entire body, Melyn reckoned. One of his outstretched wings could have sheltered her completely. No wonder he had considered her a kitling.

For her part, Frecknock looked up at Caradoc with a mixture of fear and longing in her eyes. She had not moved from the spot where she had begun her spell, but she had taken the book up and held it close to her body as if protecting it.

'You are no kitling, it's true.' Caradoc's voice was no less impressive than when Melyn had heard it in his head. 'Your face shows more experience than a few summers would allow. And the strength of mind required to make such a powerful calling is not learned in an afternoon. But why are you so small? Gog's balls, Lady Frecknock. Are all your kind like you?'

'I am all of my kind. There are none left. But before . . . before they died, yes, they were much like me.'

'And you say this is the Ffrydd? That it's been this way for all your life?'

'It has.'

'Then what in Rasalene's name has happened to me? Have I died and gone to hell?'

'I do not understand, Sir Caradoc. What do you mean?'

Melyn edged from his bush as silently as his old bones would let him, heading for the spot where Captain Osgal stood. Frecknock had only to keep Caradoc distracted a minute and all the warrior priests would be in place. Still, he couldn't help himself listening to the huge dragon's words. They sounded lucid, not the mad ravings of a blood-crazed beast. Looking across the clearing, he could see now his arm-stump was bandaged. With a cloak ripped from the back of one of his victims, Melyn guessed. The stump was held to his chest with a complicated sling.

'You call this world Gwlad, but it's no Gwlad I know,' Caradoc said, seemingly oblivious of Melyn and the other warrior priests. 'Where are the rest of my tribe? And where did all these men come from? Who taught them such brutal use of the subtle arts?'

'No one taught them. Men have always wielded the power of the Grym. They have always hunted us. They killed my parents, my village. They will kill . . .' She fell silent, staring up at the massive beast. Caradoc reached out with his one hand, cupping her head in his massive palm as Melyn reached the captain. Osgal stared open-mouthed at the winged mountain, but pulled himself together when he saw the inquisitor. He said nothing, only moved silently away through the bushes to approach the dragon from behind.

Melyn held his position, waiting until the first warrior priest appeared from the trees on the far side of the clearing. Then, taking a deep breath and making the sign of the crook, he stepped out into the light.

At first Caradoc didn't notice him, so entranced was the dragon by Frecknock's face.

'You have a strange beauty about you, Lady Frecknock,' he said. 'Nothing like the rough females who fly with my tribe. You are more delicate, like a spring flower. But how can you bear never to soar through the skies?'

'I can't miss something I've never had,' Frecknock said, and Melyn could see her shake as she clutched the magic book close to her. 'And there's no point wishing for something that can never be. I'm sorry, Sir Caradoc. I truly am. But what you do, what you have done – it is an abomination.'

'I am not Sir Caradoc. My father still heads our family. I –' Frecknock's words seemed to sink in at the same time as Caradoc noticed Melyn standing not more than ten paces away. The beast dropped his hand away from Frecknock's face, then with a casual flick of the wrist sent her tumbling head over heels.

'So, you not only wield power that isn't yours, you turn my own kind against me,' he roared at Melyn, drawing himself up to his full height, spreading his wings until they shadowed the inquisitor completely.

Melyn stared up at the beast calmly, any fear he might have felt before stepping out into the clearing now gone. His mind was calm and ready. With a thought he manifested his blade of light, felt its power warm him, chasing away the last few aches and pains of the past month's riding.

'You are a creature of the Wolf,' he said, forming the words carefully, the Draigiaith sounding alien and awkward compared to the way Caradoc spoke it. How it should be spoken, he realized. 'The Shepherd has charged me with your destruction. I do not fear for my soul setting one of you to catch another.'

'Shepherd!' Caradoc laughed. It was a terrible sound, like the screaming of trees crushed by a landslide, but it was a laugh nonetheless. 'You know nothing of the Shepherd, little man. Your precious god is no more than an—'

The noise of a dozen more blades of light burning into existence stopped the dragon in mid-sentence. He whirled, seeing that he was surrounded, and Melyn took the opportunity to strike.

He ran forward without a noise, ignoring the book that lay in the flattened grass and the overturned cauldron of herbs. Raising his blade high, he brought it down in an arc that should have severed Caradoc's other arm. At the last moment, as if sensing the attack, the dragon flinched sideways, and Melyn's blade clattered down the scales on his chest, raising sparks. A smell like burning rocks filled the clearing.

Caradoc let out a scream of rage, sounding far more like the feral beast Melyn had taken him to be. With impossible speed, he whipped out his wings, their tips striking two warrior priests and knocking them to the ground. His tail slashed round in a wide arc, the sharp scales at the tip slicing the legs out from under another one, who fell to the ground screaming as blood pumped from his severed thighs. Then the screams fell silent as Caradoc's tail came back again, this time taking off the man's head.

Melyn stepped closer still, bringing his blade up, point first, to stab the beast through one of his hearts. Again the blade skittered off the dragon's scales, and a sharp pain ran down Melyn's arm. He ducked and rolled out of the way as Caradoc tried to grab him with a sharp-taloned hand. The dragon spun again, knocking down three more warrior priests with his wings as he lifted up a huge foot to stamp on the inquisitor before he could regain his feet. For an instant Melyn was paralysed, lying on his back, staring up at a foot the size of a barn door coming down towards him, all leathery skin and razor-sharp talons.

All leathery skin. No scales.

Melyn thrust his blade up. The heat welled up in him as he channelled the power of the Grym into cutting. Caradoc bellowed in agony, pulling away from the blade. Warm blood spattered out of the wound on to Melyn's face.

'Damn you! Damn you all!' the dragon screamed, hopping like some great mythical bird as it smashed its wing tips out again, forcing the remaining warrior priests back. Melyn rolled away as rapidly as he could, gathering his feet under him and finally standing just out of the dragon's reach, his blade fiery with his rage, pointed at his quarry.

'For Queen Beulah!' He ran forward, raising his blade for a renewed attack as his remaining men did the same. Caradoc crouched as if preparing for the onslaught, then leaped into the air with a bound that would have cleared a house. He threw his wings out to their fullest extent, bringing them crashing down with a force that knocked all his attackers off their feet. Once, twice, three times they battered at the thin air, with each wing beat gaining a little more height. The wind pinned Melyn to the ground, helpless to do anything but watch as the creature rose straight up. Blood still poured from the wound in its foot, falling to the ground in a stinging crimson rain that thinned to a mist and slicked the grass all around them.

'To your feet, men!' Melyn struggled against the wind from those massive wings, which lessened only slightly as the dragon rose. All his life he had dreamed of fighting a real dragon, the kind of beast that Brynceri and Balwen had faced, not the cowering animals he had slaughtered by the dozen with casual ease. Now confronted by Caradoc, Melyn had a renewed respect for his ancestors.

When it came, the attack was far faster than he could have anticipated. One moment the dragon seemed to be struggling to lift its great bulk above the treetops, the next it was pirouetting on a wing tip and swooping towards him. Singling him out. Melyn stood his ground, knowing there was nothing else he could do but rely on his instincts and decades of training.

Caradoc was off balance, reaching out with only one arm, the stump of the other still strapped to his chest. Melyn watched his eyes, judging the moment as if this were no more than a childhood game of catch. At the last possible moment, when he could almost feel Caradoc's talons at his throat, he twisted back and to the side of the dragon's missing arm, dropping to the ground as the beast swept over him. Too quickly to see, let alone think, he hacked his blade of light around in an arc, feeling it bite into something, then pass through. Then he threw himself to the ground as that lethal tail followed, sweeping over the top of his head with no room to spare.

Melyn looked up, expecting to see the dragon wheel and come back for a second attack. But instead he flew away, heading for a rocky outcrop that rose out of the forests away to the north. Fleeing from the fight.

On the ground beside him lay three talons, each as thick as his fist, each tapering to a needle-sharp point.

13

When the Shepherd left them, journeying to the stars, his followers were bereft. Grendor and Malco fought with each other. Wise Earith turned in upon herself, speaking to no one. Only brave Balwen found the strength to cope with his master's departure. Summoning them to the throne chamber, he addressed them all.

'Friends, these are dire times indeed. But did not our master the Shepherd bid us continue his great works? Did he not gift us with such powers that we might spread his love throughout Gwlad? He has left us, true, but in time he will return. What poor servants we will seem to him if he finds us like this. Or worse, if he finds that we have failed in our duty to protect his works.'

And so saying, Balwen stepped up to the great throne and, turning to face his companions, took the seat.

The Book of the Shepherd

Errol hobbled down to the ford slowly but without his crutches. Each step was an experiment, as if he had forgotten how to walk and needed to learn all over again. His ankles were stiff, a little sore if he was honest with himself, but the dragging pain that had been his constant companion through the months since he had escaped from Tynhelyg was now little more than a memory. Still, he was determined to take his time recovering, not to make the mistake he had with the chest.

Reaching the water's edge, he slipped his shirt off over his head, dropped his trousers on to the grassy bank and stepped into the water. It had become a daily routine to swim in the river, building up his strength and stamina by fighting against the current. As ever, the water was cold against his skin, but he ignored his shivers, wading right in before plunging under the surface. Flashes of light were salmon darting away from him, swimming to the bottom and hiding in the fronds of weed that swayed in the flow. He held his breath and let the river carry him slowly downstream, watching the fish through eyes made bleary by the water. They slowly overcame their fear, emerging from the weeds, darting forward and back, each movement a flash as if they didn't swim but rather jumped from point to point.

Thinking of them brought the lines into his vision. Where everything else was blurred, they were clear and strong, painting the shape of the river bed. He reached out to the nearest, pulling the power of the Grym into him, feeling it warm his cold skin and push the dull ache from his bones.

'Come to me, dragons of Gwlad. Come to me.'

Errol nearly choked on a mouthful of water. Kicking off from the bottom, he burst through the surface, coughing and spluttering, water pouring out of his nose. He fought his way to the bank and hauled himself out on to the grass, shivering as the wind tugged at his bare skin. He reached back to the lines for warmth, touching them lightly, wary of any more surprises.

'Dragons of Gwlad, come to me. I await you.'

This time Errol was a little more ready to hear the voice, which spoke in perfect, eloquent Draigiaith. It was familiar, but at first he couldn't place it, distracted by the power behind the words. He felt like he needed to leap to his feet and run off into the woods in search of this damsel so obviously in distress. But that was absurd. He was naked, his clothes a hundred paces or more upstream. And he had no idea where this dragon was, what direction to set off in. Shaking his head to dislodge the mad impulse, he felt out along the lines, trying to see where the strange calling came from.

He had a memory of something similar, but it took a while to dredge it up from the confusion of his past. He remembered Melyn's chambers, a meeting with the inquisitor abruptly cut short. He had stood guard outside his chambers, but why would he have done that? Surely Osgal was never far from Melyn. But Osgal had been ill, had eaten something that disagreed with him. Errol could picture the captain's face almost perfectly, green where usually it was florid and sweaty. He had stood guard outside Melyn's chambers while the captain took himself off to the privy. The lines had drawn him in, past whatever magical wards Melyn had placed on his door, and he had seen the inquisitor in conversation with a dragon, pretending to be one himself, tricking the creature into giving her location away.

The memories slotted themselves back together out of

the maelstrom of images and voices that assaulted him whenever he tried to think back to his time at Emmass Fawr. Errol knew that Melyn had worked some terrible magic on his mind, filling it with false ideas and thoughts skilfully blended with the truth until he could scarcely tell which was which. But now, here, with this strange voice calling to him through the lines, some of it began to make sense.

'Come to me, dragons of Gwlad. Come to my side.'

Like straining his ears to try and pinpoint the source of a noise, Errol tried to determine where the voice he heard directly in his head originated. It was coming to him along the lines, of that much he was sure, but it seemed to come from all directions. Even the pull behind the words was formless: it filled him with an unsettling urge to act, to move, but gave no indication of where he should go. Frustrated, he pulled away and struggled to his feet. He walked slowly back to his clothes, letting the wind dry him as he went and scanning the skies all the while. He needed to talk to Benfro – perhaps he would be able to throw some light on the mystery – but the dragon was nowhere to be seen.

Pulling on his trousers and shirt, Errol went back to the cave and stoked up the fire, warming himself as best he could without touching the Grym and that unsettling call. He sat for some time wondering about the voice. What could it mean? Were there other dragons out there? Had Benfro heard the call himself and flown off in search of this female? Was she still calling? His natural curiosity, so long suppressed by Melyn's influence, niggled at him until he just had to find some answers. He brought the lines back into his focus, felt out along them, savouring the different textures each one presented to him, always trying to keep himself centred. He wanted to listen, not to be drawn down any one path, or worse, all of them at once.

'Dragons of Gwlad, hear my call. You who walk the long road, I am Frecknock, daughter of Sir Teifi teul Albarn. Come to me.'

For an instant Errol thought he heard something else, then the dragon opened her eyes. He could see what she saw: a small clearing in the middle of the forest, a clear blue sky. In the distance a rocky outcrop speared out of the trees like the bleached and dried hulk of some long-dead leviathan and overhead, descending on outstretched wings, Benfro?

Startled, Errol almost lost whatever strange connection it was he had made through the lines. The vision dimmed and he could see the cave, the fire flickering as it ate into the dry wood. Closing his eyes, he concentrated on the sense of longing that Frecknock seemed to exude. At once he was back with her, watching as a huge creature wheeled and swooped down. Now that he could see it properly, Errol realized that the dragon was not Benfro. He, and it had to be male, was twice Benfro's size, his wings larger still, blanking out the sun high overhead as he came in to land. Errol was buffeted by a great wind that knocked him back both physically and in his mind. He was pushed away from the scene into his own body, falling back on to his bed in the cave, with such force that he tipped over backwards, knocking his head against the stone wall. Dazed, he sat back up again, felt his skull for lumps. He tried to reconnect with the dragon, but he could hear nothing, though the lines were there as clear as ever. The feeling of longing was gone too, which Errol supposed made sense. If Frecknock had found what she was looking for, then she would of course stop her calling.

A noise outside the cave distracted Errol from his musings. He levered himself up off his bed and went to see what was happening. As he emerged into the light, he saw Benfro pick himself up off the ground at the far side of the clearing. Dusting himself off with a shake like a wet dog, the dragon slung something over his shoulder and started the long walk to the cave. It was unusual for him to make a bad landing these days, Errol thought.

As the dragon came closer, Errol could see that he carried a large deer, already gutted and cleaned.

'Good hunting, I see.' He nodded towards the dead beast. Benfro said nothing, slapping the carcass down on a flat-topped rock and beginning the process of skinning, jointing and butchering. Errol ignored the silence; Benfro was always a bit surly when he fluffed a landing. 'Did you fly far today?'

Benfro continued to hack away at the deer with his talons. They were formidable weapons, Errol could see, and the dragon would have made a fearsome enemy for even a skilled warrior priest, such was his size now. But he was a child in comparison to the dragon Errol had just seen.

'I almost didn't come back.' Benfro didn't turn as he spoke, and his voice was so quiet Errol had to strain to hear him over the roar of the waterfall. 'I was chasing eagles in the morning, and it wasn't until midday I realized I was heading south, to Cenobus.'

'Cenobus?'

'You know, Magog's ruined palace. Where his repository is, and all those jewels. I was so near I could see it sticking out of the trees like a great stone finger. As soon as I realized, I turned away, but it's taken me all day to fly back. I only stopped the once, when I spotted this deer a few miles south of here. Every time I think I'm beginning to fend Magog off, he finds a new way to get to me. I didn't even feel him this time, just a strange compulsion to fly south.'

'It might not have been Magog.' Errol tried to make out Benfro's aura and the almost invisible loop of the rose cord that tied him to the red jewel hidden in Corwen's cave. That he found it almost impossible to see showed that Magog's influence was minimal, and the colours shifting and swirling around the dragon were far more vibrant than he had ever seen them. Benfro was in rude health.

'What do you mean?' Benfro finally turned, still holding a slab of venison in one hand, dark blood dripping from his claws and covering the top of the flat rock.

'I heard a dragon make a calling this afternoon.' Errol told Benfro all that he had seen and heard, watching the expression change on the dragon's face from weary resignation to wonder and perhaps fear.

'This dragon you saw,' Benfro asked when Errol had finally finished. 'Was there anything noticeable about him? Apart from his size?'

Errol thought back to the brief glimpses he had seen, trying to build a picture of the creature beyond his sheer size. Details came to him now – the shape of his ears and the tufts of hair that sprouted from their ends like in the pictures of mountain cats he had seen in the library archives at Emmass Fawr. The dragon's wings had been patterned too, each one showing an image of a dragon with its wings outstretched, and on them a pattern of a dragon, and so on in mesmerizing detail. But there was one detail he had missed before, though rebuilding the image in his head, it was strange that he could have overlooked it.

'He had one hand in some kind of bandage, strapped to his chest.'

'Then he's the same dragon I saw before, flying over Cenobus. And you're sure it was Frecknock who was calling him?'

'That's what she said her name was: Frecknock, daughter of Sir Teifi teul Albarn. I didn't see her, but her voice was familiar. I think I saw her once before, when she spoke to Melyn.'

'But that doesn't make sense. Melyn captured her and took her off to Candlehall in chains. There's no way she could have escaped from the queen.'

Errol's hand went up to his chest, feeling the pain of Beulah's knife sliding between his ribs even though there was no longer even a scar to mark its passage. Most of his memories of that time were a haze of drugs and pain, but he remembered a dragon, small and frightened, chained to the Obsidian Throne like some obscene parody of the toy dogs favoured by court ladies.

'I saw her at Candlehall,' Errol said, dredging up the past. 'I spoke to her, but she didn't reply. She couldn't have escaped from there alive.'

'So what's she doing in the forest not more than a day's flight from here?'

*

Corris was a miserable little town clinging to the highest navigable reaches of the mighty River Hafren. Even so, seeing its low defensive wall surrounding a motley collection of two- and three-storey houses clustered around the unimposing bulk of the castle, Beulah could have wept for joy.

They had dumped the dead mercenaries in the woods after searching them for any clues as to who might have paid them and finding nothing more illuminating than a large supply of narcotic leaves, which explained the berserker rage of the attack. Two warrior priests had been killed, and they were given a proper burial, then the wounded had been loaded on to one of the carts and the whole royal procession set off once again, silent and more vigilant. Beulah herself had refused to ride in a wagon, taking the horse of one of the dead warrior priests and hoping it would last her longer than her previous mount.

Her arm hurt constantly, the jerking of the horse's walk making it almost impossible to concentrate on tapping the Grym to speed her healing. At least the crossbow quarrel that had hit her had not been poisoned and the wound had been clean. Once the field surgeon had stitched it up and the bleeding had stopped, she had gritted her teeth against the discomfort and tried to show a brave face to her guard.

There had been a small but noticeable shift in the hierarchy of the group. In the days before the attack the captain had taken his orders from her and passed them on to his men without so much as consulting Clun. That was fair enough, Beulah supposed; Captain Celtin was an experienced warrior priest, and despite what Melyn might say, Clun was still a novitiate who hadn't finished his training. But since the fight the captain had deferred to Clun in almost everything. The whole troop looked up to him now. For his part, Clun was bemused by their sudden change in attitude, unaware of the stir his use of two blades of light had caused.

Beulah had asked him about it, and he had merely replied that he had needed two blades to fight off so many attackers. No one had ever told him he couldn't have two at once. It had seemed the natural thing to do.

She smiled at the memory as her horse walked slowly down the well-used track towards the sleepy little town. Ahead of her, the gates stood closed, but Corris promised hot water to wash in, clean linen and dry beds, and food that hadn't been burned to a crisp over a campfire. It had never been part of the plan to spend long there; their itinerary took them swiftly downstream, first to Beylinstown, then to Castell Glas. Beulah would send a messenger ahead, warning Lord Beylin of their delay and requesting more patrols on the roads. Meantime she had business to attend to in this backwater.

As the party approached the gates, they flew open and a band of mounted soldiers rode out at a gallop. Without a word, the warrior priests formed a shield around the main party, fanning out to cover the road and the verges alongside. As the soldiers neared, the warrior priests conjured their blades, ready for an attack. But before they were closer than a half-hundred paces, the troop of soldiers reined to a halt, their leader leaping from his horse and kneeling in the road, where he remained until the travellers halted in front of him.

'Your Majesty, I have just received word of your visit. Please forgive me. Had I known, I would have ridden out to meet you days ago. The woods around here are not as safe as . . .' He trailed off as he looked up and saw the state of the royal party, his eyes widening, his mouth hanging open. Beulah nudged her horse forward, noting idly that it responded much better to her commands than the previous animal. She rode through the line of warrior priests, Clun at her side, and stopped within sword reach of the kneeling man.

'And you are?'

'Captain Herren of the Corris Guard, Your Majesty.' The soldier bowed even lower.

'Look at me, Captain Herren.' He complied, and Beulah stared into his eyes. He wasn't a man given to fear; battle didn't worry him, she could see. And yet he was plainly terrified of her. She brushed his mind, trying to discern whether what he said was true. It was possible that their messenger hadn't arrived, that he lay somewhere in the woods, feeding the animals, naked and dead at the hands of the same brigands who had attacked her party. Possible but unlikely.

'When did you hear of our visit, Captain?'

'Your Majesty, are you wounded? What happened?'

'Answer the queen's question.' Clun conjured his blade of light, thinner and longer than normal, and pointed it straight at Herren's head, the tip just a hand's breadth from his sweat-sheened brow.

'Just this morning.' The captain gulped. 'We'd heard you was going to Beylinstown, thought you might come by this way, since it's on the road. But we didn't hear nothing. Then we got word of a big party attacked out on the moors. We've been tracking a group of bandits around there for months now. I swear, Your Majesty, if I'd known I'd have been out there myself waiting for you.'

Beulah tried to keep up with the man's racing thoughts, fighting against the pain from her wound. There was some subterfuge in him, she could tell, but it wasn't aimed directly at her. It was true that he hadn't known she was coming, true too that they had been hunting a band of brigands in the nearby woods for months now, but the reason he hadn't been out on the road was less clear, as if the captain wasn't quite sure himself. She would let him live, at least for now.

'Send word to your lord. We will be taking up residence for a few days. Our wounded need tending.' Beulah nodded, and Clun extinguished his blade to the captain's palpable relief.

'Of course, Your Majesty. I will see to it myself.' He bowed and rose.

'Oh, Captain. One more thing.'

'Your Majesty?'

'You needn't worry about that band of brigands any more. We left their bodies for the crows.'

The captain nodded his understanding, swinging up into his saddle and turning back towards the town. He rode off at a similarly frenetic pace to the gallop that had brought him, his men falling in behind. The gates stayed open behind them, and the royal party passed through at a more leisurely pace.

Beulah's impression of Corris worsened with closer inspection. The three-storey buildings she had seen from afar were almost all warehouses ranged along the river-bank, and all of them were run-down. Some had no roofs, only weathered grey timber rafters reaching for the sky like skeletal fingers. Crumbling eye-socket windows stared sightlessly on to the streets and one terrace end had collapsed, spilling rubble into the swollen river. As they rode past, children stopped playing among the stones to stare open-mouthed at the warrior priests. Clothed in rags, they wore no shoes on their feet.

Tightly packed houses lined the narrow streets leading from the riverfront up to the castle. Beulah saw occasional flickers of movement from windows, the odd door pulled hastily closed, but otherwise the town seemed deserted. Tufts of grass and small flowers grew between the cobbles. Everything had about it an air of seedy decay.

The castle itself wasn't much better. Two elderly guards stood at the open gates, but it would have been as easy to get in over the rubble where a section of the wall had collapsed. Wooden scaffolding suggested that repairs were under way, but there was no sign of any workmen, no mixing of mortar or shaping of stones, and the rickety structure erected around the breach looked like it would crack under the weight of no more than an apprentice.

Though the royal party was not large, it was not possible to fit them all into the courtyard. The castle itself consisted of an ancient round tower five or six storeys high, with slits for windows and a narrow wooden door at the top of a steep flight of stone steps. Beulah recognized the design from her studies of warfare; it dated back at least five centuries. Any self-respecting lord would have demolished it and started again, or at least remodelled it into a more comfortable home. Her hopes of decent medical care for the wounded, of hot water and baths, receded. More so when the door to the tower creaked open.

Captain Herren, his riding cloak swapped for a moth-eaten herald's tabard, walked slowly down the steps ahead of a decrepit old man bent low and supporting his weight on a gnarled cane. When they finally reached the bottom of the steps, the captain once more went down on one knee – over-theatrically, Beulah thought.

'Your Majesty, on behalf of Lord Queln, I bid you welcome to Corris.'

'And is Lord Queln incapable of welcoming me himself?' Beulah dismounted from her horse, not without some discomfort, and stepped forward. The old man shuffled a bit, wheezing as if the walk down the steps had exhausted him. He coughed once, then looked up through rheumy eyes, blinking as if he had only just noticed his courtyard crammed with people, horses and wagons.

'Eh? Herren? What's all this about then? What've you dragged me down here for?'

'Her Majesty the queen, sir.' The captain tried to whisper out of the side of his mouth and smile at Beulah at the same time. Had she not been in some pain, she might have found it amusing. As it was, her anger, never far from the surface, came to the boil. Who were these people to treat her like a common traveller? And what lord could run his fiefdom so poorly that he couldn't even afford to maintain his own castle? The same sort of lord who would let armed brigands roam the roads he was supposed to protect. The sort of lord who might soon find himself without a fiefdom.

'Lord Queln, is it?' She walked to the old man, who looked up with considerable difficulty, seeing her for the first time. His back was so bent and his neck so crooked he seemed to spend most of his time peering at the ground.

'And who are you, young lady?' Queln took quick glances, tilting his head sideways in a manner that reminded Beulah disturbingly of a fly on a sunlit window-sill. After each glimpse he dropped his head swiftly, as if holding it up pained him.

'I am your queen.'

It finally seemed to sink into the old man's doddery brain. He stiffened noticeably, lifting his head once more, slowly this time, and fixing Beulah with a watery stare. Then he dropped his head back down again, bending his back even more so that she feared he would topple over into the dirt of the courtyard.

'Your Majesty, forgive my rudeness. I was not informed of your visit.'

'So everyone tells me. But it's of no matter. We have wounded who need tending, and all of us could do with a wash and a good meal. Have your staff prepare some rooms for us.'

'Of course, ma'am. At once.' Queln looked from side to side as if trying to find his servant. 'Herren?'

'I am here, sir.' The captain stood and touched his lord's arm as if he were blind rather than addled.

'Herren, it seems the queen is here,' Queln said. 'Damned odd if you ask me. I thought we had a king. But there it is. See if you can't rustle up something for her and her friends, there's a good chap. Can't have our reputation for hospitality being ruined now, can we?'

'Indeed not, sir. I've already spoken to old Missus Benton in the kitchens, and the chambermaids are airing the guest rooms as we speak.' He turned back to Beulah, who wasn't sure whether to run Lord Queln through with her blade for his rudeness or laugh at his obvious senility. 'My lord's not been a well man for many years now, Your Majesty. Not since his only son rode off to war and never came back. We do our best for him, but it's not easy. Please follow me. I will show you to your rooms.'

They left Lord Queln in his courtyard and followed Herren up the steps. Beyond the narrow oak door, the castle maintained the air of shabbiness it wore on the outside. What little light reached the window slits had to contend with inch-thick glass as green as water in a dying pond. The tapestries that hung from the thick stone walls may once have depicted hunting scenes or stories from the early days of the Twin Kingdoms but now were all a uniform grey. Clun walked up to one, peering closely at it as if he might be able to make out some detail. He reached forward and tapped the fabric lightly, enveloping himself in a choking cloud that tumbled down the length of the drape, from the ceiling to the floor, gathering momentum like loose snow in the mountains. Beulah hoped that their rooms would be better cleaned, though judging by the scurrying chambermaids they would more likely smell of recently disturbed dust.

'Who runs this fiefdom, Captain?' Beulah asked as they made their way up more narrow winding stairs to the third floor, where the main guest rooms were situated.

'His lordship does what he can, Your Majesty. I see to the keeping of law and order, and Father Tolley runs the administration, the collection of taxes and so on. Corris isn't the port it used to be.'

'This Father Tolley. He'd be a predicant of the Candle, I take it? One of Padraig's men.'

'Indeed he is, Your Majesty.'

'Correct protocol, when addressing your monarch, is to use the title Your Majesty only on first meeting. After that, you should call me ma'am. I must admit I have little time for such nonsense, but the people expect it. Now tell me, Captain. Where is this wayward Candle? Why wasn't he here to greet me?'

Captain Herren stopped mid-step, turning to face the queen. So this is his guilty little secret, Beulah thought.

'He left for Beylinstown about three days ago, Your . . . ma'am.'

'Did he say why he was going there?'

'No, ma'am. Just that we weren't to go after the bandits until he got back. I assumed he was going to ask his superior to petition Lord Beylin for help.'

'And that's why you weren't out on the road yesterday, when we were attacked?' Beulah skimmed the edge of the captain's thoughts, searching for duplicity and finding none. In truth, he was rather a simple-minded man. Not stupid, but not imaginative either. Good material for a guardsman, probably not the best choice for captain. She wondered whose decision that had been, Lord Queln's or Father Tolley's

'Yes, ma'am.'

The rooms they were shown into were surprisingly clean and spacious, though dark. A fire had been lit in the hearth, and through a small door Beulah found an ancient but large bathtub already filled with hot water. She had expected to see a stream of serving girls bringing pitchers up from the kitchens, but wide copper pipes snaked around the walls, disappearing through the stone to the back of the fireplace. Such sophisticated plumbing was so out of place in the crumbling old castle, she almost laughed.

Stripping off her road clothes, she dropped them in a pile by the door and lowered herself into the hot water, sighing in delight at one of the simpler pleasures life could bring, soaking away the dust and the aches of being so long in the saddle, while Clun attended to the wound in her arm and the ugly blistered burn on her palm.

'Do you not find this place a little strange, my love?' she asked as he knelt by the side of the tub and massaged her shoulders.

'Corris has been going downhill for years. The river's silted up and the big barges can't make it further than Wright's Ford these days. Lord Beylin spent his money improving the road from there, rather than fighting nature and dredging the river.'

'I didn't mean the poverty.' Beulah had once again forgotten that Clun was a merchant's son. His knowledge of the geography of the Twin Kingdoms was the equal of her own, perhaps even better as he seemed to know more about the commercial wealth of each town they visited, whereas all she could remember were the names of the local aristocracy. 'I meant Lord Queln. He's plainly senile, and yet no one has stepped forward to take his place. If Padraig had heard of his state, he would have petitioned me to appoint a successor.'

'Maybe it slipped his mind.'

'You don't know the seneschal well, my love. Nothing slips his mind. If he hasn't brought this to my attention, it is because he is unaware of it.' Beulah climbed out of the now-lukewarm water, accepting a towel and drying herself. Wrapped tightly in a clean bandage, her arm ached but was largely pain free; the same could not be said of her palm, which throbbed in time with her heartbeat. She would have liked a chance to meditate and focus the power of the Grym on healing herself, but she needed answers to too many questions to settle her mind.

The great hall was like something from an ancient fairy tale. A huge open fireplace burned logs the size of small trees, casting a flickering light on two long tables arranged in parallel with low benches along both sides of each. At the far end of the room, raised on a dais, a smaller table sat in front of a large carved throne. Made of oak or a similar wood and almost black with age, this was a facsimile in miniature of the Obsidian Throne back at Candlehall. Two smaller chairs with ornately carved high backs were placed one on either side. All three were unoccupied.

At first Beulah thought that the hall was empty, but a noise from the fireplace, barely audible over the crackling logs, caught her attention. Sitting on a low stool by the hearth, staring into the flames, was Lord Queln.

'My lord, I must thank you for your kind hospitality,' Beulah said, crossing the hall with Clun and feeling the fierce heat of the fire on her face from ten paces away. How could Queln bear to sit so close? 'I was particularly impressed with the plumbing.'

'Eh? Oh?' Queln looked round as if trying to locate the source of this new noise. Perhaps he truly was blind, Beulah thought. It would explain a lot.

'Your Majesty. I must apologize for my rudeness. No one told me you were coming. Had I but a day's notice . . .'

'It's no matter, Queln. I'm not so pampered that I can't cope with a little hardship. But heralds were sent out over two weeks ago. Are you telling me none made it here?'

'I don't recall meeting one, ma'am. My memory's not what it was. Tolley normally deals with day-to-day things like that, but I can't seem to find him.'

'Captain Herren tells me Father Tolley left a few days ago for Beylinstown. Why would he go there?'

'Herren. He's a good man. A good soldier. He's my grandson, you know.'

Beulah was almost distracted from her question by the admission. Almost, but not quite. There was something not quite right about Queln. She had thought him senile, but perhaps there was a deeper malaise.

'Father Tolley, Lord Queln. Why did he go to Beylinstown?' Beulah tried to catch the old man's eyes, brushing the edges of his thoughts to see what reaction the priest's name provoked.

'My son. My lovely Gerrid. He had a bit of a roving eye, you see. Always after the serving lasses. Who knows? Half of the town might be his children. It wouldn't surprise me. But Herren's the one I can be sure of. He has his father's eyes.' Queln's face slackened, and his head turned back to the fire as if he had been speaking to a page rather than his monarch. Beulah's anger flickered at the snub, and she used that surge of power to push deeper into his thoughts.

He wasn't senile, of that much she could be sure. His mind was a mess, but only because someone had made it that way. It was as skilled a working as any she had seen Melyn perform, taking snippets of memory and mixing them together, jumbling up the order of things, confusing an old man to make him more suggestible.

Beulah knelt in front of Queln, putting her hands on his knees. Instinctively he looked straight at her, and she gazed deep into his eyes.

'Father Tolley. Where did he really go?' An image flickered in Queln's thoughts, a series of fragments that assembled to form a person. Short, thin, wearing the traditional robes of a predicant, black hair slicked back over a pale almost pointed skull, a nasal, weasely voice that seemed to fill her head.

'Your reign will be short, Queen Beulah of the stolen throne.' Queln's voice was completely different, hard and cold. He reached forward, grasping Beulah's hands with his own. In the flickering orange glow of the firelight his face was contorted, veins bulging at his temples, sweat beading on his forehead and nose. 'The true king is coming, and he will wipe all but his own followers from the face of Gwlad. Enjoy your days while you can. They won't last.'

Riding Queln's thoughts, Beulah felt the full impact of the words. It was as if they had been planted in his head, waiting for the moment when she uncovered them. And whoever had put them there had left a small surprise too. She saw it just in time and leaped back, pulling her hands free, wrenching her mind away as Queln went into a spasm. Clun jumped forward to shield her, but the old man posed no threat now she had released him. He writhed, his bent back twisting and buckling until he fell off the stool and on to the floor. His breath came out in gurgling choking coughs, as if something were stuck in his throat. Blood leaked from his nose and ears, then from his eyelids, streaming down his cheeks in a parody of tears.

'Lord Queln.' Clun knelt down beside the old man, grasping his arms to stop him convulsing. Beulah just looked on; she knew that there was nothing anyone could do to save the man. Someone had killed him a long time ago, but it took a few more minutes for Lord Queln to die.

14

And the Shepherd, leaving his Hall of Candles, went out into Gwlad, even to the lair of the Wolf. And here he called out to his old foe, saying, 'Wolf, you are cowardly, attacking my flock in the night. Come, fight me cleanly, fairly. In the light. And if you can defeat me you may have your feast of all.'

Taunted by the words of the Shepherd and greedy for his offer, the Wolf came snarling even from the very depths of his lair. Though it was day, he launched himself at the Shepherd with fangs bared and claws drawn.

But the Shepherd was wise. He had prepared for this. And seeing the Wolf's evil spread all over his beloved Gwlad had determined to rid the world of it for ever. And so he gathered the Wolf to his breast and carried the snarling beast with him to the stars.

Their fight may last a thousand thousand years, but when it is done the Shepherd will once more return to his chosen, and the Wolf will be vanquished for ever.

The Book of the Shepherd

Melyn steered his horse through the rocks, leaning forward to keep his balance as the beast struggled up the steep path. They had cleared the treeline about an hour earlier and now he could look out over the sprawling mass of the forest as it spread away from him.

The track was narrow, picking a path between huge boulders that seemed almost to have been carved. At first they had been able to ride three or four abreast, and the warrior priests had spoken quietly among themselves, sharing their experiences of the fight with the dragon. Now they were down to single file, Melyn in the middle of the group with Frecknock walking ahead of him, and everyone was silent. Overhead, the sun beat down on them through hazy clouds, heating the air and making everything seem heavy. A storm was on its way.

The climb took far longer than he had expected. From the clearing where they had battled Caradoc the rocky ridge had seemed no more than a half-hour's ride away, but as with everything else in the forest this was a deception. Four or five times higher than he had estimated, it had taken them all morning to reach. Now, making their slow way up towards its spine, Melyn imagined they must look something like a line of ants headed back to the nest with their spoils. The thought of riding towards a nest made him uneasy. The creature they hunted was somewhat larger than an ant.

The little column stopped, and Melyn almost rode into the back of Frecknock. She had said little since the failed ambush, and he couldn't find it in himself to blame her for the fiasco, even though he had lost a good man. She had done all that he had asked of her, perhaps even more. If there were blame to be apportioned, then it was his. He had underestimated his enemy twice now. He wouldn't make that mistake a third time.

'What's going on?' Melyn saw Captain Osgal dismount and pick his way back along the track towards him.

'Can't ride any further, Your Grace,' Osgal said. 'The path's too narrow and steep. A horse could break its leg with a man on its back. We'll have to lead them from here.'

Melyn knew Osgal doted on his horse, but he could also see the wisdom in the man's words. It was a long way back to the main camp and the spare horses. This diversion to track down and kill the renegade dragon had already taken too much time; he couldn't afford to waste more while half of his troop walked back through the forest.

Nodding his agreement, Melyn dismounted, his knees creaking. The other warrior priests followed suit, and they were soon off again, trudging up the winding path. Ahead of him Frecknock appeared to be paying a lot of attention to the rocks, occasionally tripping over her feet as she wasn't looking where she was going.

'What is it?' Melyn asked. 'What can you see?'

She turned back towards him, forcing those behind him to stop while the rest carried on ahead.

'These rocks and boulders. They were once a building. A vast building. But something destroyed it.'

Melyn looked at the nearest boulder. It was almost square, its edges chipped and rounded by the wind and rain. Twice as high as him, its flat surfaces were dimpled and cracked just like any other boulder. He couldn't see how it could have been part of anything. It was far too big.

'Nothing could move a rock this size. Not even that creature Caradoc. It's just tumbled down in an earthquake.'

'Begging your pardon, Your Grace, but if you look more closely, you can see where it's been carved out of a quarry. See, here, and here?' Frecknock pointed with her long taloned finger, the claw extruding from its tip in an unconscious reminder of her beastly nature. Melyn moved closer to the rock and peered at its surface. There were striations, marks that could have been made by a chisel, but he wasn't convinced.

'You're imagining things,' he said, pulling his horse by its reins as he stepped forward.

'Then what about these?' Frecknock pointed to a jumble of smaller rocks a little off the path. Wondering why he was humouring her, Melyn allowed himself to be led towards them. They were made from the same stone as the ridge. Everything around him was the same material, dark red granite made friable by endless wind and rain. There was nothing remarkable about them, and yet as Frecknock bent down, grasped one of the rocks and heaved it over, he couldn't help but feel a tingle of anticipation.

'There. I thought so.' The dragon stepped back so he could see.

It was ornately carved; no weathering this. Quite plainly a craftsmen of great skill had chipped and smoothed out an image in the surface of the rock. Kneeling before it, Melyn traced his finger over the form, trying to work out what it could be. This piece was obviously just a small chunk broken off a much larger whole.

'What is it?'

'I think it's part of a wing tip.' Frecknock crouched

down beside him, reaching out to the stonework and tracing her extended claw over the shape. 'See. You can make out the scales on the leading edge, and here's the last joint.'

'No, it's part of an arm, and a spear.' Melyn looked back at the enormous square block and the hundreds of others like it scattered all over the ridge. 'But you're right: at least some of these blocks have been cut for building.'

He pushed himself back up on to his feet and went to retrieve his horse. Frecknock looked like she wanted to explore the rubble more, but she dragged herself away and rejoined the line.

Melyn noted more obvious carving as they continued up through the afternoon. A light wind built up with their increased altitude, whipping a fine dust into little whirlwinds that skidded across the path, alternately blanking out the view ahead or plunging them into choking, eye-watering darkness. And still they climbed.

He had thought himself fit, but Melyn was sweating profusely by the time they neared the crest. The larger boulders thinned out, leaving a barren desert of smaller rocks and more dust for the wind to play with. The path widened, no longer constricted by the big blocks, but still they couldn't see the top, each new rise just revealing another false summit. And then, finally, they crested the last ridge, and the warrior priest at the head of the troop stopped in his tracks, forcing those following to fan out into the rubble. Angered, Melyn pushed his way through to see what could break the discipline of his elite troops.

It was an arch not unlike Brynceri's back at Emmass Fawr. Only where that rose over the road away from other buildings, this one had been incorporated into a massive wall that stretched across the top of the rocky outcrop, reaching more than five hundred paces across to the cliffs on either side. The wall was crumbling in places, almost completely gone near the western edge, but in the middle it climbed three or four storeys high.

'What is this place?' Captain Osgal spoke the words, but Melyn knew all his men were thinking the same thing. It felt wrong, as if it had been hidden away for a long time and still didn't want to be discovered.

'I think this is Cenobus, the fabled palace of Magog, Son of the Summer Moon.' Melyn looked around to see Frecknock standing beside him. Her expression was even more rapt than when she had first seen Caradoc.

Melyn laughed. 'Magog is a myth, Cenobus too. And even if it did exist, it would be far more remote than this. Prince Lonk searched the forest for months, and when Father Keoldale left the party they still hadn't found it. I've ridden these woods before and never seen anything like this.'

'Can't you see? It's been protected by incredible workings. I've never seen such skilled use of the subtle arts.' Frecknock stepped forward, looking at the air, her hands reaching out to things that weren't there. 'But something's broken the spell. And recently, too. It's slowly leaching away.'

Melyn shifted his focus, letting the lines come to his view. Despite the absence of anything living, they covered the ground more densely than he had seen them anywhere outside the Neuadd or Emmass Fawr. It was almost as if this barren ridge, poking out of the middle of the forest, was a focus for all the life concentrated around it, sucking it in like he might tap it to conjure his blade of light. But why would a ruined building do that?

'You're looking at it wrong. How do you call the sight? The aethereal?' Frecknock looked back at Melyn, who was wondering just how much of his magic she knew and understood. Still, he took her advice and slipped into the trance that would let him see the aethereal, viewing the palace as he had directed their passage through the forest.

And then he understood why so many men had tried and failed to find this place, why so many had disappeared in the search. The whole ridge swirled with patterns of light. It was as if it were not rock but some sleeping giant, who had lain so long that the forest had grown up around him. There was no other way Melyn could describe it – the mountain was alive. But it was dying too. The colours were fading, their power seeping back into the land. The power of the Grym was reclaiming the rubble fields, pin-pricks of light showing where mosses and lichens were beginning to grow.

'Do you see it now, Your Grace?'

Melyn looked at Frecknock and almost slipped out of his trance. She was still recognizably the dragon who had betrayed her own in search of a mate, who had made herself so pathetic that even he hadn't the heart to kill her. But she was also a regal creature, glowing with an energy that surrounded her like a great halo. The assembled warrior priests were shadowy flickers in comparison, their self-images poorly formed. He doubted that they saw anything more than a jumbled mess of ruined buildings. The flow of power through this place was lost on them.

Then he realized what it was that had been with him ever since he had begun the long slow climb up the mountain to this ancient ruin. He felt in the presence of his god. Not the all-enveloping peace, the healing power and sense of omnipotence, but more the comfort of prayer. This whole place was holy ground, sanctuary.

And the beast Caradoc had sullied it by taking refuge here.

Melyn pulled out of his trance. 'With me, men. We've got a dragon to slay.' To his normal sight the ruin looked dead, uninviting, almost daunting. It seemed to shrink in on itself as he stared at it, the last vestiges of its protective magic trying to turn him away.

They picked their way across the rubble to climb wide shallow steps towards the arch. Cut into the steps were channels wide enough apart to allow wagons to negotiate the gradient but also designed to drain rainwater from the steps. All around lay the remnants of a settlement built on a vast scale: great halls delineated by the lowest stones of their walls; passageways wide enough to let a half dozen horses pass now choked with rubble; columns toppled, their constituent blocks stretching out for dozens of paces, exaggerating their already impressive length. Some incredible catastrophe had befallen this place; something had razed it to the ground in a single instant, casting blocks of stone as big as houses down the hillside for miles, turning almost everything up here on the summit to rubble and dust. And yet ahead of Melyn the arch still stood and the wall towered over his men. How could they have survived when all around had crumbled?

It was the Grym, of course, the force that flowed

through everything. But the workings that could have bent it to this purpose made him shiver. They were so far beyond anything he had ever imagined possible. No wonder this place reeked of the Shepherd; this had to have been a place of great importance to him, like Candlehall and the Neuadd.

But that thought troubled him. If this place was the work of the Shepherd, then what had destroyed it? And why had his god allowed a dragon, a creature of the Wolf, to take up residence in this place, even if it was a ruin?

Melyn stopped on the threshold and all his warrior priests hesitated too, as if something held them back. The power about the place was a heady sensation, like the befuddlement of too much Fo Afron wine. It was all too tempting to dive in, to lose himself. Only a lifetime of control held him back.

'Captain Osgal, I want you to take two men and guard this gate,' he said. 'The rest of us will go inside, including Frecknock.' He nodded at the dragon, who was still staring wide-eyed at things no one else could see. 'If we're not back in two hours, send one man into the courtyard, but only as far as you can see him from this gateway, and have him perform a summoning spell. Keep doing that every hour for two days. After that return to the main camp and take our forces back to Candlehall.'

'Your Grace, surely you can't –'

'This place is a magical gold mine, Jerrim.' Melyn used the captain's first name to calm his obvious agitation. 'Our dragon's gone to ground in here somewhere. I aim to track him down and destroy him. But there are powerful spells beyond this archway, and they're collapsing in on themselves. Don't worry, old friend. I will come back, but I must plan for every eventuality.'

Osgal nodded once, shouting to two men, who split off from the main group. Melyn turned to the remaining warrior priests, searching their faces for signs of trepidation and finding none. Good, he thought. I've trained them well. Now let's put that training to a real test.

Without a word, he stepped through the doorway into the courtyard beyond.

For the briefest of instants Melyn thought he had stepped under an ice-cold stream of water. His whole body tingled and shuddered involuntarily, as if someone were walking on his grave. And then he was standing on the other side of the arch, looking across a nondescript courtyard towards what had no doubt once been a large building. One by one, as if they had pushed through heavy drapes, Melyn became aware of the other warrior priests entering the courtyard, and then the dragon Frecknock came through. Such was the power of her presence that he had to turn and face her, to reassure himself that it was the same slight self-effacing creature he had brought with him.

She looked the same, still staring open-mouthed at things that weren't there, and yet he could see a difference in her posture that should have infuriated him. She looked confident, unconcerned about the men surrounding her, any one of whom could have cut her down in an instant. She was no longer afraid, and that should have been reason enough for him to have her killed. Yet Melyn couldn't help feeling a strange elation. He had won her over completely now. He could see it. No matter that he had killed her extended family; no matter that he represented all she had feared and despised for the whole of her life. He had shown her things she had never thought possible. She would follow him to the ends of Gwlad just for the chance of more.

'Do you have any idea where the beast is?' Melyn asked the dragon. It took her a while to realize she was being addressed.

'No, Your Grace. I'm sorry. But this place is so confusing, so full of memories.

'It's no matter. We'll just have to search the old-fashioned way. We know Caradoc's large, so we can ignore the smaller passageways. We'll split into groups. Return here in one hour regardless of whether you've found anything or not.'

Melyn nodded to one of the warrior priests to follow him and gestured for Frecknock to join them. They set off across the courtyard for the door directly opposite the archway. Shards of ancient dried oak hung from hinges rusted almost to nothing, but the step was free of dust, no doubt blown clean by the endless wind that whistled across the ridge. Stepping into the darkness, Melyn conjured a ball of fire to illuminate the room. The warrior priest with him did likewise, but the dragon hung back, seemingly unwilling to cross the threshold, certainly not about to use magic without permission.

'Come, Frecknock. I have need of your expertise here.'

She hesitated for a moment, then ducked through the doorway, even though it towered over her, easily big enough for a wagon, or an unusually large and feral dragon, to pass through.

It was cool inside after the heat of the afternoon sun. Melyn sniffed the dry dusty air, hoping for some small scent of Caradoc, but he could make out nothing past the smell of cold stone. As his eyes adjusted to the low light, he could see he was in a large hall with a huge open fireplace at the far end. A long table, too high for men to use comfortably, stood by the cold hearth, with a single chair of the kind he had seen in the dragon village positioned at one end.

A place had been laid at the table. Melyn hoisted himself on to the chair and peered at the remains of a meal. It had dried rather than rotted, leaving desiccated vegetables and a curled piece of what looked like fish laid out on a wide gold plate. A heavy tankard sat empty beside it.

'Do you think it was here, sir?' Melyn looked down at the warrior priest who had joined him, noticing as he did that Frecknock had moved to the far side of the hall and was peering into a darkened doorway. He thought of the cottage in the woods back at Pwllpeiran, the bowl in the ground formed by the roots of an overturned tree and filled with the rotting carcasses of dozens of sheep, cattle. The two human skeletons picked clean.

'No, this is too civilized.' Melyn jumped down from the chair, feeling a bit like a child, dwarfed by its size. 'And whoever started this meal did so many months ago.'

'It was Benfro.' Frecknock was perhaps thirty paces away, but her voice carried as if she were standing right beside him.

'Benfro?'

'He came through here some time ago.'

'How do you know?' Melyn walked swiftly across the room to where Frecknock was standing. The doorway opened on to deeper darkness with the faintest of breezes stirring the air, bringing up with it odours of dry emptiness.

'It's hard to explain. He left his mark here. Something happened. Something extraordinary. You've seen how the wards and protections are dissolving. Somehow that was Benfro's doing. Or he was involved.'

'You're making no sense. Can you smell him? Did he leave some kind of sign?'

'Not a physical one, no.'

'Then what are you sensing?' Melyn tried to curb his anger at Frecknock's vagueness.

'I can't describe it. I just know he was here.'

'And what about the other dragon, Caradoc? Can you sense him too?'

'He's been in here more recently. I can smell him all over this room. But he didn't stay long.'

'Where did he go?'

'Down there.' She pointed into the darkness. 'I can't tell if he came back the same way.'

Melyn raised his arm, the light from his conjured flame pushing the shadows back enough to reveal a wide spiralling stairway. Upwards, it was blocked with fallen rubble; the only way was down.

There were several openings as they descended into the

heart of the hill – entrances into basement levels that leaked chill darkness. Frecknock stopped at each one and sniffed before shaking her head and continuing down. Finally they reached the bottom, and a long corridor stretched out ahead. The floor was laid with smooth flagstones, and lifeless iron sconces hung from the wall at regular intervals. Walking forward, his light only ever reaching a few paces ahead, Melyn could feel the hairs on the back of his neck prickle. While the vaulted ceiling was high over his head, and the walls were more than fifteen paces apart, the space was relatively confined for a dragon the size of Caradoc. He wasn't sure he wanted to corner it without the back-up of the rest of his warrior priests.

'Can you still smell him?' Melyn asked. Beside him Frecknock paused for a moment before answering.

'Caradoc? He came this way, but I don't think he's down here any more. He was bleeding when he fled from you this morning, but there's no smell of blood here. His scent's faded too. Like he came here a while back. Perhaps he was exploring and didn't find a suitable place to sleep.'

'So what's down here that's so interesting?' Melyn's irritation grew as he realized they had been wandering the depths of the ruined castle for no reason. Why could Frecknock not have told him earlier that their quarry was not down here?

'Can't you see it? Aren't you looking?'

'See what? There's darkness apart from my flame, and that's hard enough to conjure down here, so far from the lines.'

'I'm sorry, Your Grace. I assumed you would be using your aethereal sight.'

'To see the aethereal requires a great deal of skill and even greater concentration. I can't just drop in and out of it at will.' Melyn wondered about the dragon. She seemed to know of the aethereal, obviously had a means of seeing it herself, and yet she had no conception of the effort it took for him to achieve the necessary trance. Was it something she could do with barely a thought?

He put the idea aside for later consideration and slowly centred himself, letting the trance take him. His conjured light faltered and went out, leaving the party in total blackness. And then the familiar sensation passed over him as the higher world of the aethereal swam into his perception.

Melyn could see the passageway clearly now, stretching away to a point some hundred paces away. The iron sconces held short oil-burning torches, their flames strangely motionless yet casting light over the rough-hewn stonework. Leaving his body behind, he floated to the nearest torch, seeing up close that the whole thing was formed from a swirling mass of colours. The stone walls, too, pulsed and glowed quite unlike anything he had ever seen before, everything streaming towards the end of the corridor. Looking back, Melyn almost fell out of his trance. He could see his own body, lifeless now that he had moved away from it. Beside him the warrior priest was a hazy form, and Frecknock was that strangely regal and elegant dragon he had noticed before. But it wasn't his companions that drew his attention, it was the corridor itself.

The colours that defined it faded away to blackness as they stretched back towards the stairs. And as they did so, the definition of the passageway altered, becoming an unformed, spiralling circle. It reminded Melyn of the way water ran down the hole in a sink, but it was as if he was sitting in the drain rather than watching from above. The aethereal view was being sucked towards him, and as he watched, a torch on the wall a dozen paces behind twisted and bent. It stretched like it was made of tar, the unmoving light of its flame still bright but elongated and curved. Then it became just another part of the smear of colour, slowly spiralling inwards.

Then he noticed the pull. It was a subtle thing, the lightest of breezes tugging him away from his motionless body. His aethereal self had no need to touch the ground, but whereas normally he delighted in the freedom of flight, now he felt helpless and adrift as that gentlest of forces moved him along the corridor towards its end.

Melyn tried to move back to his body, but some unseen hand prevented him. For the first time in many decades he felt a frisson of real fear. He knew all too well what happened to adepts who failed to return to their bodies after travelling the aethereal. Their empty husks would fade away and die eventually, but it could take many years. He would rather be devoured by a feral dragon than become one of the mindless. But he was being pulled further and further away from himself, and there didn't seem to be anything he could do to stop it. And meanwhile the tunnel itself was being devoured, that cone of darkness getting closer and closer to where they had all stopped.

Holding back the edges of this unaccustomed panic, he looked around, trying to fix himself in the shifting scene, all the while moving further away from his body. He could see a stout wooden door at the far end of the passage, great gouges scratched out of its surface as if it had been attacked by a wild beast or a man wielding an axe in a frenzy. The slow spiral of colour leaching out of the aethereal view of the corridor sank into the great door, making it pulse with a life of its own. Melyn could feel it pulling him in along with everything else, but now a presence radiated from the door that relaxed him completely, soothing away his growing panic and giving him back the courage that had so uncharacteristically failed him. The Shepherd was close by, all around him, watching over him as he always did. Melyn sensed the power of his god just beyond the door, locked away behind it. Could this really be the fabled spot where King Balwen received his instructions before the Shepherd withdrew from Gwlad? Suddenly hungry for answers, where before he had been near-paralysed with fear and self-doubt, he reached out for the wood, speeding towards it, intending to pass right through and into the arms of his god.

The impact came as a shock to his very soul. In his aethereal form he had no physical presence, so to be solidly rebuffed was a blow unlike anything he had felt. Where before he had been pulled inexorably towards the door, now he was propelled away from it with alarming speed. He could see his body, the wispy half-formed image of the warrior priest and alongside them Frecknock. They were frozen, as if all that had happened had passed in an instant, but the spiral of colours twisting away into blackness had almost reached them.

As he hurtled towards himself, wondering whether he could find his way back into his body, Melyn saw the darkness take the warrior priest and start to pull at his own image, twisting and stretching it as if it were warm toffee. He reached out for his own arm, hoping that contact would snap him back to himself, but he was moving too fast, passing his flailing aethereal arm, heading for oblivion. At the last moment he felt a tingling in his hand, another unexpected sensation, and he saw Frecknock, her arm outstretched, reaching for him. She rose from the ground even as the darkness ate it away, and he stretched as far as he could, grasping her leathery hand.

The world turned upside down as he touched her. For a brief instant he saw through her eyes, knew something of her thoughts, and then he was pitching into blackness. There was a moment when he truly believed he had died, and then Melyn crashed into the hard stone floor, knocking the wind out of his lungs.

'Inquisitor, are you hurt?' The voice of the warrior priest came to him in the darkness. Still trying to make sense of what had happened, he didn't answer at first. Melyn looked for the lines, seeing nothing at first, then the faintest of glimmers clinging to the walls. It was too little to work with. Then a different voice beside him spoke.

'If I may, Your Grace.' An orb of light more powerful than anything he could hope to control burst into being in front of him. Frecknock knelt close by, the light casting shadows on her face as she reached out to help him to his feet. The same hand he had grasped in the aethereal, he noted as he took it. She was strong, and not for the first time Melyn wondered why it was that all of the dragons he had slain had gone so quietly to their deaths. Only the creature Caradoc had ever put up a fight, and Melyn was beginning to suspect it wasn't a beast of Gwlad at all.

'What just happened?' Melyn noticed that the air was full of dust, and his ears were ringing as if he had been close to a great explosion, even though he could remember nothing of the sort.

'There was a cave-in up ahead.' The warrior priest pointed down the corridor in the direction of the door. Only now it was blocked with huge rocks, creaking as they settled into their new positions. 'I think we should probably get out of here before the rest of the passageway comes down.'

Melyn thought about the door and how it had thrown him away. The Shepherd's last remains on Gwlad lay behind it, he knew, and yet he was being given a very direct hint to leave it well alone. It was a curious kind of torment to be shown that briefest of glimpses, then to have it cruelly taken away. But who was he to question the will of God?

'Let's go then.' He reluctantly turned away. 'The beast's not down here anyway. And we've been gone long enough.'

They climbed the long slow winding steps in silence as Melyn tried to sort out the jumble of images in his mind. He had seen something of the dragon's memories, felt something of her emotions, and they puzzled him deeply. As they neared the top, Frecknock stooped, her head bowed close to his in submission.

'I am sorry, Your Grace,' she said.

'What for?'

'I suggested you look at the tunnel with your aethereal sight. No sooner did you do so than the whole place started to unravel.'

'Was that your doing?'

'No, Your Grace. I've never seen anything like that before.'

'Then you've nothing to apologize for. If anything I should be thanking you. I was adrift like a novitiate back there. You helped me back, even if I did crack my knees in the process. You didn't have to do that. You could have left me to die.'

'How long would your men have let me live if you'd been lost in there?'

It was true. As soon as anything happened to him, his remaining warrior priests would dispatch Frecknock without a second thought. But there was more to her actions than simple self-preservation. Something else drove her to help him.

He would have questioned her more, but as they stepped out of the stairwell and into the dining hall, a great roar of anger came bellowing through the doorway to the outside. The warrior priest, who had been in the lead up the steps, conjured his blade of light and ran forwards stopping only briefly before leaping out into the courtyard.

'Stay in here.' Melyn waited only long enough to see Frecknock's nodded agreement before he too ran across the hall, summoning his own blade with a thought. He paused at the doorway, listening to the fracas outside, then stepped through.

Caradoc was cornered at the far end of the courtyard. The great beast was surrounded by all the other warrior priests and backed into a corner, clutching the stump of his severed arm to his chest, the cloak wrapping it dripping now where the wound had started to bleed again. As one of the warrior priests darted forward, lunging with his blade, the dragon roared in defiance and lashed out with its tail. But the man was ready for the counter-attack, leaping out of the way and swinging his blade down as it swept past. Caradoc let out another howl, this time in pain, as a chunk of scale and flesh slapped wetly on to the dusty ground. Melyn walked slowly across the courtyard, and by the time he reached the line of warrior priests, the great beast was hunched against the wall.

'Accursed men. My tribe will hunt you down and crack your bones for what you've done.' Caradoc spoke Draigiaith with that strange inflection Melyn had noticed the first time.

'And where are your tribe now, Caradoc, son of Edryd?'

'They will come. They will have missed me already. They'll be looking for me, and they won't stop their search until they've found me.'

'Then they will find us waiting and ready.' Melyn looked the beast in his huge eyes. He could tell Caradoc was in considerable pain, reacting rather than thinking. Perhaps that was all he had ever done. He reached out to the dragon's mind, mixing fear with a certainty that he was going to strike to the left. The dragon's eyes shifted almost imperceptibly in that direction, but it was enough for Melyn to know.

'Your jewels will make a fine addition to the queen's

collection,' he said, stepping to the right, turning and striking where he knew the dragon's head would lunge.

His blade passed through thin air. Caradoc had disappeared.

15

Many histories have Balwen, Earith, Grendor and Malco as the original Guardians of the Throne, charged by the Shepherd himself with spreading his love through Gwlad and preparing for his eventual return from the stars. The title Guardians of the Throne is, however, a later addition to the scriptures. Balwen famously united the Hafod and Hendry into the Twin Kingdoms, and slew Malco in the process. Grendor fled north to what is now Llanwennog, establishing the heresy which eventually led to that benighted place abandoning the teachings of the Shepherd altogether. Earith was reputed to be wise beyond compare, and maybe she was to flee south back to Eirawen. Little is known of what became of her or her people; naught remains of that once-great civilization but jungle-devoured ruins.

The true Guardians of the Throne are a much later invention, a romantic folly of noblemen with nothing better to do with their time. Built on a shifting-sand foundation of obscure religious texts and the unintelligible ravings of an insane woman who spent most of her short life living in a cave deep in the forest of the Ffrydd, the so-called order has nevertheless proved remarkably resilient.

Barrod Sheepshead, *The Guardians of the Throne – A Noble Folly*

The sun warmed his back as Benfro spread his wings wide, feeling the air ripple and curl over their edges. He scarcely needed to think to turn now; it was as natural as breathing or walking. He was even beginning to read the invisible currents, predicting where lift might be found and where he could suddenly dive. His muscles felt strong, no trace of his injury left as he climbed higher and higher with powerful wing beats.

Bright and clear, the morning was perfect for flying. Benfro could see the great bulk of Mount Arnahi rising from the lower mass of the Rim mountains. Snow capped the highest peaks, but much of the lower hills had thawed, greening up in a thousand different shades. He was still drawn to the great mountain, but not by Magog's influence. It was more that it represented the furthest point of his travels so far. He longed to go there, and then push on further, over the rim and on into the plains of northern Llanwennog. That was where his father had gone, after all. Finding Sir Trefaldwyn was still his best chance of ridding himself of the red jewel and that treacherous rose cord that linked him to it.

Wheeling in a thermal updraught, Benfro wondered how he could even begin his search. Gwlad was a big place, and the dragons in it had long ago learned to stay hidden. Corwen's words had been so vague, and in the weeks that had passed since last the old dragon had appeared, their meaning had only become more confused. What if Sir Trefaldwyn had actually succeeded in his quest, had found his way into Gog's world, then not been able to get back? Wouldn't that explain why he had never returned?

Part of the reason why Benfro hadn't set off yet on his search was the need for both him and Errol to heal properly, to rest and build up their strength. But Benfro had to admit that he had also been held back by the sheer size of the task he faced. If he could find his father, he might be able to find Gog's world. If Gog still lived, Benfro might be able to persuade him to lift the spell of protection on the clearing where the two brothers had hatched. If he could find the clearing again, he might be able to recover some bones from long-dead Magog – as long as they hadn't mouldered away to nothing. And if he could bring the red jewel and the bones together, he might be able to breathe the Fflam Gwir, the true flame of reckoning, and undo once and for all the damage that Magog had wreaked. There were so many things that could go wrong, and that was without worrying about the men who would hunt him down and slay him without a second thought.

Lost in thought, it was a while before Benfro realized he had been gliding south, away from Mount Arnahi and towards the ruins of Cenobus. At first he thought he had let his guard slip, been drawn in by Magog's subtle, malign influence. But he could see his aura, strong and bright, surrounding him in a healthy glow that mirrored his renewed strength and vitality. He hardly needed to concentrate at all to maintain the knot that choked off the rose cord these days; it was second nature. Something else had drawn him south, something he had seen but not registered consciously.

Scanning the horizon as he flew, Benfro tried to make out the all-too-familiar hump of barren rock that poked from the sea of green like a thumb stuck through a hole in a blanket, but he was too far away still to see it, and a dull haze obscured the line between tree and sky. He sped on, looking down to see his shadow sprint across the canopy and flash across the larger clearings that linked the trees here in a vast patchwork. Over to his left, looking east, he could see the Rim mountains etched clear by the morning sun; to his right, far to the west, they continued their march round the Ffrydd, white-tipped peaks like the jagged teeth of some long-dead gargantuan fish. They were hundreds of miles distant and yet so clear he could reach out and touch them.

Only straight ahead, to the south, was the horizon obscured. As Benfro headed towards it, he could see that the haze was not due to the weather, but dust rising high into the morning air, disturbed by something below and much closer than he had realized.

His swift glide had lost him considerable altitude, and he had dropped to a level where the slow undulation of hills and valleys obscured his view of the distance. Benfro swept his wings together again and rose swiftly towards the thinnest of clouds that wisped across the sky far higher than the peaks of even the tallest mountains. He had gained so much from his time in the mountain retreat, not least the ability to cope with thin cold air. Truly he could have learned all he needed to know from Magog, had the long-dead mage not been insane.

Now Benfro could make out the rock upon which Cenobus sat, still far to the south. The great mass of dust he had first taken to be morning haze rose between him and the ancient fortress; it would be directly beneath him in just a few minutes, given the speed he was flying. Birds wheeled and dived in the dust as if they had been disturbed from their rest, or were keen to feast on others who had been dislodged. Whatever it was that moved through the trees was huge and heading steadily north.

The canopy here was thick, blocks of ancient oak and beech, their heavy boughs spread wide, obscuring the ground beneath. Benfro wheeled, trying to work out what could cause so much turmoil, but there was no way to see through the lush growth. Ahead, about a mile, the trees opened up into a series of raggedy clearings, and he climbed high above them, circling in the warm air as he waited for the beast to appear.

It was the slightest tingling sense of fear at first, an almost imperceptible thing, like the faintest of aromas carried on the breeze. Nevertheless, it brought the memories crashing back. He was hiding under a laurel bush, watching as a dozen or more men surrounded his mother, forced her to the ground, humiliated her and then killed her. He watched as they hacked away at her severed head like a pack of wild pigs, blood spraying on their cloaks and faces in their frenzy to get at the jewels within, and he knew with terrible certainty what it was that fought its way through the forest.

They rode on horses and hacked their path wide with

their terrible blades of light. Row upon row of men emerged from the shade and out into the clearing, increasing their pace as the terrain allowed more speed. Waves of terror swept over Benfro as he gazed down on more men than he had ever seen before, but he knew they could not fly, could not even hit him with a bow from this distance. The angle of the sun took his shadow far from the clearing, so the chances were they didn't even know he was above them, all their attention fixed on making swift progress through the trees. Fear was just another of their weapons, and once he understood that, he could put it aside.

He studied them as best he could, though seen from directly above they all looked much the same. They reminded him of nothing so much as a swarm of ants as they moved across the clearings in a seemingly random swirl. Benfro had disturbed enough ants' nests as a kitling to know that they were a most unpleasant foe, thousands of individual bodies all acting as if controlled by one omniscient mind. And he knew that mind was down there somewhere, deep in the middle of the flow. Inquisitor Melyn, his sworn enemy.

Before he knew what he was doing, Benfro was sinking in the air, getting closer and closer to the moving mass, until he could begin to pick out individual men. From above he could still not see faces, and he doubted he would have remembered many of them except that of the inquisitor. His face was etched across Benfro's memories in all too terrible detail. He fancied he might also recognize the tall guard with the big horse, mainly because of the animal rather than the man, and he suspected he would be able to identify the young man who had been placed in charge of Frecknock.

Almost at the moment he thought of her, he saw her step from under the trees. Just in front of her a man rode the largest horse in the whole army, and behind her, his head a shock of white hair, was Melyn. A rage such as he had never known before gripped Benfro. The heat boiled up in him, its flame ready to be spat out at his tormentor. He swooped lower, eyeing up the best angle for a dive, trying to remember the long hours he had watched hawks stoop for he kill.

'Benfro! You have to flee. Get away from here. As far as you can. They're coming to kill you.' The voice spoke directly in his mind, and he knew it as well as he knew his own. Frecknock. So intent had his focus been on the inquisitor that he had momentarily forgotten that she walked among the men, unshackled as if she were their equal.

'Dragon!' This time he heard the word shouted aloud in the language of men. The heads of the warrior priests all tilted up, following his movements as he was spotted. There was a series of sharp twangs and a dozen arrows speared towards him. For a moment Benfro froze, but he was well out of range. The arrows dropped away, falling uselessly into the canopy.

'Don't waste your shots.' The unmistakable voice of Inquisitor Melyn rose on the still air, and with it came a redoubling of the fear that he had felt before. It reached into his brain, making it almost impossible to think, freezing his muscles, robbing him of the fine control needed to stay aloft. Benfro fought against it, but it was as if he was submerged in a great deluge that overwhelmed him. He could feel his control over his aura slipping away, and Magog taking the opportunity to renew his attack, almost as if the dead dragon mage were coordinating his onslaught with that of the inquisitor. Through the haze of his battered senses, Benfro knew that he was falling again. Perhaps not quite as uncontrollably as when he had ended up in the river, but losing precious height all the same.

'You can fight them, Benfro. You have to. Use those wings of yours and fly away from here. Save yourself.' Frecknock's voice cut through the fear just enough for him to focus. He brought his wings together in a massive sweep and the movement eased the panic, strengthened him against Magog. He beat at the air again, feeling himself rise away from the trees. Down below he could see the warrior priests milling around, their progress brought to a halt as their leader cursed and railed against the sky.

He took one last look down, seeing Frecknock standing between the inquisitor and the tall man on the big horse. Part of him felt she had brought her predicament on herself and deserved whatever fate threw at her, but he also pitied her, to be at the mercy of men. Benfro struck out with his best speed, heading for the clearing, wondering as he went what Frecknock had done to keep herself alive.

'There's nothing here, Your Majesty. Just some spare clothes, a few religious books.'

Beulah stood in the middle of a dingy little room built into the thickness of the wall on the ground floor of the castle. A tiny windowless chamber leading off it was dominated by a narrow sleeping-pallet. There wasn't even a personal privy; Father Tolley, it seemed, was expected to mix with the rest of the castle staff when it came to ablutions.

Like most of the rooms in the castle, the predicant's cell was lit by a single narrow slit of a window. This cast barely enough light to see by, which didn't matter as there wasn't much to see. A plain desk with parchment and quills laid out on it, two chairs, a tall bookcase filled with leather-bound books and rolls of parchment, and a stout iron-hooped chest. Breaking this open revealed only a collection of neatly pressed but threadbare predicant's robes, socks and underwear. Father Tolley didn't even own a second pair of boots, it appeared.

'What of these books?' Beulah moved to the bookcase, conjuring a small flame to see what reading matter interested a working predicant of the Order of the Candle. Beside her Captain Herren winced as if he had never seen magic before. Perhaps, she thought, he never had. She pulled out a heavy tome, dropping it on to the desk. '*The Eleven Principles of Administration*. I remember being forced to read this as a child.'

The other books were equally riveting, the parchments if anything even drier – reckonings, revenue summaries and the like – exactly the sort of thing she would have expected. With the exception of the threadbare robes, these could have been Seneschal Padraig's rooms back at Candlehall.

'My lady, is it safe down here on your own?' Beulah turned to see Clun step through the doorway, which opened on to one of the service corridors.

'I'm perfectly safe with Captain Herren here. And I'm not exactly helpless myself.'

'Of course. It's just . . .'

'That you worry, my love? Yes, I know. I wouldn't have it any other way. But I needed to search these rooms, and Herren was good enough to show me where they were.' Beulah couldn't be quite sure of the expression on Clun's face as he looked over at the captain. It might have been jealousy. 'Anyway, where have you been?'

'The people are in shock, some are angry. They loved their lord very much, it seems. I've been trying to organize the mourning party.'

'Is there no one else to do this?' Beulah marvelled at how naturally Clun seemed to assume his mantle of responsibility, how little he complained of its burden.

'I'm sorry, ma'am. That task should have fallen to me.' Captain Herren bowed his head. 'With Tolley gone, and Lord Queln . . .' He fell silent, and for a horrified moment Beulah thought he was going to cry. The contrast with her consort could not have been more marked.

'What exactly are you looking for here?' Clun looked down at the books and scrolls Beulah had piled on the desk.

'Anything, nothing. Something that might throw a bit more light on this Father Tolley. Something that might suggest who he's working for. Corris is too small, too out of the way for Ballah to worry about. But Tolley learned his magic somewhere, and it wasn't from the Candle.'

'May I try something, my lady?'

Beulah nodded her assent, and Clun settled himself down into the chair behind the desk. She watched him enviously as he relaxed, settling his breathing down into a steady pattern and closing his eyes. For the briefest of instants she saw a swathe of colour around him, the ghost of his aethereal self.

'Be careful, my love,' she said, feeling the subtle change in the air around her. With an effort she brought the lines to her vision, noting how the chair was placed at a point where two thick ones intersected. The other lines flowed around the room, far more of them than she would have expected in such a lifeless place.

'Fetch Captain Celtin,' Clun said. Beulah shifted her focus to see Herren nod a quick assent and dart out of the door.

'What is it?'

'Behind the bookcase.' Clun pointed at the now-empty wooden shelves. 'There's some form of chamber, but it's protected by wards. I don't want to tackle them without a second opinion.'

Beulah studied the bookcase. It seemed firmly fixed to the wall, but she had seen the skill with which the palace joiners had hidden doors at Candlehall. It was quite possible that there was some form of mechanism that allowed it to swing open. Now she looked, it was obvious. The room was small, each item of furniture in the best place possible, but there was an unusually large gap between the bookcase and the desk, a patch of empty floor that meant the chest was too close to the fireplace and obstructed access to the sleeping chamber.

'Curse this pregnancy,' she said. 'If I could see what's going on here, I could have it open in an instant.'

'Don't say that, my lady,' Clun was on his feet and at her

side in an instant. His hand touched her stomach, warmth spreading through the thin fabric of her dress. Something inside gave a palpable kick.

'Ow!' Beulah was more surprised than hurt. Clun started to laugh, stopping only when they were interrupted by a discreet cough at the door. Turning, Beulah saw Celtin and Herren standing outside.

'You sent for me, Your Majesty, Your Grace?' Celtin nodded a simple salute, clasping one fist to his chest.

'This bookcase.' Clun pointed. 'It's hiding a passageway, protected by charms. You've been dealing with these things for much longer than me.'

Celtin nodded, walked slowly up to the bookcase, felt around its edges, peering closely at it from all angles. Then he leaned his forehead against the wood and closed his eyes. Everyone fell silent, feeling the charge in the air. For a minute or so there was no noise save the quiet brush of the wind against the narrow pane of glass, the occasional distant clatter from the kitchens. And then, with an audible click, the bookcase hinged an inch or two away from the wall.

Captain Celtin stood back, letting out a long breath. 'There's your passage,' he said, and Beulah could see the sweat on his scalp. 'Well protected too. I'd probably have missed it meself if it hadn't've been shown me.'

'I'll go first.' Clun swung the bookcase open to reveal dark steps descending through the stone. He conjured a blade of light, the glow chasing away the shadows. Beulah followed him down, the two captains behind her.

It wasn't far, twenty steps at most, and then the passage opened up into a small round chamber. The four of them could just about fit inside, huddled around a small altar carved from the rock wall. A slim book lay open on it. Beulah picked it up, turned it over and read the title etched in gold letters on the blood-red leather.

'*The Prophecies of Mad Goronwy*.' She flicked the book back over, taking in the page that had lain open. The margins were almost black with scrawled writing, impossible to decipher in the gloom. Sections of verse had been underlined, linked together with looping lines and arrows. 'Stanza thirty-five. "The return of the true king".'

'"When Balwen's last sits on the stolen throne . . ." Is that the one?' It was Captain Celtin who spoke.

'Yes,' Beulah said. 'Do you know what it means?'

'It means nothing, like the rest of the tosh that old witch spouted. It's so vague you can make it apply to anything. But here, in this place, I know what it means. The Guardians of the Throne.'

'You're sure?' Beulah felt ice trickle down her spine. 'I thought they all died in the Brumal Wars.'

'What's this?' Clun asked. 'The Guardians of what?'

'The Throne. Least, that's what they call themselves,' said Celtin. 'They're a bunch of freaks who reject the Shepherd's teachings and worship the Wolf. Way I heard it, they believe he's going to come back and claim his kingdom. Apparently all of Gwlad will burn, except those who pledge allegiance. It's standard nutter stuff, and they just love Mad Goronwy.'

'They worship the Wolf?' Captain Herren's voice was very quiet, almost incredulous. His face looked very pale in the light from Clun's blade, and Beulah wondered whether he might faint.

‘That they do,’ Celtin said. ‘Only they don’t call him by his true name. No, they have another name for the beast. They call him Gog.’

Beulah let out an involuntary shriek, simultaneously realizing why court ladies sometimes clasped a hand to their mouths. She felt ashamed at her lack of control, but Herren and Celtin were hardly better. Both of them had gasped and stepped away from the small altar, back towards the steps and the exit.

‘What?’ Clun stared at them all, oblivious to the change in illumination, seemingly unaware his blade of light had turned dark crimson.

The walls of the castle glistened with damp, sparkling like diamonds in the light from the torches. Errol moved slowly along the corridor, straining his ears for any sound that indicated he had been discovered. He didn’t know what monsters lurked in this place, but he was sure he didn’t want to meet any of them.

It was hauntingly familiar, but he couldn’t quite place where he had seen a corridor like this before. Nor could he remember how he had come to be in this one. All he was sure of was that he needed to get to the other end, and he needed to do it unseen.

He darted from shadow to shadow on light feet, flitting across the patches lit by the torches. Something troubled him about that: it shouldn’t have been so easy. But he was concentrating too hard on not getting caught to worry about such things. And anyway he had reached the staircase now.

The steps were wide but shallow, spiralling up. Even

keeping close to the central column, he had to take two steps on each tread. The stairs went on and on, carrying him up with slow monotony. Only the rapid dash past the wide opening to each floor punctuated the weary tedium of the climb. At each one Errol would stop briefly to catch his breath and peer down yet more lifeless corridors coloured sooty yellow by ranks of flickering torches. He wondered who lit them all and who kept them topped up with oil.

He paused for a while somewhere between the eighth and ninth floors. The corridors were four times as high as most he had seen and reminded him of some of the older parts of Emmass Fawr. In fact a lot about this place reminded Errol of the monastery of the Order of the High Ffrydd, but there were differences too. No warrior priests wandering about, for one thing. But there was no time to ponder such mysteries; he had to get to the top of the tower.

It took both for ever and no time at all. One moment he was tramping up uncounted steps, no end to them in sight, and the next he was at the top, looking into a chamber. He took a moment to catch his breath and then weaved his way through piles of strange-looking brass instruments, past tables so high he couldn't see what was on top of them, and out to the far side.

'So you made it past my children again, Xando. Well done.' The voice spoke Draigiaith with those strange inflections, and as he heard it, Errol realized where he was. He must have fallen asleep again, and now he was dreaming. Only everything was so real, as if what he saw was actually happening. He wanted to look up, to see if the vast golden cage still hung by its chain from the rafters, but he was not in control of his body. It wasn't his body at all. That was why it hadn't ached to climb all those steps, why his feet had felt so light.

'Master, they're all asleep at this hour. I was more worried that Mister Clingle might spot me. I don't much fancy working down in the sewers again.' The voice that spoke was not Errol's. It was considerably younger, higher-pitched, and spoke perfect Draigiaith with that same unusual accent. Errol found himself looking down at his hands and feet, seeing the limbs of a boy of perhaps ten.

'I will have words with the major domo when next I see him. You've been promoted, Xando. You work for me now.'

Errol looked up at the words and saw the ancient dragon standing by the fire warming his tail and back. He felt a surge of excitement and happiness at the news, no doubt the boy's feelings towards his advancement in this place, wherever it was.

'Errol!' He spun round at the word, looking up to the see the cage hanging high in the rafters. A pale face framed by straggly black hair looked down at him through the bars. He wanted to shout, 'Martha, I'll get you out of here,' but no words came out.

'What is it, Xando? Worried my little pet will escape and hex you? Don't be. She can't get out of my cage.'

'Errol!' The voice was more insistent, but Errol saw no movement from Martha's lips. She stared down, an expression of puzzled curiosity on her face, but she hadn't spoken. And if not her, then who?

'Who's Errol?' The boy Xando's voice filled his ears. 'I thought I heard someone calling.'

'I've no idea, Xando. You must have imagined it. Now come, we've work to do.' The ancient dragon shuffled away from the fireplace and headed for his massive desk. Errol felt a strange sensation, as if someone had taken him by the shoulders and held him firm while Xando walked away. He was still looking up at Martha, but out of the corner of his eye he could see a young lad dressed in an ill-fitting assortment of rags, walking away towards the desk. Up above Martha's eyes widened. She mouthed, 'Errol?' But no sound came out. And then he could feel the grip on his shoulders tightening, shaking him. The scene in the tower room began to fade, melding into a close-up view of a familiar cave wall. Martha's silent pleading face stayed with him only as a memory.

'Errol, you've got to wake up!' He blinked, rolled over and gazed up into the face of Benfro, which was perhaps too close for comfort.

'What?' Errol tried to gauge the time by the shadows at the cave mouth. He hadn't been asleep for nearly long enough.

'Melyn's coming. We have to flee.'

16

> The Grym persists throughout Gwlad. It links all livings things, from the tiniest gnat to the vast whales that dive the far depths of the Great Ocean. The most visible manifestation of this power is the Llinellau, and even the youngest kitling instinctively knows how to use them. How then might it be possible to remove a living creature from the Grym? And what effect would such a wrenching-apart have?
>
> From the working journals of Gog,
> Son of the Winter Moon

Melyn watched the retreating form of the dragon dwindle to a small speck in the sky, his anger cold in the pit of his stomach. They had been so close to success. It had succumbed to the fear like a first-year novitiate, tumbling out of the sky towards five hundred armed and ready warrior priests. It wouldn't have stood a chance. But at the last moment it had found a way, had gathered itself together and fled. Something had come to its aid.

'How did it escape us?' he asked Frecknock, who stood motionless, her eyes fixed on the fast-dwindling figure.

'We don't feel fear the same way you do.' Frecknock turned and faced him. 'Benfro would have been taken by surprise, but he would have known that what he was feeling wasn't real.'

'Benfro? I thought that was Caradoc. Are you sure?' Melyn didn't wait for the answer. He knew that Frecknock's sight was keener than any man's, and she would have been far more likely to recognize Morgwm's hatchling than any of the warrior priests. If that had been Benfro, his refuge couldn't be far away.

Melyn slipped into the trance that let him see the aethereal. The colours shifted and the whole scene took on a slightly unreal air. Patterns swirled in the sky, an indication of the powerful magics that had formed this place, that formed it still. He was loath to move far from his body, in part because of that treacherous continuously changing power, and in part because of his memories of the collapsed passageway. He didn't want to lose himself, but neither did he want to lose this chance to locate his quarry.

He rose straight up out of his body, climbing into air strangely thick, like warm water. Looking down, he could see his army among the trees, no longer advancing. A few of the figures were vaguely man-shaped, but none had the sharp sense of self required to master this place. Only Frecknock stood out.

As he climbed, Melyn searched for landmarks he could use to return to his body. He could see the bright swirl of colours that was Benfro, speeding off to the north, and the great bulk of Mount Arnahi. Melyn didn't want the dragon to get much further away, but he had to be careful. He moved slowly in the same direction, marking the relative sizes and positions of the few notable hills so as not to lose his men. The ground beneath him was an undulating mass of green punctuated by the living force of uncounted millions of small animals.

Benfro still headed straight for the huge mountain, while directly behind Melyn, almost as if his army travelled a line drawn between the two, the barren bulk of the rock where they had lost Caradoc rose out of the forest. He could return simply by heading for that, looking down until he saw his men and their horses. Melyn now sped forward like a bolt from a crossbow, his only focus the escaping dragon. And yet, for all his skill, his years of practice in travelling through the aethereal, Melyn found himself struggling. The forest writhed and shifted. Colours spun in the corners of his vision, making him feel sick. Far more so than in the lowlands of the Hafod, he felt the distance between himself and his body as a growing pull, an elastic that wanted to snap him back to himself. He was gaining on Benfro, but he wondered how much longer he could keep up the pace.

The ensuing hours were the most exquisite form of agony. Not a torment of the flesh so much as a harrowing of his soul. Melyn fought against the pain, the self-doubt, worry and fear that assaulted him in waves, even as he struggled against the ever-growing force that wanted to pull him from the sky. He began to lose control of his self-image, watching as it dwindled away to little more than the sparks he saw in his warrior priests. But it was no matter as long as he had enough left to see where Benfro landed. If he ever landed.

And then, finally, the dragon wheeled and dived, swooped over a low tree-capped hill and dropped down into a wide clearing beyond. Melyn recognized the place from when Benfro's aethereal self had fled the Neuadd. He was just in time to see the dragon land, running for a cave mouth close to a river on the edge of the trees.

He moved closer, waiting for Benfro to come back out of the cave. And then it occurred to Melyn that the dragon might be able to see him. Might even be able to fight him. He remembered the fire that Benfro has used to throw off his attack. Melyn had pushed that aside with a thought back in the Neuadd. But here, this far from his body and assaulted by the strange magic of the forest, he was weak. He might even be defeated.

It was too risky. All he needed to know was where the dragon had gone to ground. Now he must get back to his body as soon as possible. A small troop of warrior priests, riding fast ahead of the main army, could be here in two, maybe three days. The sooner they got started the quicker they would arrive. Melyn only hoped that Benfro would still be here when he returned.

And then he saw something that made his heart leap. An unmistakable figure, as pin-sharp in the aethereal as he was in real life, hobbled slowly out of the cave.

Errol.

Melyn snapped back into his body with such a jolt, he nearly fell over. It was getting dark, he noted with some irritation. All around the clearing he could see fires, smell cooking meat. They were settling in for the night.

'How long?'

'You've been away for about six hours, Your Grace.' Frecknock sat nearby but not too close. 'I watched over you.'

Melyn wasn't sure whether that was a good thing or not. She had saved him once, it was true, but he doubted he'd ever trust her. Especially after Benfro's mysterious escape. But there were more important things to worry about.

'Osgal,' he shouted. The captain came running up.

'Sir?'

'I want you and a troop ready to ride out before first light. The hatchling's holed up in a clearing about two days north of here. I want to cover that ground in considerably less.'

'I'll tell the men to get some rest now, sir.' Osgal looked up at the darkening sky and Melyn followed his gaze. There were only a few thin clouds, high up. Already the first stars were beginning to show; the Night Messenger and Blaidd yn Rhedeg.

'We'll leave when the moon's in the second quarter. It'll help us along. Tell Captain Pelquin to bring the rest of the army due north at his best speed. Keep heading for Mount Arnahi. He should catch up with us on the third day; if not, we'll find him. I don't want to waste too much more time chasing these damned dragons.'

Captain Osgal nodded his understanding and strode off to carry out his orders. Melyn pulled himself to his feet, noting that Frecknock stood at the same time. Her deference was welcome, but it could get tiring sometimes.

'Have you eaten?'

The dragon shook her head. 'I can survive for several days without food.'

'I'm off to get something, then you and I are going to have a little talk.'

If Frecknock was worried by the threat, she didn't show it. Melyn turned away, heading to the nearest fire, where a warrior priest was turning a deer carcass on a spit over the blazing coals. He took the proffered plate of meat from the man, then returned to the dragon. She said nothing, simply watching him as he settled back down and began to eat.

'Benfro wasn't alone in that clearing,' he said once he had taken a few mouthfuls and summarized what he had seen.

'I know the place. I stopped there on my way through the forest. With my parents before they had been killed.' Frecknock's gazed dropped to the ground as if the memories were too heavy for her head. 'There was an old dragon. His name was Corwen.'

'I didn't see any other dragon, but I did see young Errol Ramsbottom.'

'Who? Oh.'

'Yes. Oh. What do you suppose he was doing there? And more importantly, how did he get there?'

'Your Grace, I remember the boy from my time at the Neuadd. But I'd never met him before you brought him before the queen.'

'He disappeared into thin air right in front of my eyes.' Melyn put his plate down on the ground, leaning forward. With a thought he conjured a blade of light, extending it so that its point hovered just in front of Frecknock's face. Its white glare was reflected in her wide black eyes as she recoiled.

'Sir. I –'

'Don't try my patience, Frecknock. I've no love for

your kind, and I know you have dark magics. I saw Caradoc vanish just the same as Errol. Where did he go? How did he do it? Is this the hiding spell that you promised to show me?'

Silhouetted against the fires dotted around, Frecknock was shaking. Her eyes were still fixed on his blade, and her voice was very quiet when she spoke.

'I too saw Caradoc make his escape. It is something dragon mages can do. But it's not possible for a man to master the art. I mean no disrespect, Your Grace, but your minds cannot cope.'

'Can't cope with what? Explain yourself.'

Frecknock sat silently for a few moments as if fighting some inner battle. Or perhaps deciding how best to deceive him. He was about to poke her with his blade, make her scales sizzle a bit, when she finally spoke.

'May I show you something?' This was her way of asking permission to perform some magic, Melyn knew. He nodded his assent, and she held out her hand. In the pale light cast by his blade he could see that it was completely empty. She closed her fist and her eyes, muttered something under her breath that made his skin crawl, then opened her hand again.

A fresh apple lay in her palm.

'I've seen quack conjurors more convincing.' But Melyn could see she had no sleeve to hide anything in. And there was nowhere she could have found a fresh apple anyway; it was the wrong season.

'I took this apple from a tree in Eirawen, on the other side of Gwlad. It's autumn there now. They'll be bringing in the harvest soon.'

'And are you going to explain to me just how you performed this miracle?'

'It's a bit like the way you conjure your weapon.' Frecknock placed the apple on the ground and pointed at Melyn's blade of fire. 'You take power from the Grym, the life force that is all around us. When you create that sword, you take a little life from everything.'

'I learned all this as a novitiate,' Melyn said, his patience wearing thin.

'And you learned to see the lines – what we call the Llinellau Grym. But you see them only as a diffuse source of power. They're much more than that. They are the source of life itself. They link every living thing in Gwlad. With sufficient skill and mental discipline, you can reach out along the lines to anything, anywhere, and bring it back to you. Like the apple.'

'I know the theory of magic, Frecknock. I've even used the lines myself to communicate, as you well know. But they are dangerous, complex. Try to push your thoughts too far down them and you risk losing yourself. It's a far worse fate than being stuck in the aethereal.'

'What you call the aethereal is just an extension of the Grym, just another way of seeing it. But it's true that men find it impossible to master the finer points of manipulating the Llinellau. Don't ask me why; I suppose it's just the way you are.'

Melyn let his blade extinguish itself, the shadows crowding in so that all he could see was distant firelight reflected in Frecknock's eyes. He found it hard to skim her thoughts; they were so alien to him. But he sensed no lie in what she said. And the trick with the apple had been impressive. He picked it up. It was firm and weighty, with a warmth still in it that spoke of hot sunshine. Sniffing it brought him the aroma of autumn orchards. He was almost tempted to take a bite out of it, but a sudden suspicion stopped him. He dropped it back on to the grass.

'So you can bring this apple to you. You still haven't explained how Caradoc could disappear, or how Errol Ramsbottom can turn up in a clearing with Morgwm's hatchling.'

'It's all the same magic. If you can find the apple and bring it to you, then you can find the apple and go to it. There is no distance between two points in the Grym.' Frecknock's words came out in a whispered tumble, as if she were divulging some naughty secret at the back of the classroom. 'At least that's how Meirionnydd explained it to me. I never did manage to do it myself. Not all dragons can, and I've only studied for a hundred years.'

Melyn leaned back against a tree. He remembered his plate of meat and took it up, then put it down again when he saw it had gone cold and greasy.

'You can't do this?'

'We call it walking the lines. And no, I can't do it. Do you think I'd be here with you if I could?'

'What about the book? Is the secret in the *Llyfr Draconius*?'

'Almost certainly.' Frecknock's voice betrayed a tiny quiver of hope that instantly put Melyn on his guard. 'But it's not like a normal book. You can't just open it up and read it. You'd lose your mind.'

'So you say, but how do I know you just don't want me to know what's in it?'

'I can't stop you from reading it, sire. But I must warn you that it is very dangerous. You and I are very different. Men don't think like dragons. Your kind have never been able to master the subtle arts.'

'And yet somehow Errol Ramsbottom managed to walk your lines. Not just once, either. He escaped Tynhelyg and ended up at Emmass Fawr, disappeared from there a couple of times too, and then went from the Neuadd to the depths of this forest. He shouldn't have been able to do any of those things.'

The darkness was almost total now, and Melyn could see nothing of Frecknock's outline. She was motionless, silent, the only thing showing her presence the twin sets of low embers reflected red in her glassy eyes.

'No, Your Grace. He shouldn't have.'

'We can't very well just ride into Talarddeg, Dafydd. Not like this. They'll think we're an invasion force or something.' Captain Pelod voiced the problem that had been weighing on Dafydd's mind for several days now, ever since they had crossed the pass on their back-road route to Fo Afron and seen the sparkling blue waters of the Sea of Tegid stretching out to the eastern horizon. They had dropped back down into the trees now, but every so often a turn in the road would offer them another breathtaking vista.

Still, it had been a long journey. Dafydd was beginning to tire of the mountains and the endless forest. After the initial few days of worrying that a messenger from his father would catch up with them, ordering him back to Tynhelyg, he had relaxed enough to start enjoying himself.

It was a bit like some of his more daring childhood escapades, when he and Jarius had taken horses out at first light to hunt boar – that same sense of wrongdoing, that frisson of danger. But this was ten times as perilous, and at the same time even more exciting. He had the king's blessing for this quest, but also the king's expectations weighing heavily on his shoulders and a troop of the king's elite guard riding at his back.

'How exactly are we supposed to get from Talarddeg to Abervenn, anyway?' Jarius asked, nudging his horse closer to Dafydd's. Iolwen rode on his other side, silent but smiling. She had changed noticeably on their trip, becoming brighter and happier as the miles grew from Tynhelyg. Dafydd wondered how much of the reason for this was the thought of going home, and how much sheer relief at being away from the city and royal court.

'We'll be sailing on one of Master Holgrum's merchant ships.'

'Oh joy. A sea journey. You know how much I hate getting my feet wet.'

'I've never been to sea.' There was perhaps a note of trepidation in Iolwen's voice as she joined in the conversation. 'Is it as bad as people say?'

'Only during the winter storms,' Jarius said. 'And even then the Sea of Tegid is fairly calm, at least up the west coast. It's deep there, you see, and sheltered from the worst of the weather by these mountains we've just ridden through.'

'But what about the rest of the journey? Aren't we going out through the Spires of Idris?'

'It can get a bit choppy there, and there's a tricky bit

around the Caldy peninsula between the southern sea and the Great Ocean. But we're not going to be on a little rowing boat, Iol. And the sailors will know what they're doing.'

Dafydd said the words to comfort himself as much as his wife. He had sailed from Talarddeg before, but only north, up the coast to Kais. Jarius had more experience of the sea, but there wasn't much call for sailors in Llanwennog. It was landlocked on three sides, and the sea that formed its northern border was frozen for most of the year.

'Seriously though, Dafydd, we need to think about how we approach the city. Beulah will have plenty of spies there, and Tordu too. If we don't want either of them to know where we are, then we need to split up, arrive at different times and through different gates. There're a dozen taverns I can suggest where we can regroup, and when we know which boat we're sailing on, I can pass the message on.'

'That's a sound plan, Captain Pelod. But I have a better one.'

Dafydd, Iolwen and Jarius stopped their horses in unison. They had been riding down a long straight track with wide grass verges to either side. Nothing and nobody could have approached them without being seen. And yet there, standing in the middle of the road, was a man.

'Usel. By the Shepherd, man. You might have got yourself killed.' Dafydd turned slightly in his saddle. 'It's all right. He's a friend.' The soldiers riding behind him were in disarray, pulling up their horses and stepping off the track to avoid riding into the back of them.

'They haven't seen me yet,' Usel said, and Dafydd could

see the truth of his words in the actions of his guards. They had been taken completely by surprise and even now didn't seem to know what had caused their leaders to stop so suddenly. He turned back to the plain-robed medic and for the first time noticed that he had a horse, standing patiently behind him.

'How . . . ?'

'Magic, Your Highness. Misdirection. Please forgive me my little game, but I could think of no other way to come among you. I hadn't anticipated you would be accompanied by the king's best men. Ah, yes, they've seen me now.'

Within seconds Usel was surrounded by two dozen mounted soldiers, all wielding swords of bright white flame. He stood in their midst motionless, seemingly unconcerned. Dafydd thought it would serve the man right to let him sweat a bit, but the medic merely waited. In the end it was Iolwen who broke the impasse.

'Stand down, won't you. Can't you see he's no threat?'

The guards extinguished their blades and turned their horses away, falling back behind the royal pair and their captain.

'Thank you, Princess,' Usel said. 'And thank you, gentlemen, for not running me through.' He swung himself up on to his horse and wheeled it round so that he was alongside Iolwen.

'You were saying you had a better plan?' Jarius spoke as if the whole incident had been no more than a horse stumbling over a pothole.

'Indeed, Captain, I have. Talarddeg is, as you rightly said, awash with spies – Beulah's, Tordu's, Padraig's. Even the merchants keep an eye on each other and sell whatever information they glean. It's not a good place to go if you don't want to be noticed.'

'So we should avoid it, is that what you're saying?' Dafydd asked.

'No. Well, not all of you. I'm sorry, Your Highness. This might seem a bit strange, but I think you and Iolwen should be seen entering the city, just not in an official capacity. News must get back to Tynhelyg of your whereabouts eventually; we just need to manage the process. Perhaps Captain Pelod might accompany you, and Master Teryll as well. Her Royal Highness the princess is in a delicate condition, after all, and where better to build up one's strength than Talarddeg? You should have rooms at the most expensive inn, take the waters and be seen in the spa. Then you might charter a boat to take you across to Fo Afron. There are interesting ruins in the Gwastadded Wag that a young prince might wish to explore.'

'And you'll pick us up somewhere in the middle of the Sea of Tegid, where even the loosest-tongued sailor can't tell a soul.'

'Exactly so, Prince Dafydd.' Usel smiled as if everything had been settled to his liking.

'But what of my guards?' Dafydd asked. 'What of my safety? What of Iolwen's? If Talarddeg's as full of spies as you say, might there not be assassins too?'

'We hadn't counted on you bringing so many men,' Usel said. 'But Holgrum's ship is more than capable of taking them all. I dare say he wanted to fit in a paying cargo as well, but he might have to accept a small loss on this journey. The ship will put into a small harbour not two days' ride south of Talarddeg. They can board it there without fear of being discovered. Local tongues might wag, but only the sheep will hear them.'

'And the assassins?' Dafydd noticed that he medic hadn't answered his question.

'I won't deny that Talarddeg can be a dangerous place. But my people are in place, have been for many months now. And Master Holgrum has contacts throughout the city. If anyone was plotting an attack, we'd know about it and deal with it. People disappear all the time in busy coastal ports. The city guard tends not to get involved.'

Dafydd knew it made sense. Riding into town at the head of a troop of King Ballah's finest soldiers would bring the wrong kind of attention. He would be invited to stay at the castle, watched by his uncle, the odious Duke Vern, his every move reported back to his father. It would be all but impossible to do anything without half the local aristocrats following him around. But if he arrived quietly, unannounced but not concealing his presence, then he might well be left alone, at least for the few days it took to exchange message birds with Tynhelyg, and by then he would be gone anyway.

'How much further is it to the coast?'

'We should reach the sea by this evening. A place called Smailtown. It's a long day's ride to the city from there. We'll find lodgings for tonight and set off fresh in the morning.'

They rode on through the afternoon, arriving at the small coastal settlement as the sun dipped behind the Caldy mountains. The smell of the sea brought back vivid memories to Dafydd, not all of them good. He could almost feel the rocking of the small boat that had taken him to Kais through stomach-churning waters. That had been a miserable trip, a strange idea of his father's to round out his education by sending him to the four corners of the kingdom and beyond. He hoped that this voyage would be both more profitable and more comfortable.

Smailtown sat on the main road that followed the western coast of the Sea of Tegid. It was a small place: a few fisherman's cottages clustered around a tiny harbour, and a large inn built to cater for travellers heading to and from Talarddeg. The soldiers made camp in a sheltered field nearby while Usel accompanied Dafydd, Jarius and Iolwen into the inn.

It had been weeks since last they had stayed anywhere so well appointed, and Dafydd wasn't surprised that his wife disappeared into the bathing room attached to their chambers as soon as the maids had finished bringing up what seemed like enough hot water to fill the harbour below. He contented himself with a quick wash before making his way to the main tavern room. The endless days on the road, with only the rations they could carry supplemented by what they could catch, had given him a hunger for something more sophisticated than spit-roast deer, and a thirst for something stronger than water.

There were few people in the long low-ceilinged room; Jarius had yet to make it down. Usel was waiting for him, however, and they retired to a private room at the back of the building. They sat at a heavy-topped oak table and a serving girl brought two tankards of foaming ale. Dafydd drank deeply from his, washing away the road dust.

'You look like you needed that.' Usel sipped at his own drink with slightly more decorum.

'It's been a while since I've had real ginger beer,' Dafydd said. 'It doesn't travel well to Tynhelyg, and the brewers there don't know how to make it with the dried ginger root that gets brought in.'

'Well, this is all right, I suppose, but it's not the best. Remind me to take you to Plentin's when we get to Talard-deg. He makes the finest ginger beer in the whole of Gwlad.'

'Listen to you two. You sound like a couple of old merchants discussing their next trip.' Dafydd looked up from his tankard, then reflexively stood up. A familiar fair-haired woman in a long dark gown stood by the unlit fireplace. He was certain she hadn't been there before, though he hadn't heard the door.

'Ah, Lady Anwyn. I was wondering where you'd got to.' Usel stood as well, and pulled out a chair so that she could sit.

'I was here all along, Usel. I've been practising.'

Dafydd looked at the young woman and back at the grey-haired medic. He was nothing like as powerful in the ways of the Grym as his grandfather – no one in the whole of Llanwennog could hope to match the king – but he was nevertheless a skilled adept. He could conjure a puissant sword and knew how to feel out another man's thoughts. He could even communicate over long distances using his aethereal form, though there were few people with the skill to see him thus. He had no desire to contact either his father or Tordu, and the king himself would not wish to be bothered until there was important news. But in all his years of training he had never encountered a spell that could render him invisible in the way both Usel and now Anwyn seemed able to do. He could misdirect a person's attention so as to be overlooked, could possibly even make a small crowd ignore him, but he had also been trained to know when something similar was being done to him. At no time had he noticed any of the telltale signs.

'This . . . trick. I've not seen it done before. It's new magic?'

'No, sir. It's the very oldest magic. Or the subtle arts, as those who taught it to me would prefer to call it. I've always found the term more appealing.' Usel smiled an enigmatic little smile, then disappeared from where he was sitting. Dafydd could sense nothing of him, but he reached forward and poked the area where the medic's chest should have been. As he made contact, so Usel reappeared.

'Touch will undo the spell, it's true. But it's a useful working nonetheless. It would have been very difficult to get across half of Llanwennog undetected without it.'

'Who else knows how to do this?' Dafydd asked. 'Do the warrior priests? By the tree, man, this is a terrible thing. Our armies could be attacked before they knew anything was coming their way.'

'No warrior priests know this magic, sir. Just the same as none of King Ballah's soldiers know it, nor the king himself. It's not an easy spell to cast, more difficult yet to maintain.'

'Could you teach me how to do it?' Dafydd's mind

reeled at the possibilities. He could come and go as he pleased, evade even the most persistent of Tordu's spies.

'I can,' Usel said. 'Indeed I will, once I'm convinced of your dedication to our cause.'

'Am I not here?' Dafydd was slightly taken aback at the suggestion behind Usel's words. 'Have I not brought my pregnant wife with me?'

'I'm sorry, sir. I meant no disrespect. Yes, of course you're here, and Princess Iolwen too. But there's more at stake than you perhaps realize. You rightly pointed out the danger should Melyn and his warrior priests learn this magic. They know nothing of it, and neither does your father. But if either of them even suspected the other of having such power, they would immediately launch an attack. In their minds they wouldn't be able to afford to wait until some unseen enemy slew them in their beds.'

'Surely it would bring peace? They'd know that it was pointless trying to fight, that no one could win.' Dafydd said the words, but even as he did, he could hear his father ranting on about the menace of Queen Beulah and her odious inquisitor.

'You don't really believe that, do you?'

'No, you're right. They're determined to have their war anyway. Knowing something like this would just make them more eager to get it started.'

'Which is why we need to give the people of the Twin Kingdoms an alternative, and why they mustn't learn about this magic.'

'But if they don't know about it, then who does? And who taught you?'

'I learned most of my skill in the subtle arts down in Eirawen, from a very old and very scholarly dragon.'

'A dragon?' Dafydd almost laughed. 'Dragons don't know anything but a few parlour tricks. I've seen them in the travelling circuses. Most of them can only manage a few words of pidgin Llanwennog, and they don't really understand what they're saying.'

'The dragons you see in circuses are pathetic creatures, it's true.' Usel looked sad as he spoke, his face creasing as if he felt a terrible sense of loss. 'Perhaps what you do to them here is even crueller than the treatment my people have meted out on them for centuries. At least we only kill them.'

'What do you mean?'

'The dragons you see in circuses have been drugged into mindlessness, then trained like performing dogs to do the most demeaning of tricks. In truth they are majestic, noble and dignified creatures. And they are wise in the ways of the Grym, far more powerful than men will ever be. We've persecuted them almost to the edge of extinction, and in so doing we've missed out on an opportunity to learn so much. Worse, we've made ourselves a powerful enemy.'

17

An adult dragon's brain contains, on average, a dozen fine red jewels. Curiously there is no statistical difference between male dragons and females in this respect. It is believed that the jewels form over time, much like kidney stones, and this is borne out by the fact that juvenile dragons – kitlings in their strange speech – have few or even no jewels.

Dragons being creatures naturally attuned to magic and the Grym, the jewels become imbued with some of that great power – hence their enormous value. In all the nations of men the possession of dragons' jewels has been the exclusive privilege of royalty, and a fiercely guarded privilege at that.

But there is a dangerous side to such concentrated power, for to hold a dragon's jewel is to take a short cut to the world of magic. Those with the talent and self-discipline to learn the ways of the Grym know full well its dangers and are prepared for them. A novice, or worse yet curious amateur, is to some extent protected from this danger by lack of skill. When a dragon's jewel is used to make up for this lack, then only blind luck can prevent tragedy.

Father Charmoise, *Dragons' Tales*

'Can we rest a moment, please? I don't think I can go any further right now.'

Benfro stopped and looked back to where Errol was bent over, hands on his legs, breathing heavily. His face was pale and his hair stuck to his scalp in untidy black strings, matted and sweaty. He had dropped his bag, which he had sewn together from bits of cloth found at the bottom of his wooden chest and filled with a small selection of clothes. Benfro wasn't sure whether he was going to collapse on top of it.

'All right. But only for a moment. I'll have a look round and see if the ground gets any easier up ahead.' He watched as Errol sank gratefully to the forest floor, then pushed his way through the undergrowth, peering up to see if he could find the sun and gauge the time.

They had been walking for hours, always through the trees, avoiding the path and heading just east of north. They needed to reach the Rim mountains as quickly as possible, and Benfro knew it was at least three days' walk. That was how long it had taken him to stumble back to Corwen's clearing after he had escaped Magog's influence. But he could cover the ground much faster than Errol, even without the boy's damaged ankles. And all the while Inquisitor Melyn and his army of warrior priests were getting closer.

Despite his initial panic on learning of the approaching army, Errol had insisted they take time to prepare for their journey. It made sense, of course; just heading off into the woods with no supplies and no plan would have been a disaster. He had collected as much food as possible, wishing that he'd thought to dry some meat. Errol had spent many hours fashioning his bag, then he had gone through Benfro's, picking out the coins and the golden torc and discarding everything else except the map. It was a much reduced load, but he had assured Benfro the coins would be more than enough to buy them whatever they might need in Llanwennog.

And finally they had tried to get some sleep, knowing full well that neither of them would be able to but loath to set off in the darkness. At dawn they finally gave up the pretence and headed out of the clearing.

Benfro pushed through a particularly thick laurel bush and emerged into another open area. He could hear the river far to the west, gurgling over rocks, flush with the rain that had fallen overnight. The grass was wet on his feet as he walked out from the trees, feeling slightly nervous. He kept his eyes sharp, looking for any sign of ambush, even though he knew he must be well ahead of the warrior priests.

From the middle of the clearing he could see the mountains surrounding him like a huge wall. Arnahi climbed high into the clouds to the north, and lower peaks marched away from it both east and west. Most were still snow-capped even though spring was almost over. Closer still, the foothills rose up in a series of ever larger mounds, the tree canopy making them look like green anthills. Somewhere up there was a path through to Llanwennog on the other side. A whole new country and the place where his father had gone.

Benfro dug the map out of his leather bag, opened it

up and turned it round until he could get an idea of his location. Mount Arnahi was the only obvious landmark, but a couple of the other mountains had distinctive shapes he thought he could identify. He wished that Ynys Môn were with him. The old dragon had told him to take the map in the first place, and he had always been much better at navigation.

A terrible feeling of panic hit Benfro as he thought about his old friend – about the too-small pile of jewels back in Magog's repository where he had found the map. Turning, he rushed back into the trees, knocking branches aside in his rush to get back to Errol. The boy looked up at the noise, a look of alarm spreading over his face.

'What is it?'

'The jewels. We left them behind.' Benfro was almost unable to get the words out. He couldn't believe he could have done something so stupid.

'They're safe where they are. Corwen will look after them.'

'No. Melyn will find them. He'll take them. I need Magog's jewel to undo his spell, and I can't leave my mother behind. I have to go back.'

'But Corwen said –'

'Corwen can't help us now.' Benfro picked up Errol's bag, barely registering its weight. 'There's a clearing about a hundred paces up ahead. I can fly from there back to the cave. I'll only be an hour. Get some rest and be ready to go when I get back.'

He could see that Errol was about to argue, so Benfro simply set off back to the clearing. As soon as he was past the laurel bush, he dumped his bags in a pile, unfurled his wings and leaped into the air. He turned once, twice, three times, beating hard as he climbed. Down below he could see Errol looking up at him, but if the boy shouted anything, his words were lost on the wind.

Once he had enough altitude to get his bearings, Benfro could see how far they had walked in the day. It was a depressingly short distance; Errol just wasn't capable of going at anything faster than a crawl, it seemed. They would have to pick up the pace when he got back, or they would be overtaken in short order.

He thrust his head forward, set his wings and sped back towards the clearing and the cave. He could see the arc of taller trees, their leaves a brighter green where they lined the curve of the river. He covered the distance in no time, looking always further south for any sign of the approaching army. There was no haze of dust on the horizon to mark its passage, but the day was not as clear as when he had seen it before.

The clearing opened up beneath him. Benfro was certain they had walked further, but instead of going in a straight line, as he had intended, they had walked half of a great circle, wasting valuable time and energy. Why had they not just followed the path? And why had he forgotten about his mother's jewel, and Magog's too? He could only assume that lack of sleep had affected them both more than they realized.

His eyes fell on the waterfall and Benfro swooped, preparing to land. He had not seen the jewels since Corwen had taken them under his protection, had not seen the back of the cavern where the old dragon's own gems were laid to rest. But he knew where to look.

Movement registered in the corner of his eye as he came in to land, as close to the river as he dared. Looking around, Benfro saw something on the path where it entered the forest on the far side of the clearing. For an instant he thought it was a deer looking for some good grazing and emboldened by the quiet that must have fallen over the place since they left. But with a terrible dread in his hearts, he knew that it was no deer.

Beating his wings so hard they almost hit the ground, their tips crashing together underneath him, Benfro clawed his way back up into the sky just as Inquisitor Melyn and a handful of warrior priests rode into the clearing at a gallop. Behind them Frecknock ran like an obedient dog. How had they got here so quickly?

He hardly had time to think before the fear rolled out across the distance between him and the inquisitor. It was a mind-numbing force, squeezing the breath out of him and making his hearts thump so hard he thought they might burst from his chest.

'No! You won't have me!' Benfro screamed at the top of his lungs. The words broke whatever spell it was that Melyn tried to weave, the fear leaving him as swiftly as it had come. For a wild instant he felt the complete opposite as he turned and climbed ever higher. There were only a few men – they must be an advance party and they couldn't have slept in the days since he had first seen them far to the south. He could attack them now, while they were weak and tired. He could take them all, rip them to shreds, breathe fire and watch as the inquisitor writhed and screamed in agony, consumed by flames that kept him alive while they burned his flesh away.

'No, Benfro. You can't win this fight.' Corwen's voice was right inside him, and for a moment he could sense the old dragon as if he flew alongside. It was a voice of reason. He couldn't risk attacking these men, and as if to underline the fact some of the warrior priests conjured long blades of burning white light, spurring their horses on across the clearing. Others looked to their saddlebags and produced crossbows.

Howling his rage at the wind, Benfro took one last look at the waterfall that concealed his fate, and turned to the north and fled.

'Don't let him get away! Use your bows.' Melyn shouted the orders even as he knew he was too late. The dragon had been coming in to land, but now it wheeled, pulling its unlikely bulk back up into the air with beats of massive wings that cracked like whips. Mixed in with his frustration and rage, Melyn couldn't help but feel a curious sense of wonder at the sight of such a large creature flying through the air. It was wrong, he knew, an evil gift from the Wolf. But it was magnificent all the same.

Dismounting next to a low stone corral beside the track, he settled himself down on a stray boulder, pushed away the fury that threatened to bubble over inside him at any moment. His men were already quartering the clearing, looking for signs of their quarry, but Melyn had no time for that. He had to follow the dragon, to see where it was going. Pushing all other thoughts from his mind, he slipped into the trance that would allow him to travel the aethereal.

As he rose from his seated body, he could see the track

that crossed the clearing shimmer and pulse like a vein or some central strand of a giant spider's web, pulling everything that fell into the forest to this one location. It was very much like the paths and tracks around the dragon village he had destroyed, Melyn realized. There an ancient magic had controlled the roads, so that all travellers ended up at Morgwm's cottage. Was this clearing the home of a similar creature?

A question for later. Now he had a more urgent task. He scanned the aethereal sky for the fleeing dragon and almost missed it, looking too far to the horizon and the bulk of the Rim mountains. They were closer than he had realized, the view to the north dominated by the great jagged point of Mount Arnahi. He could feel the huge mountain calling him, pulling him towards it, and had to fight to stay where he was. It was then that he noticed Benfro dropping down into the trees not far away at all. And the track beside which his body sat led straight to the dragon, curving only slightly with the rise of the hills towards another clearing in the trees.

'Osgal, take a dozen men. Head up this track at best speed. You'll find the dragon, and no doubt the boy as well, in a clearing about two hours north-east of here. Be careful; the road will try to lead you astray.' Melyn spat out his instructions almost before he had fully returned to his body. The captain said nothing, merely nodded, then pointed to the men who were to follow him. Within moments they had mounted, crossed the ford in a welter of splashing water, and disappeared into the trees.

Melyn leaned back against the stones of the corral wall.

He was tired, he realized. Bone weary. It was no surprise; none of them had slept in over two days, and he was by far the oldest of the troop. Still, it was an unwelcome sign of weakness. He pulled himself to his feet, joints protesting at their misuse, as Frecknock trotted over to his side.

'This is the place,' the dragon said. 'I'd know it any day. Though it was more than a century and a half ago, it's not changed. Well, apart from this.' She reached out and shook the top of the corral as if expecting it to crumble away. 'And I can't see any sign of Corwen.'

'Why would they come here? What's so special about this Corwen anyway?' Melyn walked stiffly to the ford and crouched down to cup water in his hands for a drink. It was cold and sweet, fed by the snow high up in the mountains and sheltered from the sun by many miles of thick forest. He splashed his face, washing the dust out of his bristly beard and long hair. This would be a good place to stop and rest.

'Corwen teul Maddau taught Morgwm all she knew about the subtle arts. He's a true mage, perhaps the wisest dragon I've ever met.' Frecknock waited for Melyn to finish drinking before helping herself.

'So that explains why Benfro would come here. But why Errol?'

'Morgwm delivered Errol. Somehow he's acquired the ability to walk the lines. I'm sure you can see how this place lures magical beings in. Perhaps it's just coincidence that the boy ended up here.' Frecknock waded upstream towards the waterfall, the deepening pool rising around her. Wet, the dull scales on her wings and arms gleamed with countless subtle colours like oil on water struck by the sun.

'Where are you going?' Melyn asked.

'I thought I would wash some of the road dust off.' She stood just before the crashing wall of water, her words almost lost in the din.

'Later,' Melyn said. 'Now we have to search this clearing for your mage.'

Somewhat reluctantly, Frecknock waded away from the waterfall and clambered out of the river. Melyn half expected her to shake herself like a dog, but the water just ran off her, the sun drying her quickly back to her usual matt black. They walked back to the corral and the cave mouth opposite. Two warrior priests stood at the entrance looking almost scared to go in.

'Benfro was here.' Frecknock stooped low to the cave entrance, sniffing the earth and the air. 'He lived in there a while.' She pointed at the corral. 'But he's been sleeping in the cave for at least a month. The boy too.'

Melyn stooped to enter, even though the entrance was more than tall enough for him to walk through erect. Frecknock followed him, and she had no difficulty either, though the size Benfro had grown must have begun to present him with a few problems. Inside, the cave opened up to the size of a large room, dominated in the centre by a hearth. Charred ends of logs poked out from the ash-pile of a dead fire. Melyn held his hand out, palm down to the ash. It was cold, but when he pushed his finger deep into the pile he could still feel warmth.

There were two rudimentary beds in the cave, and it wasn't hard to tell who slept where. Errol's low pallet lay alongside the fire, and behind it, tucked up against the stone wall of the cave, stood a stout wooden chest. Melyn conjured a light to augment the meagre illumination filtering in through the cave mouth.

'I've seen this before.' He held his light over the chest, pulling open the top. Inside were a few scraps of clothing, neatly folded. Rummaging around in the bottom revealed the ragged remains of a novitiate's cloak and a coarse white cotton shirt. Someone had tried very hard to get the bloodstains out of it, without much success, and the stitching to mend the tear in the front was slapdash. But then Melyn doubted that Errol had much in the way of needles and thread. When he had disappeared from the Neuadd he had been wearing these clothes and had nothing else with him. So where had he got the chest from?

Then Melyn remembered, the picture forming in his mind as if he were there. A home hastily departed, only this time the occupants hadn't fared so well. A room at the back of the healer's cottage, looking out on the woods that flowed down the hills above Pwllpeiran.

'This chest has come from Errol's home.' Melyn turned to face Frecknock, who looked up from her inspection of the other bed in the cave, an alcove filled with dried grass and heather that reminded Melyn of nothing so much as an ill-made giant nest.

'It's possible to use the Llinellau to bring things to you.'

'Yes, I know. An apple from Eirawen. It was very tasty. But this . . . this is different. It's huge, for one thing.'

'I saw Sir Frynwy fetch an entire cow once. Size is not necessarily a problem.'

'But could you do it?'

'No, but the boy must have.'

'How so?' Melyn could see Frecknock's expression in the glow from his conjured flame. She looked, if anything, disgusted. As if the thought of someone other than a dragon performing such magic offended her. Or perhaps it was jealousy that someone so young could do something it had taken her years to master.

'The chest is a very personal thing,' she said after a short pause. 'To bring something so specific, you would have to know where it was, know its setting intimately. And of course it's not alive, which would have made it many times more difficult.'

'So how did he do it?'

'I don't know. Corwen must have taught him how. But he must be some kind of freak to be able to master the subtle arts with such ease.'

The offspring of a union between the house of Ballah and the house of Balwen. Perhaps Mad Goronwy had been right when she had warned against any such thing ever taking place. And now there would be a second child to contend with, if nothing could be done to prevent Princess Iolwen from carrying her unborn baby to term.

'So where is this Corwen?' Melyn was suddenly angry at the endless delays, the endless failures. He should have been through the pass and into Llanwennog by now, not chasing dragons across the forest.

'I'm not sure.' Frecknock was choosing her words carefully, no doubt aware of his mood. 'It was a long time ago when my parents brought me through here. I was barely a hatchling. I remember a very old dragon with a scarred face and one tooth broken, and I remember a cave where the light swirled and danced. But I don't think it was here. This is too small, and there's no furniture.'

'But you said you were sure this was the right place.'

'It is the right clearing, just the wrong cave.'

'Well, I don't know about you, but I only saw one entrance from outside.'

'Maybe it's hidden then.'

Melyn paused, an instant from throwing his conjured flame at the dragon. She was infuriating, loathsome and calm where he was boiling with anger. And yet she had all the knowledge he needed, even seemed prepared to give it to him, but only when he found the right way to ask. She was right too. This whole clearing was a centre of great magical power, yet the cave in which they stood was nothing special. He could feel that without having to slip into a trance. But in the aethereal he might be able to track the source, to find the place where this mysterious Corwen was hiding.

Settling down on Errol's bed, Melyn extinguished his conjured light and focused his mind. Eyes closed, the cave exploded into patterns of light. Across from him, Frecknock stood, waiting patiently. She was less pathetic-looking in the aethereal, though still small, as if fear had driven much of the life out of her.

'Come with me,' he said in the same way he would have spoken to Beulah when in this form. He rose from his body and headed towards the cave mouth. For an instant Frecknock did nothing, then she shrugged free of her self and floated towards him.

Melyn looked away, feeling uncomfortable. Outside the cave two warrior priests were pale self-images, little more than candles flickering against the midday sun. The rest of the troop were similarly nondescript as they searched the clearing. It annoyed him that his best soldiers had so little skill in the aethereal, bothered him that dragons seemed to possess it naturally. And not the mindless self-assurance of common beasts either, not like dogs or horses, which appeared exactly the same however he looked at them.

Pushing the thought away, Melyn sought the telltale signs of magical working. He might as well have looked for a specific grain of rice in a bowlful. The clearing was awash with controlled power. He had already seen how the path that crossed it was part of some vast web, but the more he looked around, the more he was overwhelmed by the sheer scale of the spells cast on the place. Magic so thick he could taste it swirled around him like a fog of colour, pulled him this way and that as if toying with him. He set his mind against it, erected his barriers until the forces that spun around him narrowed and darkened. He picked one at random, a red pulsing snake that writhed between him and Frecknock, and reached out to grasp it.

'I wouldn't recommend you do that,' the dragon said.

'Why not?

'You're very vulnerable in this form, and that's a powerful spell of compulsion. Would you want to spend the rest of your life unable to stop yourself coming back to this clearing?'

Melyn felt like a young novitiate scolded in class for suggesting something foolish. Frecknock's tone took him back to his childhood; his anger returned to him.

'I'm well acquainted with the magic of compulsion.

This is not so different from the spell that makes the Calling Road so irresistible to your kind. I have every intention of following it to its source.' But he didn't touch it, instead allowing his aethereal form to follow it as it looped and dived in among all the other magic. It was hard to make out the real from the conjured, a strain to relate what his sight showed him with his memory of the clearing, but eventually he came to the point where everything seemed to merge. He looked around, trying to get his bearings in a world that was turned inside out. Only Frecknock, standing calmly by his side as if she saw such turbulent conjurings every day, looked remotely like he would expect to see with his normal sight. Only more colourful, less dowdy and black.

Unbidden, an image of her in the water came to his mind, the wetness making her scales gleam and sparkle. Wading towards the waterfall.

Melyn snapped back into his body. The whole experience had been unsettling to say the least, but he had found what he was looking for.

'Come with me.' He didn't wait to see if the two warrior priests followed, but strode down to the ford, then into the water. It was deep as he pushed his way upstream, coming first to his knees, then his waist, then his chest as he entered the bubbling, roiling froth right in front of the cascade.

Taking a deep breath, he stepped through.

Errol heard Benfro's approach long before he saw him flying in over the trees that fringed the clearing. He had regained some of his strength, but even so he didn't fancy more walking. His legs ached with months of too little use, even his daily swim was not enough to prepare him for this kind of exercise, and the bones in his ankles felt weak, like they might break again at any moment. He was wearily preparing himself for the inevitable when the dragon's hurried, ungainly landing made him pause. Picking himself up off the ground, Benfro rushed over.

'Melyn. He was there. He arrived just as I did.'

'Did you get the jewels?' Errol already knew the answer; it was written all over Benfro's face.

'There was no time. I didn't even land.'

'They're well hidden. He'll never find them. Corwen will keep them safe.' Even as he said it, Errol had his doubts. Inquisitor Melyn was both tenacious and a very powerful magician. He would surely see through the ancient spells that protected the cave behind the waterfall.

'He's got Frecknock with him. I don't know why, but she seems to be helping him. If he finds them all is lost. I'll never be free of Magog, and I'll lose my mother.' In his panic Benfro had come right up to where Errol still sat with the bags. The dragon towered over him like a small tree, shading out the sun.

'Well, we can't go back if the clearing's full of warrior priests. We have to get as far away as possible.'

'I have to get them.' Benfro flopped down on to the ground beside Errol, who felt the shock through his bones like thunder overhead. 'I can't leave them behind.'

'What about the Llinellau?' Errol let his focus slip until the lines swam into view, thick and full of the life that filled the forest. 'Couldn't you use them to bring the jewels to you? Like I did with the chest?'

Benfro dropped his head into his hands. 'I only managed that once before, back in Magog's retreat. And now whenever I try to use the subtle arts, he's there waiting for me. If I try to do anything with the Llinellau I fear I'll end up back at the top of the mountain.' He looked up at the imposing bulk towering over them. Errol followed his gaze, trying to see the peak, imagining the little room on top of the world.

'What if I were to watch over you?'

'It wouldn't work. I don't know where the jewels are. Oh, I know they're in the back of the cave behind the waterfall, but I've never seen them. It's hopeless. Why did we leave them behind? How could I have left them behind?' Benfro dropped his head down into his hands, sobbing.

'I've seen them. And I managed to use the lines to bring that chest to the clearing. I'll do it.' Errol sounded far more confident than he felt, but he had to do something. At least try.

'You will?' Benfro's voice quavered as he looked down at Errol. Then he shook his head. 'No, you can't. It's too risky. You might fall under Magog's influence too.'

'But I might not, especially if I'm careful. I shan't touch his jewel if I can help it. And anyway, what's the alternative?'

Benfro didn't answer, and Errol took that as permission to proceed. He wasn't really sure what he was doing, but he remembered some of the things Corwen had taught him. He tried to picture the darkened cavern deep in the rock behind the waterfall, and at the same time he let his mind open to the Grym, feeling out along the lines for the one that fitted.

Slowly, piece by piece, he built the image up in his head, walking around and adding detail as he remembered it. All the while the Grym was a clamour of voices, smells, flashes of scenes that threatened to undo the one calm scene in his mind. Corwen's cave was nearby. They hadn't even walked a full day, and he knew all too well that his pace had been slow. It should be a strong connection.

Bit by bit, the image of the cavern came together, and as it did so the distractions ebbed away to a dull background susurrus. Errol could see it all now, a perfect replica in his mind's eye. And there, in the middle, the rock dais with its pile of pale white jewels, one lone white gem sitting to one side, one red one to the other, spreading its bloody glow over everything.

He reached out, meaning to pick up Morgwm's jewel, seeing his hand in front of him. And then everything changed. His brain told him he was sitting, but his balance said he was upright. His feet were tangled beneath him and he pitched forward, crashing to the floor. The hard earth floor with that familiar spicy scent. He tried to open his eyes, to replace the image he had built with that of the clearing. But all he could see was the cavern lit by the glow coming from the jewels themselves. He hadn't reached out along the lines at all; he had walked himself back to Corwen's cave.

For a moment he panicked. He knew that the warrior

priests were outside. What if they had already discovered the cave, were even now creeping along the winding tunnel that led to this sanctuary? He strained his ears, certain he could hear footsteps scraping on the floor. And was that the faintest glow of light, a flickering torch outlining the exit?

He was imagining it, he told himself. The cave was silent save for the quiet rush of his breath and the hammering of his heart. He was as safe here as anywhere; didn't Corwen's magics protect it from casual discovery? Melyn would find the other cave, know that he had fled and set off through the forest in pursuit.

But how long would it take him to find Benfro? How long could he afford to spend sitting around here fretting? He had to get back and take the jewels with him.

Errol stood up, his eyes accustomed to the low light now. As he approached the stone pedestal, he could see how far Magog's influence had spread. Corwen's own jewels numbered two dozen or more, and none of them touched the small irregular red gem, yet at least ten of them had changed from clear white to a bloody pink, those nearest almost crimson. The cavern was silent, but Errol fancied he could sense an echo of some great struggle, just past hearing. That Corwen had not appeared was proof enough of the battle taking place.

Errol reached into his pocket and brought out a strip of cloth hacked from one of his old shirts. He folded it double over his hand and reached out for the red jewel. Something invisible pushed back against him. He pushed harder, and the force opposing him grew in strength, so that it felt like he was trying to move solid rock. However hard he tried, he couldn't get his hand any closer to the red jewel.

He put away the cloth, reaching out with bare fingers. For a moment the pressure was there again, a tingling against his skin. He felt the brush of something against his head, as if a bat had flown past him in the darkness. Startled, he almost closed his hand on the jewel. It now sucked him towards it where before it had repelled, but at the last moment he snatched his hand away.

Taking the cloth in his other hand, he stared down at the jewel. Remembering his lessons back at Emmass Fawr, he tried to close his mind to outside influences, and as he did so realized just how open he had allowed it to become. One by one he went through the exercises he had learned, and with each repeated mantra, so the clamour quietened. The lines came to his vision, pulsing and glowing throughout the cavern. Then he saw the glow of his aura around him and the swirling patterns of the magics that filled the place, surrounding Magog's withered gem, spreading out from it in a foul miasma, thin tendrils of red snaking out to the lines and into the pile of Corwen's jewels.

They moved constantly, probing the air and curling around the colourful shapes and swirls that Errol knew were Corwen's defences, constantly testing them, trying to break through. One particularly fat strand looped into a line on the floor that speared off into the rock, fading from red to palest rose as it went. He could imagine all too easily where that line went.

He moved his hand close to the red jewel, focused his

attention on the thin aura that oozed over his fingers and extended it out from their tips in long thin strands that slipped in between the gem's tendrils. The touch, when it came, was like plunging his hand into ice, a cold so sudden and intense he half expected his breath to mist – if he was actually breathing. Somewhere in the distance he could hear a clamouring of voices in violent argument. He did his best to ignore them, and all the other forces that whipped at him, concentrating solely on his aura and the evil red gem.

Lifting it from the stone pedestal was an anticlimax. It was almost as if the spirit of Magog, or whatever the jewel possessed, had finally admitted defeat. The red tendrils evaporated from Errol's sight as he slowly lifted the dangerous treasure and dropped it into the cloth held out in his other hand. As his contact with it was cut, so the world seemed to shift back to normal, leaving him with the feeling that he had been away for a long time. He swiftly wrapped the jewel tight, then pushed it deep into his pocket, letting out a long slow breath. It had been such a small thing to do, and yet he was as exhausted as if he had run for half a day.

Still there was one more jewel to collect, and then he had to get back to Benfro. After that there would be more walking through the forest, probably late into the night. He reached out and took up Morgwm's perfect pale jewel.

The barrage of images was all the more intense for him being unready. Errol had relaxed the barriers he had put up against Magog, and now, weakened, he suffered the full onslaught of Morgwm's memories. He saw a once-beautiful woman cry out a name and die, her body racked with pain and wasted almost to nothing save the bulge of her pregnancy. He knew that body, skin pulled taut over bone, tanned and dried by the drug that had killed her, that swelling still there, fourteen years after her death. Princess Lleyn.

The image changed, becoming a procession: a tiny dragon snuggling into a blanket draped over the body of an infant, that same infant being handed over to a woman who looked like his mother, only younger than he had ever remembered Hennas. He saw Father Gideon standing in a doorway that made the coenobite look like a child, watched a scrawny young dragon with Benfro's face as he sat at a scrubbed wood table mixing strange poultices, dropped his head in sadness as he saw Inquisitor Melyn ride towards him accompanied by a troop of warrior priests and novitiates. The thoughts and feelings came thick and fast, a terrible maelstrom: dragons, men, wars, magic and finally the maniacally smiling face of the inquisitor, his blade of light lifted high above his head, ready to swing down and finish the job that King Ballah's executioner had started.

Knowing his death was coming, and soon, Errol found he could accept it. There would be a peace in it that he had never known in life. But there was a worry too. Who would look after Benfro? How would he cope? Had Errol done enough to teach him how to survive?

The sensation of a hand on his arm cut through the onslaught of images, and Errol realized he had been sucked in completely. He looked up to see not Inquisitor Melyn, but Corwen standing on the other side of the pedestal.

'The memories of Morgwm the Green mean you no harm, Errol. But they are just as dangerous in their way as those of Magog, Son of the Summer Moon.'

'Corwen. You're . . .'

'I'm all right, yes. Thank you. And I'm impressed with your skill at manipulating your aura. But is it wise to take those jewels with you? It will be harder to keep Magog from getting his claws into Benfro.'

'He wouldn't leave his mother behind. He came back to get her, but Melyn was already here.' Errol breathlessly tried to recount the whole story, but Corwen simply raised a hand to silence him, his focus shifting away for a moment, in the direction of the tunnel.

'They're coming. You must go now.'

Errol looked up at the wizened old dragon, then spun round. He could see nothing, but a shiver of fear ran through him. 'Melyn? But what of your spells? I thought this place was hidden.'

'So it was. So it has been for many centuries. But the most potent of spells wears off in time. And I've been a bit distracted of late. Now don't hang around, Errol. You must get back to Benfro. Working together there's a chance both of you might survive. Apart, you're doomed.'

A faint noise echoed from the dark passageway. At first Errol thought he might have imagined it, but then it came again – the far-off sound of heavy furniture being moved. There was no doubt Melyn had found the second cave now. Errol looked back at Corwen, then down at the pile of jewels on the pedestal between them. Instinctively he reached out to scoop them up, but the old dragon gripped his wrist firmly.

'There's no time for that now. You have to go.'

'But they'll find you. They'll take your jewels . . .'

'And then I'll be with them wherever they go. I'm honoured that you should be so concerned for my welfare, Errol. But I've been dead almost five hundred years. Don't be in such a hurry to join me.'

Errol hesitated. He hated running out on Corwen, and yet there was nothing else he could do. He might not even be able to do that; the noises from the passageway were getting louder, and it was no longer just his imagination that could see the palest of reflected light outlining the opening in the rock wall.

'Focus, Errol. Forget what's going on around you. Remember what you did to get here. Follow that path back to Benfro.' Corwen's words were in his head, and slowly the image of the old dragon faded away to nothing, the pressure on Errol's wrist disappearing as if it had never been there. He looked once more at the pile of jewels, then summoned up the image of the lines to his sight, trying to build a picture of the clearing he had left in his mind.

It was all but impossible. He hadn't spent long there anyway, and most of that time had been spent dozing. The lines sang to him their alluring song of everywhere, and all the while the noises from the passageway grew closer and closer, more difficult to block out of his mind. Errol's panic built as his mental discipline dissolved, until it was all he could do to see the lines.

Then he noticed it, pale pink where all the others were white, a tendril of connection looping from the jewel in his pocket and connecting with one of the lines. He had felt the touch of that jewel, its cold, emotionless grasping, and now he used that memory to feel his way along the lines, following Magog's malign influence back to its target. Taking a deep breath and blotting out everything else, Errol stepped into the void.

18

Sir Flisk was very fond of the people of Fo Afron. They were scholars and artists, and treated him and his kind with respect. He was always welcome in their cities, and perhaps never more so than in Voran, far to the east.

But kind and friendly though the people of Fo Afron were, they were not always wise. Many times Sir Flisk warned the citizens of Voran about the steaming mountain overlooking their fair city. Nem-Voranar had grown restless down the centuries, its pointed crown now more often swathed in its own cloud of steam than visible. Still, it gave the people of Voran hot water, and the soil all around was fertile. No one alive could remember a time when the mountain had not been a little unruly, but neither could they recall tales of it being anything else. And so they listened politely to Sir Flisk's warnings but stayed in their paradise unconcerned.

When Nem-Voranar did finally erupt, thousands died, buried under falling ash and pumice. The distraught survivors were forced to flee with nothing but the clothes on their backs into the inhospitable lands of the Gwastadded Wag. It was here that Sir Flisk found them, hungry and dispirited, mourning their lost home. And though they had not heeded

> his warnings, he took pity on them all the same. He bade them come together, and wove a great working of the subtle arts such that each of their steps became like a thousand. In one night of walking they reached the far side of the empty plains. Indeed, so quick was their passage they even crossed the Sea of Tegid, alighting on the western shore where now stands the city of Talarddeg.
>
> Sir Frynwy, *Tales of the Ffrydd*

Benfro paced backwards and forwards, wearing away a patch of grass at the end of the clearing, willing Errol to come back. He blamed himself for the boy's disappearance. It was madness to have let him try to fetch the jewels. Neither he nor Errol was a skilled mage; something bad was bound to have happened. What if he had been drawn away to the other side of the forest? What if he had fallen into Inquisitor Melyn's hands?

Frustrated by inaction, he ran out into the middle of the clearing, snapping his wings open and beating at the evening air. Within a few strides he was aloft, climbing above the treetops with angry ease. He wheeled about, searching the canopy as if Errol might have transported himself to a nearby treetop. But there was no figure waving desperately, just a few crows heading home to roost, a lone pigeon scooting nervously along on some unknown mission.

Benfro circled wider, his arc taking him further south on each turn. He wanted to go back to Corwen's clearing, to rescue Errol, who he was sure was being tortured even now, but realistically he knew there was nothing he could do against so many warrior priests. So he wheeled, watching the sun disappear over the edge of the far-distant Rim mountains in the west, all the while his head and hearts fighting.

He spotted movement through the canopy perhaps two miles south of the clearing where Errol had disappeared. It was difficult to make out through the dense foliage, so he dropped, wide wings feeling their way through the warm air, until he was almost touching the uppermost leaves. Speeding along, he saw a well maintained path running through the woods beneath him. With mixed feelings he realized that this was the track leading away from the ford back at Corwen's clearing. It followed the contours of the river to the point where he and Errol had emerged earlier from their long trek through the woods. In their panic they had not only forgotten the jewels, but had decided to avoid the path. Now Benfro could see that they could have covered twice the distance in half the time if they had chosen differently. And something was speeding towards his makeshift camp, the place where Errol would surely return soon.

Benfro turned and made one more sweep, peering through the leaves. Directly over the path he could just about make out the shape of horses, but he didn't need his eyes to tell him what was below. He could smell the warrior priests even this high above them. Then the canopy broke and he saw them, ten or more, heads down, their horses galloping. It was obvious they knew where they were going, but they couldn't have caught Errol and forced the location from him. He had only been gone a few minutes, if that. Even at breakneck speed it would have taken them longer to get here. Which meant that Melyn must have tracked him, and must know the paths in this part of the forest. Benfro didn't want to know how that was possible. It filled him with dread to think that the inquisitor could follow him so easily. How could he ever hope to escape?

He sped away, landed swiftly in the clearing and ran towards the shade under the trees where their bags still lay. There was no sign of Errol, but now Benfro didn't even dare shout out the boy's name for fear of attracting the attention of the approaching riders. He picked up Errol's cloth sack and tied it to the leather strap of his own bag. It added no measurable weight to that of the gold inside. What use would the coins be to him if he couldn't find Errol? There was surely nowhere in Gwlad where a dragon could go to a merchant and ask for goods. Men would either flee or kill him. Still, he slung the bag over his neck, along with the sturdy woven-grass provision bag that the mother tree had given him, easing them into a comfortable position. He could wait no longer for Errol to return, though it felt like the worst of betrayals to leave him.

Benfro was walking towards the middle of the clearing with heavy hearts and leaden footsteps when a cry stopped him in his tracks. He looked round to see the first of the warrior priests burst from the trees over to his left. The rest of them appeared in quick succession, popping from the forest like wasps from a disturbed nest. Not waiting to be caught, he leaped into the air, climbing with all his strength.

He didn't look back; his sole focus was the line of trees that formed the far edge of the clearing. Once over them he would be safe, at least in the short term. Something whizzed in the air, flying past his ear, and he watched in terror as a crossbow bolt dropped slowly to the ground in front of his eyes, hitting the earth with a dull thud he could hear even over the rushing wind. He pushed harder, trying to gain height without losing speed, desperate to outrun the warrior priests. It couldn't end this way. He wouldn't die here.

Something clattered off the scales on his back, and Benfro almost looked round to see what it was. He managed to stop himself, knowing that to look back was to slow down, and to slow down was to give his attackers time to take better aim. He felt no pain, though he had no doubt that would come later, when the panic was over. *If* the panic was over. And then he was over the trees, his tail clattering off the highest branches. He put in a dozen more huge wing beats, feeling the ache of his old wound resurface at the effort, before finally turning to see what the warrior priests were doing.

To his surprise they had not only stopped pursuing him, but had regrouped and were riding like the wind in a different direction. Benfro couldn't help himself from wheeling to see what had distracted them. His hearts almost stopped when he saw Errol standing a couple of dozen paces in from the edge of the clearing. He was clearly dazed, and, as Benfro watched, he sank to his knees, oblivious to the warrior priests heading his way.

One of them was pulling ahead, riding a fine beast far larger than the others and easily able to outpace them.

Benfro didn't need to see the man who rode it to know that this was Melyn's trusted second-in-command. The man who had stood smiling as the inquisitor brought his blade of fire down in a terrible arc, severing Morgwm's head. And now that same man had conjured his own blade, holding it high as if he intended visiting a similar fate on Errol.

Benfro's wings had put him in position even before he had thought through his plan. He shot across the tree-tops, wheeling until he faced the warrior priests' charge, Errol directly between them. The boy had not yet looked up; he seemed to be fixated on the grass all around him as if he had never seen its like before. Benfro noted his position, confident he wouldn't move, and then shifted his focus to the warrior priests.

It would be a close run thing who would reach Errol first, and as he pulled his wings back, plummeting towards the ground, Benfro could see some of the riders aiming crossbows. He heard a series of twangs as the quarrels were loosed, and in the same second he released a great bellow of rage. The fire boiled out of him, pure and white, rolling out into the air as if it were alive. The crossbow bolts evaporated in little explosions of yellow flame, whipping behind him as he hurtled towards the ground.

The man on the big horse was almost upon Errol, his hateful blade held high. Benfro could see him clearly now, make out his solid features, his sandy hair greying at the edges, his red cheeks, his eyes ablaze. His horse seemed to carry some of his madness too, its nostrils flared, its stare white and goggling. Its hooves kicked up clods of earth, throwing them back like boulders in a landslide. Sweat shined its flanks and lathered up around the leather of its harness.

Benfro snapped his eyes away from the mesmerizing sight, angling his wings to speed his forward motion but slow his descent. He reached out with his arms, seeing the rider leaning forward, desperately trying to beat him to the prize.

And then Errol looked up.

Benfro could only see him from behind, but the way his whole body tensed made it easy to read the boy's reaction. He must have known he was about to die. Not even his ability to walk the lines could possibly save him now.

'Errol. Relax.' Benfro meant only to shout the words, but with them came a huge gout of flame, the fruit of his anger. For an instant he thought he had made the worst of all possible errors, had done the inquisitor's job for him. At the noise Errol had turned, his already wide eyes almost splitting open at the sight. Benfro couldn't imagine what it must have looked like, but he fancied he could see the reflection of the flame in the boy's eyes in the instant before it . . . carried right on past him, leaving him unscathed.

Benfro hardly had time to register what had happened. He was on the boy at almost the same instant, sweeping him up in his arms and bringing his wings down with all the force he could muster. Ahead of him the horse had reared at the flame, dislodging its rider and falling back on to him. As he rushed past, Benfro was disappointed to see that the flame had petered out before it could do much damage, but he smelled singeing hair, and the odour filled his hearts with a strange joy.

And then he was on the other warrior priests, sweeping over them with his wings wide. One or two of them tried to conjure their blades, dropping their crossbows, but he was over them so fast none could strike home. He brought his wings down again in a heavy sweep, feeling them hit bodies with satisfying force. Looking back, he saw chaos as men and horses fell to the ground on top of each other.

Clutching Errol close to him, Benfro sped away across the clearing, gaining height and distance. He set his sights on the mountains and settled into a steady rhythm that would eat up the distance in no time.

Only then did he notice the noise that was coming from his mouth, and it took him some moments more to realize that he was laughing.

'Don't worry about that, Iol; Teryll will bring it down.'

Dafydd watched as his wife tried to fit too many clothes into too small a bag. They had spent an enjoyable three days in Talarddeg, seeing the sights, taking the waters and sampling the many and varied types of ginger for which the place was justly renowned. A few people had recognized them, it was true, but most had simply treated them with the deference due an heir to the throne on an informal visit, and made little more fuss than that. If there were assassins dogging their every step then Usel had been as good as his word, for they had seen nothing of them at all. The only time Jarius had unsheathed his sword had been when an armourer in a tiny workshop on the edge of the industrial district had asked if he might inspect the workmanship. The sets of swords and daggers he had bought for himself, his captain and stable hand had been immeasurably superior, and he had even bought a finely wrought razor-sharp stiletto for Iolwen. It lay on the bed now, one more thing that would not fit into her pack.

'Teryll's a stable hand, not a valet, and certainly not a lady-in-waiting.' Iolwen laughed as she abandoned all hope of succeeding in her task. 'Listen to me. I sound like one of those vacuous courtiers who follow Tordu around the palace, treating servants like animals. Worse, even. Teryll volunteered to come with you and he's your friend. I just wish . . .'

'That some of your ladies had come with you?'

'No. Really, no. None of them would have lasted a day on the road. And besides, I hardly know any of them; they come and go so quickly. It's just that you've got Jarius and Teryll both to share all this with.' She held her hands up, taking in the room, the inn, the city and beyond. 'I'm alone. I've always been alone.'

Dafydd remembered the sad little girl he had first met in the palace at Tynhelyg so many years ago he couldn't begin to count them. She had been so different, with her skin so pale it was almost translucent, her fair hair and sharply angular eyes. He had been fascinated by her but at the same time just as cruel as any young boy can be, reflecting the prejudices of his parents and teachers. He had followed her around, studied her in the same way he had studied the wildlife in the shallow reed-filled water at the edge of the royal lakes. But when she had tried to befriend him, he had called her names and run away. She had been lonely then and had grown up lonely while he had made easy friends and travelled all over his grandfather's kingdom. She had been confined to the palace, served by the unwilling daughters of out-of-favour nobles, only very occasionally seeing emissaries from her own country, the people who had abandoned her when she was only six.

And then he had come back to Tynhelyg, his studies finished, his travels for the moment complete, his mind more open than ever before, to find this strangely alluring, beautiful and different creature. Everyone had thought him mad to court her; his father had even threatened to disown him. Only Ballah had understood, and agreed. And in the end that was all that mattered.

But in all her years as a hostage to peace between their two countries Iolwen had only ever made one true friend in Tynhelyg, and she'd married him too.

'Come on, Iol. Let's see if we can't find a bit of space somewhere. We don't want to miss the boat.' Dafydd got his own travel bags from the end of the bed and unbuckled them. As was always the way when he travelled, he had brought the minimum he could get away with, but it had a habit of growing whenever he tried to pack. In theory he should have been able to get everything into one of his two leather saddlebags, but for some reason it wanted to fill both. Normally he would have had servants to sort it out for him, but even then he preferred to pick his own clothes; he wasn't so old and infirm he couldn't dress himself.

He tipped everything out on to the bed and began folding crumpled shirts. Someone had once tried to explain to him that they took up less space that way.

'Here. Let me.' Iolwen took the garment from him,

smoothing it out and performing some strange magic on it that made it look like it was freshly laundered. She worked her way through the rest of his things, placing them all back into one of the saddlebags. As predicted, the second one lay empty by the time she had finished.

Talarddeg was famed for its seamstresses and tailors, as well as its ginger. Iolwen had made the most of the opportunity to buy loose-fitting gowns, the better to hide her growing belly. Dafydd thought she looked better in them anyway, rather than the tight-laced bodices and frills that were fashionable in Tynhelyg. But he still wasn't sure why she needed so many. She folded the last one, placing it in the top of the saddlebag, as a discreet knock came at the door. Dafydd opened it to see Usel standing outside, the first time he had seen the man since entering the city.

'Are you ready?' the medic asked.

'As we'll ever be.' Dafydd hauled the saddlebags over his shoulder. Usel shook his head.

'Leave those here; I'll see to it that they're put on the boat.'

Jarius and Teryll were waiting for them downstairs, also without any luggage. Dafydd wondered if this was another part of the subterfuge. If it looked like they were leaving their bags, no one would suspect they had any other plan than to sail across the Sea of Tegid to Fo Afron and spend a few days exploring the ruins there. But given the vast wagon-loads of luggage most young nobles took on their travels, he couldn't help thinking he would stick out more with nothing at all.

The sun hung high in the southern sky as they walked

among the throngs of sightseers, merchants, hawkers and loungers who made up the lifeblood of the city. Cut off from the rest of the country by the Caldy range, Talarddeg was more of a state in its own right even if technically part of Llanwennog. It was ruled by King Ballah's second son, Vern, and Dafydd was heartily grateful he had managed to avoid visiting his uncle. Wherever you were in the city, from the busy docks to the industrial quarter and out beyond the walls to the ginger fields, you could always see the castle, perched on its high rock, looking down over everything like a buzzard eyeing up its next meal. Every day since his arrival Dafydd had been expecting a summons, and each day it didn't come was a little more weight off his shoulders.

He had expected a small boat for the trip. It was a narrow crossing which shouldn't take more than half a day with a favourable wind, but the vessel creaking against its moorings on the lightly undulating sea was magnificent. Twin-masted, she was built for speed over cargo capacity, narrow in the beam and shining with new paint.

Usel guided them swiftly through the throng of stevedores and sailors preparing the ship for departure. Dafydd saw a wagon parked by the gangplank, travel chests and the usual paraphernalia of exploration being carried up and into the hold. His earlier worries evaporated as he realized just how much attention to detail Master Holgrum must have been paying. Every angle had been covered, every eventuality anticipated. So why did the medic keep looking over his shoulder nervously?

'Lady Anwyn is aboard already. If you'd like to join her, then we can depart . . . Ah, Gog's balls, what do they want?' Dafydd was so surprised by Usel's strange expletive he almost didn't notice that something had upset the medic. Following his gaze, he saw a troop of ten men marching towards them. By their polished armour and the way the people darted out of their way, Dafydd knew they could only be his uncle's men.

'Take my hand.' Dafydd felt his hand being grasped, and looked down to see Usel reaching for Iolwen too. 'Captain, Master Teryll, quickly, join with us. Form a circle.'

There must have been something in Usel's tone, for no one asked what he was doing. Instead, they just stood there like some primitive rural prayer meeting, watching as the troop of soldiers came ever closer.

And then marched straight past.

'Wha—' Dafydd began to say.

Usel silenced him with a hissed 'Quiet.'

The lieutenant of the troop, identified by his elaborately decorated armour, ordered two of his men to take up positions at the end of the gangplank, then marched the rest of them on to the ship.

'Search every cabin. We know they left the tavern, so they must be on board by now.' Looking up, Dafydd could just see the lieutenant standing on the deck as his soldiers disappeared below. After a moment a tall man with a fierce face marched down the length of the boat. He towered over the lieutenant by a head, and was probably twice his width too.

'What's the meaning of this?' he bellowed in a voice that carried across the entire dock. 'How dare you board my ship?'

'I have orders direct from Duke Vern. This boat has been chartered to carry Prince Dafydd of the House of Ballah on an expedition to the ruins. His Grace has had word from Tynhelyg requiring the prince to return immediately.'

'Well he ain't on board. An' I'm not waiting fer 'im either. I've important cargo bound for Kais. Can't waste time and tide waitin' fer no prince.'

The lieutenant flushed and seemed to be building up the courage to remonstrate with the ship's captain when his troop reappeared.

'No one on board, sir, and none of the cabins have been used. Could they have taken a different ship?'

The lieutenant said nothing, merely indicating for his men to fall in behind him. He marched them off the boat, collecting the two who had been at the bottom of the gangplank, and headed back towards the city and castle. As he walked past Dafydd noted his brow and cheeks were slick with sweat. It could have been the heat and that ornate armour, but he suspected the lieutenant feared the wrath of Duke Vern more.

'Right, you lot. Get that equipment off my boat and back in the wagon.' Dafydd looked up to see the captain striding back towards the boat's bow, handing out orders to his sailors as he went.

'We'd best get on board quick,' Usel said, letting go of his hand. For an instant Dafydd felt his whole body shudder, as if someone had poured iced water over his head. The air darkened like a cloud had passed over the sun, but the sky was clear, blue and fresh with the sea air. He couldn't see Jarius, Teryll and Iolwen, a moment's panic hitting him. Then the sky brightened and they were there in front of him.

'I've got to learn that spell,' he said to no one in particular as they clambered up the gangplank and into the cool dark confines of the ship.

Beulah wasn't at all sad to see the back of Corris. Everything about the place depressed her, from its air of run-down poverty and dirt to its dark and gloomy castle and the nasty secrets it held. Her last act before leaving the town – still mourning the death of its elderly lord – had been to officially recognize Captain Herren as Queln's grandson and heir. She wasn't sure whether that was a blessing for the man or a curse. Certainly her requirement that he field a troop of soldiers for her army was likely to prove a strain on the newly ennobled Lord Herren's meagre resources, both financial and of men. It wouldn't surprise her if Corris ceased to exist in a few years' time, and Beulah couldn't find it in her to be sad about the death of such an insignificant corner of her kingdom.

The party rode the short distance to Wright's Ferry, downstream from the crumbling town and the boundary between the lands of Corris and the fiefdom of Lord Beylin. The contrast couldn't have been more marked, with gangs of workmen busy carving out a deep pool and loading dock at the upper reaches of the river, just below the old ferry crossing. What had been no more than a small village where boats had been dragged out on to the shallow sandy banks for repairs was now growing into a sizeable town. Beulah couldn't help but notice the number of young men hard at work increasing Lord Beylin's wealth. So much for the noble houses contributing to the war effort. She made a note to contact Seneschal Padraig at the earliest opportunity to see about raising taxes in the west.

They commandeered a couple of flat-bottomed barges, the royal party and those few noble courtiers who hadn't returned to Candlehall in the first boat, the guard of warrior priests in the second, and made swift progress downstream to Beylinstown. The rain that had dogged them from Beteltown finally gave way to sunshine, and Beulah was able to relax on deck to concentrate on healing the crossbow wound in her arm and the burn on her palm. From the steep wooded hills, bleak moors and narrow valleys of the north-west corner of the Hafod, the land flowed into the more gentle contours of the Hendry. Fertile grasslands provided grazing for thousands of cattle, and occasionally she saw, silhouetted on the brow of some low rise, small herds of the wild horses for which the area was famed. Beulah missed her horse and determined to seek out a suitable replacement when they reached Castell Glas.

But first they had to endure Beylinstown. Beulah knew Lord Beylin as an odious man, constantly trying to charm his way into favour but ruthless in his exploitation of any who fell for his winning smile. In his late thirties and still unmarried, he had pressed his suit with her father, hoping to marry himself on to the throne. He had not attended her wedding, and it would be interesting to see how he dealt with the new Duke of Abervenn.

The small convoy of barges pulled into the riverbank at a set of docks some distance upstream of the town walls.

Beulah didn't wait for the rest of the party; she, Clun and a small troop of warrior priests rode on to the main gates, leaving the rest to sort themselves out in their own time. As they passed the cattle yards and auction rings, row upon row of cows looked up from whatever it was they were doing, innumerable eyes following them as they went by, none of them human. Glancing up at the sky, Beulah gauged the time at somewhere close to evening prayers, but that didn't account for the complete lack of people.

'Where is everyone?' she asked Clun, who was scanning the area with an intent scowl on his face.

'I'm not sure. I've seen a couple of young lads scampering around at the back of the herd. I think they might be preparing some kind of reception for you, my lady.'

Beulah looked up at the town walls and the spreading mass of Beylinstown behind them. The coming war had been good for Lord Beylin and his merchants; almost all the cattle raised in the north of the Hendry came through his fiefdom. Perhaps she should have married the man after all. She could have arranged for him to die shortly afterwards and would have inherited a great deal of wealth. But then Abervenn wasn't exactly poor.

'You think they're all in there waiting for us?' she asked.

'Either that or everyone's dead,' Clun replied. 'Look, the gates aren't even guarded.'

And it was true. They were approaching the gatehouse, two huge towers with an impressive battlement linking them above a great vaulted arch. The gates stood open, the road ahead obscured by a defensive kink in the way, and there was no one around the entrance, not even a beggar crying out for spare coin. As she rode into the shadow of the walls Beulah felt a shiver of unease ripple down her spine. It reminded her too much of the dead village, Pwllpeiran, where she had met the dragon.

'Your Majesty, may I welcome you to my humble home.' Lord Beylin stepped into the road from a doorway behind the huge gates. He bowed extravagantly, then straightened, staring intently at her, ignoring the man who rode at her side. If Beulah had disliked him before, she hated him now. But she knew better than to run him through. It would be difficult to placate the other nobles, and she did need his help with the war.

'Lord Beylin. I was beginning to think you ruled a fiefdom of ghosts.'

'My people – your loyal subjects – await your entrance.' Lord Beylin motioned for them to enter the city, and at the same time a page emerged from behind the gates, leading a horse. 'If I might introduce you to them?'

Beulah sighed at the theatricality of it all. She knew well enough that it was all about show. Lord Beylin would ride at her side, and the people would know he was important. His position would be strengthened and they would feel that their queen favoured them. Everyone would win, but she hated it all the same.

'You've not met his grace the Duke of Abervenn.' Beulah waited until Beylin was half-mounted before speaking. She knew it was petty, but she couldn't help herself trying to make the man uncomfortable.

'Your Grace.' Beylin bowed from his saddle as his horse skittered around, then fought with the reins to bring it under control. 'So you're the . . . young man who so caught our beloved queen's eye.'

Clun merely nodded, his embarrassment evident in the spreading redness around his ears and the back of his neck.

'Shall we get this over with, Petrus.' Beulah used Beylin's first name as a weapon. He might think her friendly at first, but the fact that she knew that much about him would play on his mind later. 'We've had a long journey down from Corris.'

'Ah yes, Corris.' Beylin nudged his horse so that he was riding alongside Beulah on the opposite side to Clun. 'I heard you'd stopped there, and about the trouble you encountered.'

'I would hope so. I sent a messenger directly to you.'

'Of course, ma'am. And I acted on his message as soon as I received it. I have a surprise waiting for you in my dungeons. A certain predicant of the Order of the Candle you might want to interrogate.'

Beulah would have answered with some suitable reply, might even have congratulated the man, but at that same moment they rounded the kink in the roadway and entered the town proper. A throng of people filled a square: some had climbed on to the roofs of buildings, others squeezed out of windows and doorways. It looked as if the whole of Beylinstown had come to greet her, and all of them were waving tiny flags bearing the royal coat of arms. As soon as they saw her, they all shouted and cheered. She stiffened in her saddle, hating the attention and adulation, despising simple-minded peasants who could get so excited about seeing a person riding a horse. But beside her Lord Beylin was in his element, waving at his people with an annoying circular flutter of his hand, as if he were an effete farmer sowing oats on rocky ground.

'My lady, I think we should dismount and walk among your people.' Beulah looked around at Clun, who had spoken loudly enough for her to hear but not enough to carry to Beylin.

'Are you mad?' she asked, but he looked straight at her, then flicked his eyes past hers. She understood then. This whole show had been manufactured by Beylin, but he wasn't the kind of man to mix with his own workers and peasantry. This was the perfect way to bring him down to earth.

'Of course, my love.' Beulah pulled her borrowed horse to a halt as Clun did the same. He slid swiftly from his saddle, handing his reins to Captain Celtin behind him. She couldn't help but notice the captain had a broad smile on his face too.

Clun helped her down and it was only then that Beylin noticed what was happening. He pulled his own horse up short, wheeling it round.

'Your Majesty, is this wise?'

'These are my people, Petrus. I can't look down on them from a horse.' And with Clun at her side she set off to walk among her subjects.

19

Perhaps another example of the confusion within and surrounding the Guardians of the Throne is the contradictory beliefs held about this so-called order. Some say that it is a precursor to the three great religious orders known today – Ram, Candle and High Ffrydd – and that its main function is the pursuit of knowledge for the benefit of mankind. There are numerous although poorly documented instances of strangers appearing in the royal court at times of crisis, bringing wisdom and saving the day. Yet there are tales too of an order working behind the scenes to hasten the day when the Shepherd returns from the stars. Of fanatical members who demand the strictest adherence to the scriptures and think nothing of killing those who disagree with them, even members who spurn the Shepherd and worship instead the Wolf. These last are the followers of Mad Goronwy, who would pursue knowledge only to suppress it. And there are supposedly yet more who claim the title Guardians of the Throne whose heresy is even more contemptible. For they deny the existence of the Shepherd altogether and believe that – of all creatures – dragons once ruled Gwlad.

Barrod Sheepshead, *The Guardians of the Throne – A Noble Folly*

Lord Beylin's castle stood in marked contrast to Queln's sorry pile of stones back in Corris. It sat on a rocky outcrop that rose strategically over a bend in the River Hafren as it swelled sluggishly through the plains of the upper Hendry. Like Corris, it had been built many centuries earlier, but whereas Queln's keep had not changed in the intervening years, Castle Beylin had been upgraded, expanded and remodelled until very little trace of its original form could be seen.

Beulah had enjoyed her walk among the simple folk of Beylinstown, perhaps because it had discomfited Lord Beylin so much or perhaps because Clun seemed genuinely interested in meeting everyone. And far from the hostile reception she had expected, or at best a restrained indifference, everyone had seemed genuinely excited to be so close to their monarch. For a while she had basked in the adulation, the rushing energy of so much raw emotion, feeding on it until she felt like she could do almost anything. However, her entrance into Beylin's castle, a place of calm in the midst of the maelstrom, had been a relief. And, still full of the power of her subjects, she had lost no time in demanding to see the prisoner.

Lord Beylin himself led the party down into the depths. Beulah followed directly behind him, with Clun and Captain Celtin bringing up the rear. They descended through several levels, the air growing increasingly still, stale and rank, until finally they could go no further.

'Were you worried he might escape?' Beulah watched as Beylin fumbled with a heavy ring of keys given to him by the dungeon master. He selected one and inserted it into the lock on a solid oak door, which turned with an oiled ease at odds with the neglected appearance of the place.

'Father Tolley proved a most slippery captive.' Beylin took back the torch that he had handed to Clun and pushed open the door. It swung silently inward, only the obvious effort required to move it giving away its weight. 'At first we just locked him in one of the guest rooms, but he managed to walk out of there as if the door were no more substantial than air. My guards only caught him because he was foolish enough to try and steal a horse from the castle stables.'

Locking the heavy door behind them, he led them along another narrow corridor towards a final door. There were no torches save the ones they had brought with them, and the silence was total. Beulah reached out for the lines, but the few that flickered through the place were insubstantial, scarcely enough to provide a little warmth, let alone anything as comforting as light. Anyone left down here for any length of time would surely lose their mind.

Beylin handed the torch to Clun once more as he searched through the key ring, looking for the right fit. As he slotted the heavy iron key home, he peered through the small slatted opening in the top of the door. It seemed a bit of an odd thing to do, Beulah thought, given the lack of illumination inside the cell. Perhaps he was trying to see if the predicant was hiding by the door, intent on rushing them as it was opened.

'Father Tolley, I have a visitor for you.' Beylin took back his torch once more, stepping into the cell and slotting it into an iron sconce on the wall. 'I think you'll be pleased to see . . . Oh.'

Beulah peered into the room. It was surprisingly large and dry, hacked out of the rock into a roughly round shape with a high uneven ceiling. On the far side a narrow shelf of stone protruded from the wall, offering a hard bed. To the left a small hole in the floor described its use eloquently in rich human odour. Opposite it a set of rusty iron manacles hung empty from a heavy ring let into the wall. There was nothing else in the room.

'Is this some kind of joke, Beylin?' Beulah pushed past him, looking around the back of the door. 'Where is he?'

'Your Majesty, I . . .' Beylin's cool exterior vanished instantly, his confusion evident as he darted around the room, searching even when there was nowhere a man might hide. He even peered down the hole, though a rat would have had a hard time escaping that way.

'I'd heard Castle Beylin's dungeons were inescapable.' Beulah stood in the middle of the cell, looking around and up. There was something not right about the place, something that niggled at the edge of her senses. She cursed the way her pregnancy dulled them. In the crowd outside she had felt alive, her old self. Perhaps that was why she had enjoyed the sensation more than she would have expected. But here, buried beneath thousands of tons of crushing rock, she felt constricted.

'They are. No one can escape. He must have been let out. But only Marchant has the keys.' Beylin held up the clanging metal bunch. 'He would never –'

'No one has escaped this cell. Well, at least not yet.'

Clun stood in the doorway, and though Beulah turned to face him, his eyes didn't meet hers. Instead they were fixed firmly on the bed shelf. 'Were you hoping that Lord Beylin would leave the door unlocked when he left?' He walked across the room, sweeping past her as if she wasn't there, keeping his gaze locked on something as if he feared he might lose it.

'And what about the other door? Do you honestly think he'd be stupid enough to leave both unlocked?'

Beulah couldn't help herself. She let out a little gasp of surprise as Clun produced a slim short blade of fire, reaching forward with it until the tip was almost touching the cave wall at about the point a man's neck might be were he sitting on the shelf. She felt the room chill and wondered just where it was he was taking his power from.

'Your Grace? Are you sure you're all right?' Beylin stepped forward, but Clun held up his free hand, then slowly inched the other forward, the point of his blade moving closer and closer to the wall.

'Please, please. Don't.' Something strange happened. First there was just the wall, poorly lit by the flame from the guttering torch. Then the shadows it cast seemed to coalesce into an indistinct shape, solidifying like candle wax dripped on to a tabletop, finally taking on the form of a man. The point of Clun's blade rested on his Adam's apple and Beulah smelled a faint whiff of burned skin over the other cloying odours of the cell.

'Father Tolley, I think.' Clun pulled his blade back a little but kept it alive.

'Indeed it is. But how?' Beylin approached the predicant, but Beulah waved him away.

'An interesting use of magic,' she said. 'One I'd like to learn more about. But first a little discipline, I think. Hasn't anyone ever told you that you kneel in the presence of your queen?'

Tolley looked straight at her. He was a small man, thin and austere like many of his order. His simple dark robe was tied around his middle with a length of rope. He wore open-toed sandals and his bare feet were black with grime. His face was nondescript; it had probably been round when he was a child, but now bones showed through his skin, which stretched over a narrow nose. The only notable thing about him was the way his skull tapered to a point at the crown. That and his eyes. They were tiny, black accentuated by the shadows, reflecting the light of the torch and Clun's unwavering blade. And they stared without blinking.

'Kneel before your queen.' Beylin grabbed the predicant by the shoulder and threw him off the shelf to the straw-strewn rock floor.

'Patience, Beylin.' Beulah looked down at the sprawled figure at her feet. He slowly gathered himself together, staying on his knees as he rose from the ground and stared back at her.

'What was it you did to Lord Queln?' She brushed the edge of his thoughts, trying to see what images the name brought to the surface. It was surprisingly difficult to find any. The man who knelt before her was in tight control of his mind.

'So you think yourself something of an adept. Do you fancy your chances against me? Against the queen of the Obsidian Throne?'

'You're a long way from your throne now.' Beulah had been expecting a thin voice, reedy and dry like the books of accountancy and management so beloved of the Order of the Candle, like the voice she had heard when Lord Queln had died. But Tolley spoke in a soft dark rumble far lower than a body his size should have produced. With his words, she felt the first whispering of his thoughts bubble through the protective shield he had thrown around them. She focused on that, looking for a way in.

'I don't need the throne to know what kind of man you are. I know you set great store by the prophecies. I've seen how you've studied them, looked for the meaning behind old Goronwy's doggerel. So who did you think I was? The warrior maid? Balwen's last? The blood-soaked sheep?' Beulah rattled off a few of the more risible names she recalled from reading the prophecies as a child.

'You are all of them. And none.' Tolley smiled, an unnerving expression that made his whole face crease. 'You scoff at Goronwy, but she was a true visionary. She saw through the great lie, this usurper you call the Shepherd. She saw the truth, and it turned her mad. But not before she had written it all down.'

If there was fire in the predicant's voice, it was nothing compared to the zeal that boiled off his thoughts. He was as mad as the prophet he so clearly worshipped, but there was an underlying logic to his delusion, Beulah was sure. And she knew also that he was part of a much larger conspiracy, a small cog in a very big machine. If she could just find a way past his barriers, then she could lay open his whole mind, pick out the names and faces of those with whom he conspired.

'Why Corris?' She changed tack. 'How could you know I would pass through there and not come straight to Beylinstown? Lord Beylin has been busy building fine roads across all of his fiefdom, after all.'

'The book told me it would happen there.'

'So you hired a gang of bandits to attack our convoy. Surely you must have known they wouldn't stand a chance against a troop of warrior priests, let alone my guards.'

'That's why they needed the drug. Call it a little encouragement. They nearly succeeded too.' Tolley's eyes dropped from Beulah's face to her arm. Covered by the long sleeves of her riding cloak, the bandaging was impossible to see, and the wound was almost fully healed now, thanks to her days on the barge. It was possible that the predicant had heard more details about the attack than were widely known, but his words sent a little shiver through her nonetheless. Almost automatically she pulled her own defences tight around her thoughts, remembering Melyn's lessons. To attempt to sense another's thoughts was to open yourself up to the risk of them influencing you in turn.

'Where is Inquisitor Melyn these days?' Tolley asked. His question could have been a coincidence. 'I would have expected him to have been at your heels.'

Lord Beylin chose that moment to step forward, hitting Tolley hard across the face. Beulah almost felt the pain of the blow, but it dislodged a few images from the predicant's mind. She saw again his hidden chapel within the walls of Castle Corris, only this time the small room was filled with other figures, hooded in dark robes.

'You will speak to your queen with more respect.'

Beylin's voice broke her concentration momentarily, and the image faded.

'Lord Beylin. If you interrupt my interrogation again I will have you sent to serve in the infantry. You can lead the first assault through the Wrthol pass.'

As she said the words, Beulah felt the first sensation of the predicant's attack. It was subtle and far more powerful than she expected. Then she realized her mistake. This man dressed as a predicant, it was true, just another lowly scribe content to exist in the lower levels of his order. But that was his cover; that was the boy who had trained as a novitiate and showed studious promise but not the drive that would take him up through the hierarchy of the order. There was another person behind that persona, though: the young man recruited to a shadowy organization, taught things no man should ever know, shown the secrets, told the truth. And he had lapped it up, bloomed under their care into a skilled adept, a powerful manipulator with a mission to hasten the return of the true king.

Beulah saw his whole life leading up to this point, and realized as she tripped through his thoughts that he was picking his way through her own. Her plans for the invasion of Llanwennog, the distribution of her armies between Dina and Tochers, Melyn's diversion.

'What? Did you think to pass a message on to your allies? Warn King Ballah?' She pushed with all her might, shook his touch from her mind. And still he stared at her, smiling.

'The Guardians of the Throne care nothing for King Ballah and his godless Llanwennogs. We answer to a higher power. We serve the true king.' Tolley's voice was all around her now, inside her. He was tearing away at her mind like some frenzied beast, reaching for her core, trying to destroy her from within. And as he spoke, she was paralysed, held fast by the power of his madness.

Beulah gathered herself in the storm that was her thoughts, preparing for one final push, knowing that if she didn't break free of Tolley's control, he would kill her. Or worse, simply destroy her mind and leave her body still alive, an empty husk to be tended, fed, wiped and cleaned until age finally took it. She knew how to do it, if only she could concentrate. If only that voice would stop grating in her head. If only those eyes would let her go.

'He's coming, Beulah of the stolen throne. And when he gets here, his wrath will be mighty to behold. He will lay waste to the whole of Gwlad, then rebuild it as his own paradise. And only those who have shown him loyalty down the centuries, those who have fought against the lies of his hated brother, only we will be allowed a place in that safe pasture. Only we will live in the presence of –'

Tolley never finished. In an instant Beulah's head was clear, as if she had stood at the edge of a terrible storm, battered by it until she could feel nothing but the wind and the rain, and then someone had closed a door, locking it out. It took a few moments for her brain to catch up with the noise her ears had heard – a sort of rasping sound like the cutting of pigskin. Then her eyes found their focus, saw the light in the predicant's eyes fade away as his pupils rose to the ceiling.

He fell sideways, crumpling to the floor like a sack of

offal, his head tilting as it toppled away from Clun's sizzling blade.

The cave was dark beyond the waterfall, but even so Melyn could feel the power flowing through it. He waded forward, hauling himself up out of the water and on to rocks miraculously dry. No damp moss clung to the walls, no smell of mould hung in the air. Everything was held back by a working of such sophistication it was staggering. He could feel the charge in the air, thickening it, trying to push him back as he walked into the darkness. It was like a solid but silent wind, making each step as heavy as if he weighed as much as a horse, but he knew it was all in his mind. He pushed on, pitting his mental discipline against ancient spells, until with a final surge he broke through.

Only faint light from outside made it through the silently rushing water, but as his eyes adjusted to the gloom it was enough to show the outline of a large cavern. Melyn moved among huge pieces of ancient carved furniture never intended for men. He heaved himself up on to a chair that made him look like a child, and looked across a table that could have sat a party of two dozen. If they were prepared to stand on boxes to eat. Letting himself down to the floor, he disturbed the dry dusty earth on the ground. A spicy aroma rose around him. He had noticed it in the other cave, and it reminded him of something, but he couldn't place it. Shaking off the thought, he went to a large wooden chest that stood against one wall close to a vast bed. It resisted all his attempts to open it, and he was about to conjure a blade of light to cut his way in when a sound distracted him.

His first instinct was to look back to the waterfall. As he did so he remembered the two warrior priests he had ordered to follow him. They stood close to the deluge, cloaks soaked through, hair matted to their heads and feeling around in the air like a pair of bad mimes. Melyn almost laughed. They obviously couldn't see the magics that protected this place and would be puzzled as to how their inquisitor had disappeared. But he realized as he watched that he could hear nothing of them or the flood of water behind. And then he heard the noise again.

It was behind him. Turning, Melyn saw that the back of the cave wasn't a solid wall but the opening of a black passage. He walked towards it, conjuring a small flame to light his way. It flared in his hand, as bright as the sun, chasing all the shadows away and filling him with a sense of power even more potent than when he conjured his blade. Focusing on the lines, he could see why this cave had been chosen as a hiding place and a focus for the powerful spells that spread from it across the forest. The Grym concentrated here like nowhere else he had seen outside the Neuadd, and its power seemed to flow down the rocky tunnel that led away from the end of the cave.

The passageway dropped slowly and turned a long arc so that he could never see more than a dozen paces ahead. The further he went, the more he was convinced he could hear a voice. He couldn't make out the words, but the inflections, the accent and pitch were all unmistakable. Errol was ahead, in earnest conversation with someone.

Melyn increased his speed, thankful for the soft dry earth that muffled his footfalls. He dimmed his light, fighting against the surge of excitement that threatened to make it blaze out again. If he could get close enough to the boy without him realizing, then a swift blow would render him unconscious. He could drug him with wine and get back into his head, find out the secrets he held, the power that had helped him survive a stab to the heart and allowed him to move from place to place with just a thought. And with the old dragon's spell book to help him, Melyn knew he could master those skills himself. Then no one would dare oppose him. He would take the whole of Gwlad in Beulah's name.

The rock caught him unawares, poking up from the floor to trip him. Melyn pitched forward. He released his light and made no more noise than the wind that was driven out of him as he fell to the ground, but in the otherwise near-silent passageway he might as well have been wearing fools' bells and banging a drum. Pain screamed at him from his foot and from both hands where he had thrown them out to break his fall. Ignoring it, he scrambled back upright and hobbled on as fast as he could, running his fingers along the wall to get his bearings until he could collect his wits enough to conjure another ball of light.

Ears straining against the hiss of silence, he listened for the slightest sound that might indicate Errol was still there. He had to believe that the boy had no control over his strange power. Hadn't he only disappeared before when threatened with immediate physical harm – when Ballah's executioner was about to swing his axe; when

Osgal had thrown him into the Faaeren Chasm? Melyn knew he was deluding himself; fear would be enough of a trigger. Cursing under his breath, he pushed on faster, all too aware that if Errol could have escaped, he would have done so by now.

The passageway opened on to a large cavern without warning, almost as if he had stepped through an invisible door. For a brief instant Melyn thought he saw movement darting away from him, a confusing shifting of perspective that made his head spin. He put his hand out to steady himself and looked up into the eyes of the largest dragon he had ever seen.

It was impossible. The cave was not big enough to hold such a creature. It made Caradoc look like a kitling and could have swallowed Melyn whole. It stared at him with a curious expression, like one might reserve for a precocious child or a dog that has mastered a particularly impressive trick.

'So you are Melyn, son of Arall.' The voice was as loud as the creature was big, surrounding him, filling him entirely, squeezing out any other thought. Melyn tried to pull himself together, but he felt like a pile of dead leaves in a gale. His mental discipline, honed over a lifetime, disappeared as if he were no more than an empty-headed little girl.

'Who . . . are . . . you . . . ?' He couldn't be sure whether he actually spoke the words or not. Melyn could feel himself slowly unravelling under that terrible stare.

'I am Corwen teul Maddau. The last of her direct line. You know Maddau, of course. From your history. We call her Maddau the Wise. She was the gentlest, most studious of our kind. And your little proto-king, Balwen, slew her like a dog.'

Melyn was transported back to his childhood, standing at the front of the class and being chided for his presumption by his teacher. He knew the burning sense of embarrassment, the mortification of being ridiculed in front of his peers even if he thought them no better than the mindless peasants who were their parents. He knew too the terrible feeling of injustice – that he should be rewarded for his achievement, not humiliated. He pushed against that humiliation, taking strength from his persecution. And as he did so, he felt his body around him. How long he had been trapped, caught by this most powerful magic of all, was anyone's guess. But as it dawned on him what he had stumbled upon, so its power waned.

He flexed his hands, feeling the rough stone of a carved pedestal under them, in front of him. He could still see the great form of the dragon, but it was shrinking in front of his eyes, its solidity fading away to a smoky wispiness, the cave wall showing through from behind. And then his fingers caressed something cold and hard and smooth.

A jolt of energy shot through him. Melyn was thrown back, landing on his backside in the dirt. But the image of the dragon had gone, and now he could see what really filled the small cave.

'Not so grand now, Corwen teul Maddau,' he muttered under his breath as he climbed painfully back to his feet and looked down on the pile of two dozen or so small white jewels. He reached out and picked one up, conjuring his light as he did so, the better to see it. Images, memories, the shadow of the creature that had left these powerful nuggets behind, brushed at his mind. Melyn was used to the way the white jewels called him, promised him great things. He was wise to them, though he knew many men who had fallen for their allure. He closed his mind to their song and studied them one by one as a gemsmith might appraise diamonds before setting about cutting them. Most were white, but of the twenty-four, six had taken on a pale pink tinge. There was a different quality to them too, as if they belonged to another creature. A puzzle for later, he put them all in a pocket of his robe before taking a last look around the small chamber.

Aside from a few scratchy runes etched into the walls and around the stone pedestal, there was nothing of interest. Then he looked down, seeing how the soft dry earth had been disturbed by feet, recently if he was any judge. Crouching, Melyn held out his light, trying to make sense of the patterns of prints. They had been made by small boots. He didn't know what size Errol wore, but Melyn was pretty sure they were his. The boy had stepped from the rock face opposite the entrance and then stumbled; there were two hand-shaped prints in the dirt, and Melyn knew there would be larger ones much the same back down the passageway where he had fallen. After picking himself up, Errol had walked slowly around the pedestal once, then stepped back into the cave wall.

Melyn studied the rock, feeling it with his hand, then let himself slip into the trance that would show him the aethereal imprint of the place. In front of him was still nothing more than a solid wall of stone; no magics hid a second chamber or escape route. Indeed the magics that filled the place were fast unravelling, their centre disrupted when he had disturbed the jewels. Remembering Frecknock's words, he concentrated on the Grym, and sure enough he could see the lines converging on the pedestal. But whereas before he had seen them only as conduits of power, now he could see how they diffused into the air, formed the shape of the cavern. There were subtle differences between the lines that criss-crossed the floor and those that ran through the rock, something he had never noticed in all his years of studying magic and the Grym.

And then it hit him. He shouldn't have been able to see the lines at all. Quite apart from being in an aethereal trance, he was deep underground, far from living things. Back at Emmass Fawr the basement levels, hewn into the granite of the mountain on which the monastery sat, were almost devoid of power. Even he struggled to conjure a light down there. But in here the Grym was as powerful as anywhere he had seen it, and it reached out in all directions, connecting this one spot to everywhere in Gwlad. From here he could eavesdrop on conversations in Candlehall. Or Tynhelyg. He could seek out Queen Beulah and check on her progress. Maybe even communicate with her as the dragons did. He could see where Errol had gone. Follow him.

'Your Grace?' The voice cut through Melyn's concentration and he dropped out of his trance, spinning to see who had dared interrupt him. One of the damp warrior priests stood at the entrance to the cavern, his companion behind him. Anger made Melyn's conjured light glow bright. The two men drew back from him, fear etched into their faces, as well it should be. He would strike them down where they stood.

'Are you all right, sire?' The nearest warrior priest was dripping on to the dusty earth, making a ring of damp darkness around him like a protective ward. Melyn's rage turned off almost as instantly as it had come. He looked down at his own robes, soaked from his entrance. His shirt clung to his skin, cold and rough, sending an involuntary shiver through him. He could see how he had trailed drips of water into the cavern, and yet he hadn't noticed them at all when he had been tracing Errol's footsteps. Crouching down again to inspect the floor, he could see no sign of the boy at all. A different shudder ran up his spine as he began to understand what had happened. He had been seduced by the strange potency of this place. He had acted like a novitiate on first being introduced to the lines, had almost been sucked into them, his mind ripped apart by their endless possibilities. If anything, the two warrior priests had saved him from a fate far worse than death.

'I'm fine,' he said, his voice sounding strange to him in the echoing space. 'I've got what I was looking for. Let's get out of here.'

They retreated swiftly along the passageway, stepping back into the main cave far sooner than Melyn expected. With Corwen's jewels in his pocket, rather than resting in their place of power, the spells that had hidden the dead dragon's home had rapidly evaporated and tendrils of mist were seeping into the dry space. It wouldn't take long for the wooden furniture to start mouldering.

'You two. Take that chest and throw it out into the river.' Melyn cast his eyes quickly over the cave to see if there was anything else worth investigating or taking, but there were no books, no gold trinkets, no hoard other than the small pile of jewels. He let himself down into the icy water as the warrior priests hauled the chest across the floor. They tipped it over the edge, jumping in after it, and he followed them through the deluge out into the clearing beyond.

Darkness had almost completely fallen, the first few stars pricking the pink sky. Someone had built a fire close to the stone corral, and the smell of roasting meat wafted across to him as Melyn waded out of the river. He squeezed out his robes as best he could while he walked, but he would have to dig fresh clothes from his pack. At least the water had washed the road dust from his face and hair.

'Where's Frecknock?' He swung his sodden riding cloak off, draping it on the wall of the corral to catch the heat from the fire. The light from the flames made everything else dark. He moved closer, warming his hands.

'In the cave, sir. She hasn't moved in hours.'

'Hours? What are you talking about, man? I left her in there just a few minutes ago.' Confused, Melyn went to his horse and pulled dry clothes from a pack before stepping into the small cave. It was pitch black in there now, just a thin band of firelight falling on the seated form of the dragon.

'How can I lose hours and not realize?' Melyn threw his dry clothes down on to the bed of grass and began pulling off his wet ones. Frecknock's eyes were two shining points in the darkness across the cold hearth.

'This place is alive with the Grym,' she said. 'There are

powerful wards everywhere. Breaking them might well have put you outside normal time for a while.'

'But I'd know, surely. I'm not some wet-eared novitiate; I've studied magic all my life.' Melyn pulled on his dry clothes, reaching out to the lines for warmth as he did so.

'I didn't begin my studies in the subtle arts until I was seventy years old, Your Grace. I'm almost two hundred now. It's possible I've been learning the subtle arts even longer than you. Corwen may well have studied them ten times as long as me. More, even.'

Melyn wanted to scoff. It was common knowledge that dragons lived longer than men, but not nearly as long as they claimed. Still, he couldn't deny the sheer sophistication of the spells that had protected the cave behind the waterfall, nor the enormously complex workings that made navigation through the Ffrydd so difficult.

'I found a pile of jewels in a cavern behind the waterfall. How could a pile of jewels maintain such magic? Surely only a living creature could manage that.'

'You found jewels? White jewels?' Frecknock shifted her great bulk, leaning forward so that her head fell within the band of orange light cast by the fire outside.

'Is that significant?'

'A single dragon's jewels, laid to rest in a place of power. That is how we honour our most powerful mages. They lie for ever at a nexus in the Grym, watching over Gwlad and offering their wisdom to any who would ask for it.'

'Well, they won't be handing out dragon wisdom any more. Not unless they're prepared to give it to me.'

'What . . . what did you do with them, Your Grace?'

Frecknock's voice was quiet, timid. She was afraid to ask, Melyn could tell. She didn't want to upset the delicate balance between them. And yet she needed to know so much she was prepared to push the boundaries a little. He went to pick up his cloak, then realized that it, and the contents of its deep pockets, were drying on the warm stone wall of the corral outside. The pause was enough for him to change his mind. He had been intending to show them to her, to impress her with his skill at breaking down the magical barriers to the final resting place of a great mage. But he realized that such bragging was unnecessary.

'That's not your concern.' He went to the cave mouth. 'Come. Have something to eat, then get some rest. Tomorrow morning we rejoin the main army. Then you'll show us this pass through the mountains to Llanwennog.'

Night was fully upon them now. Melyn took his place by the fire, accepting a plate of roasted meat augmented with a few forest herbs and roots boiled into a sharp-tasting mush. Trail food was always unpleasant, but he knew that it was necessary to keep his strength up. Frecknock emerged from the cave and hovered behind the ring of warrior priests sitting around the fire until they had finished eating, then took a surprisingly small amount of the remaining carcass. He was watching her settling down with her meal beside the corral when a commotion from the far side of the ford grabbed everyone's attention. The warrior priests leaped to their feet, blades shimmering into brightness in the dark as a band of riders swept noisily through the ford. Melyn recognized the lead horse almost instantly, as did his men, who extinguished their blades and went to meet the troop.

Captain Osgal dismounted, letting his horse put its head down and graze as he came up to Melyn. His face was black, his eyebrows and a chunk of hair from the top of his head missing.

'By the Shepherd, Osgal. What happened to you? Did you get them?'

'No, sir.' Osgal dropped his head, then went down on one knee. 'I've failed you, Inquisitor. They were there, just where you said they'd be. The dragon was flying when we arrived, and the boy . . . just appeared. We were almost upon him when the dragon swooped and gathered him up.'

'You had bows, didn't you?' Melyn found that his anger had failed him. In its place he felt a weary resignation, a fatalistic understanding that he would have to try a lot harder if he wanted to catch Errol and Benfro. 'Why didn't you shoot at them?'

'We did, sir. But . . .' Osgal fell silent as if lost for words. His eyes darted past Melyn's and the inquisitor looked around to see Frecknock looking their way, her eyes wide, her ears swivelled forward to catch every word. She had the decency to look embarrassed when she saw she had been noticed, but Melyn didn't much care if she heard.

'Go on, Captain. Explain to me how my best warrior priests suddenly lost the ability to aim a crossbow.'

'Their aim was true, Inquisitor. Every quarrel would have hit its target, but the dragon burned them all up.'

'Burned?'

'He breathed fire, sir. It melted our bolts. Hotter than the Wolf's lair it was, but it didn't touch the boy.' Osgal held out a black lump, which Melyn took from him. It was heavy and looked a little like a crossbow bolt might if it had been dropped back into the blacksmith's forge and forgotten about.

'He used it on us as well.' Melyn could hear the distress in Osgal's voice as the captain recalled the events. 'And that time it burned. Any closer and it would have killed us. By the time we calmed the horses, he'd gone, taken the boy with him.'

Melyn weighed the melted quarrel in his hand, looking back at Frecknock, who had given up pretending she wasn't listening. 'What is this? Since when did dragons breathe fire?'

'Your Grace . . . there are legends. When we were feral beasts. Before great Rasalene showed us . . . the wonders of the Grym.' Frecknock's words came out in short squeaky bursts, as if she were gulping for air, horrified at what she was hearing. 'But never . . . in ten thousand years. More. No. No.'

20

Beware the beast that knows no master
Beware the husband who has no wife
Beware the dead but ever living
Cold fingers twined through every life

The Prophecies of Mad Goronwy

Errol was too terrified even to look down. He scrunched his eyes shut and hung on to Benfro's scaly arms with all his strength. He could feel his legs dangling beneath him, battered by the wind. He was dazed and confused and very, very afraid.

After a while he opened his eyes a tiny fraction, then wished that he hadn't. They were high above the trees and moving at a dizzying speed. The canopy beneath them was changing from spreading broadleaves to dense patches of conifer, though from this new angle it took him a while to realize that was what he was seeing. Twisting his head to one side, he saw past Benfro's steadily beating wing to the bulk of Mount Arnahi, its western flank painted orange-pink by the setting sun. Straight ahead he could make out the lower peaks of the eastern arm of the Rim mountains, clear in the evening light and much closer than he had expected.

He tried to speak, but his voice was whipped away by

the wind which tore tears from his eyes and blew through his clothes as if they weren't there at all. As he took stock of his situation, Errol felt the cold loosening his grip. Benfro still held him tight, but that wasn't something he wanted to have to rely on. The dragon was carrying all the bags as well. Surely he couldn't manage all that weight for long?

And yet there was nothing Errol could do but cling on for his life, growing ever colder and more tired. He tried tapping on Benfro's arm to get the dragon's attention, but to do it properly meant loosening his hold. And Benfro seemed intent on putting as much distance between them and the warrior priests as possible. In that regard Errol could only agree; he just wished there was a more comfortable way of going about it.

The sun slipped below the distant haze of the western Rim mountains as Errol began to lose all feeling in his arms and legs. He'd long since felt his face go numb and then disappear altogether. He tried to reach out to the lines, to pull in the power of the Grym to warm him. But he was too high up, too far removed from Gwlad, to tap into that life force. And it was so hard to concentrate, so hard to keep holding on, so hard to stay awake.

He must have nodded off, for when Errol looked down again, he could see the pine trees thinning out, dark rocks rolled down from the mountains above the traces of ancient landslides. They were climbing with the hills, and the air was thin in his lungs, spreading its chill deep into his body. He was impossibly tired, fighting against the waves of sleep that washed over him. Darkness was falling, and he couldn't work out if that was because of the setting sun or just his vision fading as the cold took him.

Then they crossed a ridge and were flying over snow. Errol remembered the scraps of dirty white that still clung to the higher passes when he made the trip from Emmass Fawr to Tynewydd, and the deep drifts that piled up around the walls of the monastery over the winter. They were nothing compared to what he looked down upon now. It was a vast field of white, crystals glinting in the last of the day's fading light. It smoothed out the contours into a series of gentle folds, each climbing higher so that they seemed to reach for the star-specked sky.

Cold beyond belief, shivering uncontrollably, Errol didn't notice that they were descending towards this high plateau until they were almost upon it. The darkness made it hard to judge distance, the unblemished surface even more so. It was only when Benfro shifted his grip that he realized what was about to happen. As it was, his terror at the prospect of landing was short-lived.

They hit the ground faster than was perhaps wise. Just before impact Errol felt himself being pushed away. He tumbled briefly through the air, then crashed into the snow. It cushioned his fall, but still drove the wind out of him and smothered him in cold. He had a brief glimpse of Benfro's great bulk hitting the ground a few paces further on before his own momentum drove him down, kicking up a great powdery mass of snow into his face with an explosion of noise and darkness.

Errol lay unfeeling for what seemed like an age. He had

gone beyond cold and through fear. Now he just wanted to lie there, head down in the snow, and sleep for a little while. There was no hurry, no need to run. He was safe here, and warm. He could rest.

'Wake up.' A large hand grabbed the back of his cloak and hauled him to his feet. Errol tried to focus, but he couldn't even open his eyes. He wished whoever was bothering him would go away. Then he could settle back down into the nice warm snow and sleep.

'Come on, Errol. Wake up.' He felt himself being shaken, tingles of discomfort coming from his legs and hands. It was the first sensation he had felt from them in a long while and it stirred a warning in his memory. Captain Osgal, of all people, telling him what could happen to someone who let the cold get to them. But he wasn't cold; he was warm. He didn't need the lines. Or had that been what the captain had said – that extreme cold makes the body think it's warm? He couldn't remember, could hardly think straight at all. Had the captain said it would make him tired as well? Or was that his mother?

'Oh, by the moon!' Errol felt himself being shaken then turned round. Then an incredible sensation swept over his face and hands. It was as if he were being doused in the softest of liquids. Where it touched him, it warmed him in such a way that he realized he had actually been frozen. It washed away the tiredness, putting strength back into his arms, his legs, his neck and eyelids. Lifting his head, he opened his eyes and almost screamed.

He was engulfed in pale blue flame, which danced and shimmered over his arms and body. Benfro stood in front of him, holding him by the shoulders, staring intently at him, but all Errol knew was that he was on fire.

'How?' He opened his mouth to speak, and the flame ran in as if it were alive, plunged down his throat and into his lungs, warming him from the inside. He coughed, but more out of reflex than from any discomfort; this flame didn't consume the air he was breathing. Instead it flowed around him, through him, until he was restored to something near normal. And then, its job done, it slowly faded away, leaving only the night and the keen, cold wind.

'Did you . . . ? What did you . . . ?' Errol struggled to form words.

'I'm sorry, Errol. I was so intent on getting away that I flew too high and too far. I should have realized. You might have frozen to death.'

'But the fire. I never realized . . . Can you all do that?'

'I don't think so. I've never met another dragon who could. Most would think it disgusting, feral even. Corwen didn't think that though.'

Corwen. Errol heard the old dragon's last words echoing in his mind. He slapped his hands against his sides, feeling the two small lumps, one in either pocket.

'I got the jewels.' He reached into the first pocket and pulled out the cloth-wrapped bundle that was Magog, unwrapping it to reveal the shining gem. In the starlight, reflected through innumerable ice crystals, it was as black as coal. 'It didn't come without a fight.'

'Put it away,' Benfro said, averting his gaze. Errol hastily wrapped the jewel up again and pushed it to the bottom of his pocket. Then he reached into the other side and pulled out Morgwm's jewel. It glinted palest white; if he dropped it in the snow they might never find it again. He could feel the soft touch of the memories held within it: fierce pride, gentle intelligence, worried concern and above all else deep sadness. The touch also brought back to his memory the images he had seen before, of a newborn infant nestling with a hatchling dragon, Princess Lleyn and Father Gideon, the sun blanked out by the disc of the moon.

'Give it to me.' Benfro's voice cut through Errol's musing, and he looked down to see that he had clenched his fist over the jewel. Embarrassed, he relaxed his fingers and passed Morgwm's memories on to her son. Instead of thanking him, Benfro snatched the jewel away, turning his body as if it needed his whole bulk to protect the tiny stone.

'You shouldn't have touched her.' Benfro's tone was as cold as the snow that trickled in through a gap at the top of one of Errol's boots.

'I'm sorry. There was no other way. Melyn was coming.'

'And you left Corwen there?'

'I had no choice. I would have been captured.'

'After all he did for you, you just left him behind to be . . . to be . . . defiled by that monster. How could you do such a thing?'

'He wouldn't let me. He pushed me away. I . . .' Errol tried to explain, even though he felt terrible about what he had been forced to do anyway. Benfro's sudden mood change shocked him. The dragon had been helping him. Why was he suddenly so angry?

'Look, I'm sorry. I tried to bring Corwen's jewels, but he stopped me. He knew what was going to happen, said it was better. That way he'd be with Melyn wherever he went.'

'Don't try to explain. Don't make excuses. I should have left you for the warrior priests. I should have let you freeze.' Benfro spat the words over his shoulder, then turned his back completely and stalked off into the darkness. Errol stood and watched him go, bemused, until the cold seeping into his feet reminded him of where he was. Being stuck somewhere near the top of a snow-capped mountain was not his idea of fun, though it beat being captured by the inquisitor and his men.

He sought out the lines, trying to tap them for warmth. The place was so barren, the snow so deep, that at first he had difficulty finding any, and when he did, they were weak and thin. Still, he was able to tap the nearest, to feel the power of the Grym surge through his body, giving him energy and driving away the cold. His breath steamed in the night air as he paused a while just to enjoy the sense of freedom. Overhead the night sky was clearer, closer than he had ever seen it before. Behind him, lost somewhere in the dark mass that was the distant forest, Melyn and his warrior priests still pursued him, but they were a long way away and he had a good head start. Pulling his cloak around his shoulders to keep out the wind, Errol set off in Benfro's footsteps.

'Have you seen the Duke of Abervenn?'

Beulah walked the well-appointed corridors of Lord Beylin's castle, stopping anyone she came across, few though they were, and asking them all the same question. She suspected that many of the castle staff were avoiding her deliberately; quite often she heard voices whispering urgently just around corners or behind closed doors, and occasionally she caught sight of figures darting away. It was obvious that they were terrified of her even though she had done nothing to deserve the reputation that prompted their fears. At least she hadn't done anything in Beylinstown.

Perhaps it was news of the battle with the band of mercenaries. Perhaps these simple provincials found it hard to cope with the idea of a woman fighting, and killing, armed men. Or perhaps they were simply frightened of her because she was their ruler. Whatever the reason, it was tiresome, and her temper was fraying to the point where she might very well begin to earn her reputation. This latest page, cornered before he could make good his escape down a servants' stairwell to the kitchen wing, was not much use either. He stared at her wide-eyed, his mouth working away as he tried to remember how to speak. And when he did find his voice it was high-pitched and squeaky, like a peasant girl hawking bread in the street.

'N-no, Your Majesty. I've n-not seen n-no one.'

Beulah dismissed him with a wave and carried on down the corridor. She had woken that morning to find Clun gone from their bed and not in the bathing room either. Normally she wouldn't have worried about it; he was free to come and go as he pleased, after all. But since the incident with Father Tolley he had become more introspective, quieter even than his usually reticent self. He had taken to going off on long walks around the city in the afternoons when she retired to their rooms to rest and work on healing her wounds. But he had never disappeared so early in the day before.

From what she could tell, he had dressed in his plainest clothes, taking his old novitiate's cloak and boots rather than anything she had given him. Beulah seldom worried about others – she had never had someone to care about until Clun had come along – but this behaviour was sufficiently out of the ordinary to give her concern. Her mind raced at all manner of implausible possibilities. Had he found a young lass in the town and was bedding her on the side? Was he secretly plotting with Lord Beylin to kill her and take the throne? Maybe he had fallen for all that mumbo-jumbo about the coming of the true king and was busy learning the secrets of Mad Goronwy's prophecies.

Beulah laughed out loud at the thought of strait-laced Clun bent studiously over a reading desk, one finger tracing lines of meaningless words etched on to a parchment. He would no more betray her than cut off his own arms. But it bothered her that she even thought these things of him.

The central hall of Lord Beylin's castle was bright and airy, modelled on the Neuadd, though not on the same grand scale. Its windows were glazed with clear glass, and the morning sun shone through from a pale blue sky outside. It was early still, but Beylin sat on his throne-like seat at the end of the hall, deep in conversation with a group of men wearing the distinctive cloaks of merchants. Her entrance unnoticed, Beulah watched the noble for a moment as he negotiated. She was forced to revise her opinion of him; his skill at commerce was quite at odds with the somewhat needy and foppish appearance he presented to the world.

'Your Majesty. I didn't expect to see you so early.' The merchants scattered as Lord Beylin leaped to his feet and crossed the hall. 'Did the servants not bring breakfast to your chambers?'

'I dismissed them. I don't like to be fussed over. Nor do I need someone to help me dress.'

'Of course not. But can I offer you something now?' Beylin looked around, catching the attention of a young page who had been taking notes during his negotiations. The boy put down his pen and scurried over.

'Go to the kitchens and tell them to prepare breakfast for the queen. To be served here in the hall.' Beylin turned back to Beulah as the lad scurried off on his errand. 'Will the Duke of Abervenn be joining us?'

'Actually, that's why I came down. I've been searching for Clun since I woke, and I can't find him anywhere. Have you seen him this morning?'

'No. No, I haven't.' Beylin frowned, then turned back to the group of merchants who were hovering uncertainly around the throne-like chair at the head of the hall. 'Gentlemen, have any of you seen His Grace the Duke of Abervenn this morning?'

The merchants came forward as if they had been waiting to be brought formally into the presence of their queen. Beulah counted five men, all well dressed and clearly prosperous if the size of their girths was anything to go by. The tallest of them, a balding man with grey tufts of hair sprouting from his ears, reached the queen first and knelt extravagantly on one knee. Sighing, Beulah offered him her hand to be kissed.

'May I present Terquid Squiler, head of the guild of horse merchants.' Lord Beylin sounded almost as bored as Beulah.

'Your Majesty, you grace our humble little town with your presence,' Squiler said. 'My fellow guild members and I would like to welcome you to Beylinstown.'

'But have you seen the duke?' Beulah took back her hand before the merchant started to drool on her ring. Squiler rose to his feet, turned and looked at his companions. There was a great deal of head-shaking and shrugging. Then one of the merchants spoke up.

'I saw a young man walking through the town just before sunrise, Your Majesty. But he didn't look like no duke to me.'

'Describe him.'

'I'd say he weren't yet twenty years, ma'am. But tall and strong. He had the ruddy cheeks and fair hair of a Graith Fawr man, I'd say. I didn't recognize him, didn't pay him much heed, to be honest with you.'

'Did you see where he was going?'

'Towards the south wall and the river gate, ma'am. Down where the barges unload and the main livestock markets are held.'

Beulah was wondering how best to dismiss them before they started to press her for trading privileges or reduced taxes, when Beylin stepped in.

'Gentlemen, thank you,' he said. 'Now if you would excuse us, the queen has not yet broken her fast. Perhaps we could continue our discussion later this morning.'

As if on cue, the doors were thrown open and a small army of servants appeared. The merchants bowed and made their exit, though Beulah could see that they were not best pleased at the interruption to their negotiations.

In moments the top table had been cleared of paperwork and laid for a meal. Platters of cold meats, dried fruits and warm-smelling bread appeared, enough to feed the queen's guard let alone just herself and Lord Beylin.

'All this just for me?' Beulah asked as she was escorted to the table, given the throne-like chair to sit in.

'My cook is perhaps a little overzealous,' Beylin said as he sat himself down to her left. 'But he's worth indulging. Have some of this fruit – it comes from Eirawen, I'm told.'

Beulah looked at the food spread in front of her, then across the table to the near-empty hall. Outside the day was growing brighter as the sun climbed over the courtyard walls. She had no appetite right now, at least not for the exotic things Beylin was offering. She was more concerned about Clun.

'I'm not hungry, truly.' She stood, finding it almost impossible to move the heavy chair back. 'I must go and find my husband before he gets into some kind of trouble.'

'Then permit me to accompany you, ma'am.' Beylin stood, dabbing at his lips with a napkin even though he had not eaten anything.

Beulah acquiesced with a nod. She would have liked to have gone alone, but that would not have been wise. Even if she could look after herself in a fight, being recognized by a crowd of her loyal subjects would have been awkward at best. In the end they were joined by a small contingent of her guard, led by Captain Celtin, which meant that far from being able to move around unnoticed, their progress through the town was marked by an ever-increasing crowd of excited onlookers.

The river gate was as its name implied. Where the Hafren met the town walls, two great towers had been built, one on either bank, and a large stone arch constructed between them. The river here was relatively narrow, but deep. On either side the warehouses and loading docks of the richer merchants towered over the stream. Beylin led the party down to his personal dock, and they took a boat to the heart of the commercial sector.

Outside the gate, beyond its original walls, the town was rapidly expanding, with new warehouses and docks stretching far south. Behind them, on the low hills on either side, Beulah could see endless rows of wooden fencing: holding pens for the cattle and horses that were the lifeblood of this place. Even early in the morning the air was thick with the dust and odour of moving animals. And somewhere in among it all was Clun.

They disembarked at a particularly grand warehouse and dock complex that belonged to Beylin himself. A tall thin man dressed almost entirely in black came to greet them, an expression of near panic on his long, lined face.

'My lord. This is so unexpected. If I'd but known . . .'

'Relax, Verran. I've not come to spring a surprise audit on you.' Beylin introduced Beulah to his chief accountant, and the man's pale face turned whiter still.

'Your Majesty.' He bowed low then fell silent, lost for words.

'We're looking for His Grace the Duke of Abervenn,' Beylin said. 'He was seen coming this way at first light.'

'I'm sorry, sir. I've been in the warehouse since before dawn, doing an inventory. I've not seen anyone but my assistants.'

'Then we'll have to look for him in the livestock rings.' Beylin turned back to Beulah. 'I wanted to show you them anyway, ma'am. I thought you might be interested in the horses.'

They set off from the warehouse out into the livestock yards and towards the main auction ring. The town was a small trading centre compared with Candlehall, but Beulah was quietly impressed with how efficiently it was all run. The holding pens were neatly arranged, each separated from the next by a track wide enough for two wagons to pass. All the roads were hard-packed dirt, but drainage ditches had been dug to carry off any rainfall before it could turn them into a muddy quagmire. Thought had gone into the allocation of pens too, with breeding cattle separated from meat stock, and in turn separated from sheep. What pigs were traded in Beylinstown tended to be kept at the furthest end, away from everything else. Lord Beylin had spent a great deal of money building up this market and taken the best advice on how to lay it out. It had obviously paid off handsomely, judging by the number of pens occupied and the steady noise coming from the nearby auction ring.

'What are they selling today?' Beulah asked as their small party entered the substantial wooden barn that housed the auction ring. Several merchants were standing about, though it was not as busy as she had expected.

'I'm not sure, ma'am.' Beylin went up to the nearest merchant, questioned him, then returned.

'There's a horse auction going on, but there's some unhappiness. Seemingly the best two beasts were bought privately before the sale even started.'

'Does that happen often?'

'Not usually, ma'am, no. The auctioneers have been known to bar breeders if they do it too much. It's their fees that pay for all this.' He gestured to take in the pens, the barn and everything else. 'Sure, there are some who try to fool them – bring a few broken old nags for the ring and use the pens to showcase their quality stock. There're merchants who'll try to get a better deal that way too, but generally they know the system's there for their benefit.'

Beulah looked over to the nearest pen attached to the auction barn. A few sorry-looking horses stood motionless in the sun, their heads drooping, eyes closed. Only their swishing tails whisking away the flies showed that they were alive at all. If this was the standard of horseflesh being sold at this market, then the best of the crop couldn't have been worth much.

'I was looking for a horse myself. My old mare was killed by a dragon, and the replacement died when we were attacked by bandits outside Corris. It's a shame there's nothing here fit for riding. I wouldn't even eat some of these.'

'Those are indeed poor specimens,' Beylin said. 'But I've no doubt there'll be better inside.'

The interior of the barn was cool and airy. Lit by big open windows high up in the walls, it was arranged around a central ring about twenty paces across. On one side wooden benches climbed in tiers. Opposite them, on a low dais, the auctioneer stood behind a tall lectern, like a priest at Suldith prayers. Alongside him an assistant sat behind a table, entering details into a large ledger.

Beulah motioned for her guard to stay in the chamber behind the tiered benches, entering the main body of the barn with just Lord Beylin and Captain Celtin for company. She wanted to observe the auction with as little disruption as possible. And, who knew, there might even be a horse worth bidding for, though she was doubtful about that. If the merchants outside thought that the finest beasts had already been sold, then she didn't much fancy buying second best.

The hammer fell, signalling the sale of a pretty mare with a foal, as Beulah settled herself down on a wooden bench just a few paces away from a group of farmers. They looked at her once, nodding by way of a hello, then went back to their discussion of the livestock on sale. It was obvious they had no idea who she was, and Beulah was strangely relieved by the knowledge. Beside her Beylin wore a dark travelling cloak over his elegant courtly clothes, and Celtin was dressed like any other warrior priest of his order. Without their guards to attract attention, they could have been anyone.

'And our next lot, a pair of fine young geldings from the Nebo stud. Gentlemen, ladies, these two have been broken both to saddle and harness. They would make good carriage horses, but equally could be ridden over rough ground. Shall we start the bidding at one hundred crowns the pair?'

Beulah listened to the sum come down to fifty crowns, then slowly climb back up as the punters were drawn in. The horses were nice enough, certainly worth the initial asking price, if not a lot more. They were a little skittish in the ring, but not so bad that they would be unmanageable. No doubt they would find their way down to Castell Glas and the household of some minor noble or rich merchant. Looking around the room, she could see plenty of interest, but the gathered farmers and merchants were eyeing each other warily, not wanting to show their hands.

She had never been to a real auction before, and Beulah found the experience fascinating. There were mock auctions at court, where the nobles bid for useless trinkets, or even each other, as a sort of game. It was just another way to flaunt their wealth, as far as she could tell, like the absurd costumes and town houses large enough to sleep an entire clan. This was different. This was the commerce that fed the Twin Kingdoms. Farmers and breeders produced; merchants bought and sold; and a small fraction of every transaction made its way back to her treasury.

Beulah watched as the geldings were knocked down for a hundred and seventy-five crowns the pair. Then a huge stallion was led in, eighteen hands if he was an inch and darkest black all over. His eyes were fierce and wild; no one had managed to tame him yet. The halter around his neck was made from rope as thick as a man's wrist, and two handlers struggled to keep him in check. Sweat sheened his flanks, and he wheeled this way and that, frightened by the strange room but determined to fight rather than flee.

'A feisty one, this. A genuine Gomoran stallion from the Gwastadded Wag. As you can see, he's been habituated to men but not tamed. And he's certainly not broken. You all know how rare these horses are, so who'll start the bidding at a thousand crowns?'

The room wasn't silent: there was too much noise coming from the great horse and the scrabble of would-be punters getting as far from the front row of benches as possible. But the atmosphere changed, as if there had been a collective intake of breath. Beulah wasn't surprised. A thousand crowns was a lot of money for just one horse, however magnificent he was.

And yet he was a truly regal beast. If he could be broken, if she could bend him to her will, then he would make the most perfect of gifts for Clun.

Guiltily Beulah recalled that it was her search for her missing consort that had brought her to this place. She scanned the auction room on the off chance that he might have come here, but he was nowhere to be seen, much like the bids the auctioneer was trying to elicit.

'All right, who'll give me five hundred? No? Four fifty? Four hundred?'

'Two hundred and fifty.' Beulah looked around for the person who had spoken, then realized it was herself. The auctioneer's eyes swept the room, trying to locate her. She waited until his eyes met hers, then nodded once.

'I have a bid of two fifty from the lady in the fourth row. Do I hear any higher?'

'Your Majesty, is this wise? Gomoran stallions are renowned for being unbreakable. In all my years I've never seen one ridden.' Lord Beylin spoke under his breath as if he were worried about being overheard in the echoing noisy barn.

'There are more ways to break a horse than brute strength, Beylin.'

'Any more bids? It's a crime to let a splendid beast go for such a price.' The auctioneer was waving his gavel back and forth across the crowd, desperately trying to pluck more money from the air. Most eyes were cast down, or fixed on the stallion as he tossed and turned, pulling his handlers about as if they weighed no more than air. Beulah tried to study the beast using her aethereal sight, but she couldn't find the trance. She reached out to him with her mind, as she had done to Father Tolley. She didn't expect the horse to have much in the way of thoughts, but she wanted to calm him, to reassure him that no harm would come his way. He was a simple thing, driven by the most basic of needs. She soothed him with promises of food, the companionship of other horses and a return to the open fields where he could see the sky overhead.

'Well, if we're all done bidding here?' The auctioneer's voice was distant, unimportant. Beulah stared only at the horse, his wide black eyes locked on her own.

'At two hundred and fifty crowns. Going once.' Nostrils flared, flecked with foam.

'Going twice.' Hind legs quivered as muscles fought against restraining hobbles. Tail arched, flicked this way and that, cracking like a whip.

'Gone! Sold to the lady in the fourth row. Your name, madam?'

Beulah sent a firm command to the horse. Be still. As

she rose to her feet, it snorted, pawed the ground with its front feet, then stopped, silent, motionless.

'I am Beulah, Queen of the Twin Kingdoms.' Now there was silence in the room. The auctioneer's mouth hung open for long seconds until, finally, he closed it with an audible snap. He looked down to his assistant, who had stood up, then back at his queen.

'Your Majesty. I had no idea. If I had but known –'

'You'd have what? Taken a few bids off the wall to up the price?' Beulah enjoyed the look of horrified injury on the man's face. Around her she noticed that everyone else was standing or kneeling. 'This is why I didn't announce myself. How can you hold an auction when you're all on your knees? And who would dare to bid against their queen? Go about your business, gentlemen. I shan't get in your way any more.' And with that she stepped down to the ring to inspect her purchase.

The horse towered over her, a mass of barely controlled energy wrapped up in a glossy black coat. The two men holding his halter ropes nodded to her as she approached, but didn't kneel or let go. Still reaching out to the beast's mind, she tried not to let her own trepidation feed into his fear. It was strange trying to calm an animal, when she had been trained by Melyn to use her talents to unsettle.

'Your Majesty. Is this wise?' Captain Celtin made to accompany her into the ring. Almost instantly the stallion's neck arched, its muscles tensing.

'Stay back, Captain. I'll be all right.' Beulah didn't look to see if her order was followed, but the great beast relaxed again. She took a couple of steps closer, holding herself upright but not looking the animal in the eye any more. Finally, when she was within reach, she put out her hand, low and flat as Melyn had taught her so many years before when he had presented her with her first horse. Slowly, and with much snorting, the stallion lowered his head until he could smell the proffered hand.

Beulah stood there for several minutes, just letting the beast get to know her smell while at the same time she filled its mind with as much comfort as she could manage. It was exhausting, far more difficult than spreading fear and confusion. All around her the hall was silent, and she could feel the weight of every eye on her. This was how legends were begun, she realized, aware of how this must look. The pale thin queen conquering the savage beast. Finally, she dropped her hand down and stepped away.

'Take him back out. Let him be with other horses.' As she spoke the words, she sent the idea to the horse that he should go with the men. Snorting and bucking but still more tractable than when he had been brought in, the stallion allowed himself to be led out. As the doors closed on the auction ring, a huge cheer went up, the people rejoicing in their queen.

Returning to the town and the castle, Lord Beylin seemed oddly distracted. He wouldn't catch Beulah's eye, and she had the distinct impression he was trying to avoid talking to her. As they disembarked from his private barge, she confronted him.

'What, Petrus? Do you disapprove of my taste in horses?'

'It's not that, Your Majesty. Though I see many months, even years of trouble from that horse.'

'Then what? You've been avoiding my eye ever since I bought the animal. Why?'

Beylin seemed to consider his answer for a while as they walked the short distance up the hill to the castle gates. 'I'm sorry, ma'am. I truly am. When you came to me this morning, I lied to you.'

'Lied to me? About what?'

'About not knowing where the Duke of Abervenn had gone. About not having seen him this morning. He begged me to do it. It was his idea that I take you to the livestock markets. I made certain that various merchants would say they had seen him heading that way. But I never intended that you should buy a horse.'

'What's so wrong with buying a horse?' Beulah felt a moment of unease as they entered the castle, stepping from sunshine to shade and then back into the sun. There was something afoot, and she didn't like the way she was being manipulated.

'I think you should ask His Grace that yourself, ma'am.' Beylin bowed and indicated to his left.

Beulah looked over to where he pointed to see Clun standing alone in the courtyard. He had changed back into more formal garments, and the sun glinted in his blond hair giving the impression of a halo. As he saw her, he walked forward, and out of the shadows followed two of the most beautiful mares she had ever seen. They were palest yellow in colour, slim and athletic. Obviously well broken and docile, yet they held their heads high, ears pricked and alert, eyes bright to everything going on around them.

'My lady, I'm sorry for the subterfuge.' Clun's face was

broad with a grin she had not seen on him before, a mischievous glint in his eye. 'I'd heard that the best horses in the whole of Gwlad came from these parts. So I thought I would buy you a pair.'

21

Most workings of the subtle arts are transient, of the moment. A dragon might reach along the Llinellau to bring something to him or send a thought to a loved one. He might draw a little of the Grym into himself to ward off the cold or to help heal some small injury. More complex workings can persist after they have been performed, though these are more difficult and can unravel when least expected or convenient.

Almost all a dragon's workings will begin to unwind once they have died. Only the subtle arts of a great mage can hope to persist for longer, and even then only if that mage's jewels have been laid to rest according to his or her instructions. It is for this reason that mages tend to live apart from the rest of their kind and their jewels are not joined with those of their family upon reckoning.

Dire consequences will follow should a dragon mage's jewels be removed from their final resting place. The workings they control are complex and powerful things, and their unravelling can be profoundly destructive.

Corwen teul Maddau,
On the Application of the Subtle Arts

Even though he walked a path beaten by Benfro's tail, Errol still found the going almost impossible. The snow was soft and powdery, with a thin crust on top that mostly held his weight but occasionally gave way. He might walk for a hundred paces with only the whistling wind to contend with, then without warning he would find himself engulfed in frozen white. Each time it happened he lost his concentration and his tenuous connection with the Grym, letting the bitter cold eat at his exposed face and hands. And each time he struggled to haul himself out of the hole back on to the crust where the dragon had passed.

He had tried walking on the snow to the side of Benfro's trail, but this was if anything more treacherous still. And all the while the thin air made breathing difficult, every small effort like climbing to the highest tower in Emmass Fawr. Still he pressed on, drawing what strength he could from the Grym and praying all the while that Benfro's tracks wouldn't suddenly disappear. If the dragon took off and flew away into the night, then Errol would never find him.

Errol wondered at Benfro's mood change. His rescue had been truly heroic, and even when they had landed the dragon had been full of concern. But as soon as he saw the jewels he had flipped. Or was it as soon as he saw his mother's jewel? Or as soon as he took it? Errol knew the dangers that dragon jewels posed, but surely they were less for a dragon himself? Unless the bond was too close, like mother to son.

The night wore on as he pondered the questions. Perhaps, he thought, it was Magog trying to reassert his influence, now that his jewel had been removed from Corwen's cave. But if that was the case, then it was crucial he find Benfro before it was too late. He remembered all too well Corwen's words when he had first seen the old dragon's jewels: '*You'll know when there's nothing left of Benfro and Magog has taken his place. If that moment comes, you must kill him.*'

Shivering as much at the cold as at the thought, Errol pressed on through the snow, climbing yet another in a seemingly endless series of shallow rises. Ahead he could see the first pink tinges of dawn fading out the night stars. How long had he been walking? Not that long surely. But then he was far further north than he had ever been before, and he had read of the frozen sea where the sun never set in the summer, nor rose in the winter.

The air seared in his throat, escaping from his Grym-warmed body in gusts of steam that hung about him as he trudged towards the top of the rise. He could see the U-shaped indentation made by Benfro as he had passed earlier. Errol was all for giving up, digging himself a shelter in the snow and going to sleep, but he knew if he did that he would likely never wake up. So he struggled on, slower and slower, hoping that this last ridge would be the top and that he could go downhill for a change. Foot after foot, every muscle in his body creaking and protesting at the strain, it was all he could do to keep his eyes focused on the ground in front of him, trying to guess when next the crust would give way.

And then his foot landed lower than he expected. For an instant Errol tensed, then relaxed, accepting the inevitable plummet, the blast of icy cold as he lost his link to the lines, the desperate struggle to pull himself out of waist-deep powder. It never came, and before he could register surprise, he had started his next step, his body acting without any input from his mind. Again his foot landed lower than he was expecting, and again he tensed for the drop through the crust. This time he jarred his knee badly, sending a shock right up through his body all the way to his jaw. Crunching teeth woke him from his stupor and Errol stopped walking, looked up, gasped.

He stood on a narrow ridge where the wind had ripped the snow away, leaving hard rock underfoot. Ahead of him, difficult to make out in the gloom, a cliff dropped away into the darkness, but he was only dimly aware of it as something not to fall over. All his attention was focused on the view straight ahead.

He was looking north and east towards the rising sun, far distant and limning the horizon with orange fire. Closer, the mountains dropped away in a series of steep-sided gullies, plunging to foothills that quickly levelled off into a smooth plain. He stood motionless, heedless of the cold wind ripping at him, chilling his hands and face as he forgot all about the Grym. For that first moment, before the sun's distant glare defined the perspective, it seemed as if he could see the whole of Llanwennog laid out in front of him. Then the light shifted and the scene changed. Still breathtaking, it was somehow less magnificent and at the same time more terrifying.

The ridge on which he stood curved away north and south, heading towards higher mountains on either side. Ahead there was a vertical drop of several hundred paces. Behind, still in shadow, the trail he had followed from Benfro's landing point snaked away across snowfields glistening and glinting in the reflected light. The trail ended here, at this cliff top.

Edging forward, Errol watched as the line of sunlight moved slowly down the cliff, cracks and crevices contrasting black against the ice-rimed rock. Down below, perhaps a hundred paces from the point where the drifts lapped up against the cliff like frozen waves, there was a deep indentation in the snow, then the beaten path of Benfro's passage carried on down in a series of gentle loops. Exhausted, Errol sank to his knees. The tears froze on his cheeks, but he no longer cared.

There was no sign of the dragon at all.

'Ho, Captain Pelquin! Well met.'

Melyn relaxed in his saddle as he and his troop rode out of the forest into a clearing filled with warrior priests. It had taken them far longer to rendezvous with the army than expected. He had thought with Corwen's jewels firmly ensconced in his saddlebags the magics in the forest that confused the unwary traveller would have dissipated. But if anything their intensity had increased, almost as if the forest were fighting against him, as if the dead dragon had actually been holding back something much wilder.

He had spent most of the time in his aethereal trance, high above the canopy and looking down through the magic to the trees and paths below. At least with Frecknock able to hear him in that form, he had been able to relay commands to Osgal, keeping his men on the right track. Still, he didn't like spending so much time out of his body, fearful that he might not be able to make it back. He would be much happier when they left the forest and reached the mountain pass.

'Your Grace, it's good to see you again. I swear we've marched through the same bit of forest a dozen times since you left us.' Captain Pelquin looked as relieved to see him as Melyn felt. Looking around the camp, he could see that morale among the warrior priests was not high either.

'I don't doubt that you have. These woods are thick with enchantments. I've never seen anything like them before.'

'Did you catch your dragon, sire?'

Melyn's mood darkened. He had tried not to think too hard about Errol and Benfro's escape, consoling himself with the prize of the jewels.

'No, Pelquin. I didn't. Neither did I catch the traitor Errol Ramsbottom, even though he was there. They both escaped into the mountains. But I suspect I know where they're going. We'll catch them yet.'

We're ready to march on your orders. I reckon the men would be happy to get out of these trees.'

'I don't doubt it. But I need to rest a while. We'll camp here the night and head out at first light.'

'As you command, sire.' Pelquin saluted and headed off into the camp. Melyn dismissed the rest of his small troop, letting them find what food they could from their companions; there had been no time for hunting since they had left the clearing. Only Frecknock remained, standing slightly behind him as she always did. He turned towards her, wondering when it was that the sight of her had stopped sickening him.

'This pass of yours. It's not far, I take it?'

'If Your Grace feels able to assume his aethereal form once more, I will show the way. It is well hidden.'

Melyn sighed. He really wanted to rest, but it was more important to be certain where they were going. Leading his army blindly into the hills could cost them precious days, and they had already wasted too much time in the forest.

'Very well. Let me get settled.' He walked across to the nearest fire, sitting down on the ground with a tree at his back. Frecknock followed, curling herself down beside him like some improbably huge and loyal hound. The firelight flickered, reflecting off her scales and her eyes. Melyn tore his gaze away, centring himself and slipping into the trance.

The flames took on that strangely alive quality they had when seen in the aethereal. All around him the trees and shrubs, grass and herbs seemed to become more solid, anchored in the stuff of Gwlad, while the forms of the warrior priests dwindled and thinned, some fading to no more than will-o'-the-wisps.

'Please follow me.' Melyn turned his aethereal self to look at Frecknock. She was no longer lying down, but stood a little further off than before. As he watched, she spread wings far larger than her real ones and soared gracefully into the air. Too astonished to be angry, he rose to follow her. They climbed high over the treetops and looked down on the camp, the forest, the endless magics twisting and twining in and out of each other.

'Legend says that two great dragons warred here, casting such terrible spells that Gwlad herself was split in two.

The magic you see all around is the echo of that long-ended battle. The skilled, those with the sight like yourself, can find their way through. Some can even bend the workings to their own will, but most who enter the Ffrydd are at its mercy.'

'I care very little for your legends, Frecknock. It's enough to know that this place is awash with raw magic. Dealing with it is my only concern right now. Getting out of this place.'

'Of course, Your Grace. I too grow tired of the endless contradictory spells. In the village where . . . where I lived, the magic was tamed, ordered. It flowed smoothly around us all, and we were able to ignore it like you can ignore the sound of the wind in the leaves or water in a brook. But here the storm never ends; the river is in spate.'

Frecknock flew higher still, as if wanting to get above the colourful formless patterns that eddied back and forth below. The further they climbed the more difficult it was to make out the forest, everything blurred into the mass of swirling magic as if it was descending on the assembled army, pulled in from the surrounding forest like insects to a naked light. Perhaps it was just the concentrated power of so many warrior priests acting as a magnet, but from up here it looked as if the forest was alive. And angry.

'Where are you going?' Melyn shook the thought away, rushing to catch up with Frecknock, who had risen higher still on the aethereal wind.

'I need to get my bearings. It's been many years since I came through here, and I was just a kitling then.'

'So how could you have seen it like this? Were you hatched with the ability to walk the aethereal?'

'Far from it, Your Grace. It has taken many years of study to master the art. But I do recall the shapes of the mountains. And I remember my father saying that the pass was protected. If I can find the right location, I should be able to see the spells that hide the entrance and hopefully undo them for long enough to get through.'

'Well, hurry up about it. I'm not happy with the way things are looking down there.' Melyn peered into the swirling mass of colour that flowed around and over the army's camp. He could make out very little through it now, only an occasional glimpse of firelight and a few horses, their heads down as they grazed. His body was somewhere underneath all that magic; he would have to pass through it to get back. And all the while more and more flowed into the area.

'This way. I'm sure of it.' Frecknock tipped forward, folding her wings into a dive as if it were the most natural thing in the world. Taken by surprise, Melyn had to rush to catch up as she plunged towards the trees to the north of the camp. They travelled perhaps three miles up a narrow-sided valley with a small stream running down it from the mountains above. At its head some ancient cataclysm had carved out a wide bowl, and a round lake sat beneath an impassable cliff, rising a hundred spans or more into the air. It was just the sort of dead-end valley Melyn expected to find in the foothills of the Rim mountains; the land near Emmass Fawr was full of them. But Frecknock didn't stop, instead heading straight for the sheer wall of rock.

And then she disappeared.

Melyn hovered above the water, looking around. Frecknock had been nowhere near the cliff face, nor had she turned away from her headlong flight towards it. She had simply vanished. Slowly he inched forward, noticing as he did how the surface of the lake was mirror-smooth and black. Then something stopped him. It was as if he had walked into an invisible wall. He could feel nothing, see nothing, sense nothing, but try as he might he could get no closer to the cliff. Turning away, he floated back towards the point where the stream flowed out of the lake. That was easy, as was weaving from side to side, up and down. But when he pushed forward again, that same unflinching and unknown barrier held him back.

'I thought you were following me.' Melyn looked to one side, seeing Frecknock once more hovering in the air. She beat her wings slowly, quite unlike the frenzied motion of hummingbirds and insects, and it occurred to him that the action was more for show than necessity. An aethereal form was limited in its actions only by the imagination and skill of the adept who conjured it, or so he had been taught all those years ago by Inquisitor Hardy. But if Frecknock was showing off, then why? And to whom? Not him, surely.

'Where did you go?'

'Through the wards into the valley beyond.' Frecknock's answer was matter of fact, as if she found the question surprising.

'What wards? I can see nothing here.' Melyn strained his sight, searching the air for any indication of magical workings. He could see none, even though he knew that there must be something stopping him.

'Here, take my hand.' Frecknock flew swiftly towards him, her large hand held out, talons withdrawn. Her touch was warm, her skin softer than its leathery appearance might have suggested. As soon as she had a firm grasp, she pushed herself forward with a solid sweep of her wings.

Melyn felt himself pulled with her towards the unseen barrier, and then she began to disappear through it like an arm pushed into the surface of a still pond. He watched as more and more of her disappeared, until he felt again that strange sensation of being stopped, only this time it was subtly different, softer. The unseen barrier gave way slowly and a tingling sensation passed over his whole aethereal body as he was pulled through to the other side.

The valley continued on, winding its slow way up to a low point between two of the peaks that formed the horizon. Now there was no cliff face, only a lake formed by a silt dam choking the river flow where the valley narrowed behind them. Melyn looked for any sign of the magic that formed the illusion, but even in the aethereal he could make out no trace of its working whatsoever.

'How is it you can see this when I cannot?'

'It was made to hide the pass from men, not dragons.' Frecknock's air was not smug as much as proud, and Melyn could see from her expression that she was genuinely pleased to have been able to show him this, as if it vindicated the trust he had put in her by not killing her along with the rest of her extended family. He was reminded of young novitiates mastering their first spells and shyly showing them to their quaisters. The way she had thrown herself wholeheartedly into his service fascinated him. Had he been in her place, he would have been constantly searching for ways to thwart his captors, and yet she strove to be as helpful as possible. He would never have revealed his secrets, yet she seemed happy to teach him and his warrior priests magics which no man had ever known.

All his life Melyn had believed dragons to be base creatures, possessed of just enough intelligence to communicate with men but with an inherent ability to manipulate the Grym. He knew they were destructive and would steal rather than work to gain the things they wanted. That much had not changed, but now he was beginning to realize something else about them. They weren't just men with no moral scruples, nor children with the power of demi-gods. Dragons were different beasts entirely, with their own way of looking at the world, a way completely at odds with his own. It was a wonder men and dragons had ever managed to coexist peacefully; they were just too different.

He was about to ask Frecknock how he might be able to see the magic that had held him back, but before he could form the words, a terrible pain seared through his head. It felt like his mind was being ripped from his body, as if someone had prised open his skull and was pulling out great chunks of his brain. Everything dimmed to black, and had he not been holding Frecknock's hand still, he might have lost himself completely.

'Inquisitor? Your Grace?' Her voice centred him, though the pain still came in sickening waves.

'Got to get back.' Melyn forced the words through gritted teeth, even though his body had no physical form in the aethereal. None but that point of contact between himself and the dragon.

He would have pondered that, had he not been fighting to keep a hold on his very being. Frecknock looked at him strangely, then tugged him back in the direction they had come. The sensation of passing through the barrier was agony now, adding to the sense of being pulled apart. But at least it was short-lived. Once through, Frecknock picked up the pace, flying far more swiftly than any wings would have allowed, back down the valley and out across the forest towards the clearing where the army was camped. It wasn't difficult to find.

Magic pooled over the camp like a thundercloud of contrasting colours. It writhed and pulsed, piling ever higher, bulging out at the top as if whatever controlled it was trying to flatten the warrior priests. As they approached it, ever faster, Melyn wondered if he would be able fight his way through and back to his body. Somehow he knew that this concentration of enchantment was what caused him such agony. But what had drawn it to this spot?

'Hold tight.' Frecknock's voice was distant, lost in a rushing wind that battered his senses. He could see nothing but the swirling colours of the magic all around him, pummelling him like hailstones, screaming like tortured babies. It was hard to think, hard to remember even who he was. There was just that one point of contact, that warm hand engulfing his own.

'Relax, Your Grace. We're back.' The voice was

different this time, closer, clearer, and he heard it with his ears rather than his mind. The turmoil began to subside, like the slow return of normal hearing after a deafening thunderclap. Melyn realized that his eyes were screwed tight shut, and he opened them to see flames flickering as they turned logs into ash. He let out a long slow breath, feeling himself breathe for the first time since he had entered his trance. And then he slowly turned to face the dragon lying beside him.

She was looking up into his face, concern in her large eyes. And still in one great leathery fist she held his own small fragile hand.

'Please, forgive me.' She let go as he snatched it back, but he didn't have the heart to chastise her. And as he began to recover, so he noticed the activity going on around him. He could hear horses nickering, their unrest palpable in the evening gloom. The air felt sticky and electric, as if a storm were brewing, and when Melyn looked up he could see a great cloud overhead, dark and menacing. Yet over on the horizon the sky was clear.

'How far is that pass?' Melyn scrambled to his feet, swaying slightly as his sense of balance tried to catch up. Frecknock stood as well, shaking her pathetic wings in a manner that made her aethereal form seem all the more ridiculous.

'About four miles, I'd say.'

'And you can lead us there?'

'Of course.'

'And when we get out of the forest, up into the hills, we'll be away from this cursed magic?'

'I think so.'

'Good. Then prepare to run. I've a nasty feeling we've upset something.'

Frecknock stood calmly in the midst of the turmoil of the camp. Melyn could hear voices shouting, see warrior priests running to catch horses that had pulled free of their tethers. Panic flew around the camp like a swarm of bees.

'You took Corwen's jewels from their resting place. His power was all that was keeping the forest at bay.'

Errol wandered along the edge of the ridge, searching for a way down into Llanwennog as the sun rose slowly over the distant plains. It had looked promising to the south, but only because the clear air and bright light conspired to make things seem smaller and closer than they truly were. After an hour's hard walking, he had been forced to turn back by yet more sheer cliffs.

The ridge to the north was not much better. It wasn't sheer as it ran towards the peak, but it climbed so high that he had to crane his neck to see beyond it, the cliff only getting taller as it went, the mountain peak plunging to the land far below as if it had been hacked off with one clean blow of an enormous blade.

His stomach grumbled, filled with nothing more than melted snow since they had left Corwen's clearing what seemed like a lifetime ago. Errol couldn't be sure whether it was two days or one, but it was more than enough to make him feel weak. The thin air didn't help. At least his ankles were only sore now, not feeling like they might snap at any moment.

The wind ruffled his hair, cold on his face as he stared into the distance and rubbed at his legs. With a single thought he reached out for the nearest lines and drew the warmth of the Grym to him. It could sustain him for a while, but sooner or later he would need some of the food that they had packed, some of the food that was even now disappearing down the hill in a bag slung over Benfro's shoulders.

Errol stopped rubbing at his ankles and stuck his hands in his pockets, searching for anything that he might be able to chew. Even a blade of grass or a bit of stick would have helped to take his mind off the churning in his guts, at least for a little while. But there was nothing save a wad of cloth that served him as a handkerchief. Without thinking he pulled it out to wipe the icy rime from under his nose where his breath had frozen on to his skin. A tiny red jewel dropped on to the icy ground and skittered towards the edge of the cliff.

Errol lunged for it, grasping the gem before it could tumble away. For the briefest of instants he felt something vast and ancient and unstoppable reach towards him, and he jerked his hand back, letting go of the jewel like it was a hot coal. Fear brought pinpricks of sweat to his forehead; he had come so close to losing Magog's jewel, then closer still to falling under its influence. Still he felt an echo of that enormous presence, always questing, probing. Folding the cloth over neatly several times until it was as thick as a travelling cloak, he scooped up the gem, wrapped it tight and pushed it back into his pocket.

Then he remembered Corwen's cave: how he had fled from Melyn's approach by walking the lines back to

Benfro, and how he had found his way there by following the link between the young dragon and the jewel now nestling in his pocket. It was true that Corwen had helped him, pushed him away even. And every other time he had walked the lines since Melyn had messed with his mind had been almost by accident. But before then he had managed to do it. When Martha had shown him how. Surely he could do it again, now, on his own.

Errol searched the ridge for the lines, seeing them as a pale web against the midday sun. They were thin, spread wide over the barren land as if there were no life at all for them to feed on. Certainly there was nothing here like the life force that ran up the valley from Pwllpeiran to Jagged Leap. But was size important? He didn't know.

Shifting his focus so that he could see his aura, he searched for the thin red cord that linked Benfro to the jewel. It should have appeared at his pocket, and sure enough there it was, looping away and splitting as it joined many different lines at once. Perhaps that was the answer. He would have to follow them all. Or maybe the jewel was influencing more than just Benfro. Maybe there were others out there being slowly leached of all life. Maybe there was more than one jewel, and they talked to each other.

Errol shook his head to rid it of the endless questions. He needed to be calmer, more focused. He closed his eyes and tried once more to picture the scene. It came to him as vividly as if he were looking, perhaps even more so. And now the lines swelled, those joined by the rose cord turning pink at its touch. He built up an image of Benfro:

his shape, the way he walked, his voice, his smell and the way he sat still when thinking. Relying on his memory of the dragon, Errol started to think his way out along the lines, trying to sense him among the endless possibilities presented, always keeping the feel of that overpowering vast presence in the back of his mind.

He saw images too brief to register in his mind that made no sense. Some were close, others distant; some happening now, others long past. Sights and sounds and smells mixed into one great confusion of sensation as he searched for the one needle hidden deep within the haystack. Benfro was out there, he knew. He just had to find him.

And then he felt a strange melancholy, at once alien and deeply familiar. It was like a mother's lullaby long forgotten bringing back memories of earliest childhood. It was sad and it was angry, fractured and incomplete. It wasn't Benfro, but Morgwm – lonely, confused, defiant. Errol recalled the memories he had touched when he had taken her final jewel from Corwen's cave, the strange images of Princess Lleyn's death and the child nestling with the hatchling. She had taken that infant boy and walked the lines with him, given him over to fostering. Was he that child? Was that how he had learned the power of the Grym?

Something shifted in Errol's mind. He needed to know, needed to ask. He needed to be closer to that broken memory. His head spun, and it felt like he was being pulled in every direction, but he held on to that one simple feeling of need as the whole of Gwlad rushed past him. And then his head was filled with cotton wool. The wind stopped whistling past his ears and instead he could hear only the rush of blood in his veins. Everything external was blocked off as if he had stuck a blanket over his head. He took a breath and felt his lungs fill with a richness he had all but forgotten. The ground beneath him felt different, softer, the damp spread of melting snow soaking through his trousers.

Errol opened his eyes and found himself staring straight at the motionless snow-covered form of Benfro.

22

> The Fflam Gwir, or true flame, is nothing like the fire that cooks our evening meal and lights our candles. Or at least it need not be. When applied to the recently deceased, it reckons a dragon's jewels, setting their thoughts and memories for all eternity, but it will not consume the bier or table upon which that dragon is laid. When used upon the injured, it can heal and restore strength. When used upon an enemy it can inflict a burn that will heal slowly, if at all, and cause constant pain. The Fflam Gwir will consume only that which the dragon who has brought it forth wishes it to consume.
>
> Few dragons can produce the Fflam Gwir, though most can breathe base fire if pressed. Such common fire-breathing is considered impolite, a throwback to feral times. Sadly this narrow-mindedness has meant that those blessed with the ability to breathe the true flame have tended to suppress it.
>
> Maddau the Wise, *An Etiquette*

Melyn watched with a mixture of pride and alarm. He was proud of his warrior priests' calmness, their efficiency as they set about dismantling the camp and calming the horses. The magic storm descending upon them was enough to chill the blood of any man, and yet they went about their tasks with swift precision and attention to detail. They had been trained to be the best, of course; no man who went to pieces under pressure could hope to gain the coveted rank of warrior priest. And yet these long weeks in the forest, culminating in this attack, were far removed from anything they could have expected to encounter.

He was alarmed by the sheer power building against them. Despite their years of training, these men were no match for the raw magics that boiled in the air. Melyn himself was no match for them, and that unsettled him more perhaps than anything else. He wasn't sure he believed Frecknock's assertion that the forest was after the jewels he had taken from the hidden cave. More likely the unravelling ancient spells thick in this part of the woods were all being drawn towards the most powerful magical source around. That might be the jewels, but was more likely the combined power of five hundred adepts tapping the Grym for a little extra energy to light their way to the latrine pits or conjure a flame rather than use flint.

'Captain, pass the word to the men. No one is to use any magic whatsoever until I say they can.' Osgal nodded his acceptance of the order, though Melyn doubted he understood the reasoning behind it. He shouted to the nearest warrior priests and they all ran off to spread the word.

'It's too late for that, Your Grace. We have to leave this place now.' Frecknock stood to one side, trying to keep out of the way of the milling warrior priests. She was constantly glancing up at the sky and wringing her hands together. Melyn could almost taste her anxiety.

'Can you lead us to the valley?'

'Yes, but we must hurry.'

'Then lead on.' Melyn swung himself up into his saddle, looking out over the hastily struck camp at his men. Most were mounted, their spare horses roped behind them. Those few who were still loading saddlebags and tent rolls would have to catch up.

'We follow the dragon,' he shouted to Osgal, who waited nearby. As the order was relayed down the line, Melyn turned his horse in the direction he and Frecknock had flown earlier.

'Your Grace, this way.' Frecknock pointed to the opposite end of the clearing, downhill and seemingly back into the deep forest. Melyn felt his anger rise, but something in the dragon's voice, and her very posture, stopped him short. She was frightened of him, that much he both knew and expected. But she was frightened of the oncoming magical storm much more. He couldn't risk the time to slip into his aethereal trance, so he had to rely on her ability to see past the confusions and spells that made everything seem different. As he stared at her, torn between his hatred of all dragons and his need to trust this one, a low rumble of thunder echoed out over the trees. The wind picked up from nowhere, rippling the leaves as if a heavy downpour was on its way. Melyn's mind was made up. He turned his horse and nodded for Frecknock to lead on.

She set off at a steady run, an ungainly motion that nonetheless covered the ground with surprising speed.

With a shout to encourage his men to follow, he spurred his horse into a fast trot and then a canter to make up the distance.

It was a surreal journey. He knew it was only a matter of a few miles to the valley and the lake, and their route should have been steadily uphill towards the mountains. Yet from what little he could see through the gathering clouds, they were heading in completely the opposite direction. The path appeared to narrow down to the point where only one or two horses could pass side by side, but Frecknock never slowed, nor even looked back to be sure they were following. Glancing over his shoulder, Melyn could see only a great cloud of dust, such as you might expect from five hundred riders and a thousand horses. Even Osgal, who should have been close by, was indistinct.

The magic was all around them, enveloping them in a fog which crackled and glowed with strange colours. Shapes loomed and receded, the shadows of enormous beasts warring. The horses were galloping now, their necks straining at the reins, muscles taut and ears held flat. Ahead, Melyn could see Frecknock running, her hands outstretched, and he fancied he could hear her voice in the wind, speaking strange words that sent shivers down his spine.

Something shimmered in the air and the beat of his horse's hooves changed. Looking down, Melyn almost unseated himself. He was riding across the glass-smooth lake, each footfall kicking up a tiny spray that hung in the air far longer than it should have done. Ahead of him Frecknock had stopped running and was standing at the edge of the water, the great bowl-shaped cliff rising above her like some vast mouth full of teeth. He reined in his horse, sending calming thoughts to its terrified, simple mind, but his head filled with the dragon's voice.

'Don't stop. Keep riding. I'll hold it open until the last are through.'

Melyn didn't have time to stop and consider. He was at the bank already, and his horse showed no sign of slowing, even though the cliff reared up in front of them. He tensed himself, expecting the beast to swerve either left or right at the last moment, but it carried straight on. For an instant he knew real fear; he was too close to the rock, going too fast towards it for anything other than a fatal neck-snapping crash. He gripped tight with his thighs, dropped his hands to the horse's neck to brace himself for the impact. There was a jarring in his knees as his horse stumbled and corrected its pace on a new surface. And then everything changed.

The day turned bright, sun shining down from a cloudless sky. The air was cooler, with a gentle breeze that tugged at his hair. Melyn's horse seemed to calm in an instant, slowing in response to his pull on the reins. He looked around and found himself in a wide valley with steep sides. Ahead the mountains rose far closer than he was expecting, their tops swathed in snow even in summer. He let go of his reins and the horse immediately dropped its head to the lush grass that blanketed the valley floor. There were no trees here at all, as if someone had cut them all down and none had dared grow again.

Looking back, Melyn saw a bank of fog spread from one side of the valley to the other. It reminded him of the haar that swept in from the sea and enveloped Abervenn for days on end. As he wondered how close Beulah and Clun were to that city, he saw a mounted figure ride out of the fog, followed by another, and another. Soon dozens of warrior priests were appearing, filling the space, all with the same look of bemusement on their bloodless faces. He cast his eyes over his men, seeking out Osgal, finding him at last.

'Muster the men further up the valley. I need to know how many made it through.' Osgal nodded but said nothing. Melyn didn't think he'd ever seen the man look so terrified. It reminded him of the boy he had been. 'I'll see to the rest of them,' Melyn added. 'Just get everyone as far away from that . . . that barrier as possible.' He kicked his horse, riding slowly towards the fog bank as a few more warrior priests stumbled through. Some were on foot, and some of the horses were riderless. Scanning the grass, he could only guess how many there were, but it didn't look like five hundred had made it through.

Close up, the fog was more like a wall of ice, sculpted and carved by the wind. It didn't move like mist, but faint colours pulsed through it as if some terrible battle was going on inside. His horse whickered and threw its head about as he came closer, while his spare mount, attached to his saddle by a long rope, bucked and reared, so he turned them away, dismounted and approached on foot.

The white wall was hot to the touch, though no heat radiated from it. He tried to push his hand into it, but it was as solid as any rock face. Melyn opened up his mind, trying to sense the thoughts of anyone who might be on the other side. Instantly he snapped it shut again as a barrage of terror more potent than anything he had ever conjured himself swept through him, weakening his knees.

Then the wall shuddered, and a warrior priest fell through it, crashing to the ground. Melyn went to him and rolled him over. The man flopped like a rag doll, his bones broken or just gone. Blood seeped from his eyes and nose, and his skin was red as if he had been plunged into boiling water. He was dead.

Cursing, Melyn again put his hand to the wall, ignoring the pain as it burned his palm. He opened his mind once more, pushed past the fear that pulsed about him, searching for a thought, any thought, that might give him an idea of what was happening on the other side. It was all noise, screaming, pain and confusion as one by one his men succumbed to whatever terrible force that was ripping them apart. And then he felt it, a mind unlike the others. It was scared but calm, working some protective magic he couldn't begin to understand.

'Frecknock?' Melyn sent the question as a thought. The dragon didn't answer, but almost as soon as he had voiced her name, he began to see in his mind as if he were looking through her eyes.

It was the lake, surrounded by that great arc of cliff, trees lining its far side. Only whereas before it had been a mirror-flat surface, now it boiled like a cauldron, great bubbles erupting steam into the air. A few men and horses bobbed in the water, most still, but a few writhing in agony. On the shore a dozen warrior priests struggled against unseen foes that lashed them with invisible claws, although the bloody welts were real enough.

The storm that filled the sky with impossible colours grew ever fiercer, and with it the pain in Melyn's palm. Still he kept his hand in place, unwilling to give up on his men. At his thought the view shifted. Dragon hands reached out for the nearest warrior priest, lifted him off his feet and threw him at the barrier. Melyn's contact was momentarily lost as the man came flying through, landing with a heavy grunt on the grass. Two more arrived together, then another two, each further along as Frecknock moved down the shore. Melyn reached out and tried to renew his contact with her, but she was closed to him. Pushing harder, he saw something similar to his aethereal view of the place, only this was some hellish version surely, some place deep in the lair of the Wolf.

Dead men and horses boiled in the lake like meat in the pot. The trees on the far side were aflame, lighting the cliffs in flickering red. The air was charged with magic, countless spells bouncing off each other, merging, breaking apart again, more powerful than they had any right to be. And, huddled against the rock wall, Frecknock struggled to help the last living warrior priest.

The lake was rising, approaching the cliff edge where they stood as the dragon finally managed to push the man back through the barrier to the safety beyond. Melyn watched as she slipped, struggled to her feet and stepped towards the cliff, one hand outstretched. At her touch the rock face flexed and shimmered, then hardened against her push. The boiling water reached her tail as she hammered her fist on the rock and then drew it back with a yelp that he almost heard. She pressed herself closer to the wall, trying to keep her feet from scalding.

'Your Grace. Can you hear me? Help me, please.' The voice was a whisper in his head, a shout drowned by the turmoil all around. Melyn felt his connection with Frecknock strengthen, his perspective shift so that he saw once more through her eyes. He could sense her fear now, steadily eroding her calm, and he could also feel her exhaustion. Whatever she had done to get his men through this barrier had worn her down until there was virtually nothing left.

Well, it would be a good way to die, he supposed. He had never intended letting her live beyond her usefulness, and the whole reason for bringing her in the first place was to find this pass. What did he really need of her now?

'Please, Inquisitor. I can't find the way through. If you're there, let me know.' Her voice was tiny, distant, helpless. Melyn knelt in the grass, one hand placed flat against the burning barrier, oblivious to his own pain as he felt Frecknock's instead, wondering why he was even thinking about helping her. She was a dragon, a beast who had disobeyed the laws laid down to control her kind, who existed only at the sufferance of his queen. And yet this creature had saved his life at least twice already. She possessed knowledge that would make the success of his mission almost a certainty. And what if there were a similar barrier at the other end of the pass?

'Here, Frecknock. I'm here.' Melyn sent the thought out. Frecknock's reaction was instant. He felt like someone had grabbed him, even though it was all in his mind. The connection with the dragon strengthened as she anchored herself to him. He could feel something of those alien thoughts, that strange way of looking at the world, at life and death and the slow passing of time. He was old, had witnessed many decades in his life, but he was an infant compared to her, and she no older than a newly chosen novitiate in comparison with her extended family.

Through her eyes Melyn watched as Frecknock pushed once more at the solid rock. The water was lapping at her tail, licking at her heels as her hand slid slowly through the barrier. For an instant he experienced the strange sensation of feeling both her hand touch his and his touch hers, then he was back in his own mind, clasping her hand tight and pulling her through the wall.

It resisted like soft mud on a river bottom. Frecknock's arm came slowly through, then her other hand. Melyn looked round, seeing Captain Osgal a half-hundred paces away, not willing to come any closer.

'Grab her hand. Help me pull her through.' For a moment Melyn thought the captain was going to disobey his order, such was his fear. But with a shake almost like a dog ridding itself of icy water, Osgal jogged over. He took Frecknock's other hand, reluctantly the inquisitor thought, and put his back into the task of pulling her through.

Whether it was the captain's strength or the touch of Melyn's mind helping the dragon to anchor herself, she came through in a rush that had them all tumbling to the ground. Osgal was the first to his feet, and Melyn rolled slowly on to his side before struggling up, holding his burned hand out from his body as if it was contagious. Frecknock stayed motionless, slumped on her front in an undignified pose, breathing heavily, her eyes closed tight. Finally she pushed herself up into a crouch, holding the tip of her tail off the ground as if it pained her, and looked round at the inquisitor.

'You saved me, Your Grace. For that you have my eternal gratitude.'

Melyn wasn't sure whether to be pleased or ashamed. He had returned the favour, had saved her for his own selfish purposes, but he couldn't help thinking that he had also betrayed his order and all it stood for.

There was a strange comfort to be had in sorting through the great pile of jewels. It wasn't as big as once it had been, thanks to his diligence. Benfro didn't look around – he didn't need to. The endless rows of alcoves, each home to a single dead dragon, were testimony to months of hard work. It was an achievement, something to be proud of. Something that in years to come they might write ballads about.

'Benfro.'

The voice was a whisper, somewhere out in the cold dark. He didn't like the place beyond the walls of the repository. It was frightening, hostile and icy. There he was chased by demons in the shape of men, beasts who murdered and butchered his kind just because they could. It was safer in here, with his jewels and the wonderful memories they contained.

'Benfro.'

More insistent this time, the voice buzzed in his head like an insect on a hot sunny day, constantly niggling away, never leaving him alone. Benfro shifted slightly, or at least tried to. He seemed to be stuck where he was, held in place by invisible hands. Cold hands.

'Benfro.'

Louder. Benfro thought he recognized the voice now, but he couldn't put a name to it. Just a feeling. He was angry at the voice, hurt by it. It was the voice of a man, for one thing, and all they did was kill. But it had betrayed him too, betrayed his only friend and kept him away from his mother.

'Benfro!'

He saw a blade of purest white light arcing through the air in a parody of the sun, descending with unstoppable force. He tried to close his eyes, to stop them seeing what came next, what he knew would happen, but his eyes were closed already. He was seeing this in his mind, watching as Inquisitor Melyn cut off Morgwm's head. Watching as the band of warrior priests descended on it like wolves around a wounded deer, ripping it apart for the goodness deep within. The memories of his mother. Her jewels.

Something changed then. He still sat in front of the pile of jewels, but the one crystal he held did not belong there. He knew it like he knew his own wings, could picture that first time he had touched it, after he had set the Fflam Gwir about his mother's body and burned it away to ash.

'Benfro. Wake up.'

For an instant the room darkened. Benfro felt a chill pass through him so intense it could have killed. It was like the fear that the warrior priests used to immobilize their enemies, but his mother had protected him from that before. Surely she could do it again. He clasped the jewel firmly in his hand, squeezing it tight until it dug into the tiny scales on his leathery palm. He waited for that familiar touch, the sense that she was standing in the next room just waiting for him. But all he could see was that arc of light endlessly falling.

He tried to shake his head to chase away the image, but he was bound with ropes, his neck stiff and heavy. His legs were still stuck, and as reached out for the pile to take another jewel, he realized his arms were fixed too. He could flex his fingers, squeeze his palm tight on that one tiny point of agony, but nothing else worked.

'Benfro, please.'

Panic flickered around the edge of his thoughts like a fox skirting a henhouse, looking for the right place, the right moment to dive in and reduce everything to swirling feathers. How had he come here to Magog's repository?

Magog. Even the name filled him with alarm. How could he have thought this was a good place to be? How could he have been proud of the work he had done here? Benfro struggled against the ties that bound him. He was stronger now; he could fight the dead mage, push off his influence. He just needed to get moving. But he was stuck fast, held in place by something cold and unyielding. He fought it, but nothing worked. How had he come here? He racked his brain, trying to remember what he had been doing. Obviously he must have fallen asleep, but why wasn't Errol watching over him?

'Benfro. Wake up. Please.'

Errol. It was Errol's voice that he heard, distant but insistent. And he had been furious with the boy, had stalked off into the cold night. The memories started to slip back into place: the argument, his mother's jewel overwhelming him with its need, the cliff he had not noticed until his wings had snapped open automatically, gliding him down to the ground far below, and walking, endless walking until exhaustion had taken over and he had sat down.

'Benfro, please.'

Errol's voice was fading, and with it the view of the pile of jewels, as if their light was dying as the memories were plucked away. But Benfro could see beyond the pile, to the scroll stacks and the ancient writing desk. They too were fading, dimming to black. The cold he had felt was gone now, replaced with a relaxing warmth that soothed away his worries. So what if he couldn't move? He could just sit here and drift off to sleep. Magog was no threat to him any more. He could sleep.

'Benfro?' The voice was barely a whisper, distant and unimportant.

Benfro was drifting off into a dream where his mother was waiting for him. She was somewhere nearby, he knew. Just round the next corner perhaps. And she would protect him from harm for ever. All his struggles were over now; there was nothing left to worry about. Morgwm was with him. She was . . .

He felt a snatching feeling somewhere in the region of his hand. His mother, so close he could almost see her, disappeared in an instant. The warmth left with her, its place taken by cold that made him shiver uncontrollably. It was as dark as a moonless night, his eyes gummed shut, and when he tried to open them, they wouldn't move.

Nothing would move any more, not his legs, nor his arms, his head or neck.

'Come on, Benfro. Wake up. Do something.' This time Errol's voice was muffled, as if he was on the other side of a thin wall.

As the words trickled into Benfro's mind, he felt something collide with the side of his head. It wasn't a hard blow, barely enough to register, but for the briefest of instants he saw in his mind a small gully filled with deep-drifted snow, and sitting in the middle of it covered in ice, a dragon. He thought at first that it was dead. And then he realized it was him.

'Don't die on me, Benfro. I'm stuck in these mountains without you. There's no way down.' Again the voice was accompanied by the weakest of slaps to the head, only this time the image Benfro saw was of a boy, a young man, his face so pale it looked almost blue, his arms and legs hanging limp and useless, covered in snow.

'Now you get it. Use that foul talent of yours if it will keep you alive. Then you can be mine.' This time it was Magog who spoke to him, unmistakable even though he sounded like he was shouting against a storm. His presence, however slight, filled Benfro with anger and hatred. He could feel it boiling in his stomach, devouring the last of the food he had eaten so long ago. Without even the strength to open his mouth, Benfro let go of the fire and breathed out through his nose.

Errol couldn't have said what made him leap to one side the instant before Benfro coughed up a great belch of yellow flame. Some sixth sense, perhaps, an inbuilt mechanism for self-preservation. Unlike the flame the dragon had breathed before, which had left him unscathed, this one roared with an angry heat, melting the ice and snow all around. He felt it sear his face even as he scrabbled to the edge of the gully, the smell of freshly singed eyebrows wafting under his nose.

Then the flames died away, finding nothing to burn. A patch of cleared ground steamed gently in the cold mountain air. Behind Benfro there was still snow, but in front of him and to the sides was clear. He didn't move for a few seconds, then without opening his eyes he reached out with the hand that had held his mother's jewel. Errol looked down at the tiny gem resting in his own palm. He had hardened his aura to it, not quite understanding how he had done so, and its siren song of patient wellbeing had stilled as soon as he had taken it from the dragon.

Benfro leaned further forward, his eyes still closed, and then lost his balance. He tried to fight the inevitable for a few seconds, then gave up the struggle and fell gracelessly on to his face. When he didn't get up again, Errol slid back down the gully and on to the bare patch of ground, now icing up again and threatening to trap the dragon once more. He reached out and touched Benfro's shoulder with his free hand, hastily shoving Morgwm's jewel deep into his pocket with the other. Benfro didn't stir, and Errol could feel just how cold the dragon was. How long had he sat in the snow, asleep or otherwise immobile, while the life slowly leached out of him?

Errol couldn't begin to guess, but he knew that a man with no knowledge of magic would have lasted no longer than a couple of hours after dark in these mountains. He would have grown sleepy and weak, then drifted off into unconsciousness and died. If it was the same for dragons then Benfro had come perilously close to death and still hovered at its edge. However, if he just reached out to the lines, drew some of their power to him and used it to restore his energy, he might warm his muscles and bring himself back. Then again, what if he didn't know how? Was it possible that the dragon was less skilled in magic than he was? Errol doubted it, but then nothing Benfro had done since they had met suggested that he was an adept.

Errol's stomach gurgled, reminding him that he hadn't eaten in far too long. It was likely that Benfro hadn't either, weakening him further. The bags were still on the dragon's chest, though the straps of the food bag were charred and snapped as Errol pulled it around. He delved in, finding frozen strips of meat and handfuls of herbs and leaves. He took out a steak of raw venison solid with ice. It needed cooking, and for that Errol needed a source of heat, but he had never learned to conjure a flame the way Inquisitor Melyn did. The Grym gave him heat, though, so maybe he would be able to pass some of that on to the food. And if so, perhaps he could do the same for Benfro.

Excited at the prospect of trying something new, Errol reached out to the lines he had been unconsciously tapping, feeling them all around him. He did his best to ignore their pull, instead trying to tap their most basic energy and bring it to himself. He felt his stomach warm, the heat spreading out through him until a few pinpricks of sweat beaded on his forehead. Getting warmth and energy from the lines had never been difficult, but how to transfer that to the steak in his hand?

He shifted his focus so that he could see his aura around him, noticing as he did how palely Benfro's clung to him. He imagined those swirling colours stretching away from him not in a thin line that could be used to hold back Magog's influence, but as a wide sheet that enveloped the food he held. With a little extra effort he managed to lift it completely off his outstretched hand, away from his body. And then he pushed the energy of the Grym towards it.

What happened wasn't quite what he had been hoping for. A loud bang echoed off the nearby cliffs and the meat shot away from him, trailing a line of smoke that marked where it landed in the snow. He fell back as if pushed by a far greater force than that which had hurled the steak, and landed on his backside. Slightly winded, Errol picked himself up and hurried to retrieve the food before he lost sight of it in the snow. It had melted its way quite deep, and cooled off considerably in the process, but it was cooked to a crisp. It could have been charcoal and Errol wouldn't have cared. He chewed his way through it as if it were the tastiest meal he had ever known then turned his attention back to Benfro.

For a moment he thought he was too late. Even straining his vision, he could make out no aura surrounding the dragon at all. And then he saw the thin red cord that stretched from the jewel in his pocket and snaked around the gully to a spot just between the dragon's eyes. Magog would not be still there if there was nothing of Benfro to leach, but by the fierce red colour pulsing along the line, the dead mage was encountering almost no resistance.

Errol reached out with his aura, stretching it to meet the cord close to its source and tying it tight. Almost instantly the line faded from red back to palest pink and Benfro let out a low moan, slumping further to the icy ground. Errol could feel Magog now, pushing and questing, testing the Grym, searching for a way around the blockage. The power and subtlety were daunting, but Errol knew Magog's evil power would not be able to touch him. At least he hoped so.

Now all he had to do was save Benfro.

The dragon was far too big for Errol to envelop entirely in his aura. He wasn't sure that he could do much at all while concentrating on holding Magog at bay. Still, he had to try, so he reached out as best he could, wrapping Benfro's upper body and arms as if he were covering him with a vast cloak. Errol felt strange, like he was made of toffee and someone was stretching him out of shape. It wasn't painful in any conventional way, but it ached with wrongness the further he pulled his own aura away from himself. When he had gone about as far as he could without collapsing, Errol imagined the Grym flowing into the space he had created, filling it with the same warmth that made his skin slick with sweat.

It felt like he was running uphill with a bag full of rocks on his back, and at the same time it was as if he were doing nothing at all. Errol could feel the power of the Grym coursing through him so much that he should have burned himself to a crisp if the teachings of the quaisters at Emmass Fawr were not exaggerations. And yet if anything he began to feel the cold around him more. It seeped in at the points where his aura was strained thin, like a winter wind finding the seams in an old jacket. A thought began to form in his mind as to how the Grym worked, but it was interrupted by another long groan from Benfro.

Slowly the dragon rolled over on to his side, head still drooping. Errol pushed a little more of the Grym into his outstretched aura, feeling the strain in his mind like nothing he had ever known before. Then his own knees gave up without warning and he crumpled to the ground, his aura snapping back close around him. He sat there, confused and exhausted, staring as Benfro first pushed himself upright, then shivered in the renewed cold and finally opened his large eyes.

23

The northlands of Llanwennog are a barren and bleak landscape stretching from the Rim mountains in the west all the way to Kais and the Tegid River in the east. On their northern edge they are bounded by the Frozen Sea, and nothing grows there but rock. Southwards, the land flows into great plains covered in high sharp grass that only the native wild cattle can graze. Many hundreds of rivers cut deep gorges through the soft rock, making travel through this inhospitable land nigh on impossible. Yet people cling to life here, in small villages, rough towns and even one or two cities. The reason, as was ever the case, is gold.

Only a few have made their fortune from the northlands goldfields, mostly through the sale of provisions and prospecting tools. And yet the lure of that precious metal drags in the foolish, the desperate and the hopeless with undiminished strength. Those who survive are tough and uncompromising people, wary of strangers and mistrustful of even those they call friends.

From the travel journals of
Usel of the Ram

'It's nice to get off that barge. I was beginning to think I'd forgotten how to ride.'

Beulah kicked her horse lightly, spurring it into a trot. Clun, less skilled in the saddle, took a while to catch up. They were riding the pair he had bought for her at Beylinstown down a long straight tree-lined road that ran parallel to the River Hafren. At this point the river was at least two hundred paces wide, deep and swift-flowing. Had they stayed on the barge, they would have been in Castell Glas already, but Beulah didn't like the idea of entering one of her cities like so much freight. The bulk of her entourage had been sent on ahead, including the fine Gomoran stallion she had bought for Clun, which no one dared go near. Now she and her consort rode at the head of a small troop of warrior priests.

'Lord Beylin certainly has opulent tastes, my lady. And yet he spends little time enjoying his luxuries.'

'You'd noticed that too?' Beulah nudged her horse into a slow canter, relishing the feel of the wind in her hair and the smooth ride of a well-bred beast beneath her. This time Clun must have anticipated her; that or his horse didn't want to lose its companion. They rode abreast on the wide road.

'I'm used to rising with the first light, but I don't think I ever entered his hall when he wasn't already there, discussing some deal or other with the local merchants.'

'He works hard, and he's a clever man. I could do with more nobles of his calibre. Alas, most of them are like old Queln of Corris. Or worse.'

'Worse, my lady?'

'You never met Angor, your predecessor at Abervenn. Unless you saw his head on a pike at the Ffrydd Gate.'

Clun said nothing, but Beulah could see his hands tense on his reins. His horse sensed his unease and stumbled ever so slightly, making him lurch forward and grab at the creature's flowing mane. She chuckled under her breath, enjoying the sense of superiority her riding skills gave her.

'Relax your hands on the reins a bit. Use your thighs to control the beast, not the bridle.' She let go her reins, squeezed her legs just so, and her own horse dropped to a trot again. Clun pulled back like a novice, his feet pressing forward in his stirrups, reins held high. Beulah laughed again.

'My love, you can ride better than that.'

'True, but this horse has its own mind, unlike the old beast they gave me at the monastery.'

'Well, we'll have to work on your skills if you're ever to master that stallion.'

'I thought the whole point of Gomoran horses was that they couldn't be broken.'

'Any beast can be broken. You've just got to find the way. You'll not tame a wild creature like that with ropes and whips, mind. You've got to treat it like your equal.'

'My equal, is it? It'll be a long time before I'm halfway there.'

Beulah's reply was interrupted by the arrival of Captain Celtin, who overtook her at a canter, his warrior priests surrounding both of them in a swift well-drilled manoeuvre.

'Your Majesty, we have company. Riders coming fast.'

Beulah looked ahead down the arrow-straight road, and sure enough a great cloud of dust rose from the ground. At the base of it she could make out the forms of mounted men.

'Hostile or friendly?' Clun moved his horse close to Beulah's and they all stopped. With the river to one side and fields tall with corn to the other, there was not much they could do but flee the way they had come or fight.

'I'm not sure, Your Grace,' Celtin said. 'Though I'd hazard a guess at the latter. I'll go and find out what they want.'

The warrior priests parted to let him through, then resumed their guard around the queen. Beulah watched, annoyed that her afternoon ride had been ruined, as the captain rode some distance towards the approaching group and halted. About half a thousand paces away, just as the noise of approaching hooves was beginning to rise above the rustle of the wind in the trees, all but two of the approaching riders stopped. Celtin waited for them; there was a brief conversation, then he turned, trotting back to his queen with the two riders behind him. As they drew near, Beulah saw that one wore the uniform of a captain, his tunic bearing the arms of Castell Glas. The other man was a herald, his tabard a blaze of colours. Both stopped a good twenty paces away, dismounted and knelt on the road. Celtin rode slowly forward to the line his warrior priests still held.

'An honour guard from His Grace Duke Glas,' he said. 'And a messenger too, ma'am.'

Beulah walked her horse forward through a gap between the warrior priests that appeared without command. The two messengers remained kneeling at her approach.

'Rise, gentlemen. You are sent by Duke Glas. Why is it he feels unable to come and greet me himself?'

'Your Majesty, His Grace would have liked nothing more than to have escorted you all the way from Beylinstown, but he has sustained a grievous injury and is currently confined to bed by his surgeon.' It was the herald who spoke, continuing before Beulah could question him, 'He has sent his most experienced men to safeguard your passage into the city.'

'And does he not think his roads safe enough for his queen to travel unguarded?'

'Had you travelled them just a moon's phase ago, ma'am, then the answer would have been yes, though he would have wished to offer you his protection anyway. But these past weeks our lands have been harried by a great flying wyrm. Our cattle have been slaughtered, crops destroyed.'

Beulah felt a chill in her heart. Was it possible that Melyn had not succeeded in tracking down and killing the beast? The inquisitor had not contacted Clun since the day he had ridden north into the forest, though she hadn't truly expected that he would until he reached Llanwennog. That would not be for at least a week yet, but the dragon should have been slain over a month ago. So what was it doing down here in the Hendry?

'Have you seen this creature?' Beulah addressed the question to both men. The herald shook his head.

'No, ma'am. I've not, though I have seen the destruction it has wrought. Captain Tole here has, though.'

'Describe it to me.'

The captain took his time replying, as if he needed to gather his memories. Or maybe he was simply in awe of his queen.

'It was big, Your Majesty. As big as a house, mebbe bigger, but I don't need to describe it; you can see it fer yerself.'

'I can what?'

'Tha's how His Grace was injured, y'see, ma'am. We cornered the beast in the swamps to the south. Hunted it down.'

'It's dead?'

'No, ma'am. Better'n that. We captured it. Well, Duke Glas did. It's in chains in the city waitin' fer you.'

'Have we got a head count yet, Captain?' Melyn walked among his men, camped in the long grass a good distance up the valley from the great barrier that had separated them from the magic storm. Melyn had decided that a day's rest was in order; they needed to reorganize and redistribute their provisions, as well as tend to the injured men and horses.

'Most have reported back now, Inquisitor. So far we've lost twenty men and three dozen horses.'

'Twenty men, by the Shepherd, is that all?' Melyn scanned the camp. 'I thought we'd lost at least a hundred.'

'No, sir. Most got through before . . .' Osgal trailed off as if he didn't want to think too hard about what had happened. Melyn dismissed him with a wave of his hand, noticing for the first time the blisters on his own palm. He felt no pain, in fact felt nothing at all, but as he looked at the mess of red shiny flesh, a wave of nausea swept over him and his knees started to buckle. A steady hand caught him.

'Delayed shock, Your Grace. Perhaps you'd better sit down somewhere.'

Melyn looked around to see Frecknock just behind him. Her support should have angered him – she was too familiar – and yet he couldn't muster the energy to punish her. Had her constant presence over these long weeks on the road, their shared adventures, so inured him to her presence?

'It's nothing.' He pulled away from her. Nearby several troops of warrior priests clustered around their fires or tended their horses, but none of them paid either him or the dragon any heed.

'It's not nothing, Your Grace. You've serious burns to your hand. If you don't do something about them, and soon, then you'll lose it.'

'Why are my men ignoring me? They should have cut you down for laying a finger on me.'

'They can't see you, sir. I've hidden us both.'

'You've what? How dare you?'

'I thought it would be bad for morale, after what your warrior priests have just been through, for them to see their inquisitor collapse.'

'Why would you care?'

'I swore a blood oath. I am bound to that until one of us dies. As long as I'm useful to you, that time may yet be some way off. If I don't help you, then you'll just kill me. I want to stay alive, Inquisitor Melyn. I can't embrace my death calmly like the others. They'd lived for centuries, made peace with Gwlad and settled down. If you hadn't killed them, they would all have faded away soon enough. But I'm still young; I've not been given the choice they all took.'

Her logic was as cold as his own. Meanwhile Melyn was not so stupid as to ignore her obvious power, and the fact that she seemed willing to do his bidding opened up all manner of possibilities.

'This enchantment that makes me invisible to my men. This is the same spell that you use to hide yourself?'

'It's similar, yes.'

'Show me how it's done.'

'Of course, Your Grace. But first you need to heal that hand. May I?' Frecknock held out her own hand. For the first time he noticed that the palm was not the thick leathery skin he had thought, but hundreds of tiny flexible scales that rippled as she moved her fingers. Not quite knowing why he did it, he let her take his injured hand.

Her touch was gentle, but even so it brought an explosion of pain that tensed his muscles. Then she muttered something under her breath and the pain vanished. Holding his palm open, she waved her free hand back and forth in the air above it, still mouthing those strangely soothing words. He felt a tingling warmth in his fingers, not unpleasant so much as mildly irritating, like a faint itch that won't respond to scratching, and a somehow disturbing sensation ran over his skin, rippling it like water pulled by a light breeze. The tightness in his knuckles eased, letting his fingers flex properly for the first time in weeks. Looking down, he saw the blisters dissolve in front of his eyes, as if his hand were absorbing them, healing with a speed far faster than even his skill at magic could have managed.

Finally Frecknock stopped her murmuring and let go of his hand. Her release was like a huge disappointment. He almost reached out to touch her again, but at the last moment he stopped himself, instead lifting his hand to his face the better to inspect her working. There was no sign of the burns and no lingering pain. If anything his hand felt better, freer than before, no longer cramped by long hours clutching his reins.

'You still need to rest, Your Grace. I can heal your hand, but I can't do anything about the shock. That will take time to pass.'

Melyn wondered what she was talking about. Then he realized that his knees were damp. Looking down, he saw that he had sunk to the grass. Or had she lowered him? He couldn't be sure, and that bothered him more than anything else. Slowly he hauled himself back on to unsteady feet, turned to look for his campfire, saw it at least a hundred paces away and suddenly felt very old.

'May I help you once more?' Frecknock asked, holding out her hand to give him support. Melyn looked at it, then at the dragon's face.

'No. I can get there on my own. And I don't need you to hide me any more.' He felt the air ripple around him as she dropped whatever enchantment it was she had worked.

'You're going to teach me that spell, remember,' he said, and hearing his voice the nearest troop of warrior priests leaped to their feet. Melyn turned his back on

Frecknock, muttered, 'At ease,' and walked slowly to his fire and bedroll. And all the way he tried not to look at his hand, tried not to think about the dragon's healing power, tried not to think how much it had felt like the touch of his god.

Errol decided early on that he didn't like flying. There was certainly a thrill in sweeping down the mountains at high speed, but it was nothing compared to the sheer terror. Benfro held him tight, and in turn he gripped on to the dragon's enormous scaly arms with all his strength, but his feet still dangled in the buffeting wind. He felt like he might slip out of the dragon's embrace and plummet earthward at any moment.

Benfro had recovered fairly quickly from being frozen, as soon as Errol gave him the remaining food. Neither of them had said anything about the events which had led to the dragon stalking off on his own in the first place; Errol suspected that Benfro was embarrassed about it, and about being saved yet again. But neither did he ask for his mother's jewel back. Errol had wrapped both gems tightly and put them in the bottom of his clothes bag along with the hoard of gold coins.

They had set off on foot at first, heading down the gully and out of the deep snow. It was hard going, pushing through the tightly packed conifers, clambering over rock falls and scrambling down scree slopes. The view Errol had seen of the grassy plains laid out to the east disappeared behind lower mountains and foothills as they descended, and then finally they reached the end of a hanging valley, where a vast waterfall tumbled into an abyss, and could walk no further.

It had been awkward trying to work out how best Benfro could carry him. They hadn't given it any thought before; there hadn't been time. But standing on that cliff top Errol had needed every ounce of his self-control to let the dragon pick him up. It had reminded him all too much of Captain Osgal hauling him to the edge of the Faaeren Chasm like a sack of rotten potatoes to be dumped. In the end he had closed his eyes tightly and tried not to gasp too much when Benfro had grabbed him. Only much later, after the initial feeling of falling had been replaced with the steady up-down motion of proper flight and the regular whooshing beat of huge wings, had he dared to open his eyes.

Now they soared over the foothills, looking out across a landscape of open grassland and occasional copses. The contrast with the endless forest on the other side of the mountains was very marked, as if this were the true face of Gwlad, clean and unblemished. The forest of the Ffrydd was a mess of scars and ancient wounds poorly healed, a rent in the fabric of the world caused by some cataclysm he couldn't begin to understand.

They flew on for what seemed like hours, until the rolling hills smoothed out to flat plains intersected here and there by deep gullies cut by rivers and streams. A herd of animals that looked like great shaggy cattle spooked at the sight of the dragon flying overhead, some ancient instinct triggering them into stampede. Benfro stooped into a dive, dropping low over the backs of the running beasts.

Errol, apparently forgotten, choked and coughed on the thick dust kicked up by thousands of frightened hooves.

The cattle scattered, some turning back the way they had come, others flooding down a series of shallow cuts that dropped into a deeper gully with a sluggish brown river running through its middle. As they shot over it, Errol saw one of the creatures trip, tumble down a cliff and come to a halt at the bottom. From the angle of its neck and the way it had landed, he assumed it was dead.

Benfro banked sharply, wheeling so that Errol's legs swung forward. His heart leaped as for a moment he thought he was going to fall. They were close to the ground, not more than thirty paces or so up, but the drop would still have killed him. He held on tighter still as the dragon continued to turn, losing height all the while. And then, with a final lurch, Benfro pulled his head up, dropped his legs and landed. Two steps forward, his wings beating the air to counteract the force of his landing, and they were down.

'My thanks indeed. But next time could you maybe give me a little more warning.' Errol rubbed at his chest, sore from being held so tight for so long, and stamped his feet on the ground to get some circulation back into them. It came on a wave of pins and needles that made him hop and shuffle. 'If there is a next time, that is.'

'I thought we could eat. And this is as good a place as any to make a camp for the night. Looks like there's a settlement a few miles east, so I couldn't have flown much further anyway.' Benfro turned away, and Errol looked back past him to where the dead beast lay. It was bigger than any cow he had ever seen before, with black shaggy hair and huge shoulders. The rest of the herd had disappeared, no thought in their flat-faced heads but flight.

Errol found some long-dead dry branches on the shingle bank of the stream and built a fire while Benfro gutted and butchered the cow. He cooked and ate a large slab of the rich pungent-smelling meat, trying to ignore the unsettling noises as the dragon set about the rest. By the time the sun had set and the stars begun their wheel over the night sky, they had both descended into a contented silent stupor.

'How are we going to find him?' Benfro's deep rumbling voice roused Errol from his half-asleep musings.

'Find who?'

'My father. Sir Trefaldwyn. That's what we came here for, isn't it?'

'I suppose.' Errol cast his mind back over the past few days and their flight from Inquisitor Melyn. Now that he thought about it, he could remember Corwen's last words to Benfro before he had disappeared: '*Find your father, find Gog.*' But in the ensuing turmoil he'd completely forgotten about Benfro's father and the quest to find him. Everything had been lost in the need to escape, and then he'd been struggling just to survive. 'Do you know where he was going?'

'I don't know anything about him at all. He left before I was even hatched. About the only thing I do know about him is that he was called Sir Trefaldwyn of the Great Span. He had unnaturally large wings and could use them to glide short distances. I wonder what he'd make of me.' Benfro stretched his own enormous wings out, their scales catching the firelight and reflecting back a thousand shades of orange and yellow. Errol stared at the patterns, trying to work out what they reminded him of. Maybe two dragons fighting.

'Why exactly are we looking for him?'

'Ah. I don't know. It's a fool's errand really. But it's the only hope of getting rid of Magog.'

'How so? Can't you just destroy the jewel. I don't know, crush it or something?'

Benfro laughed, a deep-throated hollow chuckle that nevertheless had no mirth in it. 'If it were that easy, don't you think I'd have done it already? Magog's jewels are spread throughout Gwlad. I've no idea how he did it, but he managed to extract them while he was still alive. I found a whole pile of them in a cavern at the top of Mount Arnahi, but I'd be surprised if there weren't more.'

'So what was your father doing, looking for these missing jewels?'

Benfro fell silent, peering through the flickering flame light at Errol with a look of puzzlement on his long face.

'Did Corwen not tell you? But you were there.'

'Tell me what? When?'

'When Corwen left us, when he told me to find my father. He thought he understood the truth about Magog.'

'What truth? He exists, doesn't he? I mean, he's dead, but he's still about, like Corwen or Sir Radnor.' Errol was about to say *and like your mother*, but he stopped himself at the last moment.

'No, not like them at all. Magog's presence is far more powerful, far more pervasive than that. But he exists, and if he exists, then Gog must have existed too.'

'I never assumed he didn't.'

'But you know the story. How Gog and Magog fought over who would have Ammorgwm, and then when she died they couldn't bear to be near each other, so they split the world in two and went their separate ways.'

'Sir Radnor said it was a fable, meant to teach the perils of too much pride and too much power.'

'And so it was, but like all our fables it seems it was also true, to an extent. Magog existed, we know that. It's likely that Gog did too. So maybe they really did split the world in two. Maybe somewhere there's another world where dragons haven't been hunted almost to extinction, where men know nothing of the subtle arts and where Gog still lives.'

Something stirred in Errol's memory then, a feeling of connection as if he knew what Benfro was talking about.

'But surely Gog would be impossibly old. How long do dragons live anyway?'

'I really don't know. Sir Frynwy was a thousand years old, or so he claimed. Even Frecknock's two hundred.'

Errol didn't know who Sir Frynwy was, but the sadness in Benfro's eyes as he spoke of him suggested he must have been one of the dragons Melyn had slaughtered. He tried to change the subject.

'So your father was looking for Gog.'

'Well, in a way. He was looking for a window between the two worlds, a place where he could slip through. I guess if he'd found it, he would have come back for the rest of us. We could have escaped. Corwen thought he was a fool, chasing fairy tales.'

'But then Magog showed up. So maybe your father wasn't as much of a fool as everyone thought.'

'Yes, but he's also been gone for more than fifteen years, so it's likely this window never existed. Or if it did, he never found it. Likely he's dead, his unreckoned jewels mouldering in the dark.'

'Unreckoned?' Errol remembered the word but couldn't for the life of him recall its meaning. It was something Sir Radnor had told him or he'd learned before he'd been taken into the Order of the High Ffrydd, but like so many reollections of that time it was jumbled and unclear, mixed in with all the false memories Inquisitor Melyn had foisted on him.

'When a dragon dies, his body is burned with the Fflam Gwir, the true flame. Only then are his memories set, and his jewels turned white. A reckoned jewel is still a powerful thing. It can influence you as long as you are in contact with it. But an unreckoned jewel is much more dangerous. It will attach itself to you, try to change you or destroy you as it seeks to be reborn.'

'But the warrior priests collect the jewels from the dragons they kill. They don't burn the bodies or anything.'

'I don't know what influence an unreckoned jewel would have on a man, but Magog's jewel has its claws in me, and the only way I can undo that is to reckon it.'

'So burn it in the Fflam Gwir. Better yet, I'll throw it on the fire here.' Errol reached around for his bag to pull out the gem.

'If only it were that simple, Errol.' Benfro laughed again, but it was a sad, tired sound. 'I need a part of Magog's body to burn with the jewel, and the place where his bones lie is protected by powerful magics. No one can hope to find it unless invited by one of the twin brothers hatched there. Magog invited me in once, but I doubt he'd do that again.'

'So you need to find Gog. And to do that you need to find the window to his world. You need to follow your father.'

'Exactly. But I don't know if my father found it, or if he's still alive. I don't even know if there is another world, let alone a window that leads to it. And even if there is, the chances are that Gog died millennia ago.'

Benfro dropped his head as if weighed down by the impossibility of his task. But something stirred in Errol's memory.

'What would Gog look like, do you suppose?'

'I don't know. Old. Far older than Corwen. But probably not small and withered like the dragons here.'

'No. Corwen told me that dragons made a choice many centuries back, and had been shrinking ever since. And he showed me what he looked like when he was young. So it's possible that Gog would be able to fly still.'

'I'd think so, yes. Why?'

Errol remembered his dream of the strange castle, climbing endless stairs inside the head of a boy called Xando, coming to a huge room at the top of the tallest tower. He'd seen an impossibly old yet still vigorous dragon there. And that was where Martha was trapped.

'I think Gog is still alive, and I think there must be a way to his world. I've seen it in my dreams.'

Benfro's head rose at Errol's words, and his ears swivelled forward.

'Your dreams?'

'Well, I say dreams, but they were more.' Errol told the dragon all about his encounters in that strange world, and as he did a glint of hope, or perhaps understanding, shone in Benfro's eyes.

'I've seen this place too,' he said. 'I've flown over it. But I was attacked by a group of dragons.'

'Four of them? Three male and one female?'

Benfro nodded. 'It was the last time I was in Magog's repository. You were there too – just lying there. I tripped over you and found myself flying through mountains I didn't recognize. But how could you have been in my dream?'

'How could you be in Magog's palace and yet still be sleeping in the cave? How could I be in a castle in another world? I can't begin to explain it, but I know these aren't ordinary dreams. Martha's been calling to me, I'm sure of it. She's trapped there, in Gog's world, with Gog himself.'

'Then there must be a way of getting there. But how? And where is it?'

Errol didn't answer at first. He was trying to sort all the pieces into some semblance of order in his mind. There was so much he couldn't even begin to understand, but he knew that Martha was depending on him. He and Benfro both needed to find a way across to this other Gwlad, and if that meant trying to follow a fifteen-year-old trail, then that's what they would have to do.

'You said you saw a settlement a way off, just before we landed.'

'To the east, yes,' Benfro said. 'And there's a road not much more than a mile from here. I'm going to have to be careful from now on. I don't want to escape Inquisitor

Melyn just to be hunted down by men from a different country.'

'Right. But I can speak their language, and I look like them. So tomorrow I'll walk to this town and ask a few questions. If a dragon came through this way, even fifteen years ago, someone's bound to remember.'

24

The dragon tongue, Draigiaith, is a rough and uncultured language. Little more than a sophisticated form of birdsong, it lacks the subtlety of the languages of men. This is most noticeable should you encounter a dragon and it try to converse with you in Saesneg. Its grasp of our language is like that of a young child, much like its understanding of the higher concepts of honour, loyalty and trust in the Shepherd. The study of Draigiaith is thus the study of the nature of these beasts. It does not take the student long to realize that dragons have no true intelligence, only an innate ability to mimic coupled with the moral sensibilities of an infant.

Father Castlemilk, *An Introduction to the Order of the High Ffrydd*

The road was narrow, dusty and straight as it cut a swathe through the endless long grass. Errol had been walking since dawn, and the sun was now well on its way to the top of the vast sky. His ankles hurt, his throat was dry and the makeshift cloth bag hanging over his shoulder weighed him down, its strap beginning to chafe through the thin fabric of his tunic.

He had seen no one all day, heard nothing but the soft

rustling of the wind as it played through the grass. Distant herds of the shaggy black cattle roamed across the plain, and now and then he would come across a small clump of trees, usually clustered around a spring or a dry gully. It was an empty landscape, but a strangely peaceful one too. The mountains rose at his back, distant and sharp, as if magnified by the clear air. They separated him from Inquisitor Melyn, and while Llanwennog was not much safer than the Twin Kingdoms, this remote, empty corner seemed to hold no threat for him.

Evidence of the town began a good couple of miles before he saw the first buildings. Stone cairns marked field boundaries, the grass much shorter here and grazed by goats. Closer in, drystone walls protected fields of vegetables from livestock, and here Errol spotted the first people he had seen since fleeing from Captain Osgal. None spoke to him as they laboured at their rows of carrots and cabbages, instead just pausing long enough from their toil to give him a suspicious stare. He tried to wish them a good morning, but got nothing in return.

As he trudged past the first few ramshackle houses, Errol thought that he had come upon a small village, a crossroads and staging post, perhaps, between larger settlements. But the seemingly flat plain held many surprises, and as he crested a low rise, following the road between rough wooden barns, he was suddenly confronted by the sight of a medium-sized town, certainly far larger than Pwllpeiran.

The bulk of the place was built on the gently sloping sides of a wide gully. There were no houses at its bottom, presumably because it flooded regularly, but a long stone bridge spanned the wide river that cut through a flat expanse of shingle and larger boulders. A few scrubby trees clung to the rocks, marking a recent high-water line. The bridge would have comfortably spanned even a swollen meltwater flow.

Errol followed the road past two-storey wooden houses that, while faded and perhaps in need of a little maintenance, were nonetheless substantial homes. Halfway down the slope the ground levelled out into a wide flat area that formed the town centre, and here the buildings were of stone. He wondered what local enterprise could support such wealth; there was no sign of any industry here, and neither were there holding pens for animals.

There were few people about, though at least here they responded to his greetings with polite if suspicious nods. He eventually managed to extract directions to an inn from an old lady washing her front step. Her accent was thick, and Errol hoped that his grasp of the Llanwennog language had not faded in the months since he had last heard it. He walked on to a central square, where the road he had been following met another travelling north and south. The inn was a large building on the west corner, and it was the only place in town showing any signs of life.

Errol entered a bar where about twenty men sat drinking, clustered around tables in groups of four or five. For a moment the buzz of conversation dropped away, but it soon picked up again as the townsfolk decided he was of little interest. The barman eyed him with the same suspicion he had seen from everyone else, not rude but wary.

'I'd be grateful for a pot of ale. And perhaps some

food,' Errol said. Behind him a half-dozen conversations tailed off again.

'You've coin to pay for it?' The barman's accent was thick, like the old lady's, but understandable. Errol reached into his bag, rummaging around for one of the smallest gold coins he had sorted out of Benfro's hoard earlier. Now was the difficult part. This wasn't Llanwennog money, and it was probably worth a year's salary to a labourer.

'After a fashion.' Errol put the yellow disc down on the counter. 'And I'd be looking for a place where I might change this. I used my last sovereign getting here.'

The barman picked up the coin, weighed it in his hand, then peered closely at the markings stamped into it. He stared back at Errol with quizzical piggy eyes, as if trying to make a decision. Then he put the coin down on the bar, pushing it back.

'You'll need to see Querel, the gold merchant. He should be in his offices right now. You can't miss them – it's the big building on the other side of the square. Come back when you're done with him and I'll have a meal ready for you.'

Slightly bemused, Errol thanked the man and headed back out of the inn. Sure enough, directly across the square stood the tallest building in the town. A short line of people sat outside, but they seemed more intent on basking in the sun than waiting for anything to happen. A set of large double doors lay open, and a brass plaque let into the stone architrave read: *Mertimus Querel, gold merchant – by licence of the office of the royal house.* The letters were etched in a flowing script that Errol doubted most of the men loafing about the square could read. He nodded briefly to those who looked at him, then quickly darted up the steps and into the building.

It was dark in the hall after the brightness of the sun outside. Errol waited a moment in the entrance, letting his eyes accustom themselves to the gloom. Dark wooden panelling framed numerous doors leading off the hall, which was floored with polished stone that made the air echo to every small sound. A staircase climbed the back wall of the hall to a gallery above. As he stood there uncertainly, a slight cough caught his attention.

It came from a small man in spectacles who sat at an enormous desk a few paces back from the door.

'May I help you, young . . . erm, man?' After the thick accents he had heard since entering the town, Errol was surprised to find this man addressing him in the language he had grown used to in Tynhelyg, the Llanwennog of high society and the court. The man who had addressed him was considerably older than Errol. He had thin dark hair with grey beginning to show at the temples, and wore a loose gown of what looked like heavy silk, embroidered with interweaving abstract patterns. His hands were long-fingered and sported many heavy rings.

'I was looking to sell some gold. Are you Master Querel?'

'Oh dear me, no. No, no.' The small man laughed with a wheezing sound as if he were out of breath. 'Master Querel. Ha ha. No. I am Tibbits, Master Querel's secretary. I deal with the day-to-day running of things. Gold, you say?'

Errol pulled out the coin. It seemed very small and

insignificant in the richly furnished reception hall. 'It's not much. A family heirloom. My grandfather gave it to me when I was a lad. Truth is I'd rather not part with it. But I've got no choice, really.'

Tibbits took the coin, scarcely looking at it as he pulled open a drawer in his desk and took out a small set of scales. He was slow and meticulous in his weighing, making a note in the ledger open on his desk. Then he brought out a glass beaker and poured a clear liquid into it from a flask, peering through his thick-lensed spectacles as he made sure of the level.

'To see how pure it is, don't you know. I put this in here.' He dropped the coin into the beaker. 'And read off how much the level rises . . . So.' With a flourish he noted down something more in his ledger, then picked up the beaker and gave it a swirl. 'If there're any impurities, the acid will eat them away. But it leaves gold untouched. Clever, eh?'

Errol flinched at the mention of acid. He had assumed the liquid was water, but now he could smell a faintly acrid odour. There were chairs in front of the desk, he noticed, but Tibbits had not offered him one. Instead the small man carefully poured the acid back into the flask, leaving the coin at the bottom of the empty beaker. He tipped it into a small bowl, poured another liquid on top of it, then picked the coin out, wiping it dry on a cloth. Still without really looking at the coin, he returned to his notes, making swift calculations in his ledger. Errol waited patiently, trying to read the numbers upside down as Tibbits crossed his first answer out and recalculated it three times. Only then did the man actually look at the coin.

'It's not pure,' he said. And somehow Errol knew he was lying. 'I've never seen the design before. Old, I take it? Pre-King Ballah, no doubt. Possibly even foreign. You might get more for it from a collector. Master Querel would only be interested in its value melted down. And as I say, it's not pure.'

'Would I find a collector in this town?'

Tibbits laughed again, and once more Errol wondered if the man was going to expire. 'I can tell from your manner of speaking that you're an educated man, Mister . . . ?'

Errol hesitated. He couldn't very well give his real name, which was recognizably from the Twin Kingdoms. For an instant, perhaps too long, he could think of nothing at all. Then he remembered Princess Iolwen up in her tower, and the name she had uttered when first she had seen him.

'Balch,' he said. 'Errol Balch.'

'Well, Mr Balch, there aren't any collectors of ancient coins in Cerdys. There aren't any collectors of very much at all any more. Not since the last gold seam gave out. But Master Querel is always open to a business opportunity. Tell me, do you have any more of these?' Tibbits picked up the coin, which gleamed after its acid bath and polish. Errol revised his opinion of the man's accent. It was city Llanwennog, that much was true, but the refinement was a sham, put on to fool the locals, no doubt.

'No. I've only the one coin,' he said, and for a moment he thought Tibbits might have believed him. Right up until the point where the man stared down at the bag hanging from Errol's shoulder and made a little 'Hmph' through his nose.

'Well, as I said, it's not pure gold. But there's enough to make it worth melting down and refining. I could give you . . . let's see . . . seventy-five sovereigns for it?'

Errol tried not to laugh. From what little he knew of Llanwennog money, he knew that seventy-five sovereigns was a derisory sum. The coin might well be worth ten times that. But he didn't want to raise too many questions, didn't want to be noticed at all. And he could live a long time on less money than that. Still, he realized that if he took the first offer he would seem desperate, and that would make him just as memorable.

'Is that all? Grandpa always said it was worth a king's ransom. Surely it must be worth a hundred sovereigns.'

'Well, grandparents like to exaggerate, don't they? Let me see.' Tibbits made another note in his ledger, crossed it out and scrawled some more numbers. Every so often he would mutter, 'Let me see, let me see,' under his breath as he made a great pretence of coming to a difficult decision.

'Master Querel might be able to give you a little more; he's sometimes willing to dabble in antiquities. But he's away right now. Perhaps if you came back next week?'

'I can't. I have to move on. If my horse hadn't died on me, I'd probably not need to sell the thing at all. It makes me sad to have to part with it.' Errol didn't know why he was making up such a woeful story. It seemed like the right thing to do, as if he was supplying answers to questions that Tibbits wanted to ask, but before he could ask them. The man was very transparent, his greed obvious as well as his suspicion. Errol just wished that he had Inquisitor Melyn's skill at manipulation. Then Tibbits would pay a good price for certain. A hundred and fifty sovereigns, and no need to make any more notes in his ledger.

'I like you, Mr Balch. You have an honest face. And I can see that you're in a situation that's, how shall I put it, a bit delicate?' Tibbits smiled a humourless grimace. His spectacles reflected the light coming in from the door, making his eyes look like two great burning orbs. Errol said nothing, letting the man make his play.

'I've been in a spot of bother myself before. I know what it's like when the world's out to get you. So I tell you what. I'll do you a bit of a favour. I'm heading to Tynhelyg myself next month, for the King's Festival, and I reckon I might be able to make a bit on an artefact like this. So here's the deal. I'll give you a hundred sovereigns of my own money. It'll be just between the two of us. No need to involve Master Querel, see. No need for anything to go in the ledger. You get a better price for your coin, and I might just be able to turn a small profit at the end of the day. Everyone wins, eh?'

Errol kept silent for a few moments, as if he were thinking it over. In truth he wanted to get out of the room as quickly as possible. He wanted to get away from the town too, though he knew he would have to get a few supplies first, and possibly a horse if he could find an honest dealer. But there was one other thing he had come to town for, and he'd more likely get a straight answer from Tibbits if they did the deal.

'All right,' he said. 'Thank you. You've no idea how much help that is.'

Tibbits smiled again, with a little more warmth this time. 'Sit yourself down then, Errol. You don't mind if I call you Errol, do you? It'll take a moment to count out the coins.'

Errol sat and watched as Tibbits pocketed the gold coin, slipping it expertly into a fold in his gown as if this was something he had done many times before. Then he opened another drawer and heaved out a bag full of sovereigns and smaller change. From another drawer he produced a thin leather purse with a simple drawstring and began counting money into it with a practised ease.

'Tell me, Mr Tibbits,' Errol said. 'Do you hear much around these parts about dragons?'

Tibbits stopped counting for a moment, looked up at Errol and laughed again. 'Dragons? Why of course. Everyone's talking about them right now. We had one through just last week. Great big old fellow he was, wings on him that could reach across this room. Flapped about the ring like a huge monster, he did. Almost managed to take off. What a sight.'

'The ring?' Errol couldn't quite understand what Tibbits was talking about. Was this some aspect of the Llanwennog language he had missed?

'Where've you been, Errol? Camping out in the Rim mountains all your life? The circus ring. Where else are you going to find a dragon?'

Hiding in a gully not half a day's walk from here, Errol thought, but kept this to himself. He remembered something he had heard in King Ballah's palace in Tynhelyg, an off-the-cuff remark about circus dragons. At the time he'd thought nothing of it, but now it came back to him.

'No, not circus dragons,' he said. 'Real ones, living in the wild. There must be some out there.'

Tibbits counted the last coins into the leather purse and pulled it shut, reached across the desk and handed it to Errol. 'Well, I guess there must be. Never given it much thought, really. You'd be better off asking the circus master. He might tell you where he gets them from.'

'I might just do that. Thanks.' Errol took the purse, putting it carefully in his bag before standing. 'You don't happen to know where the circus is now, do you?'

Tibbits laughed his asthmatic wheeze again, his face creasing up in a knowing smile. He tapped the side of his nose in a gesture Errol didn't understand. 'I see how it is, Errol. You fancy a life on the open road, eh? Got to be better than page to some incontinent old lord in the northlands. Well, don't worry; old Tibbits won't tell a soul. And as for the circus. Well, I heard they were headed towards Tynhelyg for the King's Festival, same as me. Only they'll take a month or more getting there. Put on a few shows on the way, like.'

Castell Glas smelled of cattle dung. Beulah's nose wrinkled as they approached its massive gates, through which flowed an endless stream of people and livestock. Inside the city walls, away from the breeze that flowed in from the Gwastadded Wag to the west, the smell built up in intensity until you could almost taste it.

Duke Glas's soldiers cleared the road so that the royal party could make swift progress to the castle high on its hill above the winding river; there was no great welcome from the people here. During the short canter through the northern quarter Beulah could see clearly the source of the city's wealth and its unpleasant aroma. Cattle waited in endless pens, some patiently, most in a state of high anxiety. Nervousness spread among them like a disease as groups were rounded up, driven to slaughter and butchery. Their hides would end up in the tanneries, smoking off to the south, while the meat was cured or salted, packed into barrels to be shipped downriver and across the Twin Kingdoms. Once more Beulah appreciated the foresight of Lord Beylin in keeping livestock out of his city.

Things improved marginally as they climbed the hill to the castle. The centre of the city was filled with houses, small manufactories and the occasional warehouse, but mercifully devoid of animals. The higher they rose, the more of the westerly breeze made it past the buildings, sweeping the fetid air away and replacing it with the sweeter smell of warm grass.

Duke Glas was meant to be in bed, at least that was what the fawning surgeon kept saying as he fussed about his patient. Glas himself had obviously decided that he wasn't going to greet his queen from his bedchamber, and Beulah was grateful to him for that at least. He was however confined to a litter, borne by several strong men, and he wasn't a pretty sight.

'Your Majesty, please forgive me for not kneeling. My legs aren't quite as supple as once they were,' Glas rumbled in a deep voice that was in better times jovial. He was probably a lot of fun to be around, Beulah thought, a bluff honest counterpoint to the more devious politics of the court. But he was in obvious pain, and one leg had been amputated at the knee, the bandaged stump red with leaking blood.

'Given the circumstances, I think I'll let you sit, Glas.'

Beulah dismounted, handing her reins to a page, then walked across to the litter and proffered her hand to be kissed. The duke took it in a massive paw rough with scars and dry-scabbed cuts. His other arm was strapped into his chest, its weight held by a sling. He kissed her royal ring lightly before releasing her hand and looking up at her. One of his eyes was covered with a patch, raw flesh and bruising around the socket suggesting that he wouldn't be seeing from it again soon. If ever.

'May I present His Grace the Duke of Abervenn.' Beulah stepped back, letting Clun come forward. Her consort's efforts not to stare at Glas's injuries were perhaps not as successful as they would have been had he been born to the nobility.

'So you're the young lad who stole our queen's heart.' Glas slapped Clun on the arm, then collapsed forward, coughing heavily. He tried hard to conceal it as he spat into a clean handkerchief, but Beulah saw the blood and wondered whether these were injuries even a bear of a man like the Duke of Castell Glas could survive.

'Your captain tells us you captured the dragon, Your Grace,' Clun said.

'None of this "Your Grace" nonsense, lad. You're a duke too, you know. Act like one. Call me Glas; everyone else does. Except my old mother. She insists on calling me Derryl. Can't think why.'

'Well, I'd very much like to hear how you trapped it. And I'd like to see it too, if that's possible.'

'Of course, of course. But let us go into the hall. There's food and drink after your journey.' Glas clapped his hands lightly together, wincing as he did so, and his litter was lifted. Beulah followed him into the great hall of the castle, which was laid out for a banquet. She was given the place of honour at the top table, with Clun at her right and Glas laid out on his litter off to the left. Servants brought food and wine, but Beulah had little appetite. As she picked at some beef, the meat cooked until it was soft and flaking off the bone, Glas recounted his tale, his booming voice occasionally cut off by bouts of horrible coughing.

'Blasted creature appeared about three weeks ago. Right out of nowhere. It has a liking for beef, so I suppose it was attracted by our cows. It certainly took enough of them. And those that it didn't get damned near killed themselves in terror. I sent men out after it, but it's blasted hard to catch a beast that flies away at the first sign of trouble.'

'It flew away?' Clun asked the question, but Beulah had been thinking it too. The dragon that had attacked them had not seemed afraid of a troop of warrior priests; why would it be wary of ordinary soldiers?

'Oh yes. Every time. Usually with a prize bull or heifer in its claws. So I put guards on all the collecting pens. That kept it away for a while, but then it turned nasty. Killed two men and a herder's boy. Tore 'em in two. Begging your pardon, ma'am.'

Beulah put down her knife, all thoughts of food gone. 'So you laid a trap for it, I take it?'

'Oversaw it myself. Couldn't expect my men to face it while I stayed at home. It took a while, but eventually we surrounded it in a small wood not far from the city. Couldn't take off for the trees. We pelted it with arrows, but most of them bounced off. So I went in close and kept it nice and distracted while Captain Tole and his troop sneaked round behind and dropped an oak tree on its head. Knocked it stone cold. Would have killed it there and then, but I knew you were coming. Thought I'd let you see it first.' Glas descended into another fit of coughing, and Beulah had to look away. The sight of his freshly spewed blood was enough to turn her stomach. She wished he would go back to bed but hadn't the heart to dismiss him. His bravery might have been born of stupidity, but it still deserved reward. It was just a pity that he most likely wouldn't live to enjoy whatever boon she chose to bestow.

'Perhaps Captain Tole would be able to show us the creature,' Beulah said. 'I think your surgeon will have a heart attack if we keep you out of bed any longer.'

'Ah, horse shit, ma'am. If you'll pardon my crude language. I've got at least two ribs floating around and making a mess of my lungs. It'll be a miracle if I live out the night. But I wanted to welcome you to Castell Glas. It's been too long since a monarch of the Obsidian Throne came out to the Hendry.'

'Too long indeed, Glas. But you must rest. You can heal if you let yourself. Give it a few days and you'll be feeling much better. I'll send my own physician to help, and meantime the captain will show us your dragon.' Beulah stood, prompting the whole hall to do the same and effectively cutting off any further protest from the duke.

'I will await your return, ma'am. There's much yet in the way of hospitality we have to offer.'

'I don't doubt it, Your Grace.' Beulah nodded her

thanks and descended from the high table, walking across the hall to the corner where her warrior priests had been eating with the Castell Glas guards. Captain Celtin bowed his head in salute and she motioned him close, whispering in his ear so that the duke's men couldn't hear.

'You've some skill at using the Grym for healing, Captain. See what you can do for Duke Glas, and don't suffer any nonsense from his surgeon.'

'Of course, Your Majesty.'

'And if he's too far gone, make his passing easy.'

Celtin nodded in understanding, bowed once more and hurried off to carry out his assignment. Healer or assassin, Beulah wondered which he would be, finding herself hoping for the former.

Captain Tole looked terrified as he led the royal party back down into the city. There was nowhere in the castle with a big enough doorway for the beast to pass through, he explained, so Duke Glas had commandeered one of the largest stone warehouses in the old merchant district.

The stench of the city was thick in the narrow streets between the tall warehouses, but the nearer they came to their destination, the more Beulah could smell something else. It was an odour that made the hairs on the back of her neck stand up, a stench she had first smelled in a little village a thousand miles from here, the overpowering reek of dragon. It was not something she had noticed with the creature Frecknock that Clun had brought to her. Perhaps it was something to do with the male of the species. Or something different about these new beasts. They had appeared from nowhere, after all.

'Your Majesty, in here, please.' The captain's wavering

voice interrupted Beulah's musings, and she turned to see a small opening in a much larger set of heavy wooden doors. They towered twenty paces over her, and together were wider than they were tall. The Shepherd only knew what wares were so large they needed such an entrance, but whatever they might have been, the market for them had dried up years ago. Stepping into the cool expanse of the warehouse, Beulah saw only a vast empty space lit by sunlight from windows set high in the walls and torches hung from sconces in the thick stone pillars that supported the slate roof high overhead. Nervous-looking soldiers snapped to attention as she was announced, and then her eyes fell on the reason for their discomfort.

It might have been sleeping, or more likely was simply weighed down by the mass of chains attaching it to the floor. Glas's men had taken no chances with their trophy, using the heaviest links they could find and anchoring them in the flagstones. Yet even sprawled out, flattened like a dog run over by a cart, the dragon looked bigger than she remembered.

'Your Majesty, please be careful. It could wake at any moment.' Captain Tole sounded more nervous by the minute, and Beulah had to remind herself that he had been part of the party that had captured this creature.

'It's already awake.' Clun stepped forward, perhaps the only person in the warehouse who didn't exude any kind of fear.

'Have a care, my love,' Beulah said, watching as her consort walked calmly up to the dragon and hunkered down just out of reach of its enormous head.

'I know you can hear me, dragon,' Clun said. 'Do you remember me?'

Somewhere in the warehouse a soldier let out a high-pitched gasp. Not quite a scream, but not far off one either. The dragon opened its eyes with a slow arrogance, as if it could scarcely be bothered, and flexed its limbs against the chains holding it down, testing their strength, then relaxed before opening its mouth. A stream of sounds came out which might have been language, though Beulah understood none of it. Instead her head filled with scenes: flying over an unfamiliar landscape, swooping and diving with other dragons, approaching a huge castle on top of a mountain. She shook the images out of her head, seeing the soldiers around her staring mindlessly into space. Only the warrior priests who had accompanied her looked alert. Then she heard more of the strange tongue and realized that it was Clun talking.

'What are you saying? What language is this?' Beulah walked towards the dragon and her consort, hearing more words in what she realized must be Draigiaith, the language of dragons. But when had Clun learned it? Only a few of the senior quaisters and Melyn himself had any understanding of it.

'My lady, this dragon is not the creature who attacked us before. This is not Caradoc, son of Edryd.'

'How can you be sure?' Beulah looked more closely at the huge beast, trying to compare it with her memories of the dragon that had attacked her in the mist. It seemed bigger, but that could have been because it was indoors. However, it had both hands, and no mark of where Clun had scored his hit before. But if half the stories told of dragons were true, then they were capable of growing back whole limbs. She tried to remember something of the markings on the creature that had attacked her, but her most abiding memory was of her beloved horse dying in agony.

'She told me so.' Clun's voice broke into Beulah's horrified thoughts, and she realized that her mental guards had been brushed aside as if they were no more than paper. She pushed them up again, stronger than before, staring at the prone dragon.

'She?'

'She is Morwenna the Subtle, apparently.' Clun turned back to the dragon and spoke once more to it, his voice oddly compelling as it formed the alien sounds. Beulah felt the pressure on her mind ease as Morwenna turned her attention back to Clun. And then it – she – let out a mighty bellow of rage. Rearing up, flagstones popping out of the floor like corks, chains snapping as if they were made of thread, she rose to her full height, thrusting her wings out until they hit the warehouse walls and punched on through.

Beulah leaped back as her warrior priests conjured their blades of fire. Glas's soldiers still stood stupefied, either by fear or by some ensorcellment. It didn't matter; the result was the same. The dragon used her wings as weapons, cutting down the men where they stood as she tried to manoeuvre in the tight confines of the warehouse to strike at Clun.

'Clun, your blade!' Beulah shouted, then ducked, throwing herself to the floor as a wing swept through the space she had been occupying. She rolled, leaping to her feet and diving away as the dragon brought her wings above her head and then swung them down at the floor. Flagstones split, the whole building shuddered, and still Clun stood motionless, right beneath that head, as if waiting to be struck down. Beulah reached the relative safety of the nearest pillar, where she could gather herself. Over the other side of the warehouse two of her warrior priests had taken similar refuge. A third lay broken on the floor, his head split open.

The dragon roared, rearing up to the ceiling as she threw off the last of her chains. She looked down at Clun, who returned her stare with a curiously calm expression on his face. He appeared defenceless but unafraid as the dragon hurled what had to be insults at him. The words echoed around the warehouse, much more painful on the ear than even their intense volume should have allowed. They rattled around Beulah's head, making it hard to concentrate.

Clun said something then, and the pain stopped abruptly. The dragon roared once more, this time just a simple cry of rage, and smashed her head down to crush the man who stood before her.

Beulah was certain he was dead. But at the last possible moment Clun moved with a swiftness she would not have thought possible. Stepping sideways, he produced two long blades of light, swinging them with an economy of motion that was both beautiful and terrible. The dragon's scream was cut short, but her head carried on down, striking the floor with a crash that dislodged slates from the roof and sent them clattering to the floor. The few soldiers still standing fell to the ground, and Beulah had to clutch the pillar to stay on her feet.

And then the dragon's head parted from her shoulders. It bounced on the stone, rolling forward in a spray of hot red blood that filled the room with a tang of iron. Once, twice it rolled over, then came to a halt, eyes wide open in surprise, staring directly at Beulah.

25

Take camphor wood, dried at least a season and flaked into thin slivers. Add essence of melar and wormwood berries ground to a fine powder. Crumble in some leaves from a year-old deaney bush and blend together well. This mixture when added to the embers of an oak fire will produce a thick smoke that will render a dragon insensible in moments.

From the personal papers of
Circus Master Loghtan

Benfro sat in the small patch of scrubby trees and looked out over the empty gully. The ash pile of their fire from the previous night was the only sign that anyone had passed through this place in a hundred years. That and the bloody skeleton of the beast he had butchered. He had tried cutting strips of meat to dry, but as the sun's heat filled the day a thousand, thousand tiny biting flies had appeared, attracted by the rich tang of spilled guts. Unlike the flies he knew from the forest, these ones didn't seem deterred by the meagre smoke from the fire, and once they had gathered around the carcass, spoiling the meat, they had begun to pester him too.

In the end he had been forced to retreat to the shelter

of the trees, both by the flies and the intense heat of the midday sun. There was no wind in the gully, and the rocks soon shimmered with reflected warmth. At least he was in the shade, but he fretted that Errol would return and not find him, so he sat at the edge of the copse and stared out at the dead fire.

Benfro had managed to sleep a little, dozing but never allowing himself to fall into a deep sleep. He constantly checked his aura and the thin traitorous cord that linked him to Magog. As the afternoon progressed, he became more and more obsessed with it. How was it that Magog had such a hold on him, and yet Melyn and his men had handled his mother's unreckoned jewels unscathed? If what he had heard about men was true, then they collected vast hoards of jewels, stolen from countless smashed skulls, and stored them in their palaces. It horrified him to think of his mother's jewels cooped up in some dark place, incomplete and bewildered, but at least they were reckoned. To be dead, unsustained by a living mind and yet still open to new experiences, still hungrily absorbing all that went on around them, all that came through the Llinellau; would that not drive a dragon mad? Perhaps that was what had happened to Magog, his original character supplanted over hundreds, thousands of years by the cruel presence he had become. But it still didn't account for how the dead mage could attach himself so firmly to Benfro's mind, how that dreadful rose cord could be so firmly fixed to his aura.

The afternoon progressed to evening in a series of jumps, as he napped, woke with a start, checked he had not succumbed in some way to Magog's influence, then fell back to his musing. Eventually Benfro would doze again, his thoughts jumbling in unlikely combinations until some subconscious sense of self-preservation kicked him awake once more.

As the light began to fail he left the shade of the trees and went back to their campsite, wondering whether Errol might have returned, seen the place deserted and left some kind of message. He was being daft, of course. The boy would have had to walk down through the wood to get to the bottom of the gully anyway, and the trees weren't so big that Benfro could hide himself completely. But with each passing hour the dragon worried more. What if Errol had got himself into some kind of trouble? What if he had been attacked on the road?

When the first stars began to prick the darkening sky overhead, and still Errol had not returned, Benfro panicked that he might have lost the jewels. They had left the empty food bag back in the mountains, its woven grass handle burned through. Errol had taken his cloth sack with him, leaving Benfro's leather satchel with the remaining gold coins and the map from Magog's repository. Benfro emptied it out on to the ground, picking through the treasures, looking for the small cloth-wrapped bundles. No matter how many times he looked as darkness fell and the cool night air dropped into the gully, the jewels were not there. Errol had taken them with him. And now Errol was gone.

Benfro slumped. He hadn't realized just how much he had come to rely on the young man, just how alone he was without him. Only the night before, as they had talked about their dreams and the possibilities they presented, he had dared to hope that he might succeed, that he might rid himself of Magog once and for all. But even if he did, his mother would still be dead. Melyn would still be hunting him. He would still be hated and feared by the people who covered Gwlad. And if he found Gog's world, where dragons ruled supreme, then what? He was just a kitling, not much more than sixteen summers old.

Such was his gloom, Benfro didn't at first notice the noise. Only when he heard the first shout did his brain catch up with what his ears had been hearing. The faintest of breezes brought both familiar and strange odours to him. He smelled horses even as he heard their hooves on the dry ground, their urgent whinnying. And he smelled men too, their bodies unwashed and sweaty, unrecognizable. Or was that a familiar odour mixed in with the rest?

Swift but silent he got to his feet, holding his wings in tight by his sides as he crept up to the lip of the gully. Heavy clouds had obscured the moon and most of the sky, but a few stars shone through the gaps. Enough for him to make out dark shapes in the night.

A voice spoke, gruff and demanding, in a language Benfro didn't understand. He sneaked closer still, relying on the steady swish of the wind in the grass to mask his approach. He needn't have worried. Three horses stood riderless by the edge of the road, one laden down with bags, the other two lightly harnessed. The voice came from the long grass to the side of the road, and as he crept closer Benfro made out movement – a scuffle. He heard what sounded like wet cloth being slapped against a rock and a series of low grunts. Then silence.

The voice spoke again, and a dark shape rose from the

grass, heading back towards the horses. Another bent down and hauled up something heavy. Benfro stole closer still, tasting the air like he had been taught by Ynys Môn, keeping himself as silent as possible, hunkered down in the swaying grass. And then two things happened at once. A stiff breeze blew up, taking his own scent towards the horses, and the clouds rolled back, spilling moonlight over the scene.

Two of the horses reacted instantly to his presence, their ears going flat to their heads, eyes opening wide in fear. They would have run, but they had been hobbled; instead they tried to kick out, wheeling and snorting, and finally crashing to the ground in terror. The third horse, laden with packs, reacted more calmly, simply ambling out of the way of its panicked fellows. But Benfro's attention had been drawn swiftly away from the horses by the man still standing in the grass.

He was no taller than Errol, thin, with a narrow face topped with very little hair. He wore spectacles that glinted in the moonlight, and was dressed in a long flowing gown. More importantly, he held an unconscious Errol by the throat, and seemed to be trying to choke him to death.

Benfro let out a bellow and leaped forward. The man saw him but didn't react until it was far too late. He dropped Errol, who slumped to the ground unmoving, and tried to flee. But Benfro was upon him already, and all the frustrations, all the anger and fear and pain he had felt since that terrible day when his mother had been slain, all his rage came out at that point. He grabbed the man by his shoulder, feeling a savage glee as he sank his talons into soft flesh, crushed brittle bone. He picked the man up off his feet, twirling him around so he could look straight into his eyes.

'Why are you doing this? Why can't you just leave us alone?' Benfro shook the man violently, then threw him away from him, disgusted by the bloodlust that had come over him. He turned back to see the second man un-hobbling one of the kicking horses, jump on to its back as it scrabbled to its feet, and gallop away down the road. Benfro would have given chase, but Errol let out a moan of pain.

He knelt down and picked the boy up carefully. Errol's face was covered in blood, seeping from a wound on the top of his head, but otherwise he appeared unharmed. Benfro carried him out into the grass, away from the horses, and laid him down again. As he did so, Errol opened his eyes and said something in words Benfro didn't understand.

'What did you say? Are you all right?'

A brief moment of puzzlement flashed across Errol's face, and then he spoke again, this time in Draigiaith.

'Thank you, Benfro. I think you just saved my life.'

'Who were those men? What did they want?'

'One of them is a gold dealer called Tibbits. The other I don't know, though he might have been a friend of the ostler who sold me the horse.' Errol sat up slowly, wincing as he felt his head. 'They hailed me on the road. I thought I must have left something back in Cerdys, but when I slowed down to let them ride alongside me, one of them coshed me over the head. I guess I'm lucky they didn't use a sword.'

'But what did they want? Why attack you like that?'

'Gold, of course. I should have expected it, I suppose. Tibbits never believed me when I said I only had the one coin. What happened to them?'

Benfro looked back towards the road. The hobbled horse was still struggling, but less frantically now that he had moved away. The other had ambled out into the grassland and was grazing quietly, as if seeing dragons was an everyday occurrence. It was too dark to see far down the road, but at a gallop the second of Errol's attackers would be a couple of miles away by now. The first man still lay in the long grass where Benfro had thrown him.

He was sprawled on his back, one leg tucked up behind him in a manner that suggested it was broken. His back was twisted, and a dark stain spread from the wound in his shoulder where Benfro's talons had pierced skin and broken bone. But it was his head that gave the game away; it was never meant to point that way.

Errol held a finger to the man's neck for a few moments, then reached out and picked up the shattered spectacles that lay beside the body. 'He's dead. Poor old Mr Tibbits.'

Benfro felt a shudder run through him and was unsure what it meant. Part horror, part elation. He had killed a man, had picked him up and shaken him until he broke. Admittedly he had been no warrior priest; it wasn't Melyn lying there with his neck broken. But he had killed him nonetheless.

'We have to hide the body where it won't be found. The other man got away, you say?' Errol scanned the open plain as if his eyes were able to make out anything distant in the pale moonlight.

Benfro nodded.

'Then he'll tell anyone who'll listen that there's a wild dragon on the loose. It won't be long before there's a whole gang of them out here looking for you. We have to get away from here tonight.'

Benfro looked down at the dead man and remembered the rage that had swept over him when he had seen him choking Errol. His stomach gurgled, still full of meat, and he knew instinctively what to do.

'Stand back,' he said, and when Errol had moved to the road Benfro took a deep breath and let it out. Flame burst from his mouth, billowing around the dead body like a thousand caressing fingers. It gave off no heat, left the dried grass untouched, but swiftly consumed the man and his clothes. In a matter of minutes there was nothing left save the spectacles, their lenses cracked and hazed, at the head of a small pile of fine white ash, already being dispersed by the wind.

Melyn couldn't be sure at what point on their journey through the pass they had crossed over from the Ffrydd, which was technically part of the Twin Kingdoms, and become an invading army in Llanwennog. The trail through the mountains was fairly easy going, twisting and turning through steep-sided valleys, though their horses left behind them bare earth where scrub grass and heather had grown.

The first couple of days were hard work. Although his injured hand was completely healed, the inquisitor suffered from a kind of numbing exhaustion as his body caught up with the magic that had been performed on it. He spoke little during that time, dozing in his saddle whenever the road was smooth enough to relax. On the third night they pitched camp in a large clearing where two valleys intersected. Water was plentiful, and the horses were allowed to roam free in search of feed. Captain Osgal posted guards to look out for wolves, but so far the only creatures they had seen were eagles, soaring and screaming in the clear air. It was cold this high up, and wood for fires was hard to come by. Melyn wasn't concerned for the wellbeing of his men – they were used to such conditions at Emmass Fawr and could tap the Grym to keep themselves warm – but he did worry about the horses. They couldn't afford to lose any more before they reached the first of the Llanwennog settlements.

As night began to fall, he took a walk around the camp, talking to his warrior priests and casting an eye over their mounts. In truth he needn't have bothered; his men were trained for worse conditions than these. They knew how to look after themselves and understood the importance of keeping their horses fit. But Melyn needed some time away from the busy centre of the camp, needed some peace and quiet to develop his strategy for sowing panic in the northlands. Soon he would need to contact Beulah too. Loath though he was to admit it, Melyn knew that he couldn't do that without help.

He found Frecknock huddled in the lee of a boulder. She was curled up as if asleep, but at his approach opened her eyes, looked up and then struggled to her feet. In the darkness her black colouring disguised her bulk.

'Your Grace. How is your hand?'

Melyn could have done without the reminder of his debt to her, but her concern seemed genuine. He held up his palm, unsure whether she would have been able to see it.

'Better. Though you could have warned me about the side-effects of the healing.'

'I'm sorry, Your Grace. I underestimated the severity of your injury. Most men would have passed out from the pain long before they could damage themselves so.'

Melyn supposed it was a compliment of sorts, though he wasn't about to acknowledge it.

'I want to know about this spell of concealment. Is it hard to learn?' He sat himself on a smaller rock beside the boulder and indicated for Frecknock to be seated too. She hunkered down, trying to lower her head to his eye level, then slumped on to her belly instead.

'Not especially, no. At least I didn't find it so. It's something we teach our kitlings almost as soon as they can speak. You might think it cowardice, but being able to blend into the background is an effective way of staying alive in a hostile world.'

'It doesn't surprise me that your kind would resort to such tactics, but I can assure you avoiding a fight is not my intention. So, tell me how it's done.'

'Well, Your Grace, the principle is quite simple. All life flows from the Grym, as you know, but the Grym also flows from living things – trees, animals, dragons, men. Anything that lives, really. Dragons are constantly aware of that connection, but other creatures, it seems, are not, and only a few men such as yourself and your warrior priests are skilled enough to perceive the Grym in any manner at all. So your kind rely on the more physical senses – sight, touch, smell, hearing. You define your world by them; your language is full of references to them.

'But what you don't perhaps realize is just how much you rely on your unconscious knowledge of the Grym to get by. It affects you subtly but constantly, and if manipulated the right way it can confuse those other senses so much that you will ignore something that is quite plainly there.'

'So this hiding spell, it won't work on dragons. Is that what you're saying?'

'Not on all dragons, and not all the time. But you and your men are possessed of superb mental discipline simply because you have to work so hard to manipulate the Grym. Your blades of light are fearsome weapons forged by sheer concentration. That same quality is the most important factor for success in turning the Grym to hide you from sight, so I'd guess once you understand the principle of the working, you'll be far better at it than most dragons.'

'Then what is the principle? How is it done?'

'Well, consider your blade of light. To conjure it you reach out to the Grym and bring as much power as you can imagine back into yourself. But instead of burning you to a crisp, you turn the Grym on itself and channel it into your blade. Imagined as an extension of your arm, it becomes a terrible weapon. The art of hiding is, in a way, the complete opposite. Instead of taking in the Grym, you must try to turn it away. You want to divert it around you so that you become a hole, a black spot in the fabric of Gwlad. And you need to close down your thoughts so they don't leak out into the Llinellau. Then when people look at you, their subconscious will tell them there is nothing to see.'

It sounded easy enough, but Melyn could remember the excitement he had felt on first being told how to conjure the blade of light and how it had taken him many months of diligent study and practice after that to produce a faint glow for a couple of heartbeats. And two of his fellow novitiates had burned themselves to death, cooked from the inside, trying to master that same skill before they were ready.

'So what are the dangers in this working? How can it go wrong?'

'There's no danger, as far as I know. It's a skill we teach our kitlings long before they are allowed to study any other subtle arts. I suppose if you separated yourself from the Grym completely then you might die, but you would more likely become unconscious first, and then the spell would unravel.'

Frecknock fell silent, and Melyn thought about her words. He considered the lines about him, thought about how he tapped them to conjure his blade of light. Then he imagined pushing the Grym away from himself instead of welcoming it in. It was an odd reversal, and almost immediately he felt the cold mountain air chill his bones. He tried to lift himself above the Grym, even though to distance himself from it was the complete antithesis of everything he had been taught, and everything he had ever experimented with in magic. And at the same time he pulled his thoughts in tight, as he did when dealing with

Seneschal Padraig or Archimandrite Cassters, men who were adept at reading and manipulating the minds of others.

'I'm impressed, Your Grace. I know you are there, and yet I can barely see you at all.' Frecknock's eyes were still fixed on him, but as he stood, then stepped to one side, she struggled to follow his movements. He said nothing but turned away and walked back into the camp.

The first group of warrior priests were huddled around a tiny fire, enjoying the light of it more than any warmth. Melyn walked up to them quite openly, standing in the light from the flames in a space between two seated men. That they didn't immediately leap to their feet was confirmation enough of the success of his conjuring, but he stayed where he was, intrigued to hear what their conversation might be in the absence of their leaders.

As it happened, they were complaining about much the same things he recalled moaning about when he was a warrior priest out on a long mission. They missed the food and facilities at the monastery; they grumbled about long hours in the saddle, but they were excited about the mission and pleased to be out of the forest.

Leaving the troops by their fire, Melyn wandered through the camp past other small groups with similar concerns. He noticed that even the horses paid him no heed, their heads down and grazing hard at the thin grass even though they should have been able to smell him. It gave him a certain thrill to be able to move about unnoticed, but at the same time it bothered him that nobody, no creature, could sense him at all. For now this was a fine new weapon, but sooner or later his enemies would acquire it, and he needed to know how to see through it before then.

Captain Osgal was attending to his horses, which were close to Melyn's own animals. As the inquisitor stood right in front of him, he looked to his left and right, then straight ahead, his eyes focused on something in the distance. Melyn was about to say something when the captain turned away, walking quickly over to the fire where Captain Pelquin sat with a couple of warrior priests.

'Have you seen the inquisitor?' Melyn heard Osgal ask as he approached the group.

Pelquin stood up, scanning the small fires dotted about in the darkness. 'He was walking the perimeter earlier. Then he went to talk to that dragon. Damned creature gives me the creeps. I thought we were supposed to kill them.'

'That's not what you were saying two days ago, when she got us all out of the forest.'

'Yeah, well, I've been thinking about that. I reckon all that trouble was down to her in the first place. I mean, we've had no end of problems since she's been about. We lost good men back at that lake.'

Osgal made a non-committal noise and turned away to look around some more. Melyn let his mental guards down, relaxing some of his control in much the same way as he would in order to extinguish his blade of light. Osgal almost immediately stopped. His eyes swung this way and that, trying to focus on something in the darkness, never quite falling on Melyn's face.

'What is it, Osgal? You look like you've seen a ghost.'

Pelquin looked straight at the inquisitor with unseeing eyes. 'There's nothing out there, man.'

'Actually there is.' Melyn released his control on the Grym surrounding him, then pulled its energy back into his cold body, shivering at the sudden influx of heat. It was worth it just to see the look on his captains' faces.

'Your G-grace, how . . . ?' Pelquin stammered. Osgal made the sign of the crook and bowed his head. Behind the two captains the warrior priests at the fire struggled to their feet.

'You think the dragon Frecknock has brought us bad luck, Pelquin. But I know that the opposite is the case.'

'Your Grace . . .' Osgal began, his tone betraying what he was about to say.

Melyn waved him quiet. 'I know our teaching, our sacred charter. I still hold to them. Nothing Frecknock has told me has changed my mind on that. But she has knowledge that I mean to extract before I carry out Bryn-ceri's orders and send her soul back to the Wolf. This magic will be of great use to us in the days ahead. Tomorrow you and all the other troop commanders will learn it from the dragon, and then you will pass it on to all your men. Once you have all mastered it, then we will descend upon the godless Llanwennogs and destroy everything in our path.'

In the end they left the horses behind, and most of the provisions Errol had bought. It was too risky to travel on the roads near Cerdys, given that one of Errol's attackers had escaped. Errol freed the hobbled horse, which staggered to its feet and limped away to join the other animal.

Benfro then left him to sort out the provisions while he went back down into the gully and fetched his own bag. By the time he got back, Errol was ready to go, though he wasn't enthusiastic about flying. Benfro was confident he could hold a good course across the grasslands, if he could see the stars, but the clouds that had parted so conveniently earlier on had grown thicker.

Taking off was easy enough in this flat land, even with the added weight. But with the moon obscured by clouds, it was difficult to get any bearings. After circling a few times to gain a little height, Benfro decided the best thing was to follow the road at least until the outskirts of the town. Hopefully there would be enough light spilling from windows and doors for him to skirt it and then pick up the road on the other side.

Errol kept silent as they flew, his hands gripped tight around Benfro's arms. Travelling more slowly in the darkness, Benfro thought he might have been able to talk, but after a couple of remarks went unanswered, he decided that it was perhaps better to concentrate on flying. As he had hoped, the town was a blaze of lights. If anything there was rather more than he would have expected, suggesting that more people were up and awake than normal. He flew around it, going far to the south and crossing the dark ribbon that was the river as the first fat drops of rain began to fall from the sky.

Benfro had walked through enough rain to know that he didn't like it, but flying in it was a whole new experience. Quite apart from his speed making it feel like he was walking into the teeth of a howling gale, the rain made his wings heavier and reduced their efficiency. His muscles had to work harder and harder just to stay up, and as the weather worsened, so it became increasingly difficult to see anything at all. In the darkness it was impossible to tell if the rain was a passing shower or part of a much larger system. He was going to have to land.

No sooner had he admitted that truth to himself than Benfro saw the problems he faced. His vision was seriously impaired, making it hard to gauge distance to the ground. The darkness made it impossible to see any obstacles that might make him trip and break his neck on landing. And the grass was waist high anyway, swirling and swaying in the wind and rain.

Then he saw, a good way up ahead, more lights. At first he thought it was the same town and he had turned full circle in the night. But the closer he approached, the clearer it became: a much smaller settlement than Cerdys, little more than a village judging by the size of the buildings. As he neared it, the rain eased a little, then stopped altogether. Benfro soared over a dozen rooftops and then he was speeding away on the other side, headed towards a small clump of trees that sat on the landscape like a tumour.

Almost as if it had been sent to help him, the moon poked out through a small gap in the clouds, illuminating the grassy plain surrounding the woods. Another gully cut through the grass and trees, narrower than the ones they had encountered before, deep and steep sided. Benfro banked hard, losing height as fast as he could, all too aware that the moon would be gone again in seconds. His wings were too heavy to consider flying on, even if the rain held off, so he swooped down in a series of tight turns, coming finally to a heavy landing on the grass.

Errol dropped to the ground like a discarded sack, muttering something that sounded very much like 'Never again,' and they walked quickly across the dark grass to the woods, reaching the trees just as the first heavy drops of rain started to fall again. They found a cave in the side of the gully, surrounded by trees and boulders. In the darkness it was impossible to tell how far back it went, but it kept the rain off, and Benfro couldn't smell anything inside that suggested it was already occupied. He would have liked to build a fire, but he knew that any light would attract attention from the village.

'How far do you suppose we came?' Errol asked after they had settled themselves into what little dry space there was.

'Not far enough. A rider could cover the distance in half a morning, I'd say. Quicker if the road's good.'

'Which it is. I'm sorry, Benfro. I've got us into rather more trouble than we needed right now.'

'It's not your fault.' Benfro shoved his fist in his mouth to stifle a yawn. Now that he had settled down, he could feel sleep tugging at him, the weight of his exhausted muscles dragging him down.

'Here, you should get some sleep. I'll keep watch.' Errol shuffled himself upright against the rock wall to make more room. Benfro was too tired to move. Muttering a quiet, 'Thanks. Wake me after an hour or so,' he settled down on the hard dry earth and was asleep in moments.

*

The sun was shining down through wet leaves and birds were singing a loud dawn chorus when he woke. Benfro stretched, pushing his wings wide as it occurred to him that Errol had been awake all night and that he had not dreamed a thing while he slept. Looking round, he saw the boy still wedged against the cave wall, his eyes drooping slightly, his brow creased in concentration much like Sir Frynwy's when he tried to remember a particularly obscure bit of lore. Benfro reached out with his aura, automatically knotting it around the ever-present rose cord and erecting his mental defences against Magog. As he did so, Errol's frown relaxed and he looked up.

'Did you sleep well?'

'Very well, thank you. You look like you could do with a nap yourself.'

Errol struggled to his feet, knees popping like an old man's as he stretched. 'I could. But I think I'd better check out that village before word gets out from Cerdys. I might be able to pick up some food too. I can sleep all afternoon and we can head off after dark.'

'Won't they be suspicious if you walk in from nowhere?'

'Villagers are always suspicious. But they're usually more hospitable than townsfolk. At least that's been my experience. I should be fine.' And with that Errol heaved his bag over his shoulder, scrambled out of the gully and was gone.

26

To a citizen of the Twin Kingdoms, the Llanwennog circus is an inconceivable thing. Dour Hafod and rural Hendry take their entertainment from travelling minstrels and mummers, or else celebrate with drinking and eating to excess. Our cousins to the north, however, enjoy a different kind of amusement.

So how to describe the circus to one who has never encountered its like before? Well, there are minstrels and mummers, it's true. But there are also magic acts and freaks of nature on display: bearded women of terrifying demeanour, scaled men who live underwater like fish, dwarves who can lift ten times their own weight, acrobats who can walk along a thin wire suspended over a killing drop as casually as if it were no distance at all. And there are animals, the wildest, rarest creatures from all the corners of Gwlad, caged, tamed or at least controlled, trained to perform such tricks as would give anyone wonder who could not see the cruelty in their entrapment.

But the most prestigious circuses, and there are very few of them today, are those that have dragons. For whereas we have persecuted these magnificent creatures by hunting them down and killing them, in Llanwennog they have perfected the art of humiliating them.

From the travel journals of
Usel of the Ram

As Errol had predicted, the villagers were wary of him to start with, but hospitable. The small tavern at the centre both fed him and provided him with provisions for his journey. He hadn't been able to buy another horse, since none were available, but this was probably not a bad thing as most seemed to be skittish around dragons. Errol had thus concluded his business in the village by midday and was about to leave when a small band of rough-looking men rode into town.

Their arrival caused much excitement, and it wasn't long before Errol heard the word 'circus' whispered among the grubby children who played at the roadside, chasing chickens and hitting each other with sticks. The men went into the tavern, laughing among themselves and ignoring everyone else. Errol ducked back in behind them. His empty plate and tankard still sat uncleared at the table by the unlit fireplace where he had eaten, so he quickly sat himself back down again, pretending he had never left. The men didn't seem to notice him, too intent were they on shouting for the barmaid to bring them ale. She bustled around, drawing several tankards from the barrel and banging them down on the bar.

'It's not often we see the circus here these days. Will you be giving us a show?'

'Sorry, love. We're just camped up for the night. Master

Loghtan's got some bee in his bonnet. Reckons he's found a new act and wants to make sure it's all ready for the royal performance.'

The barmaid's disappointment was obvious even to Errol. 'How long you staying, then?'

'Not long, I'd wager. We've not made a proper camp or anything. We'll probably push on down to Gremmil first thing tomorrow.'

'So you're here for the night, then?'

'Oh, aye. If you're looking for a show, why not come out to the camp? We're always practising something or other. An audience is always welcome.'

Errol could see what was going on as plain as day. No doubt the barmaid would go out to the circus camp, and if she didn't come back until the morrow morning, then that was her business, he supposed. Still, it gave him an idea. He slipped once more out of the tavern and headed off up the road in the direction from which the men had ridden. There was only one road running through the village, itself no more than a dozen small houses clustered around a central green with a spring feeding into a small stream. The road rose gently to a ridge about a mile distant. Errol climbed slowly, the midday sun hot on his head, until he reached the top, and there, spread out over the grassy plain below, was the circus.

Having only ever read about such things before, the circus looked to Errol very much like a small travelling army. There were perhaps four dozen large wagons, drawn up in lines just off the road. Horses grazed the grass, tethered so that they didn't wander too far, and a couple of large tents had been set up. Smoke rose from a fire near the centre of the camp, and as he approached Errol could smell cooking meat.

Closer to the circus, he saw people wandering about, busy at tasks he couldn't begin to comprehend. A group of children juggled and skipped over a long rope, their play skilled and graceful in marked contrast to the village boys. He supposed they were practising, but as soon as they saw him, they stopped, running off between the great wagons screaming with laughter. Errol felt a bit awkward just walking around staring. He could see now that many of the wagons were ornamented, painted in vivid colours and hung with cooking implements, shovels, water barrels. It struck him that they were people's homes and he had no right nosing around them.

'Can I help you, young man?' The voice almost made him jump out of his skin. Errol turned to see an old woman, her face darkened by a lifetime in the sun and wrinkled like dried fruit. Her hair was white, but her eyes were sharp. She was dressed plainly, and held herself upright with all the vigour and self-importance of a noble.

'I was in the village over there.' Errol pointed back up the road. 'I heard the circus had camped here and thought I'd come over to look. I've never seen one before.'

'Never seen the circus before?' The woman's face relaxed and she smiled, revealing perfect white teeth. 'Why, where you been all your life, young man? The Twin Kingdoms?'

Errol tried not to start at the suggestion, but something of his alarm must have shown. The woman laughed.

'Tis a joke, young man. For sure, they're so tied up with their Shepherd over the hills, they don't know how to enjoy themselves. But I'm forgetting my manners. Please. Any traveller's welcome in our camp. Can I offer you a bite to eat? Some tea perhaps? I'm Griselda, by the by. I work with the lioncats.'

Errol 's eyes widened in surprise, and he almost forgot to introduce himself.

'Errol. Errol Balch. And thank you, but I've just recently eaten. Did you say lioncats?'

Griselda laughed again. 'That I did. Would you like to see them, Errol Balch?'

'I . . . well . . . yes.' Errol nodded his head, wondering why he was acting like an imbecile. He had read of lioncats as a child, knew that they were savage, untamable creatures that lived in the arid plains of the far east. He had never expected to see one.

'Well then, come this way. They're due a feed anyway.'

Errol hesitated as Griselda marched off down a narrow alley formed by two lines of wagons. After about a dozen paces, she stopped, turned and saw him still standing at the roadside.

'Don't worry. I'm not going to feed you to them.' She laughed again, beckoning him on.

The circus animals were housed in large wagons arranged in a square. Errol recognized a few of the creatures lolling in their cages in the midday heat, but most of them were completely new to him. Griselda mentioned a few names as she led him past sleeping wolves, brown bears, gibbering apes. At one cage she stooped to pick up a bucket of water, throwing it through the bars into the darkness beyond. Something barked at her, a bit like a dog, and when she threw in a second bucketful a fat nose with thick whiskers poked out, snuffling the air. An overpowering odour of rotting fish wafted over him, making Errol cough and gag.

'Ah, don't mind the smell of old Bogey there. You get used to it after a while.'

'Erm, what is it?'

'That's a genuine sealrus, from the Sea of Tegid, that is. Loghtan picked him up the last time we were in Kais.'

'Loghtan?'

'The circus master. Loghtan's been running this show more 'n forty years now. His father and grandfather afore him. They're a proud family of carnies, they are, even if young Tegwin don't take much after his old man.'

Errol let the information wash over him as Griselda spoke. He had only the vaguest idea of what she was talking about, but she was friendly and kind. Instead, he looked around at the wagons. Some were open-sided, with heavy iron bars keeping the beasts within from escaping. Others were solid, with tiny windows. One or two of the wagons rocked slightly, as if the creatures hidden within were pacing restlessly back and forth. Most were silent and still, the horses that pulled them hobbled and grazing the long plains grass a way off from the camp. Occasionally a strange moan or an ear-splitting roar would shatter the quiet, sending shivers down his spine even though the day was hot and sticky.

'Here we are. Callias and Pello, my two mountain lion-cats. We caught them as cubs, ah . . . it must be ten years ago now. Out in the wildlands to the west of Mount Arnahi.'

Errol approached a low-slung wagon, open-sided at

one end but with a closed area up where the driver would sit. Two lithe creatures lay in the shade of the roof, panting in the heat and flicking away flies with their long tails. They were the colour of burned sand, their fur smooth over strong muscles. Their heads were broad, pointed ears ending in long tufts of hair, whiskers short and thick, eyes yellow and piercing. He stared at them, entranced.

'Aren't they magnificent?' Griselda's voice was heavy with love and pride, like a mother clucking over her children. And yet there was something terribly wrong. Errol could feel the frustration of the animals as they looked through their bars to the endless plain beyond. He could see how they pined for the open spaces, and how their coats were not as glossy as they should have been, their muscles not as taut.

'Here, would you like to feed them, Errol?' Griselda knocked the lid off a small barrel beside the wagon, and the stench of rotten meat filled the air. She dug around inside, pulling out a haunch of some unidentifiable animal, and offered it to him. He could see flecks of white on it where the flies had laid eggs, and as he took it from her several plump yellow maggots fell to the ground.

'Just push it through the bars. They won't bite you.'

Errol moved closer, anxious to get rid off the fetid meat but unsure whether giving it to the lioncats was any sort of kindness. He hoisted it through the bars, throwing it towards the nearest of the two animals, who yawned wide and revealed broken, chipped and blackened fangs. As the meat slapped on to the straw-strewn wagon floor, the poor beasts roused themselves, showing swollen joints and bone under thin skin. Errol could see sores through their fur where they had lain for too long, and his initial sense of wonder was erased completely.

'Magnificent, aren't they? I raised them myself. They treat me like their pack leader.' Griselda spoke with quiet pride, and when Errol looked at her, he could see that she was completely blind to the suffering she inflicted. He looked back at the two lioncats, gnawing at the rotten carcass, withering away in their cage and taunted by the sights and smells of the unreachable wilderness just beyond their bars.

I'd free you, if I could, he thought, and for a moment they both stopped their chewing and looked straight at him with intelligent sad eyes.

Tearing himself away from their gaze, Errol looked around for something, anything at all, to get him away from the lioncats. Across the camp, set away from the other animal cages, there was a single wagon twice the usual size. It was a heavy construction, thick oak planks held together with black iron plates. Tiny windows, no more than air vents really, were set into the sides high up, where no one could peer inside, and from where he stood, Errol could see no way of getting in.

'What's in that wagon?' He waited until Griselda tore her gaze away from her beloved lioncats and pointed. She looked momentarily annoyed, then her smile crept back on to her face.

'That. Ah yes. I'm not surprised you noticed that. In there, young Master Errol, is our dragon.'

'Dragon?' Errol realized he sounded like an awestruck child, which was probably for the best. He hadn't dared hope he would find a circus so soon after beginning his search, let alone one with a dragon in it. He wanted to rush over and speak to the creature, to ask it how it came to be here and whether it knew of others of its kind, but he had to contain his excitement.

Trying to make himself sound slightly scared, he asked, 'Can I see it?'

Griselda's smile faded from her face, but her voice was still kind when she spoke.

'I'm afraid not, Errol. Only Master Loghtan can open up the dragon cage, and he rarely shows off old Magog between performances.'

'Magog?' Errol nearly fell over when he heard the name.

'That's him. Magog, Son of the Summer Moon. The greatest dragon who ever lived. They say he raised the Great Barrier Range of mountains, split Gwlad in two so that Llanwennog would be safe from the madmen to the south. Surely you must have heard the tale?'

'Of course,' Errol hastily agreed. 'But the version I was told was a bit different. And surely Magog's long dead. If he ever truly existed.'

Griselda laughed. 'Dear me, Errol. You take everything so literally. There never was a dragon called Magog. That's just a myth. But this old creature claimed that was his name when Loghtan captured him. So Magog he is to this day.'

'Is Master Loghtan here. Might I meet him?'

'Why would you want to do that, Errol? Here, you've not run away from home hoping to join the circus, have you? Master Loghtan's got no place in his circus for dreamers, you know.'

'No, nothing of the sort. It's just, well, a dragon. I've read so much about them, but I never thought I'd get the chance to see one. Or even to meet someone who knew about them.'

'Well, I doubt there's anyone knows more about dragons in the whole of Gwlad than does Master Loghtan. How else would he manage to keep one under control all these years, let alone track one down and catch it in the first place?'

Errol doubted that anyone knew as much about dragons as Andro, and he himself was probably more knowledgeable than most, but if this Master Loghtan was an expert on the subject, even if he did seem to use that knowledge to control and trap the creatures, then Errol could think of no better person to ask about the whereabouts of any dragons in Llanwennog.

'He sounds like just the man I'd like to meet. Would you introduce me?'

'I think I would, Errol. You seem genuine in your interest, not just some spoiled noble-born running away from the king's service. But Loghtan's not here. He stopped and made us camp this morning. Went off on some errand with his son Tegwin, and I've no idea when he'll be back. Here, you could wait for him. I'll introduce you to the rest of the troupe, if you like.'

Errol was tempted, but he was beginning to feel the effects of a sleepless night and looking up he saw that the sun was well past the midway point in the sky. Benfro would be worrying about where he had got to.

'I'd dearly like to, but my friend's waiting for me back in the village. He'll start to fret if I'm not back soon. Perhaps you could tell me where you're going and I might be able to catch up with you later?'

'Well, that's easy enough. We're headed south and east to Tynhelyg. Loghtan wants to be there in six weeks' time so he can get a fortnight's rehearsal in before the King's Festival. I don't think we'll have much time to stop anywhere for long enough to put on a show before then.'

Errol was about to ask what the King's Festival was, his heart almost stopping at the thought of going anywhere near the capital, but just before he opened his mouth to speak he remembered the gold merchant, Tibbits, mentioning the same thing. At the time he had let it slip by as an unimportant detail, but from the way Griselda talked, it was an important occasion and something everyone would know about.

'Well, my friend and I are heading for the capital,' he said. 'So I'll look out for you when we get there. Or maybe we'll catch up with you on the way.'

Benfro lay for a long time in the cave, enjoying the warmth and the sense of security. It was low-ceilinged for his bulk, though a man would have found it spacious. The floor was flat packed earth washed in by ancient floods. At the thought of water his stomach gurgled. He had gorged himself the day before, but he had also breathed fire, and that always left him empty. He would have to see about finding some food before Errol returned.

A slow river ran through the gully, and Benfro found a deep pool at the bottom where a rockslide had trapped the flow. Slipping into the cool water as quietly as he could manage, he swam to the middle and then let himself sink to the bottom.

Unlike the fish in the river that ran through Corwen's clearing, these had no memory of being hunted by dragons. Soon Benfro had a haul of five fat salmon, cleaned and filleted. He ate three raw, then took the others back up to the cave. If he found enough dry wood, he could probably make a fire without too much smoke and cook the remaining fish for Errol.

The sun had climbed high into the sky by the time he had collected enough dead branches and twigs. Benfro piled them in the mouth of the cave and then retreated into the cool darkness to escape the midday heat. The woods were silent, all the animals hiding away until evening brought cooler air, and Benfro settled down to rest as well. Errol would be back soon, he was sure.

A noise woke him. Or perhaps it was the smell of smoke. For a moment he thought that Errol must have returned, seen the wood and the fish and started a fire without waking him. That he could feel nothing of Magog's presence reinforced this idea, but there was something wrong. The smoke smelled sweet, perfumed like the herbal preparations his mother had burned to cleanse the house. And when Benfro tried to see his aura, to check that it still knotted around the rose cord, he found he couldn't focus.

He tried to push himself to his feet, but his legs wouldn't work. It was as if he had lain on them badly and they had gone to sleep. When he reached out to massage them back to life, his arms felt like they were made of stone. And now the sweet smell of the smoke was inside his head, making it hard to think.

Darkness moved across his vision. Benfro looked up and saw a man standing silhouetted in the light from the cave mouth. It wasn't Errol.

'Well, well, well. It looks like we've got ourselves a mighty prize here.' The man spoke Draigiaith with a strange accent. Benfro fought against the lethargy that pulled him down. He weighed ten times more than normal, but still he managed to haul himself off the ground. He tried to concentrate, to summon the fire in his belly, even as his head whirled and spun.

'Oh, a fighter. Good.' The man turned away and shouted something in another language. More smoke billowed around him, so that he looked like he was on fire. It filled the cave, making Benfro's eyes water, his throat sore, his head even more muddled. He barely registered the movement of more people entering the cave, holding something between them. They threw it at him, and the weight of it on his shoulders made him collapse to the ground.

Blackness flooded his vision, and Benfro could feel himself slipping out of consciousness. All he heard as he struggled in vain against the smoke that smothered him was the man's voice, bold and sneering.

'You are mine now, dragon. Remember that. You are mine.'

Griselda was all for making Errol stay. She led him back through the camp a longer way, taking him past the fire and the two large tents, introducing him to a strange bunch of people. He finally managed to escape half an hour later, and hurried back up the road to the village. The horses of the circus men still stood outside the tavern, patiently waiting for their owners to finish drinking. As Errol passed he could hear raucous laughter that made him think it would be a long wait.

The smell of smoke wafted faintly on the breeze as he approached the trees. He couldn't see anything in the air and wondered if Benfro had caught some food. Ducking under some branches, the smell of smoke was stronger, and it was a strangely sweet aroma, like burning herbs rather than the acrid taste of woodsmoke. A tingle of fear ran up Errol's back. He slowed, trying to be as silent as possible, listening for any sound that might be out of the ordinary.

He hadn't even reached the mouth of the cave before he realized that something was very wrong. The ground had been churned up as if a tree trunk or suchlike had been dragged along, sweeping aside all the leaves and other litter, taking the topsoil off in places. It swept in a wide curve from the cave, turned sharply back up the hill on the opposite side from where Errol made his way down.

Two small fires had been lit just inside the cave. They were all but burned out now, but Errol could smell the sweet taint coming from them. A faint bluish haze filled the air, made his head swim. He took a deep breath away from the fires, held it and walked into the darkness.

The cave was empty. Even Benfro's bag had gone. As he was about to leave Errol spotted something glinting in the dirt. Stooping, he picked up a small ring. It was simple in its design, three bands of different-coloured gold wound in a tight spiral and flattened at one point to bear a tiny coat of arms. He remembered finding it among the gold that Benfro had brought from Magog's repository and putting it in the smaller haul as something which might be easily pawned for coin. Whoever had taken the bag must have spilled its contents and missed this when they were collecting everything up. Numb with shock, he palmed the ring, bunching his hand around it into a fist.

Errol scurried out, following the torn-up ground as it wound through the trees. Even in his agitation he could piece together what had happened. Somehow someone had tracked Benfro to this place, and that person knew how to put a dragon to sleep. There was no sign that Benfro had put up a struggle in the cave, and then he had been dragged away. It had to be the smoke, though it seemed strange that something which only made him light-headed could knock a dragon the size of Benfro out cold.

It was too much of a coincidence that the circus had stopped so close to their hiding place just a few hours after they had arrived. This must be the work of Loghtan; hadn't Griselda said he knew more about dragons than any man in Gwlad? But how had he known about Benfro? How had he tracked him?

These questions still unanswered, Errol pushed past the last of the trees and stepped out on to a well-made road. He hadn't realized that the copse adjoined it, but this must be the same road that passed through the village, the same road the circus was travelling on its way to Tynhelyg. Its surface was still slightly damp here, shielded from the drying sun by the trees. Errol stooped and peered, making out the hoof prints of several horses. Some of them were wider than his splayed hand, and they sank deeper into the wet dust than the smaller ones. Cart-horses would make such marks, he reckoned. And now he looked, he could see parallel tracks where the wheels of a heavy wagon had passed.

Errol straightened up, looking both ways along the road in the vain hope that he might catch sight of the wagon. Not that there was anything he could have done to help Benfro. There was nothing to be seen. And then he felt something, a familiar sensation but one mixed up with the confusion of false memories that Melyn had filled his mind with. It came to him a fraction too late: there was someone else nearby. Very close.

'I thought you'd be along soon enough, if I just waited.'

Errol started to turn, caught a fleeting glimpse of a man's leering face. Then something hard connected with his skull, and everything stopped.

Acknowledgements

It's my name on the cover, and if you don't much care for tales of talking dragons and evil sheep then I'm the one to blame, but a vast army of people have helped take my initial story and mould it into the book you have just read.

Writing acknowledgements is always fraught with difficulty, as no matter how hard I try, I always forget someone and end up insulting them. That said, this book wouldn't have appeared in the form it's in without the tireless work of my agent, the admirable Juliet Mushens. Neither would it have been as polished without the boundless enthusiasm of my editor Alex Clarke and the rest of the team at Penguin. A huge thanks to all of you.

The Golden Cage first saw life as a self-published ebook under my DevilDog Publishing imprint. A lot of people bought it, and many of them liked it enough to get in touch, keen to know when Book Four in the series would be published. My sincere apologies for the delay – life and the adventures of Detective Inspector McLean rather got in the way. My thanks though to everyone who contacted me. Your enthusiasm for Benfro and his tale has been inspirational, and Book Four, *The Broken World*, will be along soon.

And last, but never least, thanks to Barbara, who first planted the idea of a dragon called Benfro in my mind, and gave me all the support I needed to grow that idea into this wonderful, sprawling adventure.

J D OSWALD

THE BALLAD OF SIR BENFRO

I

Grendor's great-grandson, King Ballah I, while still waging the war that would forge the land we know as Llanwennog, needed to identify his messengers and spies to those nobles he most trusted. To this end he had six rings made, each bearing his personal seal. Any noble, on being shown this seal, was to render up whatever aid the wearer of it required.

Such is the strength of the magic woven around these rings that all attempts to copy them have ended in failure. Nor will the seal reveal itself should the ring be worn by an enemy of the Llanwennog throne. It is said that the wearers can communicate with each other over vast distances and that the rings will summon them back to Tynhelyg should the king's life ever be in peril. Few have ever seen these rings, but to be charged with wearing one is the highest possible honour.

The Taming of the Northlands –
A History of the Kings of Llanwennog

'Fetch his lordship. He's coming round.'

Errol heard the words as if he were dreaming them. He wasn't sure where he was, but it was warm and comfortable. It smelled clean, the air fresh with a hint of dry grass.

He had been sleeping, he was sure, but he couldn't remember going to bed. Rolling on to his side, he opened his eyes and was nearly sick as waves of pain rushed over him. He had just enough time to register the vaguest image of a person standing over him, then everything dimmed again.

'Be careful. You've had a nasty blow to the head.' Strong arms cradled his shoulders, pulling him forward. Then something cool, more soothing than a mother's lullaby, pressed against the back of his skull.

'Fetch those pillows over, Mentril. Let's make our guest comfortable.' Errol felt himself pulled upright, but he still didn't want to open his eyes. Finally he was let back down again, sinking into soft cushions. The coldness was pressed to his forehead now, a dampened cloth that felt wonderful. He tried to relax into it, letting the pain slip away as he settled. Only when he was sure it was safe did he try to look upon the scene.

His first thought was that his mother had found him. A pale woman stared down at him, her concerned face framed by straight dark hair flecked with lines of grey. But as he regained some degree of focus, he could see that it wasn't Hennas. This woman was far better dressed than he had ever seen his mother, with the exception perhaps of her wedding day. She wore a fine silk dress in rich brown colours with a white shawl hanging loosely around her shoulders. His mother had never possessed such finery.

Without moving his head it was hard to take in much more than that worried smiling face, but Errol could see that he was in quite a large high-ceilinged room, lit by a pair of windows. Even moving his eyeballs made his head swim, so he could take in no more than that. Perhaps he would be better speaking.

'Where am I?' The words sounded wrong, faint and hoarse in his dry throat. The woman leaned closer to him, bringing a soft lavender smell with her.

'You shouldn't try to speak. Rest. Conserve your energy. You've been badly injured.'

She was speaking Llanwennog, and as if that one realization was the keystone to a dam inside his head, Errol was flooded with memories. More than anything else, he feared for his life. He had spoken in Saesneg, the language of the Twin Kingdoms. His voice had probably been too quiet to be understood just now, but what if he had been muttering while unconscious?

'Where am I?' he tried again, this time in the local tongue, forcing the words out louder even though it made his head ache.

'You're safe. You're in Castle Gremmil, on the edge of the northlands. My husband found you dumped in woodland beside the Tynhelyg road. I guess you must have been attacked by bandits and left for dead.'

Errol tried to piece together his last memories, finding only snippets of images. He needed time to sort through it all, but now he knew he was on the spot. It didn't seem like these people realized where he was from; if they had, he would most likely have been in a dungeon. He needed to come up with a good story, and fast.

'I don't remember much. I was heading for the capital. Came down from the mountains. I've urgent news for King Ballah. Stopped off at some village for food; I think the circus was there. But after that it all goes a bit blank.'

'An emissary for the king, eh. Well Poul said you were carrying the king's seal. Rest a while and I'm sure everything will come back to you. Do you remember your name?'

'My name? Why yes. Sorry. It's Errol. Errol Balch.'

'Well, Errol. It's nice to meet you. I'm Isobel, Lady Gremmil. And this, if I'm not mistaken, is my husband.'

Errol looked up at a noise from the far end of the room, and immediately wished he hadn't. His brain felt like it was too big for his skull and was trying to fit in by squeezing out his eyeballs. Sparks flashed across his vision, and when they cleared it was to see a short broad man peering at him myopically.

'So you're a Balch, are you? I thought you had the family look. Pleased to meet you. I'm Poul Gremmil.'

'It was you who found me?' Errol took the man's proffered hand, squeezing it rather limply in his own.

'Well, it was one of my dogs, to be honest. Thought he'd flushed out some game, but when we went in after it, there you were, dragged under a bush with not a stitch on. Thought you were dead, but I guess you Balches are made of sterner stuff.'

Errol found that moving his arms eased the pain a little. He reached up to touch the back of his head, feeling a crusty mess of blood and hair.

'I'm very grateful to you, and your dog. But tell me, have I been unconscious long?'

'A day, maybe. Have you any idea who might have done this? Only it's a bad show, bandits attacking travellers on the king's road in my bailiwick.'

'I'm not sure, truly. I had to change some gold in Cerdys

and I'm fairly sure I was followed from there. But there were a few rough types in the circus. Did you see it when you found me?'

'The circus? No. They'd shipped out south before I came through. Seemed in a bit of a hurry to get to the King's Festival, by all accounts. But Cerdys? What in Gwlad were you doing up there?'

'Came down from the mountains; I was up there on a mission for the king. It's all very secret, really. I need to get back on the road as soon as possible so I can deliver my report in person.'

'Well, of course. But I doubt you'd stay on a horse more than five minutes with your head the way it is right now. You must stay with us at least another day or two. Give your brain time to recover.'

'You're right, of course. Thank you, my lord.'

'None of this "my lord" nonsense. We don't stand on ceremony out here in the wilderness, and any man bearing the king's seal will find aid here. It's Poul, please.'

'The king's seal?' Errol was puzzled. Now that he thought about it, Lady Gremmil had mentioned something about that too, and they were being far more hospitable than he might have expected, even if his face did make them think he was of royal birth.

'Your ring. I guess whoever attacked you must have missed it. You were clutching it so tight in your fist.'

Errol looked over at Lady Gremmil, who had reached for something lying on a small table beside the bed. She handed him a plain ring, and as he saw it, he remembered picking it up from the floor of the cave.

'It's a long time since I've seen one of those. King

Ballah doesn't grant that kind of boon to just anyone.' Lord Gremmil paused a moment as if trying to find a way to phrase the question Errol knew he wanted to ask. 'I don't suppose you can tell me anything about this mission, can you?'

Errol didn't answer straight away. Partly because he needed time to pull together the strands of the lie that had sprung so easily to his lips, and partly because he didn't want to seem too eager to give up state secrets. He rolled the ring around his palm for a moment, then slid it on to the little finger of his left hand. It was a bit too big, but it stayed in place.

'I can't be specific, you understand. It concerns the war with the Twin Kingdoms. We had intelligence of a possible route through the northern Rim mountains. King Ballah asked me to investigate, but quietly so as not to spark any panic. I've been riding the old trapping routes all spring and summer.'

From the look on Lord Gremmil's face, Errol knew he had the man convinced already. Lady Gremmil reinforced the lie by shuddering visibly, holding her hand over her face.

'And did you find . . . ?'

'Let me just say that it would be unwise to send all your able-bodied men to the southern passes. I think only a madman would lead an army through the great forest of the Ffrydd and over a poorly-mapped high mountain pass, but we all know that Inquisitor Melyn is insane.'

'I hear what you're saying, Errol. And you're right. This is the most important information. Rest now. I'll have a servant bring food. Then we'll see about getting you some clothes and a horse. This is grave news indeed. You must get it to the king with all haste.'

Melyn settled down by his fire, calmed his breathing and prepared to enter the trance state that would let him travel through the aethereal. They had reached the northlands of Llanwennog, and his scouts had reported back with the locations of the nearest settlements. Now it was time to contact Beulah and let her know how their plan was progressing.

It was not a task he was looking forward to. Back in the comfort and security of Emmass Fawr, or even the Neuadd, he wouldn't have thought twice about it. He'd even slipped away from his body while riding his horse along the Calling Road before, borrowing some of its energy to boost his own. But here he was in enemy lands, and the distance to Castell Glas, where the queen should now be, was far greater than anything he had travelled before. Neither could he contact her directly; he had to rely upon Clun. The boy had a natural talent for the aethereal, it was true, but nothing compared to the ease with which Melyn could communicate with Beulah. She was so close to him; he had trained her, moulded her for so long, he knew he could always find her. Clun was a new entity for him; it would be far harder to track him down.

And then there was the forest. He would have to traverse it, find his way through all that magical turmoil without losing sight of his own true body. All along the way he had been marking points that he could use to navigate. He should be able to retrace the path they had taken since parting with the royal procession, but he was not convinced that anything in the forest stayed the same for very long, especially when viewed in the aethereal.

Still, it had to be done. Without communication between his small army and the larger forces massing on the border, the whole invasion plan would grind to a halt. And so he relaxed, focusing his eyes on the flickering flames to help steady his mind.

The hubbub of the camp drifted away, not fading to total silence but sounding as if it were a good distance off. Melyn stayed in his body for a while, memorizing how he felt, setting it in his mind until he was confident he could return. Then, with a last look around the camp, he rose out of himself and into the air.

'Your Grace, I hope I'm not intruding.'

Melyn turned his aethereal body and looked down to see Frecknock a few paces away from his unmoving physical body.

'What do you want?'

'To help, if I may. Am I right in thinking you are about to contact His Grace the Duke of Abervenn?'

Melyn felt a tinge of his old anger rising; this creature had grown increasingly familiar and impertinent over the weeks and months of their journey together. She should be put in her place, should really be executed, as the queen had ordered. But she had also been of great help, and he found himself far more tolerant of her than he would ever have thought possible.

'What if I am?' he asked.

'Well, sir. I could watch over your mortal body while you are gone from it and do everything in my power to protect you from harm, but if you would permit me to accompany you on your journey instead, I could show you a much quicker way to reach Master Clun.'

'Very well, show me.' Melyn was surprised at how readily he accepted the offer of help, though any companionship on his difficult journey would have been welcome. Frecknock too was obviously taken aback by his consent, as she took a moment to compose herself before spreading her aethereal wings and leaping into the air. They were too small to support her bulk, Melyn noted, at least in the slow, almost lazy, way she used them. But there was an elegance about her aethereal flight that contrasted sharply with her waddling walk.

He followed her up into the air, over the camp and back towards the long valley down which they had travelled. When they had perhaps gone a mile, she descended to the ground, beckoning for Melyn to do the same.

'We needed to get a bit of distance from the camp, Your Grace. There's too much interference in the Grym with so many warrior priests around.'

'Why should it matter? I wasn't proposing to use the Grym.'

'Ah, but the aethereal is as much a realm of the Grym as the physical world. If anything it is more closely linked to it, since here you can do so much more.'

'How so?'

'It's easier for me to show, Your Grace, than tell. Please take my hand.'

Melyn did as he was asked, once more feeling that touch that should have revolted him, should have made his skin crawl, and yet was instead oddly comforting. Frecknock squeezed his hand, and he could see that she had closed her eyes in concentration. Then the aethereal view of the valley began to dissolve. There was an instant when Melyn thought he could see the whole of Gwlad laid out beneath him, a moment of darkness so complete it sent a shudder down his spine; and then he was somewhere else.

It was a small arena, roofed over and with a dry dirt floor. A few people sat around the edges, their forms more or less distinguishable in the aethereal, but it was the two figures in the centre that caught Melyn's attention. The first was quite obviously Clun; his features were unmistakable, even if he seemed to have matured years, rather than the months they had been parted. The second figure was something altogether different.

Melyn didn't think he had ever seen a horse so proud and magnificent. Like all simple creatures, its aethereal form was detailed and rich, as if it was aware of nothing but itself. It held its head high, neck arched, tail jutting out as a warning to anyone who might approach from behind. As he watched, it pranced around the arena in a wild manner, throwing its feet out and tossing its head from side to side, circling and circling the boy, eyeing him up for the kill. Clun however seemed unconcerned, almost ignoring the great beast, refusing to make eye contact, turning his back at times.

Melyn looked around and spotted the queen sitting in the gallery overlooking the action. She glowed as if someone had placed a candle inside her, and her aethereal form showed the slight swell of her belly. Without thinking, he moved across to her, settling himself down on the bench beside her.

'Beulah.' Melyn spoke softly, in the way he had always

done when trying to attract her attention to the aethereal. It was as much a game as a method of teaching, though normally she was aware of his presence even before he spoke. This time it was as if he didn't exist. The queen ignored him, her eyes only on Clun, and he felt a strange jealousy at her obvious devotion to the boy.

'She can't sense you, Your Grace. The child growing inside her . . .' Frecknock stood a short distance away, trying to make herself look small.

'I know. She's pregnant and that stops her from being able to see the aethereal.' Melyn turned his attention back to Clun. 'We were always going to have to communicate through the boy, but it looks like he's distracted at the moment. I could always attract Beulah's attention, but Clun needs to be a bit more focused.'

'You're very close to Her Majesty, Your Grace.'

'Her father put her in my care when she was only eight years old.'

'That would likely explain it. But if you will allow me, Your Grace, I should be able to alert Master Clun to our presence.'

Melyn nodded his assent, aware that once more he was depending on the dragon. He would have to kill her sooner or later, he realized; her influence on him was growing too great. But for now her aid was the only thing keeping his mission on track. And she fascinated him.

Frecknock stepped down into the arena, her aethereal form floating a hand's width off the dirt floor. Melyn watched the horse kick and stamp as it rushed round in a great circle. Then, when it was about to pass the spot where Frecknock's form stood, she stepped into its path.

The effect was instant. The stallion reared up, almost falling backwards as it recoiled. It backed off several slow paces, then stopped, staring at the dragon with wide eyes and flared nostrils. Clun watched it, an expression of concern spreading over his face, and then his gaze moved around the ring as if he were looking for something. He swept over Frecknock and Melyn, then did a double take, his eyes going out of focus for a moment before finally coming to rest on the inquisitor.

'Mistress Frecknock. Your Grace. I'm very glad to see you.' Clun bowed, then stepped away from himself, his aethereal form leaving behind an almost identical double as still as a statue.

'You've been practising, I see. Good.' Melyn floated his own form down to meet Clun. He was dimly aware of motion all around him: no doubt people in the arena reacting to the sudden stillness of the Duke of Abervenn. He trusted the queen would understand what was happening, but no doubt some fool would try to go to Clun's aid and distract the boy. Or get himself kicked to death by the horse.

'Now listen to me carefully. We don't have much time.'

There was no doubt about it, the horse was magnificent. He was also completely wild. Beulah still wasn't sure why she had bought him and doubted he would ever be broken. But he might be put to some of the more tractable mares, she supposed. Foals with a bit of Gomoran fire in them would make fine warhorses.

Still, Clun was determined to try, and he was going about the task in a most unusual manner. It had taken ten men with ropes and a great deal of swearing to bring the stallion from the stone stable he had been trying to destroy and down to this training arena. At least two of the stable hands had broken arms, and by the way a third was walking his ribs were badly cracked. Those brave enough to watch had climbed to the back of the raised seating around the arena. Only Beulah herself dared to lean over the railings; Captain Celtin sat nervously behind her.

Clun stood in the middle of the ring as if it were the most natural thing in the world to be so close to an animal that could run him down in an instant. The stallion's hooves were each the size of his head, and tore up great clumps of dirt as he pounded round. And yet the horse didn't attack him, just ran and ran. Round and round.

After about half an hour of this, the horse began to settle down, perhaps no longer afraid of the strange situation, but more likely just bored. Beulah wasn't sure such a creature knew what fear was. At this point Clun turned his back on the beast and Beulah felt a surge of trepidation. Surely that would invite an attack. But the horse continued its pacing, snorting and shaking its great flowing mane. Then, finally, it stopped, breathed heavily a few times, and walked slowly towards the centre.

Whether he sensed the approach or just heard a change in the beast's breathing, Beulah didn't know, but when the stallion was within ten paces of him, Clun turned and faced it, eyes with an expression of cold fury that reminded her of the battle he had fought with the dragon. The stallion kicked up instantly, but instead of attacking, backed away, resuming his mad running round the arena. And all the while Clun kept his eyes on him, swivelling slowly on his heels to mark the endless circles.

Beulah watched, fascinated. She had never seen anything like it before. Breaking horses was a brutal business, she knew. This horse should have been haltered and hobbled, then made to accept a breaking saddle; then brave men would have attempted to ride it until it was beaten into submission. Until its spirit was broken. That was how it had always been done at Emmass Fawr and Candlehall. But experience said Gomoran stallions could never be broken that way. At least no one had ever succeeded. What Clun was doing was completely different, and apart from the fact that he was as yet unharmed, seemed to be completely ineffectual. Since he had never before owned a horse, let alone tried to break one, what surprised her most of all was that he should even be trying.

'By the Shepherd!' Beulah jumped and felt Celtin behind her tense as the stallion suddenly reared, almost falling over in its desperation to get away from something she couldn't see. Clun looked confused, as if this was not something he had expected. He looked around the ring, and then his eyes seemed to go out of focus. His hands dropped slackly to his sides and his head drooped so much she thought he was going to collapse. But he stayed on his feet, looking for all the world like he dangled from an invisible rope with his feet just touching the ground.

Captain Celtin was the first to move, stepping reluctantly forward to jump down into the ring. Beulah stopped him, her touch making him visibly flinch.

'No, Captain. Wait a moment. I think I know what's happening.' She looked once more at Clun, then back at Celtin. 'Do you have any skill at the aethereal?'

'No, ma'am. I'm sorry.'

Beulah cursed her pregnancy once more. She tried to sink into the trance, tried to sense the presence she expected, but it was as if her head was wrapped in blankets. She looked around the arena, half expecting something to appear to her normal sight, but there was nothing to see apart from the curiously dangling Clun and the remarkable sight of a Gomoran stallion held motionless by fear.

'Be not alarmed, my lady. Inquisitor Melyn is here.' The words sounded distant, echoing from Clun's mouth without his lips moving. They were hard to hear above the muttering of the crowd. Beulah shouted, 'Silence!' and a strange quiet fell upon the place. Even the stallion stopped his snorting.

'How is it you can speak, my love? Are you not in the aethereal?'

'I have news from His Grace the inquisitor, my lady.' Clun either hadn't heard the question or chose not to answer it. 'He has reached the northlands and will begin his planned actions in a few days' time.'

'Has he killed the dragons?' There was a prolonged pause after Beulah asked the question, minutes passing as if some long conversation were being held elsewhere.

Finally Clun spoke again. 'No. The wild creature Caradoc escaped, as did Benfro. Frecknock is helping the inquisitor.'

'She's with him? Here, in the aethereal?'

'She is, my lady.'

For some unaccountable reason this made Beulah shudder. She hated not being able to see and move about the aethereal herself. It was a double torment to know that dragons might be spying on her, influencing her while she was so vulnerable. And why was Melyn allowing the dragon to accompany him? What could possibly have happened that could have made him trust her so? She longed to ask him more, but she was constrained both by the crowd of nobles who had come with her to the arena, and by the knowledge that anything she said would be heard by the dragon too.

'Tell Melyn that we will leave here tomorrow and sail directly for Abervenn. And tell him he would be wise to remember what we discussed before we parted. He knows what I mean.'

Clun fell silent once more, still dangling like a puppet in the exact centre of the ring. Again Beulah strained her senses to catch anything of the inquisitor, or even the dragon. Was that why the stallion had reacted to fearfully? Was it an ethereal presence that it sensed, that had it almost cowering? Beulah had thought herself an adept, a master of the skill, but now she realized she knew very little about the worlds of magic at all.

'My lady, they are gone.' Clun's voice was back to normal now, and he pulled himself upright, turning to face her. 'The inquisitor said to tell you that he hasn't forgotten your words. He will carry out your orders when he feels the time is right.'

'Did he say why he had brought the dragon with him?'

'Mistress Frecknock has sworn a blood oath to protect the inquisitor. She wants to stay alive, and she knows the only way she can do that is by being useful. She is teaching Melyn and his men what magic she can to help them with their campaign, and she's doing everything she can to protect the inquisitor himself. I suspect she knows that if he dies, she will lose her head soon afterwards.'

If he dies. The enormity of what Melyn was doing hit home with those three short words. Beulah knew that the mission was a brave one, if not plain foolhardy. Five hundred warrior priests against an entire nation was not good odds. And the whole plan depended on them drawing the attention of a large proportion of Ballah's army. It would be a miracle if any of them survived.

'Do not fear, my lady. His Grace is very resourceful. He has his best warrior priests with him, and now he has new magic to help too. You'll see him again. I know it.' Something about Clun's voice, his choice of words, made Beulah believe him. There was more to the Duke of Abervenn than the brave young man who had captured her heart.

Beulah's gaze was so fixed on him that she completely forgot about the stallion on the other side of the ring. Only when he moved did she notice him, no longer afraid but striding into the centre. The horse was huge, his coat black and shiny with sweat. He had an aura of unstoppable power, of untapped menace and single-minded obstinacy. And before she could shout a warning, it was upon Clun, who simply turned, calmly staring into those huge eyes, reaching up with his hand, letting the horse get his scent.

Slowly, calmly, the stallion lowered his head and allowed his ears to be scratched.

There was something wrong with his head. No matter how hard he tried to think, how much he shook the water out of his ears, still Benfro felt like he was muffled in thick, soft blankets. Neither was he quite sure where he was, though oddly that didn't seem to worry him much. Wherever it was, it was moving, lurching from side to side with a monotonous rhythm that swirled the fog around his brain and made it harder still to concentrate.

He tried to see what was going on, but wherever he was it was dark. A tiny sliver of light splayed in through a hole high above him, painting a fan-like pattern on a ceiling that appeared to be made of wood. But that couldn't be right. Hadn't he been sleeping in a cave? He'd lit a fire. No, he hadn't lit a fire, but there had been smoke. He was fairly sure of that. Or had he dreamed it? He remembered being tired, heavy, like he'd eaten too much. But he'd only had a couple of fish, and not that big. He remembered catching them in the river, filleting some to cook later when Errol got back.

Benfro started to piece things back together, bit by bit, memory by memory. It was slow work; he seemed to be able to hold only a few things in his mind at once. He had no idea how long it was since he had been in the cave, nor how long he had been in this moving wooden box.

This cage.

The idea came to him at the same time as he started to notice the sensations in his arms and legs. It was as if he had forgotten what discomfort was and it had taken him that long to put a name to the feeling. Now that he had made the connection, he realized he had been uncomfortable ever since . . . when? He couldn't remember waking any more than he could remember going to sleep. But he must have done both at some point.

Benfro shifted his body, tried to sit up from the unusual

lying position he found himself in. It was harder than it should have been. Not only was his sense of balance not working, but his arms and legs appeared to be tied together. He rocked back and forth, rolled over on to his front so that he could lever himself upright, but in the confines of the cage it was near impossible given the way he seemed to feel things only long moments after he had touched them. Finally he managed to reach some sort of tipping point, realizing as he did so that he had no way of staying upright. With a graceless certainty he toppled over, landing partially on something slightly softer than the wooden floor.

A voice muttered something harsh that he didn't understand.

'What? Is there someone there?' Benfro's words sounded oddly thick to him, slurred and heavy.

'I said watch where you're sitting. You're not the only one in here.'

'Sorry. I didn't realize.' Benfro shuffled himself as best he could away from the voice, backing himself into a corner. Only then did he realize that the words had been spoken in Draigiaith. Not only that, they were perfectly formed, the voice itself deep and old, slightly reminiscent of Sir Frynwy. Not the speech of men.

'I don't mean to be rude, but where are we? And who are you?'

'I am Magog, Son of the Summer Moon. But you can call me Moonie.' Something shifted in the darkness, a looming presence dragging itself across the floor towards him. The light playing on the ceiling should have been enough for Benfro to see by, but the same cloud that fogged his thoughts robbed him of his keen eyesight. All he could make out was a glint, perhaps the reflection of an eye. Then he felt hot breath on his face, rancid with the taint of rotten meat. 'And you must be my brother Gog. I've been waiting for you. Where have you been all these years?'

'No, I'm Benfro. Sir Benfro.' The presence in front of him withdrew; there was a shuffling sound and something slumped against the far wall, upsetting the regular motion for a moment.

'A shame. And I was so sure. I was –' But whatever the creature was, Benfro didn't find out then. The cage stopped suddenly, throwing him forward so that he sprawled painfully on the floor. He heard the noise of bolts being drawn, a key turning in a lock, and then light flooded over him.

Benfro looked up to the far end, where the creature was slumped. It was almost impossible to make out the dragon who sat there, his colouring so perfectly matched the dark wood. He seemed thinner than Benfro, though otherwise much the same size. Except for his wings, which, while large for the dragons of the Ffrydd, were pathetic in comparison with Benfro's own. But what grabbed Benfro's attention most, what filled him with fear and pity and anger, was the expression on the dragon's face, the look in his eyes. He was frightened, broken and quite, quite mad.

Something hit Benfro square in the back. Whatever it was that had been distancing his mind from his body dissolved in one instant of exquisite pain. He yelped, turning to see what had happened, and saw a man standing in the open doorway clasping a long whip in one hand. The man said something in a voice that sounded like it was used to being obeyed.

'I don't understand.' Benfro held up his hands. His wrists were cuffed in iron, a short length of chain looping between them.

'He says you're to behave yourself and stop spooking the horses. Otherwise he'll –' Benfro felt the tip of the whip fly past him across the room and saw it hit the other dragon square in the face. Magog, as he called himself, shrieked, dropped to the floor and covered his head with his hands, speaking quick words in the same language as the man. He in turn hurled what sounded like abuse at the dragon, then turned to Benfro.

'So. Not speak Llanwennog, do you. Will learn. Not learn, not eat. Now be still.' And with that he slammed the door shut, plunging them once more into darkness. Moments later the regular rhythmic motion started again with a first sudden lurch that had Benfro sprawling on the floor once more,just as he was beginning to lever himself upright.

'Hee hee. You upset Tegwin. You don't want to be doing that. He can be nasty. And old Loghtan's worse still.'

Benfro started to struggle up again, then remembered the man's words and the pain of the whip. Perhaps when his head had cleared a bit more he'd teach this Tegwin a lesson, but for now it might be best to get rid of these chains. Taking a deep breath, Benfro held his arms up in front of him and pulled them apart to stretch the links taut. He thought of how they were an affront to his dignity, how they would be better off gone, and he tried to remember the feeling that had spread through his stomach before. Then he breathed out.

There was no flame.

Puzzled, Benfro took another deep breath and tried again. And still he failed to produce so much as a spark. It should have panicked him, should have angered him. Thinking about it, he realized that being in chains should have angered him too, and yet he had accepted it as merely a bit of an inconvenience. Something was deeply wrong with his mind, but he couldn't bring himself to care. Instead he settled himself back down on the floor, the weight of his body coming down hard on his arms. They would hurt later, when the circulation came back into them, but right now he was too tired, too confused to care. He closed his eyes, for all the difference it made in the darkness, and tried to sleep, but the other dragon kept muttering under his breath.

'Magog?' Benfro said, wondering how this pathetic creature had come by the name. The muttering stopped, so he assumed he was being listened to. 'What is this place? Where are we? And who's Loghtan?'

'Loghtan is the boss man. Oh yes. You think Tegwin's nasty with his little whip. Just wait till you meet Loghtan. Takes away your thoughts, he does. Takes away your mind.'

'But where are we? How did I get here?'

'We're in the circus, brave Sir Benfro. Oh yes. In the circus.'

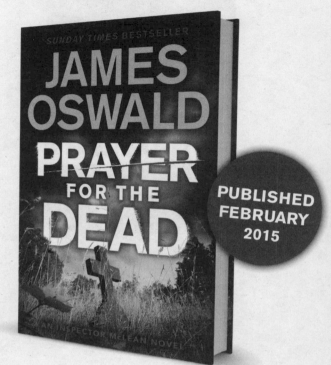

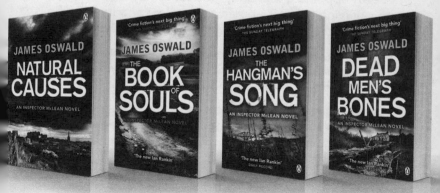

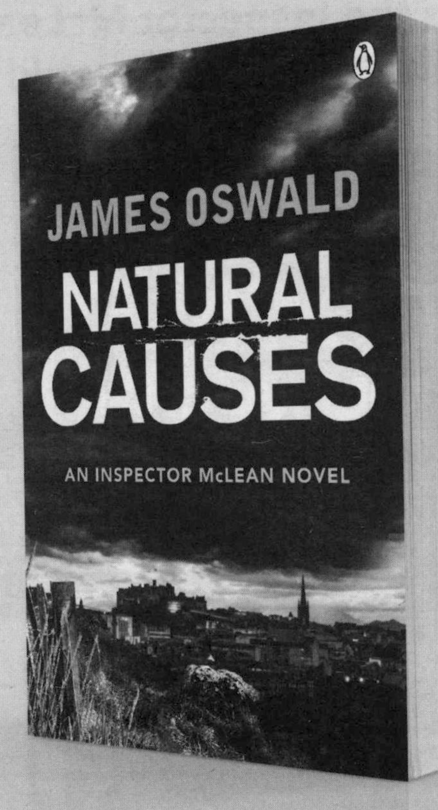

A young girl's mutilated body is discovered in a sealed room. Her remains are carefully arranged, in what seems to have been a cruel and macabre ritual, which appears to have taken place over 60 years ago.

For newly appointed Edinburgh Detective Inspector Tony McLean this baffling cold case ought to be a low priority – but he is haunted by the young victim and her grisly death.

Meanwhile, the city is horrified by a series of bloody killings. Deaths for which there appears to be neither rhyme nor reason, and which leave Edinburgh's police at a loss.

McLean is convinced that these deaths are somehow connected to the terrible ceremonial killing of the girl, all those years ago. It is an irrational, almost supernatural theory.

And one which will lead McLean closer to the heart of a terrifying and ancient evil . . .

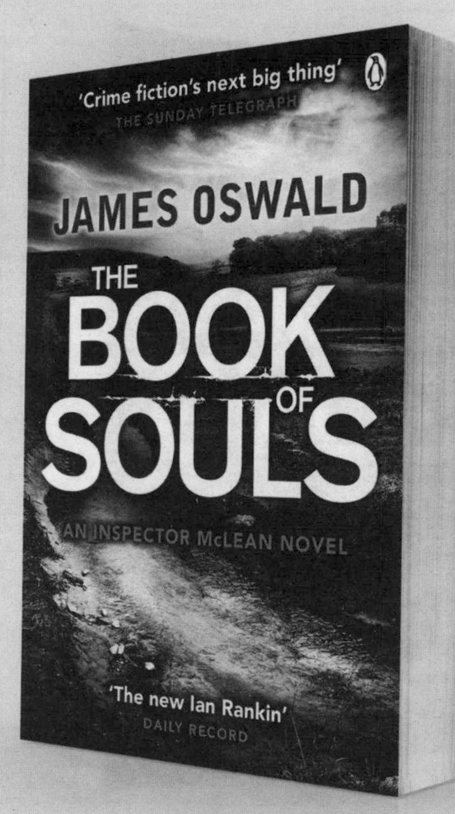

'Crime fiction's next big thing'
THE SUNDAY TELEGRAPH
JAMES OSWALD
THE BOOK OF SOULS
AN INSPECTOR McLEAN NOVEL
'The new Ian Rankin'
DAILY RECORD

Every year for ten years, a young woman's body was found in Edinburgh at Christmas time: naked, throat slit, body washed clean.

The final victim, Kirsty Summers, was Detective Constable Tony McLean's fiancée. But the Christmas Killer made a mistake and McLean put an end to the brutal killing spree.

Twelve years later, and a fellow prisoner has murdered the Christmas Killer. But with the festive season comes a body; naked, washed, her throat cut.

Is this a copycat killer?

Was the wrong man behind bars all this time?

Or is there a more sinister explanation?

McLean must revisit his most disturbing case and discover what he missed before the killer strikes again . . .

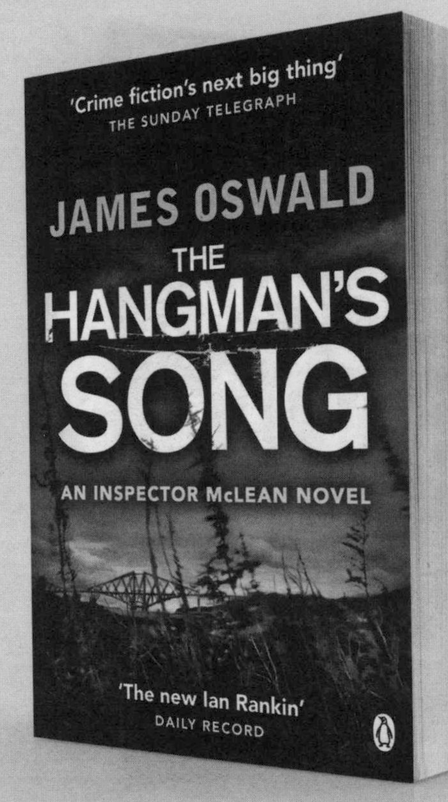

The body of a man is found hanging in an empty house. To the Edinburgh police force this appears to be a simple suicide case.

Days later another body is found.

The body is hanging from an identical rope and the noose has been tied using the same knot.

Then a third body is found.

As Inspector McLean digs deeper he descends into a world where the lines of reality are blurred and where the most irrational answers become the only explanations.

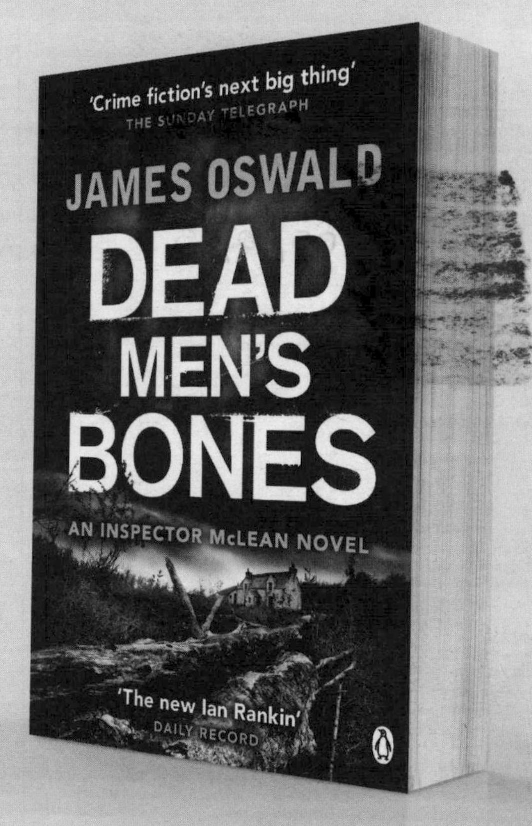

A family lies slaughtered in an isolated house in North East Fife . . .

Morag Weatherly and her two young daughters have been shot by husband Andrew, an influential politician, before he turned the gun on himself.

But what would cause a rich, successful man to snap so suddenly?

For Inspector Tony McLean, this apparently simple but high-profile case leads him into a world of power and privilege. And the deeper he digs, the more he realises he's being manipulated by shadowy factions.

Under pressure to wrap up the case, McLean instead seeks to uncover layers of truth - putting the lives of everyone he cares about at risk . . .